I0691825

Marin in the Moonlight

Revel Pointe Romance, Volume 1

A.E. Merriweather

Published by Spoonbill Publishing, 2024.

This is a work of fiction. Similarities to real people, places, or events are entirely coincidental.

MARIN IN THE MOONLIGHT

First edition. October 1, 2024.

Also by A.E. Merriweather

Revel Pointe Romance
Marin in the Moonlight
Summer in the Snowfall

Watch for more at www.aemerriweather.com.

For friendship reasons and romance readers.

Prologue

The Secret Reveler
A Blog Devoted to All Matters Reve

The 2011 Revel Review

It's been a tragic year for the Reve family, especially for our favorite ne'er-do-well, Ethan. He lost his older brother and heir apparent, Wade, in Afghanistan, and his father, Gaspard, is currently recovering from a stroke. Ethan's lovely lady songstress, Revel superstar Bree Brooklyn, dumped him via social media after catching him *in flagrante delicto* with a busty bartender in New Orleans. Now he's back at Revel Pointe, ostensibly to run the family business.

Ethan Reve, CEO?

Ethan has the academic credentials, but does he have what it takes to run the beloved institution that is Revel Pointe? The studios, theme park, and cruise line? He hasn't lived up to his father's expectations thus far. Re: the very public fight at Wade's funeral, in which the patriarch was heard yelling, "The wrong son is in that grave!" Ouch, Papa Reve.

A Real-Life *Game of Thrones*

To add more grist to the gossip mills, Ethan's stepmother, the terrifyingly competent Tilda Olsen-Reve, is vying for the position of top dog. Her social media has been on fire since tragedy befell the Reves last year, and she certainly paints herself as the stable eye of the storm.

What about Ethan's younger half-siblings, James, Henri, Dominic, and Elsie? Are they cool with their big bro taking the reins, or will they want a shot at it?

Stay posted, my fellow Revelers. Intrigue is afoot.

Chapter One

Marin

The sun casts a warm pink light through a canopy of live oaks, where Spanish moss drapes along the large drooping branches. A cool breeze waves the tendrils back and forth, a welcoming gesture, beckoning me down the gravel path, flanked by red roses, toward the park entrance. The enormous wrought-iron fence and the bright pink crepe myrtles help to slow my breath. The tension in my shoulders releases. As I plant my feet on Revel Pointe ground, my favorite place on Earth, I know I made the right choice. This "silly theme park," as my family calls it, feels more inviting than the home I ran from.

I'm a Vandersee, and I just did something a Vandersee never does: I quit. Grad school, to be precise. I didn't intend to blow up my own life, but on my drive back to Tulane University, when my eyes clocked the *Bienvenue à Revel Pointe* sign on the interstate, my body responded as if on autopilot; my own hands steered my car down the off-ramp about thirty miles outside New Orleans, and my feet negotiated the gas and brake pedals. Before I knew it, my whole body was out of the car, in a sunny parking lot surrounded by the famous Revel Oaks. Home at last.

The wonderful world of Revel has always been my escape, so I suppose it makes sense I'd seek refuge here, especially after my disastrous trip back home to Vermont for Christmas break.

The whole family was there, which was rare. Even so, I barely saw them the entire trip. Our home, nestled in the Green Mountains, is cavernous with distinct wings, like the house itself doesn't want us to interact. Mom spent most of the time skiing, working from her home office, or meeting with clients. Dad spent most of his time in town working or drinking Old-Fashioneds in his den. My older sisters were also specters in the house. Alana, the eldest, worked on her dissertation and bit anyone's head off who had the audacity to speak to her. Arista trained for her triathlon and posted pictures of green and red smoothies online. When she wasn't sculpting her body, she worked on her research. Once I asked her about it, hoping to connect, but it involved shocking mice, so I stopped asking questions.

As a result of the Vandersee clan being preoccupied with their many pursuits of excellence, I spent most of my Christmas vacation hiding in my room, rewatching my favorite Revel movies, including my most recent favorite, *Island of Sirens*. Reverting to my younger self at home, I always end up in my Rose Red PJs, hiding from my family, escaping into my cocoon. It remains to be seen if I'll ever emerge a butterfly.

Prognosis: not likely.

The problem is my entire family is extraordinary—kings, queens, and princesses in a world of paupers. Unfortunately, I am barely a serf in their estimation. Maybe a common tavern wench. They all pray to the god of credentialism, attending the "good" Ivys, Yale and Harvard. I earned a degree in Marketing from the University of Vermont before applying and getting into Tulane's MBA program. No one mentions the "State" school I attended. Tulane is a step in the right direction, but the Vandersees feel business school is for the "kids who can't do hard math."

I had somehow gotten through the entire winter break without a pile-on and thought I might just make it the rest of the trip without any incidents.

Oh, I was so wrong.

The night before I was set to drive back to New Orleans, they finally acknowledged me, as if by some unspoken decree, and they all wished to discuss my lackluster pursuits.

"So, how's *Bid*-ness?' My dad thinks he's funny. He is not. He was on his way to drunk.

"It's actually great," I replied quickly, lest they lose interest. "The Finance class was a beast, but I did well, and I really liked my Organizational Behavior class."

Arista snorted, her brown eyes rolling dramatically under her ash-blonde bangs.

"What?" I should've ignored it, but I couldn't help it; I engaged.

"Nothing." Arista shrugged her perfectly sculpted shoulders and pushed around the baked chicken and kale concoction she had made instead of eating the spaghetti I prepared. She was in ketosis.

Mom chimed in. "It's just that course title, Organizational Behavior. What does it even mean?"

"It's about how to manage people and run an organization. It draws on social science," I explained.

"*Soft* science, you mean," Arista added, cutting her chicken into minuscule bites. Mother's eyebrow raised skeptically under slightly ashier blonde bangs before she snickered and took a sip of cabernet.

"I think it's great that you've found something you're good at," Alana said, smiling and nodding. Alana is a less toned, more waif-like copy of Arista. She was trying to help, but her comment made me feel like a kid at the grown-up table.

The whole dinner went like this, a cold war punctuated by unexpected shots across the table. Mother occasionally looked up from a journal article, but nothing, not even my disappointing path, could hold her attention long. I should be used to the thinly veiled scorn, the reminders that I'm the odd one out, but their indifference still hurts.

Hell, I don't even look like them. Jokes have been made about "the mailman."

"Wink, wink, nudge, nudge," as my Dad liked to say.

My family are tall, thin, and blonde with brown eyes like woodland elves from *Lord of the Rings*. And then there's me. A weed amongst flowers. A red-headed hobbit with an ass and a chest that Arista once told me were "obscene."

"You look like a lady in a porno," she told me in high school after I wore my first bikini to a neighbor's pool party. "Please don't make 'slutty' your thing."

The next day my mom pulled me aside and told me I had grown up and needed new clothes. We went to the mall and brought back baggy shirts, sweaters, and sweatshirts. Jeans two sizes too big. I didn't start wearing the right size until my best friend, Flora, forced me to during my senior year in college.

To avoid conflict, I essentially lived in my Revel sweatshirts and joggers at home. I'm not proud of this behavior, but it's easier. Fighting with them never works. It's four against one, and I'm the dyslexic ginger who took the ACT three times to get a 30. I'm the intellectual and physical runt of the litter.

But that's not my worst trait, according to my family. It's not my mediocre scholarship, my lightweight graduate program, my untoward curves, or my learning disability. The worst of my qualities is my obsession with all things Revel Pointe:

"Put that book down and finish your actual work."

"Why are you obsessed with kids' toys and shows?"

"Last time I checked, Revel is for children, Marin."

Do they know that being mean to me is the glue that binds them together? What would they criticize if I wasn't there? They'd start gnawing at themselves like bored dogs without a bone, I thought, when Arista brought my attention back to the present conversation.

"Maybe you should drop out of Tulane and work at Revel like your weird goth friend Flora," she suggested, and the table laughed.

Flora came home with me once, claiming she needed to "see this shit for herself." When she walked into the empty house when my parents were at a charity event and my sisters were god-knows-where, Flora sang, "When Cameron was in Egypt's land..." Apparently, I lived in Cameron's house from *Ferris Bueller's Day Off*.

Flora did not take to the Vandersees, and the family certainly did not take to Flora. Flora spent the weekend bragging about my grades, my work with Amnesty International, and my marketing internship at Burton Snowboards.

"The CEO personally told Marin that she had a job the minute she graduated," Flora said during dinner. The reception from the Vandersees was cool at best.

"That's nice," my mother replied. "Alana, did you get access to Johns Hopkins' lab?"

Flora fumed. I could see an epic Flora-takedown fomenting. Our eyes locked, mine pleading with her to let it go. It wasn't worth it. Her eyes said that she thought it was, that *I* was. Fortunately, my father got a call and that meant dinner was over. The Vandersees fled to their separate wings.

Flora and I sat at the now-empty table, silent for a moment, before she hissed, "We are getting the hell out of here. Right now."

In Flora's beat-up yellow VW bug, she placed one hand over mine. "We will talk about all of this," she said, gesturing to the house with her other hand. "But now, now we are going to listen to the entire *Portia's Power* soundtrack." Portia was the first "hear-me-roar," late 60s, Women's Lib princess. We angry-belted the entire way back to campus. Flora was my hero, but she wasn't at this particular Christmas dinner to swoop in and save the day or defend herself.

Arista made another disparaging comment about Flora: "Well, Flora certainly dresses like a cartoon character. No costume change required for her at Revel."

And that was it. I stood suddenly, my plate clanking against the table; all hazel-brown eyes were on me, and mom even looked up from her journal. It's one thing to be cruel to me, but Flora, even absent from this sham family dinner, didn't deserve their derision.

"You know what?" My voice echoed in the cavernous room. "That's a great idea. I'll drop out of school and work at Revel. See you next Christmas." I threw my napkin on my plate. "Maybe."

I didn't get a chance to see their faces, but I heard Alana say, "Nice, guys."

"Can you pass the wine?" Arista replied breezily.

In my room, I shoved my least baggy clothing into my duffel. This was the first time I said boo to those people. My hands were shaking. I am usually a go-along-to-get-along type, but something flipped. I felt giddy and terrified. How dare they talk about Flora like that? About Revel.

If they only knew that Revel is why I'm still a functioning member of society. In spite of them, Revel gave me a childhood. The heroes and heroines of the early fairy-tale films gave me my belief in the power of imagination. However cheesy it seemed to them, the artistry and uplifting themes gave me hope that somewhere, there's a world where people care about doing good because it's the right thing to do, not because it looks good on a resume.

Revel saved my life time and time again. So of course, after a grueling two-day drive back to New Orleans, filled with tears and scream-singing along to my favorite Revel movie soundtracks, I end up here, at the gates of Revel Pointe, instead of Tulane. I'm done trying to live the life my family wants for me. I'm going to be where *my* people are. And that place is the real-life, fantastical Revel Pointe theme park in the swampy dreamland of Louisiana.

Chapter Two

Ethan

Revel Pointe—this kitschy, corporate hellscape that is my life now—ruined everything. Goodbye, Manhattan. Goodbye, decent bagels. Goodbye, glamorous models around every corner. See ya, bustling city where I could hide in crowds, surrounding myself with other "rich bros" whose antics were always distracting enough to let me do my own thing.

I had a plan. Sort of. I had more of a plan to plan. And this plan did not involve being here, at my family compound, an insane replica of a Medieval castle on the edge of a theme park, searching for something strong to drink. But there's nothing in this whole damn fort that'll take the edge off. Turns out Dad's third wife, Yasmin, doesn't like her man hitting the sauce, especially since his stroke.

My own refrigerator was barren, so I headed to the shared common space. There are fancy sparkling waters and weird green juices in the open-concept kitchen, but nothing potent enough to help me deal with my new life circumstances. Gossip-rag headlines pop onto my phone screen and hover in my mind's eye: "Ethan's Home for the Unforeseeable Future"; "A Revel without a Clue"; "Minus Bree Brooklyn, Who's Next for Ethan Reve?"

If only Wade were here. If only he'd stayed home instead of going to war. My brother. Our hero. Wade would tell me to get over myself. He'd give me a pep talk about family and obligation, and I would cave like I always did whenever he asked me for something. Wade is the best Reve.

Was, I remind myself.

Before I can stop my mind from spiraling, I picture the coffin again, closed. I remember how light it was, hardly weighing anything at all. Carrying it to the gravesite with my brothers, I had a sick rhyme in my head: *All the king's horses and all the king's men couldn't put Wade back together again.*

And then the panic descends. My heart beats fast, like hummingbird wings, and beads of sweat drip at my hairline. *I'm dying*, I think, while searching frantically for anything to numb the impending attack.

Nothing. Nowhere.

I'll have to leave the compound and go to the RP Lounge, that dumb-ass exclusive members-only bar that my ex-stepmother, Tilda, insisted on marketing to our "elite clientele," a.k.a. rich adult Revelers. But I'm desperate. Maybe Bobby, the ancient bartender, will be there. He's worked at Revel since before I was born and has always been nice to me.

Checking my watch, I find the park is almost closed. Most people, and their prying eyes and cameras, will have left by now. Bobby will give me a drink and some space. Maybe even let me take a to-go cup. This is Louisiana after all.

As I jog out the door, a mantra plays in my head: "*The wrong son...the wrong son.*" I ignore the overtly jolly scenery. I can't seem to catch my breath; a barrel of snakes roils in my stomach. When I reach a rest area near the center moat that circles the iconic lighthouse, my stomach lurches. I can't find a trash can, so bushes will have to do. Then I puke, mostly bile, which stings. Leaning my arm against the brightly colored wall, I feel better. A little lightheaded, but better. Until I feel it—eyes on me.

Oh, *shit.*

I turn around slowly and find a woman, a blur of long red hair, her face in shadow. She's wearing a pink Rose Red sweatshirt.

Great, a dumb Reveler. She probably recorded the whole episode.

"Are you okay?" she asks, concern emanating from her voice.

I wipe the spit from my mouth, desperate to hide, hoping she didn't take a picture.

"Do you need me to call someone?" She closes the gap between us. With her features still shaded, her hair glows like golden embers, the sunset light behind her creating a halo. A veritable angel.

Golden embers, I think, then woozily snicker at the sentimentality. But I can't take my eyes off her. I squint, trying to see her face.

"No, no, I just ate something that disagreed with me," I lie and throw my shoulders back, donning my confident-alpha pose. "Sorry you had to see that."

"Are you sure?" she asks. "I'm happy to help—" Her voice is so sweet, so genuine, that I'm frozen to the spot, wondering briefly if perhaps this stranger could, indeed, help me.

Then that damn *Diamonds & Toads* ride starts, the waltz blaring through the loudspeakers, "*Marie, my love, let's wander...*"

The overpoweringly sweet song kills the moment, and now the need to run away is overwhelming.

"I'm fine. Thank you." I try to walk away casually, fairly certain that my spew session will be on *TMZ* or that idiotic Revel blog in the morning.

More reason for everyone to think I'm a screw-up. The wrong son.

Chapter Three

Marin

On a bench near the *Diamonds & Toads* ride, I try not to freak out that I just saw Ethan Reve vomiting on a rose bush. While he's the "bad boy" of the family, I've always thought him the handsomest son, a giant of a man with black hair and blue eyes. When someone says, "Ethan Reve," the word *hunk* comes to mind.

Of course, his wealth and celebrity have made him an unstable hedonist like most famous children, including his ex, Bree Brooklyn. As a tween, she was fabulous on her Revel TV show, *Twinners*, where she played twins who swapped places all the time to juggle their singing career. Since growing up, Bree's been in the news more than Ethan, partying, trashing hotel rooms, screaming at assistants in public. Considering his reputation, Ethan must have been vomiting up last night's booze and who knows what else.

Except he didn't look drunk, he looked sick. Less Adonis on Earth, and more lost, unfortunate soul—an actual, vulnerable human being. And there was something about his face when I asked if he was okay, like he was surprised by my concern.

Get a grip, Marin. Everyone looks tortured when they lose their lunch. You didn't come here to analyze Ethan Reve's mental health, I tell myself. With a deep breath and the smell of taffy from a nearby Roman candy cart, I take the next step towards my future. Here goes nothing. I call my advisor and officially withdraw for the semester.

Then, I text Flora: I've done something crazy. Are you at work?

Flora has been working here since August. In college, we bonded over a love of all things Revel. We met freshman year in our dorm. At an orientation week floor party, everyone's doors were open. We were all supposed to serve themed shots. I've never been much of a drinker, and my ill-matched roommate considered this a serious character flaw. So she dragged me to different rooms to try "ALL of the shots." When we wandered into Flora's room by shot number three, I was tipsy.

Flora's themed shot was based on Revel's animated classic *20,000 Leagues Under the Sea.* Her whole dorm was decorated in a nautical theme. A life-sized Captain Nemo and the Nebuchnezzer were painted on her walls. Her tiny abode was magical, and I was buzzed enough to get over my shyness to tell her.

"I LOVE this theme! *20,000 Leagues* is a classic!" I yelled at her over sea shanties playing on her desk speaker. "I had the biggest crush on Captain Nemo as a kid!"

"Thank you!" she yelled back, her bright pink head bobbing up and down. "It's one of my favorites. I mean, I love them all, but I thought this was easiest to do!" She handed me a blue shot.

I promptly abandoned my roommate and spent the rest of the night in Flora's under-the-sea dorm room, talking about everything. And that's our origin story. Flora was the eldest in a big family and the first to go to college. She was so much cooler than me, her dark hair often streaked with pink, purple, and blue. She played drums in a punk rock band, FindersKeepers, when she wasn't working behind the scenes in the drama department, and earning her BFA in Costume Design.

Boisterous, creative, and unapologetically into Revel Pointe, Flora worked at the park every summer in college. After graduation, she got the coveted Revel internship and was hired to work full-time in Character Casting & Costumes.

She's the one who bought me my Rose Red sweatshirt, handing it to me and saying, "Is it weird that I bought you a shirt with *you* on it?" Flora told me if I ever wanted to ditch grad school and work as a Rose Red princess, she'd hire me immediately.

Now I hope she meant it because I'm here pacing the park, practicing my "please hire me" speech. I didn't expect to start as a character, though. Maybe Flora could hook me up with a gig in one of the many gift shops, or maybe something in food service. Hell, I'll do anything, just as long as I get to stay here.

Flora texts back: *Yeah, what's up? Have you run away from home already?*

I write back: *Yep! I'm currently listening to "Marie's Waltz" on a bench outside Diamonds & Toads.*

Within seconds Flora replies: *Holy cannoli! I'm finishing a fitting. I'll get Tyler to swing by and get you on the cart. Sit tight.*

I tap my foot to the music and watch the few remaining families walk toward the Revel Palace Gate. Most Revelers seem tired, happy, and more than a little sunburnt. A little girl in a Rose Red costume holds hands with her sister in a Kiki the Croc hat. Their smiles could light up the park. From here I can see the ornate wrought-iron gate, the original entrance. Mick Reve had it made for his wife, Marie, a Frenchwoman he met during World War II. Much of the park is a love letter to Marie, who missed her war-ravaged home. Their first-born, Gaspard, didn't seem to inherit this romantic streak, and I guess the jury is still out on the rest of the Reve kids. *Especially Ethan*, I think, as a gangly teenager rolls up in a golf cart and yells, "Yo, you Marin?"

Chapter Four

Ethan

Turns out the RP Lounge is classier than I remembered with an old-school speakeasy vibe. Bobby, the good ol' bartender that PawPaw won't let Tilda fire, looks perfect in his red vest, cleaning glasses behind the bar. PawPaw opened this park in 1962, and Bobby was his first hire. No one's quite sure how they met, but Bobby did odd jobs, from sanitation, to ride mechanic, and now tending bar.

"You best eat something first. I won't serve you till you get some food in that belly. You're lookin' peaked," Bobby growls at me. He sets down pretzels and roasted peanuts in two tiny bowls. "Eat some of that, then I'll take your order." I sigh, then shove some peanuts in my mouth.

"There, okay?" He glares at me until I swallow and give him a curt nod.

"What'll it be? I make a mean gin fizz," he boasts, throwing a white bar towel over his shoulder.

"I'll have a Maker's Mark, three fingers, neat." I hold up three fingers, then tap them on the bar in time to the jazz soundtrack from PawPaw's first animated classic, *Ragtime Romp*.

"All right, I see it's one of those types of days." Bobby turns and grabs the Maker's bottle from the shelf. "How you holding up?" He places the drink in front of me. I don't sip. I down it.

"Another, please," I demand, trying to erase the residual panic.

"No, sir. Not until you drink this." Bobby replaces the empty glass with a tall glass of ice water.

"You know the customer is always right, right?"

"You know your PawPaw never said malarkey like that. Now drink your water."

I comply, feeling calmer.

"Now you didn't answer my question," he says. "How *you* holding up?" His big, bushy eyebrows furrow as his brown eyes lock on mine.

"Honestly, I'm just peachy." I gulp down some water. "I mean look at me. I'm rich, healthy, privileged. Nothing to complain about."

"Now don't give me that crap. Money and privilege don't mean life ain't a bitch sometimes."

"Yeah, well..." I pivot. "Tilda did a nice job with this place. Is it always this quiet?"

"At seven on a Tuesday after New Year's, it is. The lounge gets hopping, though, on weekends." He refills my water. "My shift ends soon, but I've got time if you feel like talkin'." He leans forward a bit, his voice low. "You know your PawPaw and I are rootin' for you the same way we were rootin' for Wade. Mick never liked the direction your Daddy and Tilda were takin'."

"Yeah, well, where is PawPaw anyway?" I spit out. PawPaw, Mick Reve, is a famous recluse now. Not a Howard Hughes level-hermit, but he completely left the public eye when MawMaw died, right after Henri was born. He was at Wade's funeral and with Dad in the hospital a few times, but PawPaw always retreated back to his little cottage in the woods, hidden behind the park. He sends handwritten letters on my birthday and at Christmas, but I rarely bother to read them anymore. They're just filled with the same old drivel about coming home and how to be a good man, etc., etc.

Wade once said PawPaw's like a Revel character, living in a waking dream. Wade also reminded me that PawPaw's been through a lot, with what happened during the war, MawMaw dying, and his little girl, our Aunt Alice, running away to Paris to avoid the place he built from nothing in the bayou of Louisiana.

Even as a kid, Wade was empathetic, better than me always. Everyone knew it, which is why the head-honcho position was always going to pass to our father, Gaspard, then to Wade when the time came. But with Gaspard's stroke and Wade gone...well, now it's on me to fill the spot in the interim until Gaspard gets back on his feet.

Had PawPaw actually left his hidey-hole, he'd know what a royal mistake choosing me will be. His lawyers must have determined succession when I was a baby. The whole family knows having me in charge is a legal middle finger to Tilda, Dad's second wife. PawPaw never liked Tilda, and it's apparent that he loathes her now after the money-hungry decisions she's made for the company over the years. Once, PawPaw famously referred to Tilda as "the succubus" at a family dinner. He doesn't want her tentacles wrapped around Revel Pointe any more than they are.

"A real Lady Macbeth," he'd quip and not under his breath. He's become quite bold in his elder years. Next December, he'll be 95.

Bobby's gravelly voice interrupts my wandering thoughts. "Your PawPaw's here once in a blue moon. You can always go see him at the cottage if you need him." Bobby wipes down the bar top, his sleeves rolled up now, showing an ancient anchor tattoo on his forearm.

"Nah, I'm good. Just getting used to all this." I gesture to the Revel trappings of the lounge.

"Well, you're a smart boy. Always were. I trust this place is in good hands." He refills my water glass.

I nod, not so sure.

"You got a fight ahead of you, with Tilda, with the board, with yourself." He lowers his voice, but I hear him too well. "Now finish that water. I gotta prep for the next shift."

I do as I'm told, and when Bobby turns his back, I lean over the bar, grab the bottle of whiskey, and head home.

Thinking about power, I mentally quote *Macbeth*—*Tomorrow and tomorrow and tomorrow...*

Tomorrow, I will work, collect data, look at our finances, review projects, and make a plan. I will win over the board. I will make Wade proud.

Tonight, I'll drink. I'll forget the coffin, forget Dad's face turning red as he yelled at me. Tonight, I'll push the image of Dad in the hospital, hooked up to tubes, out of my mind.

Tonight, I'll drink to forget the redhead from earlier and how the concern in her eyes and the caring tone in her voice made me feel more alone than ever.

Chapter Five

Marin

After about ten minutes of screaming and jumping up and down, Flora and I settle on an ugly brown couch in her office/dressing room. Multicolored pieces of taffeta, tulle, and satin explode from a closet. Glittery tiaras, wands, and rhinestone necklaces litter a mirrored vanity along with a cornucopia of makeup. We have to move two clear plastic bins full of sparkly shoes just to sit on the couch. I'm in Revel heaven.

"I can't believe you told your family to fuck off," Flora says, shaking her head in disbelief. With her now-natural onyx hair piled on top of her head in a messy bun, various pencils sticking out of it, she's exactly the person I need in my life at this moment. I beam at my best friend.

"Well, not like that exactly, but yeah..." I rarely swear. I'm not a prude, but cursing is considered a sign of ignorance in my family. Flora says she cusses enough for the both of us anyway.

"And you're quitting grad school? I mean, for real? Wow, Marin. That's just so not you," Flora says, worry forming in her large, espresso eyes.

"It's a break. I called my advisor right after I got here. I can take a semester off without penalty." We're both quiet for a moment. "I'll return in the fall." I'm working up the courage to ask her for a job.

"So..." I start, but thankfully I don't have to ask.

"You need a job."

"Yes, and..." I try to remember the speech I rehearsed. She pats my arm. I notice that each nail on her light brown hand is a different shade of pink. She hasn't gone totally corporate yet.

18

"I have the perfect position for you. It will royally piss off this bitchface Celeste, but that's a perk. She's already on my shit list. She's late all the time, and I've caught her texting in costume, even though we explicitly tell characters to leave phones in their lockers. The good thing is all of this is documented. So..." She gives me her evil-genius grin. "This is happening."

"What exactly is happening?"

"Operation Rose Red." She claps her hands like summoning her retinue of servants.

"I thought I'd work at a concession stand or something. Isn't there some rigorous training I have to go through?" I stammer, not wanting to cut in line. "This seems wildly unfair."

Flora hops off the sofa, opening drawers, rifling through piles of costumes, and pulling out folders.

"I am 100 percent okay with starting at the bottom," I reassure her.

In response, Flora hands me a huge white binder.

"Open it," she orders. I note the "I'm about to engage in hijinks" glint in her eyes.

The first page is titled "Revel Character Cast Manual." Below are the "Do's and Don'ts." I just stand there, mouth agape.

"The hardest part about preparing for a role is building canonical knowledge," Flora says. She pulls a pencil out of her hair. "The normal training process takes weeks, but you, my dear, nerdy friend, know more about Revel than anyone I've ever met, and you know I'm a do-or-die Reveler. So, all you need to learn is basic etiquette." She grabs a notebook and a tape measure out of her fanny pack and eyes me suspiciously. "Lucky for you, this is what I do."

I glance at some of the rules.

- *Cast members cannot post pictures of themselves in costume.*
- *When in the park, stay in character at ALL times.*

- *No phones, ever.*
- *No sitting or lounging in public.*
- *Cast members are expected to meet a guest quota per hour.*
- *Cast members are expected to maintain their current weight. Costumes are expensive, fitted, and often shared. They won't be altered if cast members gain or lose weight.*

"Yikes. Okay." I frown. Flora now hovers above me with her notepad in one hand and the tape measure in the other.

"It's not that bad. I mean, it's a lot of work. It can be hot. Kids can be brats. Dads can be handsy, and you aren't allowed to point with one finger. You have to use two fingers." She demonstrates, looking like a flight attendant telling passengers where to find the emergency exits. I laugh incredulously.

"We jokingly refer to it as *fingering* instead of pointing." Her pointer and middle fingers curl and flick quickly, back and forth.

"That's foul." I giggle, but I sober up quickly. I know there are rules and lots of work that go into making this place magical for guests, but I can't help but worry. Will working at Revel Pointe ruin the fantasy of Revel for me? Will I end up hating this place I love so much?

Flora shakes her head at me. "Stop frowning. You'll love it. Every day you get to meet little versions of yourself. You get to be a part of a kid's first experience here. You'll see families bond and teenagers forget that they should be angsty turds. You'll be a part of something dedicated to making people happy."

Yes. I smile. All of that outweighs the weird rules and possible discomfort. I can do this. I have to do this. I blew up my life for this.

Flora's black eyebrows furrow in determination. "So, stand up. Let me measure those bodacious bazongas and get you in costume. The other Reds aren't quite so busty, so I have some work to do. You start tomorrow."

Chapter Six

Ethan

The sound of my fists hitting the bag is satisfying. I jab and cross until sweat pours into my eyes. The bag sways wildly. When my arms can no longer take the pain, I hop on the treadmill and try to run off my frustration. I was late to my meeting with the Chief Financial Officer this morning. What's the most annoying thing about this is that I did not oversleep. I wasn't hungover. I simply hadn't explored the park in about a decade. The last time I wandered around was with Wade and our younger half-siblings nearly a decade ago. Always the leader, Wade wanted to take them to see the new Steampunk Coaster, for the movie with the long title I can never remember. Wade and I let them convince us to take pictures with Miss Prudence Pleasant and her Haughty Hooligans. That's the last time we were all together. Our brothers and sister—The "Pride & Joy" a.k.a. James and Henri, and the "Little Angels" a.k.a. Dominic and Elsie.

It was James who had had the idea to name each generation of siblings to "take the piss" out of each other. Wade and I were called "The Bambinos." Our mom, Bambi, was Dad's first wife. She met him in his twenties when he frequented her place of work, a strip club called Scuttlebutts. Yes, my mother was once a "dancer." Bobby once told me that Dad brought her home to piss PawPaw off, but the joke was on Dad because PawPaw adored Bambi. Allegedly, Mick liked her more than his own son at that point. PawPaw refused to turn on the Mona Moon Lighthouse for two months after mom died. I was a baby then, and Dad never talked about her. PawPaw told us stories about her, though, saying she was like a Louisiana sunrise, beautiful and warm.

A few months after mom died, Dad married Tilda, and James popped out five months later. Interesting timing. I never held it against James or Henri. They have enough to put up with as Tilda's narcissistic extensions of herself. In interviews with the press, Tilda referred to them as Gaspard's and her "Pride & Joy." We joked that she couldn't remember their names. Unsurprisingly, her Pride & Joy were shipped to boarding school around the time Gaspard and Tilda became very busy breaking ground on Spoonbill Springs, the new animation studio in Baton Rouge.

I think James and Henri coined "Little Angels" for Yasmin and Dad's spawn, Elsie and Dom. I don't know anyone who doesn't love Yasmin, a doting mother and the antithesis of Tilda. Maybe that's why Dad didn't ignore this batch. It was impossible to; Dom and Elsie were freaking cute. Now they're fresh-faced college students.

Anyway, that was the last time I can remember that we were all together, until Wade's funeral. Shit, that day in the park with Wade was the last time I felt anything remotely positive about this place.

I increase the speed on the treadmill, furious because this morning the CFO wanted to meet at the resort's conference room, clear across the other side of the park, and I showed up late despite my best effort.

Last night I reserved a Revel golf cart for an early pickup, but it never showed. There was no way in hell I was taking a horse and buggy, so I walked, making a wrong turn somewhere around the San Fran Safari, and showed up to the meeting twenty-five minutes late, sweating and out of breath.

I was greeted by the she-beast herself, my stepmother and part owner of Revel Pointe, Tilda.

"Glad you were able to join us this morning, Ethan." Tilda and the CFO sat close together, catty-corner at the end of a long shiny table. The twerp smirked like he expected nothing less than this.

"Hello." The CFO stood. "I'm Bill Symons. I've only been here about a year. Not sure we've met properly." He was tall and stupidly tan, about forty with a build that screams "body by CrossFit." His handshake bordered on aggressive.

Tilda stood as well, as tall as Bill and equally fit. Her face is always tight, her hair streaked blonde, and there's a sheen on her forehead from what I can only assume is a barrel of Botox. She is beautiful in a disconcerting way, her eyes a bit too close together, forward facing like a predator. Her voice, however, is saccharine and incredibly feminine.

She sounds like she likes you. She does not.

"So sorry I am late. I had some transport problems this morning." I moved to sit down.

"No problem, sweetheart." Tilda smiled. "Unfortunately, Bill and I have another meeting in a few minutes, so we'll have to cut this short. If you'd like, you can just flip to the last few pages and sign off." She flicked her hand, air signing a signature. "Otherwise, we'll have to reschedule. So sorry."

She was not sorry.

"I like to read things before I sign them." I opened the first page.

"Of course, you do," she replied, the condescension in her voice unmistakable.

Bill, already at the door, turned to me as an afterthought. "I have the financials here, but I also sent an e-copy a few minutes ago. Look them over, and we'll talk when you're ready."

It was clear he thought I wouldn't get through the first few pages. The guy thinks I'm illiterate.

"Just tell my assistant Sheila, and she'll set up a tête-à-tête," Tilda purred as she prowled towards the door. "We're so happy you're back home at Revel, and we look forward to all the fun new ideas you'll contribute. Ta!"

Bill held the door for Tilda and took a healthy gander at her ass on the way out. They're definitely tête-à-tête-ing on the regular.

Carrying the 300-page document, I walked back into the unusual winter heat with the sneaking suspicion that my transport problem this morning wasn't a twist of fate. Tilda's smug smile, Bill's self-congratulating smirk—they think they've won something. It's my job to figure out what.

I spent the day reading and found the smoking gun. Wade's proposal was cleverly hidden towards the end of the tome. It was only three pages long, but Wade knew how to paint a picture. Before he deployed, he proposed a new park experience based on the *Island of Sirens* movie. An immersive VR adventure with the ultimate goal of educating the public about the delicate balance in ocean ecosystems and humanity's responsibility to use sustainable building practices.

The new experience would be expensive, but it would be groundbreaking. In the proposal, there's a line with Wade's fingerprints all over it: "*What is the point of money and power if we don't use it to protect the defenseless, as well as entertain AND educate the public?*" Dad certainly didn't write that. He was about bottom lines.

I think about Wade's proposal as I slow down on the treadmill, finally ready to hit the sack. After showering, I fall into bed, exhausted. Later that night, I dream about Wade.

When I wake up, the only thing I remember clearly is us walking in the park with PawPaw, and Wade pointing at something in the distance and saying, *Can you see it?*

But I couldn't.

Try harder, Wade pleaded.

My face is wet with tears. I get up and prepare my counterattack.

~

For the next few days, I don't drink and I work out like a beast, sharpening myself. What I have going for me is that my enemy wildly underestimates my abilities. They've forgotten who I was before my years as a public scoundrel: a nerd with a degree in Finance and Business Management from MIT. A math geek who left academia for the "right kind of job for a man," as my dad said. Recruited by Goldman Sachs, I became a "finance bro." And other than the problem-solving aspect of the job and making boatloads of my own money, I hated every minute of it. A few years in, trapped and needing time to figure my shit out, I left GS and began my illustrious career as a full-time fuckboy. It wasn't all for show. Sometimes I thoroughly enjoyed myself, but it went too far, especially when Bree got involved.

Ah, Bree. Her public announcement of our breakup seemed like lightyears away. She never cared about me. She made that abundantly clear when she didn't fly to Louisiana for the funeral, citing "work" as her excuse. Too bad she failed to tell her entourage that week, who took roughly one thousand photos of her eating sushi at a new restaurant where the tables are literally naked women.

A few nights later, the bartender at Molly's, my favorite New Orleans bar, asked me to help her with something in the storeroom. We ended up fooling around on a dilapidated table while the mean old bar cat hissed at me. Drunk and grieving, I barely remembered posing for "selfies," which were promptly trending hours later.

How did I leave Revel years ago because of my selfish, cutthroat father and stepmother only to end up surrounded by selfish, cutthroat pricks? I should have run away to Paris like Aunt Alice. I think of PawPaw quoting *King Lear*. I feel like King Lear, shaking my fist at the "great stage of fools" around me, except I'm not an old man. I'm thirty and shouldn't be this jaded.

For some reason, an image of a red halo of hair pops into my mind. I shake my head, needing to focus on the problem at hand. I survey my compound apartment, which looks like an Office Depot exploded on my dining room table. Books lie half open on my couch. Dishes are piled up in the sink.

My new meeting is scheduled with Bill, Tilda, and our COO, Ernie Guidry, today. Once that's over, I'll clean.

"You make a mess, you clean it," PawPaw used to tell us as kids, so I rarely use the cleaning service provided in the compound.

I think about my dream. About Wade.

Try harder.

I am going to be the acting CEO in lieu of Dad, in lieu of Wade. Everyone's bronze medal. No one expects me to try at all.

But I am going to figure out how to honor Wade's memory.

Come hell or high water.

Chapter Seven

Marin

After I filled out mounds of paperwork while Flora altered the Rose Red costume, she leads me through a series of interconnected tunnels that allow employees to get around the park without being seen by the public. We enter the employee dormitory and head to her small one-bedroom apartment. She rolls a twin cot into her room.

"Just like college, right?" she says as she makes up my bed with Thumbelina sheets. Despite the upheaval of my life and new job anxiety, I fall asleep immediately.

The next morning, Flora shoves a cup of coffee in my face.

"Wake up, Rose Red!" she shouts. "It's time to work."

In a blur, I follow her back to the dressing rooms and sit in her alcove, reading the employee manual, and memorizing the laundry list of very specific rules.

An attractive blonde girl in short-shorts and halter top saunters into Flora's office around 8 a.m. only to walk back out five minutes later, beet red and screaming, "Screw you! That phone rule is inhumane!" This must be Celeste.

Flora comes out a moment later. "Okay, let's get you ready." She fits me for the costume, and I am in hair and make-up by 10 a.m. About to make my debut as a Revel princess, I can barely contain myself, jittery from the coffee and nerves.

"Take some deep breaths and smile," Flora coos as she walks me to my station in the French Village, an exact replica from the 1973 animated classic *Diamonds & Toads*. *Rose Red*, which came out in the '80s, doesn't have a particular station because the setting of the film, as Flora jokes, is "vaguely European village and sometimes forest."

The good news is Red and her prince get to hop around the park more than the other characters.

"I'm trying to breathe, but I may bust a seam." I laugh, hoping this corset will loosen up throughout the day.

Despite actually having red hair, I wear a red wig. It's more of a crimson red, deeper than my own, and Flora told me it saves time. "Wigs keep you from having to spend three hours getting the perfect Rose Red waves."

My corset is a deep rose pink with purple damask threading. My petticoats are white and fluffy. A gauzy material hangs down my arms. It's romantic, vaguely medieval, and uncomfortable. I fidget.

"Don't worry. You look so perfect. We both know you know this movie and the lore better than most fans. Just breathe and stay in character from now on." Flora fluffs my hair and scans my face.

My make-up is caked on but flawless. False eyelashes, red lips, rosy cheeks, and Red's famous Marilyn beauty mark. Revel historians believe this was intentional. Gaspard had a crush on Marilyn Monroe as a boy, so Mick modeled Rose Red's face on hers. I've seen some side-by-side images; the resemblance is not subtle.

We enter a rustic medieval gate, the path turns to cobblestone, other characters mill about in period dress: large tan tunics, rough brown pants, peasant dresses and bonnets. Two cows and a mule eat behind a pen. The air smells like smoke, hay, and wood chips. Everyone is smiling. I feel transported.

"Like I said, you won't always be in this location. You'll be in the Princess Palace quite a bit. But now, it's time to meet your prince. You'll work with him exclusively." Flora gestures to a tall figure, lounging in the shade talking to a blacksmith. He is dashing in a red cape, tight trousers, and gray tunic. His V-shape is accentuated by a large black belt with a brass buckle. I try not to salivate, but this man is right out of one of my fanfic fantasies.

"Hello, Roland," Flora says loudly.

Roland straightens immediately and walks into the sun. His hair is perfectly coiffed, brown with blonde streaks, longish on the top but expertly slicked back. His eyes are a startling hazel. He even has the classic Roland dimples. This is my Prince. My corset feels even tighter.

"This is your new main Red." Flora gestures to me. Casting likes to keep couples exclusive. Continuity is key. Repeat visitors like to see the same actors together.

Roland cocks his head to the side, taking a moment to recalibrate, then he bows. Flora side-eyes me. I can feel it, but I just keep staring.

"Cough, cough, Rose Red." She nudges me. "Remember the rules." She does a half-curtsy.

"I'm so terribly sorry," I manage in my best breathless voice. A little huskier than my normal speaking voice. "I'm Rose Red."

All cast members have to stay in character the minute they leave the dressing rooms. They must refer to their castmates by their character names and only engage in behavior that the characters would. I curtsy as requested.

"Do not trouble yourself, Rose Red. I am not your normal prince, and you aren't a normal princess," Roland says, quoting the movie, as he moves closer and grabs my hand. I blush like a fangirl. I'm supposed to be working with him, but I can barely string together two words around him. When I look into his beautiful eyes, his head lowers and he kisses my hand. My skin tingles as his eyes scan my face. His smile grows bigger with approval.

"It's like a frame from the movie," the blacksmith says. "She's the best one so far! Goddamn!"

"Language, Edgar," Flora admonishes. "Now, Rose, the Prince here will help you learn the ropes today. Unfortunately, he's scheduled to play the Pirate Prince for the next week, so soak up all the expertise." Princes, unlike Princesses, are not in high demand, so they often play multiple roles.

I bet he looks fabulous in pirate regalia. Heat floods my cheeks again. Damn it, being pale is like being a walking, talking mood ring.

"Thank you." Roland nods at Flora. "Rest assured that she will be taken care of." He bows briskly and holds out his hand. It takes me a beat to realize what he wants. I awkwardly place my hand on his, hoping it isn't too clammy.

The rest of the afternoon is a blur. Roland and I barely have time to speak before the photo ops consume the day. I do notice him checking me out a few times, and he also shares his flagon of water with me. Just like the movie. In the few moments we have to ourselves, he quizzes me about the rules and asks me character questions. I answer all of them correctly, and he says with raised eyebrows, "You, my dear Rose, are brilliant."

Roland makes me feel like a princess, so my acting feels natural, less stilted as the day goes on. When we part, he lifts my hand to his perfect lips and whispers, "Until we meet again." His deep baritone sends shivers down my spine as I float back to the cast compound, then back to Flora's place.

Over margaritas in her tiny kitchenette, Flora asks how my first day went. I tell her about how busy we were and how wonderful Roland was.

"A great partner. So helpful. Great with kids and parents. Just perfect." I'm beaming.

"Be careful." Flora warns and sips her beverage through a purple Steampunk Coaster curlicue straw.

"What?" I say, a tad too quickly. "It's hard to take anything you say seriously when you're drinking out of that ridiculous straw."

She laughs and takes a loud slurp. "Don't get me wrong, Roland is one of the best cast members in the park, but he's acting. He's not the real Roland. In fact, I think his name is Tim. Or Tad..." She pauses as if trying to access a database of cast names in her brain. She shakes her head, clearly not interested in Roland's real name. "Whatever. Roland. He's an actor. Just don't get too swept up in the magic of all this." She waves her hand in the air to encompass the whole park.

"I won't. Don't worry," I assure her. "I'm just so excited to be here. Thank you so much."

Flora raises her glass in the air. "To Rose Red and Flora the Fox. Back together again."

Something clicks into place as my glass clinks against Flora's. Warmth spreads through me, and it isn't the tequila. It's this place, this friendship, this feeling that I am where I should be.

Later that night, I fall asleep, exhausted but exhilarated, and I try not to replay the image of Roland kissing my hand, his hazel eyes sparkling, his voice so like the actual Roland's it's uncanny. I knew it'd be a while before I'd see Roland, again. I hoped sooner rather than later. Heeding Flora's warning, I also remind myself that I should absolutely learn Roland's actual name.

Chapter Eight

Ethan

I was ambushed, I think as I pace, thankful for the thick rugs because I'm sure at this rate I would ruin the hardwood floor. Tilda, the witch, rescheduled our meeting again, but I was not deterred. Perhaps I should have been. I underestimated Tilda's avarice. You'd think she'd be satisfied with her shares in Revel and running Elixir, the 3D computer-animated film division. Oh, and the already lucrative cruise line. But no. She's a menace. I tug at my hair, so pissed off I'm sweating.

I felt prepared walking into the rescheduled meeting, confident even. This time the meeting was at Revel Pointe Palace's conference room. But instead of just Tilda, Bill, and Ernie Guidry, I walked into a full-on board meeting. Even Luca Conti, the Italian shipping magnate who made the cruise-line dream a reality, was there. *Magnifico.*

Exhausted with frustration, I plop down on the couch and replay the meeting, word-for-word. I left knowing three things:

1) Tilda doesn't want to pursue Wade's "pet project."

2) Tilda wants to develop another cruise line, which will require Revel to buy an entire island in the Caribbean for ships to dock.

3) Tilda will play dirty to get what she wants.

She had slides prepared, business plans in shiny folders, and a killer pitch. Her venture would cost a lot, but she could guarantee a high return on investment.

After her spiel about making the company billions, she sat down, looked at me, and said, "Ethan, do you have anything to propose?"

She knew goddamn well I didn't. "I was told this meeting was about *current* proposals and finances. Also, I wasn't aware this was a full board meeting." The room was silent. Uncomfortably so.

Bill Symons looked up from his business plan. "We have this meeting on the second Wednesday of every month."

Tilda frowned at me with fake disappointment. "Yes, and this was the only time we could all meet this week."

"Well, now I know," I said between my teeth, seething. "No one thought to send me a calendar invite?" I'm supposed to be the acting-CE-fucking-O.

Ernie Guidry coughed. He had enough manners to look embarrassed. "Ethan, I can see you took copious notes. What's your opinion on our revenue streams?"

I took a breath and let loose. "I think they are very healthy. You have been doing a fantastic job the last three quarters keeping this place profitable and safe for investors. My dad would be happy with the progress."

Nods of approval from the board. Tilda's mouth formed a thin, flat line.

"However—safe?" I paused. "That's not our brand. We are innovators, or at least we used to be. We need to push ourselves. We claim to be the most creative content and entertainment creators in the world, yet it seems we've grown stagnant, scared of risks. It's all sequels and reboots, another hotel in the chain or cruise in the fleet."

Bill shifted in his seat. "Well, with the mixed reviews of the last few movies and the luke-warm response to our *Twinners* spin-off, I think we need to just take a beat..."

"I think this is exactly the time to wow Revelers. Remind them of who we are," I interrupted.

"You haven't been here in a decade," Tilda said, her voice friendly but she smiled like a snake. "How do you know who we are?"

"Fair point, but I'm a Reve, and I'm here now. And I know my brother." I paused, gathering myself. "*Knew* him. I know what my PawPaw would want. And I think—"

"I noticed you left Gaspard off that list." Tilda leaned forward. While she and my dad were terrible spouses, they were excellent business partners and still work together closely. Dad and I were not close. Obviously. And it was obvious to the board members too.

"Yes." I bit my tongue and tried not to take the bait.

"I spoke to him after his physical therapy this morning, and he was more than happy to pursue the second cruise line and island acquisition." She reclined in her seat and crossed her legs and shared a smile with Luca Conti. Smug, continental SOB.

"Well, I can't speak to that. What I can do is ask for time to put together a proposal that honors my brother's memory and Revel's mission."

I searched the faces around the table. Some were old, like Ernie Guidry and Shirleen Watson, PawPaw's right-hand woman before he retired. But, there were a lot of new faces too. I didn't know these people, and they probably only knew me from the latest episode of *TMZ* or from the cover of *US Weekly*. Hopefully, they didn't imbibe too much celebrity gossip. Either way, I was largely an unknown entity to them, or known for the wrong things.

Tilda began to speak, but Shirleen interrupted. "Excuse me, I just want to recap, if no one minds." Heads nodded all around the table.

Shirleen reviewed her notes and continued. "We have two proposals to consider. Both are big projects, both require serious time and upfront costs, not to mention the logistics of purchasing an island."

"As you see, it's all clearly–" Tilda interjected.

"Excuse me, Tilda," Shirleen said firmly with the confidence of a terrifying high school English teacher. "I don't feel comfortable moving forward with either until we have more data in front of us, especially in a time of transition." More nods around the room. Luca Conti and Tilda shared a meaningful look.

Pointing in my direction with a pencil, Shirleen added, "And as Ethan pointed out, our finances are healthy. I love growth as much as the next person at this table, but we must be responsible, and that means having all the cards on the table."

"Well," Ernie said as he picked up Tilda's plan, "I propose waiting until next quarter's meeting to hear both proposals."

"I second that," Shirleen said. "All in favor, say 'Aye.'"

Ayes won seven to five. Ernie nodded at me. Shirleen closed the meeting.

Tilda and Bill left in a huff. Shirleen came over to me, a vision in a banana yellow suit with giant red reading glasses framing kind eyes.

"You'll want to overprepare," she whispered, her chin tipping down so her eyes peered over her glasses. "There are snakes in the grass."

Ernie gave me a hearty handshake. "You bought yourself some time, boy. Best make this proposal something special."

Afterwards, I walked back to my place in a daze. Wade had outlined the *Island of Sirens* idea, but it was three pages and short on logistical details. He thought he'd have more time. Now I had three months to come up with a winning proposal, including development and marketing plans.

This is when I started pacing, my feet keeping time to the words *"Three months, three months."*

After a while, Three months was replaced by my old standby, *"Wrong son. Wrong son."*

Now, surrounded by my literal and figurative mess, my head pounds. Another panic attack creeps its way from my gut to my heart. Breaths come quick and shallow. I need to get out of here. Now. Maybe Bobby's working again.

Chapter Nine

Marin

Looking like a Revel Princess and actually being a Revel Princess are two very different things. I've nailed the walk and the pointing (or "fingering"), but I wasn't prepared for the mounds of underwear and petticoats, especially in the swampy heat. The winter weather is unpredictable. One day it's chilly and damp, a cold that seeps through to the bones; the next it's balmy. There are numerous cooling stations and hideaways from random afternoon showers. Why did Mick Reve insist on building a theme park in the swamp?

I wasn't prepared for how exhausted I would be by the end of the day, how my face muscles hurt from smiling. Even so, it's still magical to see kids' faces light up when they recognize their FAVORITE princess.

I also started to make friends with other cast members. A few nights ago, I had drinks with Lana, the girl who plays Princess Portia from *Portia's Power* and Carrie, the pixie Thumbelina. After a few glasses of wine, I told Carrie that I sleep on her at night. She batted her eyelashes and told me that I'm free to try the three-dimensional version of Thumbelina anytime. My eyes must have popped out of my head because Flora, Lana, and Carrie burst out laughing.

"She *is* like a real Revel princess!" Lana exclaimed, pouring me another drink.

"Sometimes," Flora said knowingly. "But that's one of the many reasons I love her."

"I'm not that naïve," I hiccoughed.

"Fucking adorable. Seriously," Carrie sighed. "And straight. Of course."

"Yes, she only has eyes for Roland," Flora teased.

"Oh, really?" Carrie leaned forward, preparing to divulge hot gossip. "He asked me out a few times during my first season," she admitted. "But I told him I was exclusively into princesses."

"What did he say?" I asked, a little too eager.

"He said 'Isn't that great? We have so much in common!'" Carried laughed. "A total Prince Roland thing to say."

Flora winked at me and elbowed my arm obnoxiously. I snickered and took a sip of wine. I worked with Roland the day before yesterday. My fledgling crush has become full blown. He's so courteous, so fun, so kind. Opening doors, holding his arm out for me when we walk, winking at me throughout the day when a kid is particularly cute. He compliments how I handle difficult guests. He admires my knowledge of Revel lore. When he smiles at me, I feel truly beautiful and perfect. Something I never feel around anyone, especially guys. I usually feel ogled, or I mess up potential romance by being ridiculously awkward.

I've only had one actual boyfriend. It was in college, Jonathan was sweet—sweet, it turns out, has its limits. I refer to the night I lost my V-card as "an exercise in patience." For both parties. When Jonathan broke up with me, I understood. We weren't a "good match." This made sense to me. He was just another person with whom I didn't fit.

Flora tried to set me up multiple times after that, saying I needed to play the field, but I'm just not built for it. More power to my peers for exploring, but I can't really engage in anything romantic unless I feel safe. With Roland, I feel safe. Seen, even.

A little voice reminded me that feeling seen in a costume might be a problem. I looked up and saw Flora give me a wary look over her vodka soda, her brows furrowed a bit.

Despite her clear concern about my fraternizing with a coworker, I find myself daydreaming about holding his hand, walking around the Mona Moon lighthouse, and canoodling on the benches when our shifts end. I still don't know his real name. But, hey, maybe I'm a Method actor. I chalk my insane crush up to my consummate professionalism.

Sure. Keep telling yourself that, the voice returns.

Doubts occasionally creep in. *Maybe my parents are right—I need to grow up. Grow up and out of this fantasy world, this escapist dream land.*

Now, heading back to the dressing rooms, I remind myself to enjoy this and shove the doubts away. My thoughts turn to Roland, my new friends, my new life. I followed my bliss, and it led me to Revel Pointe.

I just finished a grueling ten-hour shift, but Flora promised I'd only work eight tomorrow. Even though I'm exhausted, I want to stroll around the park in the quiet hour before the park shuts down for the night and most of the guests have left.

The truth is I want to be Rose Red for a few more moments before becoming boring Marin Vandersee again, and I know exactly where I want to wander, Mona Moon's Lighthouse. I will go to Mona Moon, toss a coin in the moat, and make my wish.

One of the first structures ever built at Revel, the lighthouse is an enormous tower that reflects the phases of the moon in the huge lamp at the top of the structure. The face of the moon is Mona Moon from Revel's first hit, *Ragtime Romp*. It's what launched Mick Reve to fame and fortune, and its success is what allowed him to start this park—*A Place for Children of All Ages*. In *Ragtime Romp*, Mona Moon grants wishes, but only to worthy wishers. It's silly, but I still plan to throw my coin in, repeat the motto, *Wish upon a moon and awake anew*, and make a wish.

When I arrive, a few crew members are still sweeping away popcorn kernels, readying the pathways for tomorrow. The sun has been down for hours, but Mona's face and the real full moon light up the night sky. I pull a quarter from my hidden pocket and take a moment to thank Flora for recognizing that even Revel princesses need pockets in their dresses. The moat is deep, more than six feet, but the water is clear, and the bottom is covered by other wishers' coins. The light shimmers off the variegated metal like mermaid scales. I am ready.

I grasp the coin tightly, close my eyes, whisper Mona's motto and wish.

I wish to find love. I kiss the quarter and throw it in the air. It makes a plopping noise and sinks to the bottom.

Suddenly I have another wish. I fumble in my pocket for another coin. I kiss this one. *Find a way to be a part of this world, Revel Pointe, long-term.* I watch the coin sink below the surface.

A moment later, I hear a splash followed by a baritone "oomph!" I look around. There's no one on the other side of the moat and no one behind me. Thank god, because I'm still in costume and Rose Red doesn't know anything about *Ragtime Romp.* I turn to leave, but then I hear another splash. I search around again but see no one until rippling waves lead my eyes to a man, who is in the moat. And not just any man—Ethan Reve.

Oh my god, it couldn't happen twice. Now I'll have to tell Flora about it. I'd had the hardest time not telling her about seeing Ethan that first night. It just felt like bad form to gossip about the guy. He'd just lost his brother last year. And there was something so sad about him. He seemed so lost. But now?

Now he's swimming in the Mona Moon moat. *What the heck?* Although I wouldn't say what Ethan is doing constitutes swimming. Swimming requires coordination. Something he severely lacks.

Oh no, maybe he's drunk and floundering. What should I do?

"Hello? Do you need some help?" I call to him, but it's eerily quiet. He has stopped flailing and appears to be sinking. One beat, two go by.

Before I think about it, I somehow hop the wrought-iron fence and dive into the water, adrenaline fueling me. Despite the warm days, the water is freezing. And it's deeper than I expected. I grab on to Ethan's arm, but instead of me drawing him to the surface, he pulls me down.

I have read about this. This is how drowning people kill their would-be saviors. They panic. They hold on too tight.

But he isn't frantic, just stronger and heavier than me. I kick him in the shin and that seems to wake him up. He shoots up, pulling me with him. We cling to the fence for a minute, our feet barely planted on the ledge when Ethan begins to wobble.

He's going to fall right back into the water. I put my arm behind him and push up. It's awkward, but I manage to encourage him over the fence. He falls onto his back with a thud.

I attempt to hop over next, but my dress catches on the fence. A tear and a swoosh, then I'm rolling onto the ground in what feels like seven thousand pounds of petticoats and a corset. I stop near Ethan Reve, who isn't moving or coughing. Needing to make sure he's breathing, I crawl over and place my right hand by his head and lightly slap him with my left.

"Ethan, Ethan," I whisper insistently. It doesn't work, so I yell, "Wake up. Ethan!"

I'm trying to roll him on his side when he takes a deep breath.

Thank god I don't have to recall the scant CPR training from health class.

Now that he's breathing, I take a minute to catch my own breath. I lie on my back and look at him in profile. He's beautiful in the moonlight. A study in contrasts. Dark hair, wet pale skin. He must be freezing. I roll over to check his pulse, then he grabs me and pulls me on top of him. I push myself up, trying not to use his body for leverage.

His eyes open and attempt to focus for a moment. They narrow in on my hair. My wig, which must be outrageous now, is somehow both huge and flat when wet. The light is behind me, so I get a good look at his face, but he struggles, squinting at me.

His hand cups my face, and he says something like "Golden ambers."

Has he completely lost his marbles?

Then he whispers, "I'm sorry." His eyes lock on mine, searching for absolution. I don't know what to do. He repeats himself, "So, so sorry."

I lean forward a bit, lay a hand on his heart, and whisper, "It's okay. You'll be okay."

Then, his mouth is on mine. I'm too stunned to move. His breath tastes like whiskey and mint. His lips are firm, and I let him kiss me until his hand reaches around to the back of my head, which deepens the kiss, and suddenly, my mouth opens for him.

I'm kissing Ethan Reve is my last coherent thought before I'm just feeling. Feeling his tongue expertly play with mine. Feeling his torso, wet against mine. Feeling his pecs, his abs, sculpted and hard, his hips. His lips leave my mouth, and he's kissing my neck. I moan, loud enough to startle myself.

He calls me his angel. *What am I doing?*

I push myself away from him, but he whispers, "More." His deep, scratchy voice betrays a hint of a Southern accent. It's sex. Pure, unadulterated sex. His hand moves from the small of my back to my ass. I am straddling him now and can feel how excited he is. We're kissing again. And moving. It's rhythmic, and my whole body feels like it's on fire. I want more. More of this feeling. More of him.

Mona Moon's dulcet voice sounds from a loudspeaker, "The clock has rung, it's time to go, we'll see you again, this I know." I freeze, the spell broken. I spring off of him as much as the weight of my wig and petticoats allow, mortified by my overwhelming response to his drunken kiss.

He moans, "Please." Then his voice gets gruffer, louder, "Don't go."

I watch as he tries to get up and falls again. Afraid of what might happen if I touch him again, I step back.

"Please, Ethan. Go home," I turn away, stumble a few steps before turning back to say, "And for god's sake, take care of yourself!"

I hobble all the way back to the dorms, holding my heavy, soaked petticoats, praying no one sees me, and wondering, *What in the ever-loving hell just happened?*

Chapter Ten

Ethan

An ugly, low-pitched squawk wakes me. Hints of the sun peek over the clouds. A seagull perches on a wrought-iron fence close by, its head cocked quizzically, its call obnoxious. Its beady black eyes seem to judge me.

"Shoo!" I yell, sitting up. Oh, god. My head. My back. My entire body.

Did I pass out in front of the lighthouse? I search for clues. There's the gross, minty aftertaste in my mouth. The ever-present scent of water on the pointe. This seagull eyeing me. The lush azalea bushes along the path. The poofy pink dress. Wait a second. *I don't remember wearing that last night.*

As the sun is still rising, I realize I only have a few minutes to get my shit together. I lean against the fence and retrace my steps. After freaking out about the board meeting, I made my way to RP Lounge. Bobby wasn't there. I sat alone in a corner booth, taking deep breaths, avoiding eye contact with the growing crowd of faux-elite Revel members, and scrolling on my phone. I remember scanning pictures of "friends" at NYC art installations, new nightclubs, and trendy restaurants where a whiff of fog is an appetizer. None of them have reached out to me. I don't miss them. Not even Bree.

This made me even sadder because what was I even doing with my life before coming back to Revel Pointe? Why did I choose to spend my time with these vapid heiresses, athleisure-wear moguls, and mercenary influencers? I should have been here with Wade. I should have spent more time with him. I should have made PawPaw engage more. The 'should-haves' overwhelmed me.

Some women sent over a mint julep. They must have been from up North, thinking all Southerners sit and sip sweet tea and juleps on porches dressed like Colonel Sanders. The truth is, stereotype or not, a mint julep is delicious. I ordered three more, drinking them in quick succession. I vaguely remember the blur of women joining me in my booth.

Then I remember feeling a crushing desire to be alone, narrowly escaping the group of pawing, spray-tanned women, wandering to the bathroom, then heading back out into the park. The rides had closed, and the pathways were nearly empty. Just crew members picking up after the hordes of tourists. I vaguely recall wanting to see the lighthouse turn on, *needing* to see it.

Wade and I used to climb the lighthouse stairs with PawPaw, way back when he could manage the twelve-story spiral staircase. We'd eat beignets, powdered sugar covering our faces, and he'd tell us stories from *Ragtime Romp*, about Theo Tomcat, Kiki the Croc, and Miss Maisy. He told us about how Mona Moon granted wishes to little boys with kind hearts. Maybe that's why I ended up there. I wanted to feel close to Wade. I wanted to remember when we were considered good, kind-hearted boys worthy of our wishes. At least Wade remained worthy. The last thing I remember is looking up at Mona Moon's face illuminated in the dark sky, wishing... And that's it. The rest is blank.

Shoving my hands in my pockets, I notice how wet they are. Could I have actually fallen into the moat? And climbed out? Or maybe someone helped me? Someone in a pink dress, I surmise, as I notice another soggy lump of a cherry-blossom pink dress on the concrete pathway. I slowly crawl to it and pick it up; it's heavy, wet, and stinking like pond water. The skirt is torn. There's something familiar about this dress that I can't quite...

Shit! A Revel princess pulled me out of the water last night. Embarrassment courses cold through my veins. I'm such an idiot.

Our cast members sign NDAs, but pulling a drunk Ethan Reve from the moat might prove too juicy for a princess to keep to herself. Now, I know I need to find this person and make sure she didn't blab this to *The Secret Reveler*. But first I need to get off this concrete, take a shower, and drink a gallon of strong coffee. Maybe the deep sense of self-loathing will dissipate with my hangover.

Mona, whatever I wished for yesterday, let's add "find the princess from last night" to the list.

Chapter Eleven

Marin

I sneak back to the dorms undetected, thankfully. I strip off my petticoats and leave them to dry on the back of the kitchen chairs. In the shower, I let hot water soothe my tense muscles, breathe deeply, and try to make sense of what happened. I'll have to tell Flora in the morning, but what am I going to say? That instead of heading straight back to our staging and change rooms, I wandered to Mona Moon's Lighthouse, wishing for true love, mooning over Roland, and then was interrupted by Ethan Reve nearly drowning? And then promptly had the most intense make-out session of my entire life?

This is too ridiculous to believe. I must have hit my head and passed out. Maybe saving and then kissing Ethan Reve will be revealed to have been a dream all along, a convenient plot device that explains the mess away. I'll wake up, back in my shitty sublet apartment in New Orleans, late for my Econ class.

Brushing my teeth, the minty flavor reminding me of Ethan, my whole body tingles in response. It definitely happened.

I throw on an oversized *Hansel & Gretel* tee and quietly tiptoe to bed. Flora, thankfully, sleeps with ear plugs and a night mask. In college, she told me being a country bumpkin meant that the tiniest sound and faintest light kept her up at night, except for the sound of wind and crickets.

I lie there tossing and turning on my cot. After what feels like a few hours, I finally drift off—only to be awakened after what feels like ten minutes by a shriek.

"The petticoats!" Flora has discovered them. It's 6 a.m. *Time to face the music*, I think as I drag myself from the bed and inch toward the kitchenette.

Flora holds the damp petticoats up, inspecting them. She drops them and narrows her eyes at me.

"What happened?"

"Well, you'll never believe this, but..." I can't hide anything from Flora. She knows me too well, and so I proceeded to tell her everything. Almost.

"I pulled Ethan Reve from the Mona Moon Lighthouse moat last night."

"Ex-excuse me?" Flora stutters. "Say that again."

"I was at the Lighthouse, and I heard a splash and saw Ethan Reve sinking in the moat, and he wasn't moving."

Flora's eyebrows take up residence in her hairline. "What!?"

"And so, I jumped in, and I pulled him out. He was drunk. I think he fell in." Flora is silent, processing. I move to the coffee maker as a distraction.

"Where's the dress?" Flora's tone isn't accusatory, more investigative and a bit concerned.

"Crap!" I just remembered. "It got caught on the fence. It tore right up the middle, and I sort of fell out of it."

Flora's eyes grow larger than an anime character's. Her dresses are her babies.

"I am SO, SO sorry, Flora. I know how hard you worked on it, and I know..."

Flora's hand flies up in the air, as she cuts me off. "Don't. We have other costumes. That was an emergency. You did the right thing."

"Yeah," I mumble, eyes on the floor.

"You saved a dude's life. That's a reasonable excuse for trashing a costume. So, you fall out of the dress..." Her black eyebrows quirk up. "Then what?"

I blush.

"Oh my god. You banged Ethan Reve!" she exclaims. Her hands pound the counter.

"No! We did not bang." I turn around, grab the coffee filter, and start scooping grinds, taking deep breaths. "I would never have sex with a drunk person."

"Do not lie to me, Marin. Something happened. What happened?" The petticoats are now cast aside, and she's leaning against the counter. "You owe me details." She gestures to the sodden underclothes.

I sigh. She's right. "Well, I sort of fell near him. I went to see if he was hypothermic, and he looked at me kind of funny, and then started kissing me."

Flora's mouth drops open.

"I didn't kiss him back at first, but then..." I hesitate.

"Then what?" Flora leans towards me.

"Then I did." I pour water into the coffee maker basin, trying to act nonchalant.

Flora squeals. "And?"

"And what?" I tap my hand on the counter, focusing on the sound of percolating coffee, willing my face to turn from red to white.

"And how was it?" she asks, ravenous for details.

I blush deeper, probably a stunning shade of crimson now.

Flora smacks the counter again. "Oh my god, he rocked your world!"

"Ssshhh! Keep it down. He didn't rock my world, he just...he's a very good kisser, and I don't know...I don't have much experience with all that, you know, and well, it took me by surprise is all. He was wasted and didn't even know what he was doing." I turn around again, pretending to focus on finding sugar and cream.

I hear her whisper, "Wow, you saved Ethan Reve."

When I turn around to face her finally, Flora's eyes narrow for a moment like she is using x-ray vision to read my inner thoughts, then she shrugs, letting it go.

"Well, hurry up then," she says. "We have to find that dress before the park fills up, and I'll have to figure something else out for you today." Flora turns toward the bathroom.

I nod, mortified by the idea that a park visitor, or another employee, could find my dress and think Rose Red was up to no good.

Later, as we walk past the Mona Moon Lighthouse, there's no pink dress to be found. *Crap.*

Chapter Twelve

Ethan

After a nap and a shower, I head to the cast offices carrying a giant trash bag filled with Rose Red's ruined dress. The ceilings are unusually high here, and the cast members enter and exit the station through a series of tunnels. I haven't been down here since I made out with one of the San Fran Safari dancing cheetahs the summer between high school and college. *Ah, memories.*

I find my way to the front desk, trying to be inconspicuous but failing. The people who work here are usually die-hard Revelers. They work here, play here, and spend half their paychecks on the merch. They have themed watch parties and know more about my family than I do. So, needless to say, I create quite the stir below decks.

A young woman dressed like Thumbelina is stretching provocatively by the front desk, obviously trying to get the attention of the pretty brunette manning the phones. I walk up, lean onto the desk, and Thumbelina does a double take. The brunette looks up from her computer. Her mouth drops when I smile.

"I was wondering if you could help me." I attempt to sound casual, hating the eyes on me.

The receptionist opens and closes her mouth a few times, and Thumbelina grins.

"Madison here is a bit flummoxed. Maybe I can help?" She has one foot in her hand, knee bent, stretching her quad. Clearly, less flummoxed.

"I found something, and I'm pretty sure it belongs to a cast member, but I don't want to get this person in trouble for losing her...things." And this is the moment that I realize this looks bad. So, so bad. I'm returning a torn princess dress in a trash bag. Public relations, as my media-savvy little sister Elsie says, is not my forte.

"What sort of things?" she asks, her brow cocked quizzically. Her eyes drift toward the enormous bag.

Abort, abort, I think. "You know what, I'll just figure it out on my own." I back away from the desk and wander towards a random hallway.

I hear her call after me, "If you change your mind, I can help..."

Most of the dressing room doors are open and cast members rush about in every direction, dressed and undressed. Most of them are theatre kids, unfazed by the naked body. I try not to gawk at the shocking amount of flesh on display as various women are fitted into costumes. Two lithe, scantily-clad women apply body paint to one another while a tanned Adonis waits on the couch, scrolling nonchalantly on his phone.

By the time I reach the end of the hall, I am ready to leave. This was a stupid idea. What a waste of time, I think, when I hear a woman yell from one of the few closed doors, "I'm sorry, but if you didn't lose that damn dress, I wouldn't be poking you in the ass at all!"

Bingo. I stop in front of the dressing room, knock three times, and wait. I hear exaggerated shuffling, huffing and puffing, and a sweet voice say, "I'm so sorry, Flora." The door swings open and an exasperated-looking woman with long black hair styled like Betty Page and four pins sticking out of her mouth, mumbles, "Yes?"

"Oh my god" comes a voice from behind her. A petite woman stands on a box. She is wearing some sort of teal swimming cap on her head, her face is painted green, and she's in a shiny, moss-green leotard. She looks like an alien. Do we have an alien experience here? I look a bit more closely. She's petite, but curvy in all the right places.

A sexy alien experience, maybe? Something out of the original *Star Trek*?

The alien looks horrified by my presence.

"I'm sorry to bother you." I turn to face the exasperated woman with the pins. "I wanted to return this. I think someone left it out last night."

I hear multiple gasps. I turn to discover four women, again, in various states of undress behind me. *Shit.* Now I'm really causing a scene.

"You better come in." Betty Page mumbles and takes the pins out of her mouth, sticking them into a ball on her wrist.

She shuts the door on the onlookers' faces. "I'm Flora, and this is Marin a.k.a. the former Rose Red."

"I'm Ethan." I extend my hand to Flora.

Instead of shaking it, Flora gestures for me to take a seat. "Yeah, I know who you are, dude." The couch is covered with costumes, so I stand there, awkwardly. Too big for the tight quarters. Or maybe it just feels that way.

"Here," she sighs, grabbing a mountain of costumes and placing them in a huge bin. "Sit."

"I just wanted to return the dress and talk to *you*." I gesture to the alien. "For a few minutes." I place the bag next to me. Marin hops off the box and quickly dons a robe. Modest, I see, unlike her fellow castmates. She must be new.

Marin grimaces as she pulls the dress out in two distinct pieces. "Um. Thanks." Then she looks at Flora with contrition in her big eyes.

"Don't worry about it," Flora consoles, sitting on a stool by the mirror.

"Could we get a little privacy?" I ask. "I just want to thank Rose, I mean Marin, and clear something up." I smile, trying my best to appear harmless.

Flora checks in with Marin, who gives a resolute nod, and Flora stands again. "Listen, you've got to get out to the Lily Pad in thirty minutes, so make it quick." Flora glares at me a moment, a warning not to fuck with her friend. I'm surprised to discover this display of loyalty makes me a little jealous. I'd like a Flora in my life to glare at basically everyone for me.

Once we're alone, I turn to Marin's green face, her earnest blue eyes as big as moons, and I can't help but laugh at this ridiculous situation.

"What?" She sounds defensive like she's used to being the butt of the joke.

"Nothing. Everything." I gesture around me and to her face. "I just wasn't expecting a frog to be my savior."

She huffs a little, but smiles. "Yeah. I'll be playing Miss Maisy Moreau for the next few days until I can get my Rose Red costume back in park condition."

"You've been demoted? From princess to frog?"

"I wouldn't say being Miss Maisy Moreau is a demotion. She's the first female character to have her own spin-off series from *Ragtime Romp*. She's also the moral conscience of the group."

"Okay..." She's a Reveler. *Great.*

"Okay, what?" She stares me down. Not impressed, not disappointed. Just a hot, amphibian Reveler who saved me from a moat presently nerding out and growing impatient with me.

What do I do with this? "You're a Reveler. You know your stuff," I respond flatly.

"Well, yeah. I wouldn't work here if I didn't love Revel Pointe." Her chin juts forward proudly, like a challenge.

"Listen, I just wanted to return the dress and also ask about last night." I lean forward, eager to get some answers.

"Yes?" Her eyes are downcast. She seems embarrassed. Not like someone who would share information with the press, but I've thought that before and have discovered no one is above making money. The sexy frog looks at me anxiously. "What about last night?"

"I was very drunk. I don't remember anything. When I woke up and saw this dress and—"

"Really?" she says, incredulous.

"Yeah," I continue. "I had some drinks at the lounge. Too many, obviously. I vaguely remember walking around the park, and then I blacked out."

Her eyes grow round. "Whoa," she whispers, drawing her robe around her tightly. "So, you remember nothing?"

"Zero. Zip. Zilch." I shrug, as if I don't find this disconcerting. As if I'm not secretly horrified that I can't seem to get a handle on my liquor or my life. "Nothing. Nil. Nada."

"Okay, okay. I got it. You don't remember anything." She's a little huffy now, her arms crossed across her chest. It's difficult to keep my eyes on her face and off her curves as she continues. "You blacked out."

"Yes."

"You do that often?" Her eyebrows arch.

I squirm. The truth is, since Wade died, I've done this more times than I care to admit.

She senses my discomfort. Her voice softens when she says, "I'm sorry. That was rude."

The silence between us is deafening, so I blurt, "I was wondering what happened last night." I lean even closer to her, my voice quieter. She stares at me, her bald head cocked to the side, reminding me of the seagull from this morning. It's cute as hell.

"Well, you fell into the moat," she says matter-of-factly.

"I gathered that."

"Then what do you need me for?" Sassy, or *sassafras*, as my PawPaw says. I like it.

"You're a bit of a smart ass for a Revel princess."

It's her turn to shrug. She pulls the robe's belt tighter and angles toward the make-up counter.

I press on. "How did I get out of the moat?"

She sighs. "I jumped in after you, helped you climb back over. My dress got caught on the fence. I couldn't lift you, and I was in my underthings." She whispers "underthings" like it's a naughty word, shifting her weight. "So, once I knew you were breathing, I went home."

I don't blame her. Revel has strict rules about cast member behavior in the park. Cavorting with me in a moat would definitely get her fired. But it could also make her some money. I stand up and take a step towards her.

"Did you take any pictures?" I try to ask nicely, but I'm already expecting the worst.

"What?" She stands up straight. Her hands are on her hips now like an angry mother from an '80s sitcom.

"You know, with your phone. Did you take pictures?" I ask, more forcefully than I mean to. This is always the hard part—getting obsessed Revelers to admit they're scum of the earth, parasites sucking on the celebrity teat.

"What would I do with pictures of you?" She's insulted, but instead of pulling away, she steps towards me.

"You know exactly what you'd do with pictures of me, drunk-as-a-skunk and making wishes at Mona Moon's lighthouse? The tabloids would pay top dollar for more compromising photos of the notorious Ethan Reve." We are even closer now. Her face tilts up towards mine.

"Oooh, I see." She nods, a look of pity flashes across her features, replaced quickly by a harder look. "I would never do anything like that."

"Excuse me, but I find that rather hard to believe." I laugh cynically, running my hands through my hair again, willing it to stay down as my body heats up.

She pushes her shoulders back. "Well then, I'm sad for you because I didn't and wouldn't do that."

Strangely, I believe her, but life has taught me not to trust this feeling. "So, no pictures? No proof?"

"No." She shakes her head. "Anyway, cast members are not allowed to have phones on them in costume."

I snicker. "Oh, like these millennials follow that rule."

"*I* follow that rule." She puts a hand on her heart. The robe won't stay closed. I try not to stare at her cleavage.

"And you didn't tell anybody?" Despite the make-up, her face is easy to read. She's getting mad.

"Just Flora, and she won't blab to anyone."

Fuck. They always have a friend. And that friend usually has an angle.

"How do you know she won't blab?" I sneer.

"Because she's my friend. And I asked her not to."

"Oh, so it's that easy, is it?" This chick must have grown up in a convent or in a little house on the prairie.

"Yes, because I don't keep friends I can't trust." Her chin juts in full defiance mode now. "It kind of defeats the purpose."

I notice a small indentation in the center of her chin. Her blue eyes bear into my own. *Who is this person?* She acts and sounds like a character in a children's book. A real do-gooder. A real Revel princess. Fuck me, no one's this nice.

"Has anyone ever told you that you're incredibly naïve?"

"Yes. All the time, but I don't care." She shrugs. "I'd rather think the best of people and be happy." She leaves me to check herself in the mirror. "Now, I have to get into full frog make-up in less than ten minutes and on a lily pad in twenty. If you don't mind, I think we're done here."

"I do mind. We're not done. One last question."

"What?"

She removes her robe as if to suggest the meeting is over. I've offended her more than I realized.

"Why?" I follow her to the vanity where she straightens various applicators. I find her eyes in the mirror's reflection.

She dabs a sponge into some paint and dabs it on her nose, huffs then bites. "Why what?"

"Why didn't you take pictures, sell the story? You could have made some serious cash."

When she turns around, we are close, inches apart. I'm surprised by how much I want to touch her, to ruin her makeup and pull the swim cap off her head and find out if she is an actual redhead.

She must see my eyes roaming across her body. Her brows furrow.

"I would never do that to someone. Because I love it here and respect your family's legacy too much, even if *you* don't."

I want to say more but am too gobsmacked by the sincerity of her words. We stare at each other for what seems like an hour. Something else is bothering her, other than my questioning her integrity.

But the conversation is cut short. The door opens, and Flora sticks her head in. "Listen, I really need to get Miss Maisy to her lily pad pronto."

Marin breaks the staring contest first, turns toward the mirror again, picks up the sponge, and starts blotting it around her eyes.

"Well, I won't take up any more of your time." Sheepishly I head toward the door.

"Hey, Ethan," Marin calls, and I whip around. "You're welcome."

I eye her reflection in the mirror. "For what?"

"For saving your life." Her voice is tremulous. I never even thanked her. In fact, I've just spent the last few minutes insulting her.

I am such an asshole.

Flora says, "Okay, bye-bye now," and slams the door in my face.

Chapter Thirteen

Marin

After eight sweaty hours in my Lycra Miss Maisy costume, undressing takes an act of God and Congress. I use a vat of Vaseline to remove the green paint from my face and chest. And even after using about thirty baby wipes, I'm sure I'll still find a green Jackson Pollock painting on my pillowcase in the morning. I doubt I'll even sleep tonight after that terrible exchange with Ethan Reve that kept replaying in the quiet moments of my workday. Flora is dying to know what we talked about, but I was so fired up after he left that I told her we'd have to chat later. I needed to get my head on straight before becoming this new character, which wasn't all bad.

In fact, it was a much slower day. It turns out that while I was excited to play such an iconic character, most people are not that interested in Old Miss Maisy. However, the Revelers who sought me out were serious fans. I met a couple in their early thirties with matching Miss Maisy and Theo Tomcat tattoos. They were getting married in the Revel Palace Hall of Enchantment the next day. Flipping adorable.

But the lack of visitors and photo ops meant that I had a lot of downtime to think. At first, I was furious with Ethan Reve. Furious that he would insinuate I would exploit his vulnerability for money. Furious that he called me naïve. And if I'm honest with myself, furious that he didn't remember the earth-shattering hotness of our make-out session.

After some heated stewing, next came pity. I felt sad for Ethan Reve. He must walk through life with everyone's eyes on him, assuming the worst of everyone. That must be hard. I'd always been invisible at home, but I remembered all the times I wasn't. The times I felt under the microscope, every little gesture or word under critical scrutiny.

"*Grow up, Marin.*"

"*Statistically, it would be anomalous for all of our daughters to go to an Ivy, you know.*"

"*Be sure to dress appropriately, Marin. Best foot forward.*"

And that's on a small scale. Ethan has the whole world monitoring him, wanting him to succeed and fail in equal measure. And to lose his brother so tragically, just recently. He's always been in Wade Reve's shadow, always mentioned in conjunction with the heroic Reve, the first son of the ambitious Gaspard Reve, and the first grandson of an empire builder, Mick Reve.

Even in the dormitory, his surname is on everything. Reve in filagree on the gates, blazoned on flags, stenciled on the ground. So much was expected of him now. He had to live up to his family's name when nothing much was expected of him six months ago. I remember the look he had after retching. Adrift. Lost.

I know what it's like to be the odd one out, to want something different, to be different.

No, I couldn't stay mad at him. Even if he didn't thank me for saving his life. At first, I thought he didn't acknowledge it because he's an entitled prick. But the more I thought about it, our conversation, the fleeting moments of real emotion peeking through the exchange, I realized he isn't grateful because he does not value his life enough to thank me for saving it.

This shift in perspective doesn't mean that I trust Ethan Reve. Not by a long shot. He's an irresponsible ne'er-do-well. He seems damaged, and damaged people hurt others, even when they have good intentions. Life has taught me that much.

See, I imagine saying to Ethan's stubborn, handsome face, *I'm not all that naïve.* I groan at the thought. Like he's even thinking about me and our conversation right now.

Fortunately, I don't have to interact with him again, now that he's brought up feelings that have left me confused and frustrated. I need to get out of this Ethan funk. So, after wiping off my makeup, I braid my hair, throw on a Captain Nemo baseball cap and a plain gray sweatshirt. Then I head out the door into my favorite place on Earth. Maybe I'll hit up Le Bleue Tortue for cafe au lait, then the *Hansel & Gretel* cottage for some Roman candy, and then see how Roland is holding up without me, as this morning Flora relegated him to pirate duty again.

Roland would get the Ethan taste right out of my mouth. I blush at my own unintentional innuendo. A little breathless, I saunter back out into the park in search of something to change my mood.

Chapter Fourteen

Ethan

The minute I leave the cast members' lair, I "New York" fast-walk back to my place. With sunglasses and hat on, I hope to avoid knowing stares. I really want to avoid running into an adorable frog who probably wishes she'd left me in that moat.

Back at my apartment, I find myself longing for the comfort of numbers, so I plop myself down in front of my computer with a cappuccino and the earmarked financial statements. It doesn't take long for me to understand that Tilda is not wrong. The cruise line is already a huge moneymaker for Revel Pointe. We run a number of ships out of the port here, outside of New Orleans, that are Revel Family cruises, but Tilda wants to create a cruise just for adults. Considering that adult Revelers are some of our best customers and most loyal brand advocates, it is hard to say no to this. However, the part of Tilda's plan that makes me wary is the island acquisition.

Here I fall down a research rabbit hole. Bodden Island is 10,000 square miles – roughly the size of Pittsburgh – and is near the Cayman Islands in the Caribbean. This particular island is sparsely populated, so that "shouldn't be a problem," according to Tilda. However, the deal between Revel Pointe and the local government is a bit vague on details. There is also mention of an environmental impact report, but that is nowhere to be found. I search for more information online, find little, then flag this section and return to Wade's proposal.

As the heir apparent, Wade interned at different departments in high school and college, starting in janitorial services then the mail room. After college and before Officer Candidate School, he worked in development. He loved the script for *Island of Sirens,* and when he saw the completed film, it lit a fire under his ass for some reason. I remember an email he wrote me about how I needed to see this film.

I wrote back, "Film? How fancy. I don't watch kids' movies, Wade."

The only thing I know about this movie is that it wasn't the massive hit Revel Pointe Studios wanted it to be. Later I found out that some senator had publicly denounced it as having an eco-terrorist agenda. Developing a park experience is expensive—not as expensive as acquiring an island and launching another cruise line—but basing it on a polarizing film would be risky. In the short term, a weaker ROI than the cruise option.

But Wade didn't care about the naysayers. Hell, he joined the Marine Corps despite Gaspard's insistence that it was a waste of time and his irate threats to disown him. He joined despite being an obvious target, the ultimate symbol of American exceptionalism and capitalism, and despite the very real threat of death. Wade could and would do anything he set his mind to. And he wanted to pursue this project. His passion for the *Island of Sirens* experience leaps off the page.

And I must face some harsh truths. Tilda is right—I am completely out of my depth. I haven't been around in ten years. I've actively ignored all things Revel. And to my detriment, I've never even watched *Island of Sirens.*

In the kitchen, I down a glass of ice-cold water. A new phase of my headache throbs at the base of my neck. I don't have time to do all the market research necessary to speak to Revel's target demographics. Not alone, anyway. I don't even know what I don't know, and who could I go to for information without showing my shitty hand? My unforgivable ignorance about my own family's legacy? James and Henri are far away and almost as uninterested in Revel as I am. The Little Angels are still in college. Other than

Bobby, and maybe Ernie and Shirleen, I don't trust anyone. With hangover shakes, I gulp down more water and spill on my splayed hand resting on the counter. Watching droplets of water trickle off my knuckles, it hits me.

Rose Red.

The green alien girl.

Marin.

She's trustworthy; she didn't contact the press. I checked the blogs and social media all day today. Not a peep about me floundering in the Mona Moon moat.

Suddenly, I feel a sense of hope. A bit of relief washes across my temples. With Marin's nerdy Revel know-how and my financial wizardry, we could make Wade's final dream a reality.

I just need to find her, grovel as much as I can swallow, and hope she takes pity on me.

Again.

Chapter Fifteen

Marin

Roland is nowhere to be found, so I pout and stroll around the park, sucking on Roman candy. The park is still crowded. It's another cool, sunny day. Normally I'd hop on as many rides as I could fit in before sundown, but candy and roller coasters are not compatible.

Out of costume, just plain old Marin, I feel a bit lost. I head to the San Francisco Safari, wanting to zone out on watching the gorillas interact. After visiting the zebras, the primate hut, and the giraffes, I sit on a bench and take stock. While I am thrilled to be at Revel, something feels off. I go into full introspection mode. It's time for one of my famous life status updates. Well, famous to me and to Flora; who when I told her I categorize areas of my life and put them into bullet points in my head to review, she told me I was her "favorite freakazoid."

In my mind's eye, I make a list of possible culprits for my feelings.

- *Family*... Radio silence from the fam, but this is not unusual. Plus, I feel good about speaking up before leaving. Nope, it's not family dynamics.

- *Friends*... I have the *best* best friend in the entire world, whose generosity is unparalleled. I'm getting to know my co-workers better and feel like I'm in a like-minded community. So...nope, it's not friends that's bugging me.

- *Love-life*... It's complicated. I like someone, but we don't spend time together out-of-costume, so I don't know what's real because it's Roland's job to be charming. And, if I have such a huge crush on him, then why did I rub my face and body all over Ethan? Ethan doesn't even remember the incident. And he was a turd when he returned the dress. The whole impending doom thing must have kick-started our libidos. So, romance is a bit rocky, but no, it's not the cause of this apprehension.

● *School...* Despite my family's constant reminders that I'm not like them, I really love learning and enjoy my classes. While working at Revel Pointe has always been a dream, playing Rose Red isn't a long-term life goal. I want to pursue Marketing, to tell stories, and in one impulsive moment just days ago, I may have just shot myself in the foot. What if Tulane doesn't allow me to re-enroll in the Fall? Then what? I start to feel panicky. This is the culprit! I breathe deeply, trying to get off this slippery slope to Panic-ville because I don't regret the decision to take a break. I had to do this, to explore, to follow my own path. *But for how long?* Hmm... As Miss Prudence Pleasant says in *Around and Far and Upside Down,* "You can't steer a cart that's not moving." I'm steering the cart one way; I can steer it back when I need to.

I stand, reinvigorated, and power walk to the Safari exit, humming along to the "Monkeying Around" song playing over the loudspeakers.

In the dorms, I hear a familiar baritone drawl at the concierge desk. "Yes, she must live here. She plays Miss Maisy AND Rose Red!"

I hang back in the hallway and watch the concierge dude, wearing a headset and Revel polo, very patiently explain, "We've no record of a *Marin* living here, Mr. Reve."

"That doesn't make sense." His voice is polite but clipped. He's clearly not enjoying the Ethan Reve Experience. Ethan towers over the concierge, no less intimidating in a gray T-shirt, jeans, and ball cap than he would be in a suit of armor. He may be even more intimidating as his tight tee highlights the broadness of his shoulders and the muscular shape of his arms.

Geez, Mare. Snap out of it. He may be hot, but he's an asshole. Remember that.

The concierge's tone is faux conciliatory. "Maybe that's not her real name," he suggests.

This isn't good. I don't think Flora officially told anyone I was staying with her. Is this even allowed? Holy crapola. Ethan Reve is screwing with my life again.

I lean closer and hear Ethan sigh. "What about Flora? She knows Flora." I hear typing and then decide to put both men out of their misery.

I run up to the desk. "Hi," I say breathlessly. "I'll take it from here." Ethan double-takes.

"It's *you!*" he yells. His eyes look like they might fall out of his face.

What the hell? Of course, it's me, I think. Or maybe he remembers...*oh god*. He remembers the hot, wet, over-the-petticoats hump!

And then I realize this is the first time he's ever seen me out of face paint, out of costume. I sober and grab his elbow, leading him towards the elevator, calling out behind me. "Thanks. He's just confused. I'll take it from here."

"No problem," the concierge replies, still unclear about who I am and why Ethan Reve would show up here asking for me. Between Ethan's visit to the dressing room this morning, and now this, I wouldn't be surprised if *I* end up on *TMZ* or *The Secret Reveler*.

I need to get him out of here, but the lobby is filling with curious cast members. When the elevator doors open, I grab his forearm and pull him in behind me. Now we are so close and alone, I smell his clean, boy-soap smell and something else, a little spicy and a lot intoxicating.

"What floor?" he asks, smirking a bit, because I clearly forgot the next step in this process.

"Three."

He clicks the button, and it lights up. Why is this elevator so slow? The word *awkward* feels too weak to describe the silence that envelops us. I can hear myself swallow. To distract myself, I think of adjectives for awkward. Uncomfortable doesn't cut it. Discomfited? Unpalatable? Maybe painful? That's it. *Painful*, I think, when the elevator dings, and he follows me to my room without a word. While I unlock the door, I feel him behind me and remember his strong hands on my lower back.

Pull yourself together.

Before opening the door, I turn around abruptly in the empty hallway, which startles him. This close, I note he needs a shave although the scruff looks good on him, especially with his tanned skin.

"Wait. What are you doing here?" I force out, attempting to keep my voice steady.

He peers both ways down the hallways and nods to Flora's dorm door, so I let us in. Ethan looks around the living room/kitchenette. "So, this is what a dorm looks like?" His eyes soak it in. "I've never been in one."

"I find that hard to believe," I retort. Something about him makes me snappy.

"Well, let's just say I never made it this far." His smile is big; his teeth are perfect.

"Nice," I huff, then turn around and move away from him, feeling the blush creep up my neck. Damm it. "I'm going to get a glass of water. Do you want one?"

"Sure, thanks." He nods and takes a seat on a stool at the tiny counter, watching me pour water. I attempt to get my wayward blush under control. On autopilot, I round the counter corner and hand him his glass. He downs it, his Adam's apple bobbing up and down. I can't help it. I stare. How the heck is drinking water sexy?

"Thirsty?" I ask and take a sip. Dainty. Like a lady. Not like a water-starved ogre. A thirsty, hunky ogre.

"Yeah, I just ran around the park trying to find you."

"So sorry to inconvenience you." He leans back and crosses his arms, then uncrosses them, then crosses them again, appearing as painfully uncomfortable as I am. *Good.* Maybe we're on an even playing field now. "What exactly do you want?" I cross my arms, now, mirroring him.

"I have a proposition for you." His voice is low, conspiratorial.

"No," I declare. Bet he never hears that word.

"What? Wait, you don't even know what it is!" He grabs the counter with both hands.

"Whatever it is. No." Knowing his public past, I can only imagine. Something risqué. Illegal maybe? Untoward, definitely.

"Hear me out." He leans in. The clean-boy smell, subtle and woodsy, makes my head spin. He needs to leave.

I head towards the door. "I think you can find your way out."

Ethan follows me but stops short, understanding dawning on his handsome face. "You think I meant a sex proposition?" He snorts. "It's not anything like that. God!" He seems horrified that I would even think he'd like to be untoward with me, which feels worse than a sexy proposition. He definitely doesn't remember our exchange by the moat.

"Who do you think I am?" he asks, offended.

My voice is frigid now. "I think you're leaving." I open the door and gesture towards the empty hallway, channeling my inner schoolmarm.

"Listen, this isn't about sex. I'm not trying to have sex with you," he says a little too quickly.

I try not to wince and remind myself that I *don't* want him to want me—the opposite of that Cheap Trick song.

Ethan raises his hands in the air, a sign of surrender. "I want your help. I need it, actually." His voice cracks on the word "need." He leans closer again, and I can see clearly that he's uncomfortable. Something more important is at play. There's sadness in his eyes. Seeing that lost look surface, remembering the pity I felt for him earlier, I sigh and shut the door.

"And I should care why?" My tone is acidic. Okay, so maybe the whole "I don't want to have sex with you" thing chafes a wee tiny bit.

"That's fair. I have been a jerk. I get it. But this isn't about me." His eyes are intense. Pleading. And so, so blue. "It's about Revel Pointe. About my *family legacy*."

He's quoting me back to me. Now, I can't help it. "What is it you need exactly?"

"Help with a business proposal. A big, new Revel experience, in the park. It was Wade's proposal. His passion project before he left. Before..." His eyes freeze on the floor for a moment, then he takes a deep breath. "I'm presenting Wade's proposal to the board next quarter. I know numbers, I can do the financial stuff, but I don't know..." He looks away, pulls his cap off his head and then readjusts it.

"What don't you know?"

He chuffs. "I don't know Revel."

"But you *are* a Reve." I'm flabbergasted.

"I'm aware of who I am, but I've spent the last ten years running away from this place. I haven't seen a movie, read a book, or watched one of our TV shows in years."

"You dated a Revel star, though."

He winces for a second, then dons a sardonic mask. "Yeah, we didn't do a lot of talking."

"Why me? Just google it or something." I groan and plop on the couch.

"I don't even know where to begin. I don't have time to do market research. Or to hire a team of lackeys who'll probably just tell me what I want to hear anyway." He sits down on the rickety IKEA chair across from me and bends forward, elbows on his knees, business-like.

"I need to work with someone who is a real Reveler. And most importantly, I need someone who will tell me the truth." He leans in a bit closer. "Someone I can trust."

I blink. I'm sure my mouth opens and closes a few times, but I'm not sure what to say. Asking for help is clearly a new phenomenon for him, but his address seems earnest with a tinge of desperation under the surface.

I shake my head as I stand again. "And you think you can trust me? We don't even know each other. I'm sure you can find someone else..." I explain, but he cuts me off, jumping up and pacing with the frenetic energy of a big cat. All I can do is watch until he stops moving and stares down at me.

"First, yes, I think I can trust you, and second, I can't find someone else. I have three months." He's close enough that I can see just how long his black eyelashes are. "The only person I could have trusted with this is dead. The other is a recluse."

I try not to freak out when he mentions Mick Reve, his PawPaw, so casually, and I focus on Ethan's blue eyes, blazing with the intensity of his plea.

"Please. I need you." His shoulders tense up, and he turns away. I feel this insane urge to wrap my arms around him, to tell him it's going to be okay, which is completely out of the question.

"How do you know you can trust me?" I ask, barely above a whisper.

He turns and looks directly into my eyes. "You saved me already, Marin."

I sit there, looking up at him while he looks down at me. The air between us is electric.

The moment breaks when he turns on the charm, his eyes all twinkly and pleading. "Please. Say you'll help. Again."

I sigh then try to exude professionalism. "I still have to do my job. I can't ditch Flora."

"We'll work at night! Over dinner, whatever..." A goofy, gorgeous smile tempts me to smile back, but I'm all business now.

"And I won't do this for free. My time is valuable."

"Of course. I'll pay you. Double, no triple what you make as Rose Red."

I nod, then stand up. He probably has no idea how much I make. Cast members make a pittance, so this is not bad news.

I remain silent.

"And if this works out, and the board accepts Wade's proposal...I mean *our* proposal..." Ethan looks at me pointedly. "Then I'll get you a full-time, salaried gig at Revel. In any department you want."

Ethan Reve is offering me my dream job at Revel Pointe and in a position where I could use my degrees and Revel knowledge. I want to squeal with joy, but I stick out my hand instead.

"Sounds like a deal to me."

He looks at my rigid hand for a moment as if confused by the gesture, then he shakes it vigorously, asking, "What's your number?"

We exchange information, and then, like a giddy 14-year-old boy, he yells, "Meet at the family compound in two hours. We start tonight!"

Chapter Sixteen

Ethan

It's late afternoon when I leave Marin's dorm. Instead of feeling overwhelmed by the crowds, I feel less panicked and more hopeful. *Maybe this will work out after all*, I think as I return to the family compound. Gaspard, a rejector of work-life balance, had this place built so he could be closer to work. It was designed with the blueprints of a real medieval castle. The exterior stone was shipped from Norman ruins. Inside, my dad had real Crusade weapons and armor hung on the walls. Yasmin warmed the place up with some tapestries and art, but the general vibe is still "Don't fuck with us." We all have our own quarters, but we Reves are rarely here together, so it is possible to never see another person in the compound. Still recovering from his stroke, Gaspard isn't working, so he's been moping on his boat.

I tidy up my place a bit then call Jenny, our family's personal concierge, to raid our supply closet and bring me all of the office supplies. I want Marin to feel like I'm taking this seriously.

Marin.

It was a shock to see her without her green face paint. She's somehow stunning and wholesome simultaneously. Her light auburn hair, in a thick braid, reminds me of Scottish farm girls. Her heart-shaped face and porcelain skin make her look like a starlet, but a healthy sprinkle of freckles across her nose and cheekbones keeps her earthy. Her stormy blue eyes appear gray from some angles and sky blue from others. Her chin I recognized. It's strong, stubborn somehow, with that tiny indentation in the center. A butt chin like Ava Gardner.

Speaking of which, I stop myself cold. I'm not about to let my dick do my thinking because my dick, as proven by the past ten years, has shit for brains. And this is far too important. I need Marin's help, her expertise. I need a confidante in all of this. Not a fuck buddy. Not another person I'll disappoint or hurt. It's strange to feel protective of someone I've just met, but I do. Maybe because she's helping me. *Has* helped me already.

In the fridge, I have essentially nothing to eat or drink unless Marin wants a protein shake or roasted peanuts. I call Jenny again and ask her to send snacks.

"Anything in particular?" Jenny's twangy voice asks. I realize I don't know anything about Marin. Her preferences, her dislikes. Does she have allergies? Oh god.

"Just a little bit of everything, I guess." Within twenty minutes, two young men dressed like yacht crew in Revel blue roll in two trays loaded with food—bagels with lox and cream cheese, seven types of potato chips, hummus with vegetables, croissants, cut fruit, an array of fancy fizzy water.

I tip them and notice a text from an 802 number. It's got to be Marin. She's arrived downstairs. I run through the door, down the hall and stairs and meet her at the front entrance.

Slow down, buddy. Don't appear too eager. I need her, but I don't want to seem desperate...even if I am.

Despite my vow to view her only as my new, platonic work partner, I take her in. Marin's hair is still in a braid, but she's changed into a pretty, light pink sweater with a cowl neck. A dark purple backpack is slung across her left shoulder. She looks sweeter than a confection.

I lick my lips and nod at Jenny, who raises an eyebrow at me, curious about my guest, my only official guest since I've been back home. I frown at her unspoken question.

To Marin I say, "You ready?"

Marin nods, thanks Jenny, and follows my lead. I turn to ask her a question, but she's behind me a few paces. Eyes big, mouth open.

"Never thought you'd visit the compound, huh?" I grin but try to temper my amusement at her wide-eyed expression.

"No." Her eyes scan the stone floors, dramatic wall sconces, centuries-old oil paintings and tapestries. "It's like an old castle."

"That was the idea. My father had it built in the '80s. He wanted a place for the family to live. Closer to work, but safe from prying eyes. There's a sister castle by Spoonbill Studios."

"It definitely has a defensive feel to it." Her voice is church quiet as we pass a display of 12th century mounted swords crisscrossed on the wall.

"It's a bit much, I know. But Dad has a thing for the Middle Ages. I think he likes the whole "lord of the manor" vibe. It's sort of a family thing. PawPaw had the bug first, obviously; it skipped me and Wade, but James, my younger brother, is also really into old architecture." I pull out my keycard. The whole family has these electronic skeleton keys, allowing the Reves access to almost the entire park. I press the card to the electronic pad above my door. We hear a click and enter.

The rooms are a lot less martial and intimidating. At least my apartment is designed in a much less ostentatious way. The exposed stone walls continue throughout, but warm rugs cover the cold floors. Books are strewn about, haphazardly placed on my spiced rum-colored Chesterfields, on end tables, on the coffee table. It's more like a city loft than medieval chambers.

The banquet of food I ordered covers the 12-foot island. "Grab yourself some food. I usually work at the dining table," I say as I take her bookbag and place it on a chair across from me. My open laptop glows. The office supplies, financial statements, and proposals litter the long mahogany table.

"Wow, you know how to throw an office party," Marin says as she nabs a grapefruit fizzy soda from the counter. "Coaster?" I give her a copy of a book about WWII submarines.

"Seriously?"

"Yes, unless you want to read it right this second?" I arch an eyebrow.

"Seems riveting, but maybe later. Right now I'd like to know exactly what we're doing tonight." She sits and crosses one knee over the other, and I can't help but notice her shapely calves in her skinny jeans.

"Not hungry?" I gesture to the spread on the counter.

"Maybe later." She throws her hands in the air, impatient. "I'm dying of curiosity over here. Now, spill." She places her drink on the book, pulls out a pad of paper and a ridiculous-looking pencil with a Captain Nemo head in place of an eraser, then folds her hands like a star pupil.

"Okay. I won't keep you waiting." I clear my throat. "The board has to decide how to invest its capital this year. Tilda Olsen-Reve, who I'm sure you know..."

Marin rolls her eyes. "Of course."

"Her proposal was pitched last week. And Wade's, which I'll show you in a minute, we will prepare to pitch in three months. But first, here's our competition." I hand her Tilda's new cruise line plans first.

She flips through the pages, deliberate and thorough, while I wait. Suddenly, she pauses. "Island acquisition?"

I nod.

"Like a whole island?" she asks, unbelieving.

"Yes."

"Wow." Her saucer eyes are back. Playing a cartoon is not a stretch for her.

"What about it?" I stand, grab a soda, and pace.

"That's just an epic, crazy thing to buy; it's like something a Bond villain would do." She picks up her fizzy water and takes a sip. "Is it normal for mega companies to buy islands?"

"I wouldn't say it's common, but it's done. Dubai and China have been making their own islands for the last few decades. I went skiing a few years back and discovered that the alpine resort owned the whole island off the coast of Canada. So, it's a thing."

"Aren't there consequences? I mean, for the people who live there? Wouldn't they be displaced?" Her mouth skews like she's eaten a lemon.

"If you keep reading, the proposal says they would be relocated and compensated for the move handsomely."

Her eyes narrow with skepticism. She leans back, taps her pencil for a moment. Her brows knit in concentration. "That seems sketchy. And presumptuous. Where's the environmental impact report?"

"Exactly!" I point at her, thrilled she picked up on this discrepancy immediately.

"Also, cruises aren't environmentally sound either. In my Business Ethics class last semester, we did a whole unit on sustainability. Cruises emit a ton of sulfur and carbon dioxide. And don't even get me started on the blackwater and sewage problems..."

"Wait," I interrupt. "You're in business school? Where?"

She blows an errant piece of hair out of her face, seemingly exasperated by the question.

"Yes, I'm pursuing an MBA at Tulane. Anyway, between the cruise line and the possible effects it would have on the island's ecosystems..."

I interrupt her again. I can't help myself. "What are you doing *here*?"

She averts her eyes, takes a sip of her soda. "It's complicated." When she picks up her pencil and taps the proposal in front of her,

I know she'd rather not talk about it. "Let's focus on this." Her gaze bores into me. *Noted.*

"Okay..." We sit in awkward silence for a moment. Before I can formulate a clear picture of this enigma before me, she lets out a breath and interrupts my thoughts.

"I just think there's something fishy about this project. Let's see Wade's *Island* proposal." She holds out her hand for the document. I place it in her hands, her cotton candy pink nails popping against the turquoise of the folder. I'm still curious as fuck about what brought her to Revel Pointe in the middle of the school year. She should be on campus in New Orleans, in a library, writing a paper, griping about her exams in a bar, not dressing like a princess or a cartoon frog in a swamp.

"I'm going to grab a bagel while you read. You need anything?" I ask, wanting to do something while giving her time to take in the material. I want her to love Wade's proposal, to see its creativity and merit on her own. Also, I know it's freaky when people stare at you reading. Or at all, I guess.

"Nope, just absorbing this." She doesn't lift her eyes from the page.

I saunter to the kitchen, slice through a whole wheat bagel, slather it with cream cheese, and make a cappuccino. I stand there eating slowly, thinking about this intriguing woman in my dining room. Rose Red is getting an MBA. She's skittish, wary of telling me why she's here. I respect that, but my curiosity may get the better of me.

When I return to the table, she closes Wade's proposal and looks at me, her eyes filled with tears.

"This is beautiful, Ethan." A tear falls down her cheek. Her skin has turned pink around the eyes. "Really, really beautiful."

Chapter Seventeen

Marin

Embarrassed by my tears, I stand abruptly. "Bathroom?"

"Just down the hall, on the right." Ethan gestures to the hallway, looking perplexed by my weepy reaction. I barely register my surroundings, desperate to hide.

In the bathroom mirror, my face is blotchy from crying. I was never a pretty crier. Arista told me I looked like a red-and-white checkerboard. I splash my face with water, reach for a towel, and take a few deep breaths. I know I'm overwhelmed by the events of the past few days, but Wade's *Island of Sirens* proposal is truly brilliant. The film came out four years ago in the summer of 2008. It's beautifully done and more dynamic than their latest movies. Revel's artistry and imagination have always been stellar, but this film is epic, heartbreakingly gorgeous, and the characters are complex. The rumor is that, while Tilda and Gaspard greenlit the production, it was Mick Reve who found the source material and handpicked the artists. It's a rumor because his name doesn't show up on any promotional material or in the credits, but the mythic, singular content lends credence to the gossip.

The original book is a revision of *The Odyssey*, which makes sirens out to be nothing more than feathery femme fatales. *Island of Sirens* reclaims the sirens' story. But that's not all it does well. The first ten minutes are crafted in moving mosaic, telling the story of a group of sailors shipwrecked in a storm and landing on the island of Naxos, home of the sirens. As Wade imagined it, the experience would center around Naxos. In the prologue, we learn that the sirens saved the sailors' lives, nurtured them back to health, and many of them formed relationships with the humans while helping them rebuild their ships. The sirens shared everything with the men. But when the ship was finished, the sailors stole away in the night. And worse, the sirens' sacred shell was stolen. The sacred shell kept the balance between the land, sky, and sea. Without the shell's powers, there were more storms, more fighting between creatures, less harmony in the environment, and the effects of this chaos rippled throughout the world.

When the men left, the sirens were heartbroken and enraged, especially since a few of them were with child. And sirens are not forgiving creatures.

Queen Acantha, one of the sirens expecting a child, vowed to never let another man step foot on their shores. They became vigilant isolationists, keeping watch on the rocks around their islands, singing songs, luring men towards them, not to kill or eat the men, but simply to search for the lost shell. However, they enchanted the wayward men so they would only remember a beautiful song about monstrous birds, using beaks and talons to rip out their innards. The sailors would tell tales of these evil creatures of the sea and song. Sigourney Weaver, the only big name in the production, voiced Queen Acantha and the prologue's voiceover.

"For the sailors would weave a tale, and *their* stories were written down, and we were glad of it; it kept others away. But *their* stories became fact although it was a fiction. This is *our* story."

In the first scene, we meet our heroine—Young Kaliope, the daughter of the Siren Queen and the Sailor Captain. As a half-human, Kaliope feels not-quite-siren enough and wants to prove her worth to her mother and sisters. She cannot use the Siren's Song, a powerful magic that all sirens can wield. She does, however, have waterpower and hears the call of the shell in the ocean waves. She sees a vision of an enormous man on a throne, wearing the shell around his neck. She sees his foot touch the shores of Naxos, then, in her vision, chaos ensues, fires, floods, blood. To prevent this premonition from coming true, Kaliope believes she must find this royal man and reclaim the sacred shell.

At this point in the film, Kaliope sings her "I Want" song—"Kaliope's Promise"◇a driving, drum-laden anthem where she sings, *"To save our island, to fight the monster, to prove myself / I'll do, I'll dare, I'll defend my place among my sisters!"* She leaves home, alone.

On her quest to the mainland, Kaliope is chased by Cetea, a dragon-like sea monster, and uses her powers to escape. Exhausted, she washes ashore a small island called Ikaria where Nestor, a fisherman and burgeoning naturalist, finds and cares for her.

Talk about an amazing meet-cute where Kaliope wakes up and attacks him by summoning water from his pail to throw in his face. Nestor has a coughing fit. Kaliope tries to flee, but weakened after the Cetea chase, she passes out again. When she wakes up a second time, he's holding a bowl of stew and asks her not to hurl it at him because it will scald him. "And, it's wasteful." Mistrustful of men, Kaliope asks Nestor why he saved her. He says that she needed help, and he's not a monster. She counters with "We'll see," then eats the nourishing soup.

Eventually, Nestor learns she's looking for a giant man who sits atop a green throne. He says, "You mean King Staffan? Trust me, you don't want to find him."

In an amazing sequence using shadow puppets, Nestor tells the story of King Staffan's rise to power. The song Nestor sings, "An Emptiness Within," is haunting and includes a warning. Staffan is a famous collector of powerful artifacts, weapons of extreme power, and more. He has the Golden Fleece, Hippolyta's girdle, and the Hydra's heads in his Jade Halls. But it's not just things he collects. He has captured nymphs, dryads, inventors, philosophers, demigods even.

Nestor sings, "*He controls the wildest beasts and men/to collect more and more / to fill the emptiness within.*" Nestor warns that waterpower will make Kaliope a valuable addition to Staffan's collection. While Nestor seems to know where the king is, he refuses to explain how he knows, nor will he take her there. She is frightened by his warning, but Kaliope plans to leave the next day.

Unfortunately, a colossal storm prevents her from leaving. Nestor and Kaliope take shelter in a cove where she uses her powers to prevent the sea from sweeping them away, thus saving Nestor's life.

While they wait for the storm to pass, Nestor explains how his island is dying. His people have overfished because the king demands tribute. Also, the islanders also want instant gratification and cannot see past their greed. As a result, many islanders have left. Those that stay are hungry. The water is rising, too. Nestor measures it, keeping track of the changes, and predicts they don't have much time before another storm sweeps the island and its people away. After seeing Kaliope's powers, he strikes a bargain. He will take her to King Staffan if, in addition to the shell, she steals the Iron Net—the magical net that replenishes fish from air. She agrees, and they embark on their journey.

One of the best parts of the movie is the friendships that develop. Nestor and Kaliope have witty repartee worthy of Nora Ephron. They encounter a dryad, a tree nymph, named Laurel, who lost her sister to King Staffan. Laurel turns into a tree when she's scared, but they discover she can regenerate limbs at will when they outrun Empusa, a monster from the Underworld. Kaliope learns to trust these new friends, and Nestor helps her embrace her humanity.

Laurel is the comic relief and helps Kaliope laugh at herself. There's a wonderful moment of levity when Laurel sings a song about how everyone thinks the way she copes with difficulties is to turn into a tree called "Chortle, Guffaw, Chuckle." She says her real defense mechanism is laughing. (This song is currently, and appropriately, Flora's ringtone.)

After some misadventures, Kaliope, Nestor, and Laurel arrive at the Chrysos Palace, only to discover a labyrinth and a chimera. They fight the chimera, but Kaliope's powers are weakened. The longer she is out of water, the weaker she becomes. Nestor and Laurel carry her, unconscious, to the gate. The king meets them and casts a sleeping spell over her friends.

When Kaliope wakes, she sneaks out of her room, walking by the king's "collection," including Laurel's sister, Daphne. Daphne, alive and chained to the wall, tells Kaliope where to find Staffan. Staffan waits on his throne, a large, handsome man with long black hair and a tall, bejeweled crown, wearing the sacred shell just as he appeared in her vision.

He tries to use the shell's powers on her, but it doesn't work because she's part siren. He recognizes her because he was one of the original marauders on the ship that wrecked on Naxos. In his song "She Chose Wrong," Staffan explains that he was in love with Queen Acantha, but she chose Captain Mikos instead: *So I stole the shell, killed the captain, and took my place as king / But there's something for which I long, something missing / She chose wrong!*

Staffan hatches a plan to fill the void—Kaliope must lead him back to the sirens so he can collect his queen. She refuses, remembering her visions. Staffan brings in his "toys," showing how he'll use the shell's power to coerce Nestor and Laurel to rip each other apart unless Kaliope helps.

In the bathroom, finally calming, I recall how the movie theatre crowd was so quiet I could hear the popcorn machine out in the lobby when Kaliope shook hands with Staffan.

In the climax of the film, to save her friends, Kaliope leads the king back to Naxos, bringing about the very vision she sought to prevent. Staffan has Laurel and Nestor chained to the mast. Nestor tells her to use her powers to flee and save her home, the way he would save his. They share a kiss before he passes out. Then Kaliope sings, "A Place Where I Belong," about being torn between loyalty to her new friends and to her home.

When the king steps on the shores, her apocalyptic vision comes to life. The sky opens, the waters surge. The animation of this sequence is heartbreaking and terrifying, and the audience watches Kaliope witness the destruction of her island home from the ship. She knows she has failed.

Honestly, it's been years since Revel Pointe has gone to such a dark place. Hence the rumor that Mick was involved. His early movies are famous for including scenes that haunt the nightmares of young children, in the best way possible.

With nothing left to lose, Kaliope frees Nestor and Laurel. She tries to escape into the water, but Staffan has created a force field around the ship, which now hovers above the fray. Kaliope must stand by as the destruction continues. Nestor and Laurel find Kaliope, sobbing. They tell her that her vision was incomplete, that saving the island is not up to one individual; it requires a group effort.

At that moment, a powerful voice rings out from the island. Kaliope's vision only showed her the doom. It didn't show her that the sirens fight back. Queen Acantha's voice calls louder to her, and the force field breaks. Staffan's soldiers attack. Since Staffan cast a spell and deafened his soldiers, they could not hear the sirens' voices. The fighting is epic. The King makes it to Acantha and tries to convince her to go with him to the Chrysos Palace, to become his wife, his queen.

She says that she always felt sorry for Staffan because he wasn't capable of love, thinking others were things to possess. Furious, he charges Acantha, but she uses her powers to throw him in a waterspout and recapture the shell. When she places it around her neck, the chaos stops. Kaliope runs in, her friends behind her. Acantha turns, smiling, but Staffan has crawled to a nearby rock formation. He spears her. Kaliope cries out, but this time it's the Siren's Song, which turns Staffan and all of his soldiers into stone. Laurel extends one of her tree limbs and pushes him into the sea.

Kaliope rushes to Acantha, who tells her daughter to protect those who cannot protect themselves and hands the shell to Kaliope. She says she can't; she's not a full siren, and she failed. Acantha tells her that the shell has returned to its rightful owner. "You belong to the home you fight for," the Queen says, then dies, drifting down to the sea depths. Nestor holds Kaliope as she cries.

Dabbing my eyes in the mirror, I remember that there was not a dry eye in the theater the first and second time I saw *Island of Sirens*.

Kaliope vows to wear the sacred shell, and she and the remaining sirens end their century of isolation to help restore balance in the environment. Unfortunately, they are too late to save Nestor's island. They help the residents relocate to another near Naxos. The last image of the film is Nestor, Laurel, and Daphne on a ship, following Kaliope and the sirens in the water as they leave the sunken Ikaria to help others, singing, "*Together we can save the sea, protect the land, and fight for our future! / Together, we fight for home.*"

The first time I saw this movie, I sat and cried through the credits, like I am losing it now in Ethan Reve's luxurious bathroom. I still can't believe this movie isn't Revel's biggest hit to date. They chose to do traditional cel animation instead of using the uncanny valley of 3D computer-generated Elixir productions that were huge hits the past decade.

Island of Sirens still made millions, but it didn't make *Rose Red* or *Camp Willow Creek* money. I'm not sure how saving the world is political, but some politicians claimed its message was indoctrination and encouraged a boycott. I feel bad for the boycotters because they missed out on a beautiful film, wonderful music, and a universal message about family, friendship, and learning to love and trust.

In the past decade, Revel Pointe has only released sequels to earlier films. They were good, but obviously safe cash-grabs. An *Island of Sirens* exhibit would be a risk, but a necessary one for the Revel ethos to remain intact.

I take a few deep breaths, apply some lip balm, and straighten my shoulders. I need to work on this project. I speed-walk to Ethan waiting for me at the dining room table—ready to fight for the future of this Revel Experience.

Chapter Eighteen

Ethan

When Marin returns, she asks a million questions, demonstrating her analytical mind and extensive knowledge of Revel Pointe as well as her deep love of *Island of Sirens*. Eventually, she stands, stretches, and yawns. I try my best not to notice her bare stomach as her pink sweater rises up.

"I gotta go. I have work tomorrow." She packs her notebook into her bag. "I need you to crunch some numbers, especially when evaluating our market-based pricing strategy versus our values-based strategy. You'll need to update the pricing that Wade provided, especially for the design budget of the Sirens' Experience. Call the design team who worked on the Miss Prudence Pleasant Steampunk coaster and Hooliganza. It provides the most comparable immersive experience."

I nod, jotting down notes on a legal pad, scribbling to try and keep up with my growing to-do list.

"Also, we need to dredge up some hype. It's been four years since this movie came out. Why does this experience need to be made now? I wonder if we can get some of the voice actors to post on social media—"

"Marin."

"But remember, we need to tell the story in a way that resonates and inspires." Her bag is now full and on her shoulders. "Revel is all about the story."

"*Marin*," I say more insistently.

"And we absolutely need..." She continues, not even looking at me, her idea euphoria spiraling.

"Marin!" I wave my hands in front of her face.

"What?" Her mouth sets in a grim line, annoyed that I stopped the flow.

"I've got it." I tap on the legal pad and lock eyes with her. We stare at each other for a beat. Her eyes are stormy, but her mouth betrays that she's enjoying herself.

She exhales. "Sorry, I can be...a little obsessive when I'm, well, obsessed." She rolls her eyes at herself. "You know, inspired." I like this about her. She doesn't take herself too seriously like the people I used to associate with. Like myself sometimes, if I'm being honest.

"Don't be sorry. I appreciate your enthusiasm. I just wanted to say thank you for your help and go get some rest. You're pulling double duty for the next few months. I need you well-rested and raring to go."

I walk her to the door, thankful that her giant backpack prevents me from touching the small of her back.

"Yes, right," She cocks her head to the side, a teasing grin lighting up her face. "'Raring to go'? What are you, eighty?"

"Darn tootin'!" I slap my knee.

Her eyes roll again, but her smile widens. "Just one more quick thing before I go."

"I know, I know." It's my turn to roll my eyes at her. She's so close now, right in front of me, her head near my heart. "Seriously, just one more thing, then night-night." I look down into her deep blue eyes, our bodies almost touching. Maybe a good night kiss?

Stop staring at her lips. Stop. Down, boy.

"You've seriously never seen *Island of Sirens*?" Her voice is incredulous, like I've committed the most unforgivable sin.

"Alas, I have not." I look down at my feet in faux sheepishness. "Am I excommunicated from the cult of Revel now?"

Marin chooses to ignore my sarcasm. "Well, put that at the top of the to-do list for tomorrow night. We're watching it. Prepare to be amazed!" she says with a flourish and shuts the door behind her.

In bed later, I fall asleep grinning. This project is still the underdog option, but with Marin, the proposal has a fighting chance with the board. She's so passionate. It's evident in the way her big eyes light up when she talks shop. God, the way she lost it after reading Wade's proposal... She gets it.

What did I do to deserve this good luck? This Revel princess is about to save my ass. Again.

Chapter Nineteen

Marin

"Are you okay?" Roland asks with concern in his hazel eyes.

"Yes, so sorry. I didn't sleep well last night," I admit. We are in the French Village again, on a quick break. Normally, Roland and I chat amiably when we get to duck away from the park guests to rest our feet and rehydrate, laughing about a particularly strange guest request or comparing notes on the best kid freak-out moments of the day so far. But I feel off today.

We lounge in rustic chairs in the cottage, off limits to the public, behind the Bleu Tortue.

"If you need to grab a cup of coffee, I'm pretty sure I can handle a few minutes without my princess." He leans towards me, smiling.

"No, no. I drank about a pot this morning." I stifle another yawn. "Oh god. I'm sorry." He must think I'm hungover.

"What kept you up last night? If I may ask..." He looks at me intently. This is the first personal question he has asked me. When we're together we're usually in character, and our breaks haven't really allowed for more than surface small talk.

"Of course, you may ask. It was just a good old-fashioned case of insomnia," I lie. Sort of. It wasn't some vague inability to sleep that kept me up, though. I spent most of the night vacillating between extreme excitement and debilitating anxiety. I'm pretty sure I broke some sort of record for the number of times I rolled from one side to another, metaphorically and literally. Again, I'm so thankful Flora sleeps with noise-canceling earplugs and an eye mask. With anyone else, they'd have sent me packing to spend the night in the tub.

"Okay. Well, just checking on my favorite princess," he drawls and winks at me. This does something funny to my stomach. He's just so damn hot. I wonder if he would kiss me like Ethan kissed me.

A very drunk Ethan, I remind myself, who has no memory of this kiss—the Ethan I work for now. I shake my head a bit to erase all thoughts of kissing Ethan.

"Are you sure you don't need a longer break?" He stands and stretches his arms over his head. Normally, I'd surreptitiously ogle him. Today, I'm too distracted to swoon.

"Yes, yes. I'm all good." I stand as well and readjust my bountiful skirts.

"Well, if you need anything, I'm more than happy to help my extraordinary, not-your-normal princess, Rose Red," he says, quoting the film. He throws his cape over his shoulder and bows ostentatiously.

"Oh, my." I throw my hands up to my heaving bosom; we're acting out their meet-cute, "This damsel appreciates your offer, but she's not in distress." I smile coyly, and Roland reaches out his arm for me to take. We walk back out into the bright sun, our game faces on. He leans closer to me. His breath smells like cinnamon.

"I'm always here to help, in and out of character, Red." He winks at me again, and I blush.

A child shrieks, "OHMYGODOHMYGOD!"—waking me up from the Roland spell—and we spend the rest of the day as a charming prince and a smitten princess.

Because I have a shorter shift today, I leave him at 4 p.m. He kisses my hand, bows, and whispers, "Sweet dreams, Red."

He looks at me quizzically again, but I don't have time to unpack his look.

I rush back to the dressing rooms and find Flora sketching on her couch, almost swallowed by at least seventeen different fabrics. She glances up at me, assessing.

"You've got that post-Roland glow about you again." Flora's voice is flat; she really dislikes him, but she's trying to be considerate of my raging crush. She sketches what looks like a new costume for Miss Maisy.

When she notices me peering over her shoulder, she shrugs and says, "You inspired me to update Miss Maisy's look."

What she's produced is beautiful and innovative, and yet somehow retains the nostalgia of the 1949 classic.

"Wow! That's amazing, Flora."

She bites her bottom lip. "You think so?"

"Yes, when did you start doing your own designs for Revel?"

Flora has always had a great eye for design, and her sewing skills are next level. She told me that growing up poor meant she had to make and alter her own clothes. Necessity turned to passion.

"I mean, I've always fooled around with my own designs, but I'm thinking of pitching these to Marta next week." Her dark brown eyes fill with trepidation and excitement. Marta is the head costume designer for Revel. Her expectations are high, and her patience is minimal. Flora has idolized Marta for the last decade, dropping Marta facts on me since our first year of college—"You know, Marta taught costume design at Parsons for ages and won three Tonys," "Revel must be paying her a fortune to leave NYC behind," and "Do you think it's too derivative if I go just by my first name like Marta? Introducing...FLORA!"

My feet are aching, so I drop onto the sofa. "Oh my god, you HAVE to pitch these to Marta!" I exclaim, sipping my energy drink.

"You've only seen one design." Flora stands and stows her notebook away on the vanity.

"I don't need to see more if they all look anything like that. Plus, I've seen plenty. I went to all of your shows in college. And, don't forget, I wore many Flora originals at Halloween."

"Stand and turn around," Flora orders and I comply. Flora tugs at my corset strings, loosening them, then steps away for a moment. She leans against the vanity and crosses her legs. "Yeah...okay. I'll do it. It's just..."

"What?" I squirm out of my top.

"Marta isn't necessarily warm and fuzzy, and she's incredibly protective of her time. I've also heard rumors that she is a wee bit territorial." Flora now picks at her lips, a bad habit I haven't seen in years.

I swat at her hand. "Flora Gonzales, you are the one who told me no one was going to give me anything I wasn't brave enough to ask for. You deserve this. Don't be like me. Don't be afraid to ask for what you want."

Tears well up in Flora's eyes. "What are you talking about, Marin? You're here right now. That's brave as hell." She pulls me in for a hug. A moment later, there's a knock at the door and it opens. Carrie stands in the frame.

"Hey, ladies. Sorry..." She stops, watching us embrace. "I mean, sorry, not sorry, to interrupt." A smirk on her face.

"Ah, c'mon, Carrie," I say as I pat Flora's back one more time, then turn around to take off my skirt.

"What's up, Thumb?" Flora wipes her face, now streaked with purple mascara.

"Were you two having a precious moment?" Carrie asks as she plops down on the couch.

"No, just your typical best friend bonding shit." Flora folds her arms, back to the tough-as-nails hard-ass most people see. "What's up?"

"Lana and I want to invite you two over for happy hour. We've got Patrick's birthday party tonight but thought we could pre-game." Carrie and Lana act as the unofficial social directors of the dorm. Their room is decked out in Christmas lights year-round, and they've apparently got seven blow-up mattresses for epic slumber parties. Sometimes, rumor has it, the slumber parties turn into sexy slumber parties. Patrick, who plays Theo Tomcat and subs for any animal that requires an actor over 6'4, is a huge Reveler. Flora calls him a kindred spirit.

"I'm sorry, I can't tonight," I reply as I start wiping off my makeup.

"Why? Hot date?" Carrie retorts, fanning imaginary heat.

Flora's eyes lock onto mine in the mirror. "Did he ask you out?" Her face remains passive, but there's a wariness in her voice. For a moment, I see Ethan's face but quickly realize she must mean Roland.

"No, no, no." I stammer and blush, and then realize I don't know what to say. I never said I'd keep this project with Ethan a secret, but there was an implied sense that the project should be on a need-to-know-basis. I will absolutely tell Flora, but I barely know Carrie, and I'd rather err on the side of caution, especially when I think about Ethan's suspicions about whether I sold pictures of us to the media.

"Maybe Ethan Reve found you irresistible in that frog get-up then?" Carries asks playfully, like it would be utterly absurd.

"Obviously. I'm definitely going over to his place tonight to watch a movie." Flora and Carrie laugh at the notion, which stings a bit.

"Seriously, Mare. Why can't you go? I need you. Patrick is doing Revel trivia tonight." Flora starts packing her makeup brushes. I avoid her eyes and lie.

"I have to talk to my advisor at Tulane to...to..."

Flora senses I don't want to share with Carrie and covers for me. "No worries! Got it."

Our eyes meet in the mirror again. Her look says *we'll talk later*. Love for my best friend overwhelms me. Flora twirls away from the vanity. "I'll have to fly solo tonight. Woe is me!" She flings the back of her hand to her forehead and sighs dramatically.

"Drama queen." I elbow her as I pull off my petticoats. I've gotten far more comfortable changing in front of others the last few weeks, but I'm still me and turn away slightly from the couch.

"We'll see you later then, Flora," Carrie says. "And Marin, you're dead to me," she jokes, then pirouettes into the hallway.

"Speaking of drama queens," Flora mutters. "I love that pixie."

I laugh as I pull on my jeans. "I gotta run. We'll talk later?"

Flora nods. "Yes. Later," she says ominously.

It's almost twilight by the time I'm out of the Rose Red getup and back to just plain ole me. I have to get across the park by six to watch *Island of Sirens* with Ethan, the not-so-charming Revel prince.

I am certainly not nervous about sitting near him, in the dark, on the plush couch in his luxury apartment, for two hours, just the two of us. That tumbling feeling in my solar plexus is simply the result of only eating a granola bar for lunch.

He better have popcorn, I think as I book it to his family compound castle, hoping no one wonders why I'm heading in the opposite direction of our dorm.

Chapter Twenty

Ethan

Per Marin's orders, I spent the day holed up in my apartment researching. After hours of looking at tables, graphs, and spreadsheets and playing phone tag with assistants of designers who were perpetually in "creative meetings," I was suspicious. By the eighth call to a Revel designer, I started to feel demoralized. Were designers told not to talk to me?

I needed to blow off some steam. I lifted heavy in the compound gym, showered, then shaved. Clean and ready to work, I head back to my apartment. When the elevator doors open into the main entrance, Marin stands there, waiting to come up.

"Well, hello!" She beams. I smile back but try not to take her bubbliness to heart. I mean, she is sweet for a living.

"Going up?" I lean past her and press the "hold open" button. I don't do the creepy hair smell thing, but damn, it's hard not to. She smells delicious, like sugary macaroons and fresh-cut roses.

By some unspoken rule, we are quiet on the short ride to the fourth floor. She holds her bag in front of her and stands in the corner. A part of me longs to tease her, to loosen her up, but I follow her lead. When we make it to my apartment, she heads right to the dining room table, drops her bag, and demands, "So, what did you accomplish today?"

I get right to business. "I updated Wade's estimated budget, factoring for inflation and access to crews. Fortunately, the costs have not skyrocketed in the last few years." I hand her an updated budget. "Here's the new and improved cost analysis."

"Thanks." She nods as she reads. "Okay. Did you contact any designers?"

"Well, yes and no."

"What does that mean?" She cocks her head to the side like a curious cat. Her long hair is a red wave against her white blouse tucked into high-waisted blue jeans. She wears red flats that make her feet look tiny. With her red hair, white shirt, and blue jeans, she's a real patriotic firecracker. *Focus on business, Ethan.*

"It means I called. I spoke to assistants. Every single designer was in a meeting or unavailable. Seven of the eight said they had some availability, but not until months from now. I only talked to one designer, some creative named Cricket of all things, who said she was leaving the country tomorrow to work on a super-secret, special project." I clutch the chair back in front of me, squeezing the wood with frustration. Explaining this out loud, I am no longer suspicious. I am certain Tilda is sabotaging this project. I let out a long breath to calm the stirring anger within me. I want to explain the whole family business history to Marin, but she doesn't need to hear about my family drama.

"I see." Her blue-gray eyes narrow. "Something is rotten in the state of Denmark."

"Definitely. And if we continue with the *Hamlet* allusions, it appears that Tilda must 'smile and smile and be a villain.'" I hint at my animosity for my once stepmother.

"You know your Shakespeare. I'm impressed." Her right eyebrow arches.

"Well, being a ne'er-do-well playboy and full-time fuck-up means there's a lot of time for reading." I bow with a flourish. "Plus, PawPaw's a big fan. He said Shakespeare was the best storyteller of them all."

Instead of laughing or being impressed that I dropped some Revel family lore, she frowns slightly. "Okay, so what aren't you telling me about this situation with your family?"

Where do I even begin? Also, how do I explain this without dumping years of emotional baggage on her? The last time I shared my feelings with a woman, she ghosted me.

"It's a long story that I'm *not* in the mood to share." I leave the room to shield my real thoughts and head into the kitchen for a bottle of red wine. Still, I can feel her staring at me.

"Cabernet?" I ask stiffly as I rifle around the drawers for the opener. Shit, I'm on edge.

"Yes, please," she replies with a thoughtful expression on her face. But I'm thankful she doesn't push me to talk. I'm also grateful, and a bit anxious, about how perceptive she is. I imagine I'll have to give her some version of the story about my family, filled with half-truths, one that won't ruin Revel for her.

I pour us each a glass. "I've got popcorn, too."

She nods, a smile relaxing her face. "Yes, please!"

"I downloaded the movie. Why don't you make yourself comfortable, and I'll bring the popcorn in when it's done." I need a minute to collect myself. This feels like a date. Although I can't remember the last time I had a movie date at home. Most of my dates were public events, in fancy restaurants or on red carpets. It's been years since I haven't had to yell over a crowd or hide from paparazzi on a date.

Also, I remind myself, this isn't a date. This is research. This is work.

This is a bad idea, I think, as I bring one bowl of popcorn for us to share and place it in her hands. Marin eyes the bowl eagerly and licks her lips. Jesus. This isn't going to work. I'm going to spend the entire movie uncomfortably fidgeting and trying not to glance at her as she licks butter from her lips. I feel all of fourteen years old as the

Mona Moon Lighthouse logo appears on screen. But then, a miracle happens.

Within the first few minutes of the movie, I'm absolutely hooked. In fact, I can't look away. The *Island of Sirens* animation is unlike anything we've done in the last twenty years. It's hand-drawn, but highly stylized in an innovative way. The music isn't cloying or childish; it is powerful and emotional, like the score to an Oscar-worthy adventure drama.

During the movie, I can sense Marin's eyes peek over at me, gauging my reactions, which must be up to snuff because she's smiling like a goofball.

When Queen Acantha is speared by Staffan, I gasp. I don't think an onscreen death of a mother character has been done since the 1960s. As far as I know.

The Queen's last words to Kaliope—"You belong to the home you fight for"— makes me think of Wade. I feel a tightness behind my eyes. When the credits roll, I just sit there. Dumbfounded. Proud of what Revel Pointe produced for the first time in a decade. And suddenly, I understand. This film is about sacrifice, and home, and being better together.

"So... What do you think?" Marin asks, facing me, leaning her head on her hand, sinking into the sofa next to me.

"I think we should watch it again."

She beams at me. "I'm game if you are."

We take a quick break and set it up again. This time, we take notes. I order pizza. We pause scenes to talk about the film's themes and interpretations, and how we can translate this groundbreaking film into an experience that doesn't water down its message. We add to Wade's proposal. It's quickly becoming ours.

I forget to feel awkward the rest of the evening. And it isn't until I'm walking her to the front entrance at one in the morning that the awkwardness returns. When I look down at her pale, lovely face and her kind, lively eyes, I can't help but pull her close, not into a passionate kiss, but into an enormous hug. "I get it now. Why Wade loved this, why you love it. Thank you."

When I pull back, her face is crimson, and she whispers, "You're welcome." She pulls at the straps of her backpack. "I have to work late tomorrow, but I'll text you when I'm free."

After refusing to let me walk her home, she gives me a little wave before rushing down the front path in a near sprint.

Interesting reaction. Women don't usually run away from me. *This woman does*, I think as I saunter back to the elevator humming "Kaliope's Promise."

Chapter Twenty-One

Marin

I'm jogging along the levee, thanking the weather gods for another cool, sunny January day. Despite the lack of sleep I've been getting, I woke up before Flora, who I left sleeping in the clothes she wore last night to Patrick's party. She won't be up for at least another two hours. I'll finish up my three-mile run and make a vat of coffee when I get home. I should have slept in, but I needed to think. I'm too riled up from last night's meeting with Ethan.

After the first few minutes of my run, my feet find their rhythm, and I'm on autopilot. I run to think, and boy, do I have a lot to think about.

I don't know which I find more confusing, Ethan Reve kissing me at the lighthouse or Ethan Reve hugging me last night? Thrilled that he saw the magic of *Island of Sirens*, I forgot to be awkward around him. I relaxed and actually had fun. Ethan Reve revealed himself to be a bit of a geek, discussing how the story mirrors Joseph Campbell's Hero's Journey, which he knew George Lucas used to write *Star Wars*. When I called him a nerd and threw a pillow at him, he threw it back at me, teasing, "Takes one to know one."

We talked a lot of shop, but we also made each other laugh. When Ethan laughs, really laughs, with his whole body, he throws his head back, with his hands on his stomach, and his eyes go all crinkly. He's actually likable. Not the arrogant rake he was just a few days ago. And when he hugged me, and said what he said, my heart fluttered. I didn't know how to respond, what to do with that level of unexpected sincerity. It felt so nice and warm in his arms.

What the hell am I thinking? I barely know this guy, and he happens to be a known philandering party boy with more notches in his belt than Casanova. Plus, we're working together on an incredible project that has the potential to change my life. A job in any department at Revel? *That's* my actual dream.

I mean, I don't even have to think about it: I want Marketing Analyst and Experience Developer. When I decided to pursue my MBA at Tulane, it was one, for proximity to Revel Pointe, and two, to make connections that would eventually lead me here. Essentially, I am currently doing what I want to do for the rest of my life, and all because I made that turn off the interstate. Well, and because I pulled a very drunk Ethan Reve out of a moat.

I remember his insistent kisses, his mouth on mine, his stubble on my chin, his hands on my back. He doesn't remember, though. But if he offered me a job fully aware of our moat makeout, I would have said no to working on the project. That scenario would be wildly inappropriate, which reminds me to tread carefully. The sweet Ethan from last night could be an anomaly.

As I run the levee path, I marvel at this opportunity. Revel princess by day, marketing whiz by night. Then I stumble. I don't fall to the ground but roll my ankle before I right myself and stop to catch my breath. This wipes the grin off my face because it reminds me not to get too carried away. I will only land this dream job IF we are successful. To be successful, I need to focus on the task at hand, not the confusing feelings Ethan Reve dredges up.

I can hear my sister Arista asking, *"Is hooking up with the boss how you plan to get ahead in life?"*

Or Alana, talking to me like a child, *"Marin, are you sure this is a good idea?"*

I pick up my pace, choosing to ignore my naysayers. Now the sun crests the flat horizon, casting a rosy color of morning light on the muddy Mississippi River. The scent of powdered sugar from the many beignet stands around the park already wafts on the breeze. I have to take stock. There's a lot to be done before I transform into Rose Red today. I find myself looking forward to the corset and petticoats now. It does something to my posture. I stand straighter, taller. It's become less costume and more supportive armor. I feel feminine yet girded. I don't have to think of what to say or do because I know what Rose Red would say and do. It is strange, but I feel more at ease as Rose Red. And despite Roland's dreaminess and my stupid crush, I feel more comfortable around Roland as well.

Far more comfortable than I do around Ethan, I think as I open the dorm door and head inside to get ready for a long day in the park.

Chapter Twenty-Two

Ethan

The cappuccino machine brews a crisp, nutty scent in the kitchen. It's doing nothing for my mood. I'm worried in a new way this morning. I got up before I felt rested, hit the gym again, showered, and when I opened my email, more design assistants had replied with possible appointment times a solid two weeks *after* the proposal pitch meeting with the board.

There is also an email from my little brother James with the subject line "Oh My Goth" that includes a picture of him and a gorgeous, raven-haired young woman at Chartres Cathedral. Looks like he's putting his architecture degree from Cambridge to good use. I reply, "Don't get too close to that church. She might burst into flames."

Most of our sibling communication is through pithy texts and emails. Elsie, the family's littlest Little Angel, had also emailed, forwarding an article headlined, "Bree Brooklyn Hooks Up with Hedge-fund Hottie, Harrison Matthews." There's a picture of Bree and Harrison on a red carpet and another of them entwined in a booth. Elsie just wrote, "Glad you dumped The Cheese, E." Looking at the photos, I feel nothing. No jealousy, no anger, nothing. Well, unless boredom is a feeling, which I guess it is. So yes, I feel something. Bored.

I shoot Elsie back a quick message: "Stop reading trash and start studying." I smile as I click on a load of junk mail and drag it to the trash. Then I see it. This one is from gaspard_reve@revelpointe.com: "We need to talk. Today. Meet me on the boat at noon."

No "Dear Ethan" or "Love, Dad." Just orders. Typical.

More than likely, despite doctor's orders, he's been working. At the very least, he's been in contact with Tilda.

After Wade's death, Dad's stroke was bad enough to require him to take a break for the unforeseeable future. He's always been a powder keg. Obsessed with work. Obsessed with expanding his father's dream, an empire builder. A cultural colonist, Wade used to say. As heir apparent, Wade bore the brunt of our father's expectations, his drive and ambition. Gaspard Reve took pride that his disciplined, hardline approach to parenting created the confident, capable, if not a tad too tender-hearted, Wade Reve. I always felt that Wade was just born a leader, and his successes were *in spite of* the pressure Gaspard exerted, not because of it.

As the second son, I've always been an afterthought. A math nerd. Too sensitive for my father's silences, his mercurial moods. I don't know what made him reject me. Dad had Wade, then Yasmin, and the Little Angels. There was little left over for me, not to mention James and Henri.

I close my laptop and exhale loudly. This is not going to be an easy conversation. Gaspard will likely reject anything I touch.

But this is Wade's project. I'll remind him of that.

Technically, it doesn't matter what Dad thinks. He's on medical leave; his vote doesn't count. However, he still holds enormous sway over the board and is always in cahoots with Tilda, who is telling him god-knows-what about my unprofessional behavior since stepping up. Gaspard's M.O. has been to ignore my exploits. Until recently. Until Wade was no longer here, then Dad's attention was hurled at me full force. I can already sense the weight of his disappointment pinpointed on me like a laser.

As I dress sharp in slacks, a white button down, and slip-on dress shoes, I check my reflection in the mirror. I look better than I did last week. Sharper, more alert. Ready to meet Gaspard head-on, to fight for this project, for Wade's project. An image of Marin's earnest slate-blue eyes waxing poetic about *Island of Sirens* hovers briefly in my mind.

Maybe I can channel the wonder and hopefulness she exudes. *Yeah, right.*

Thirty minutes later, I'm on Dad's Giraud Admiral Yacht, his home away from the compound. It's docked on pretty Little Lake on the Northshore in his private slip. A true Cajun, the man has always been more comfortable on a boat. I'm waiting on the covered deck when Yasmin greets me. Her delicate, youthful beauty always strikes me despite knowing her for years. Long almost black hair, amber eyes, high cheekbones, and gentle smile. A few wrinkles have eased into her forehead and around her eyes, but she wears them gracefully. Yasmin slides a tall glass of lemonade to me.

"You have come to see your father." she says, stating the obvious. My foot taps at breakneck speed, a nervous tic that reliably rears its head when I have to talk to Gaspard.

"He summoned me." I take a sip. It's delicious. My foot continues to tap, tap, tap.

"Good, okay. But remember, he's not supposed to work." She sits and forces me to still with her steady eyes. I press my heels onto the deck.

"I'll try, but I imagine that's the only reason he asked to speak to me."

She frowns at this, reclines back, but her eyes still gleam with intensity. She plays with a pleat in her white tennis dress.

"I'm sure that's not the case. Just remember that he's supposed to avoid stress. To keep his blood pressure steady. You understand?"

I nod.

"Good," she stands. "He's finishing up a call with Dom. He'll be out in a moment." I watch her walk away.

Damn, my dad is lucky. That woman protects the hell out of him. Tilda would have thrown him to the wolves if it'd get her money or power. What does Yasmin see in him, I wonder, when I hear the sliding door open.

My father stands there, a big hulk of a man. All the kids get our stature from him. Even Elsie is almost six feet tall. Dad's black hair is a little longer than I'm used to, with white streaks glinting at the temples. He has a Mediterranean look—brown, tan skin and deep crow's feet. My eyes are his eyes. His hair is my hair. Hell, we even have the same walk, except he's slower now. We have different noses and smiles, however. I have PawPaw's nose and MawMaw's smile. Wade didn't look like the Reves at all. He mostly took after Mom. He was also a big dude, but blonde with brown eyes. An all-American GI Joe. *A Marine, you asshat,* I can hear a frustrated Wade saying. *Soldiers are in the Army. Marines are in the Marine Corps.*

Gaspard takes Yasmin's place. He pockets his phone, and Yasmin follows, bringing him a green smoothie. He groans audibly, whether in pain or disinterest in the healthy shake I'm not sure. Yasmin puts a straw in the drink, gives him a stern look, and leaves us alone.

Gaspard pushes it away and rests his hands on his slight belly. "I hear you've been busy the past few weeks."

"Yes." Monosyllabic responses work best. Less likely to rile him up and piss off Yasmin.

"I've been told that you're working on a proposal, in competition with Tilda's cruise." Gaspard's heavy brow wrinkles.

"Yes."

"What game are you playing here, Ethan?" Gaspard's large hands grasp the armrests.

"I'm not playing a game. I think Tilda's idea has some merit, but I don't think it's as good as Wade's proposal." Gaspard's eyebrows shoot up at Wade's name, but I continue. "Before Wade left, he wrote a proposal for an *Island of Sirens* experience."

"I'll stop you right there. We're not moving forward with *that.*" He says, his voice dropping an octave.

"Why?" Genuinely curious, I scooch forward, my chair scraping against the shiny wooden planks.

"*Sirens* didn't do what we wanted at the box office. It was controversial." Gaspard rolls his eyes. Well, at least he gets that the whole controversy was inane.

"Controversial by some shit politicians who've never even seen the damn thing," I counter, feeling my hackles rise. I try to take deep breaths, to listen to the water lapping against the boat instead of the squadron of pelicans fighting over a fish on the dock.

"Doesn't matter." He shrugs as if that's that. "It's too risky. We're buying the island and doing the second cruise line." He grabs the smoothie and takes a sip. Clearly, he believes this is the end of this conversation. Behind him, I see Yasmin spying through the sliding glass door, making sure this isn't a stressful engagement. I smile wanly as if to reassure her, but I intend to fight.

"I don't think so." I say softly.

Gaspard's eyebrows shoot up again. "Oh. And why is that?" His drawl is more apparent when he's surprised. Like Yasmin, he is dressed in white, highlighting his tan and making it hard for me to believe he was in the hospital not that long ago. But upon closer inspection, he doesn't move as quickly now. His left side is stiffer than his right.

"Because a second cruise line is safe. It's what you and Tilda have been doing for the last four years. Avoiding risk. Grabbing cash, trying to please everyone, but not really pleasing anyone."

Gaspard's eyes narrow in on me. He's giving me the look, the Dirty Harry look, that used to make me cower as a kid, but I keep going.

"You're on medical leave. You don't have a vote." Gaspard tries to interrupt, but I cut him off. "This is what *Wade* wanted. It is a risk, but it could pay off. Big. The *Sirens* experience isn't as big of a financial risk. Plus, cruises are environmental disasters," I say, quoting

Marin. "Wade's idea could make us the vanguard again. And most importantly, we'd be doing what Wade wanted..."

Gaspard slams his right hand down on the table. "Stop saying his name!"

I sit quietly, waiting for the wave of criticisms. I don't have to wait long.

"You don't get to say what this company will and won't do. You've wanted nothing to do with it since you were a teenager. YOU didn't work your way up like your brother. YOU didn't give a shit about this place." His face turns red as the volume of his voice rises. "YOU don't get to say what Wade wanted."

Yasmin rushes to Gaspard, placing her hands on his shoulders and squeezing lightly. "Gaspard, calm down." Her usually soft voice is steely and stern. "Deep breaths." She rubs a hand in a circular motion on his back, then turns to me and says, "I think that's enough for today."

I stand up, look down on my father, whose eyes have not left my face. He is calmer, but no less deadly.

"You. Are. Not. Wade." he spits out, his blue eyes blazing with condemnation.

"Trust me, I know," I concede. "But, unlike you and Tilda, I will do right by him."

I attempt to walk away confidently but feel the yacht shift beneath my feet. I want to run and leap full speed off this dumb boat. I want to numb this panic and ache, beating like a drum through my body.

Later, I don't remember getting home, but I do hear my favorite mantra echoing, "*Wrong son, wrong son*," keeping time to my quickening beating heart. Shit. Here we go again.

Chapter Twenty-Three

Marin

Outside the French Village, Roland and I are posing with grumpy four-year-old triplets. Their sunburnt dad takes a million photos while the mom tells their girls to "Smile! Smile! Bigger!" The girls want to go back to the hotel pool, and the loudest triplet has not smiled yet. It's almost closing time and probably around their bedtime. "Sadie, Sara, Sophia, SMILE!"

Secretly, I admire their resistance. Sometimes I worry about this next generation of kids whose lives are meticulously documented and curated specifically for "Likes."

Roland presses his hand into the small of my back in solidarity when I take matters into my own hands, bending down and saying in my best Rose Red voice, "Do you know the first rule of being a princess?"

"Nooo," whine two girls at the same time while the other little girl wipes her nose with the back of her hand.

"It's to always be kind." I bend down even more, as if there's a great secret to be revealed. "Do you know the second rule?" I tap each of their heads.

"Noooo," they reply in unison. Their attention is fully piqued.

"Always... be... SILLY!" I stick out my tongue and tickle their bellies as all three girls giggle.

Roland nudges me and whispers, "I think they're ready for their close-up."

He spins the girls back to their mother, smiles on their identical faces. The dad gets the picture, and we do one final loop of the French Village before heading back for the evening.

Roland holds his arm out for me, which I now take without thinking twice. "Good work back there." The light in his hazel eyes is admiring as he looks down into mine.

"Thanks. We were going to be there forever if I didn't intervene."

From our hidden alcove, I see the mango-colored setting sun. We're working the late shift. Pretty soon we'll transition from greeting kids to taking pictures with adults at Revel Palace. Strangely, the vibe isn't that different. Most adults are respectful and excited to see us, but some take just as long as the kids to get the photos "just right." Rose Red and Roland represent their childhoods. The women do tend to fawn over Roland, but I can't blame them. He's devastatingly handsome and courteous, with a mischievous twinkle.

"Well, you are wonderful with the guests, Red." He stops walking and faces me. We're close together in a privately intimate way, our arms and eyes locked. Is he in character right now? I can't tell.

"So are you, Prince." I smile at him. With my face tilted up to his, he leans in, naturally. Oh my stars, I think he is going to kiss me. It would be "in character" for a peck on the cheek. Roland and Rose only full-on kiss at the very end of the movie in a complicated twirling spin into a dip and kiss. It is not to be tried by the faint of heart or the clumsy of foot. It's the *Dirty Dancing* lift of the Revel world. But surely, he wouldn't do that. Verisimilitude is encouraged, but full on make-out sessions are not.

I should want a kiss, right? I have been mooning over him for weeks now. I look up at this prince, unsure what I'd do if his perfect lips landed on mine.

"Ahem." A man coughs behind us. I turn to see Ethan Reve, of all people, wearing expensive business casual attire, his sleeves rolled up and a few buttons open on his chest. He looks hot. Hot and tired.

"Oh, hello," I stammer. These worlds aren't supposed to collide! I'm not prepared for this. I have zero excuses prepared for why Ethan Reve would deign to talk to me, let alone seek me out.

"May I help you, sir?" Roland has turned around to face Ethan, his voice polite, a total professional. But I know Roland by now and detect a bit of stiffness. His head tilts like he's trying to put a face to a name. I can hear the *Diamonds & Toads* ride playing the Marie's Waltz theme, I smell powdered sugar from the nearby beignet machine in Le Bleue Tortue. I see Ethan Reve moving towards us.

"I need a moment alone with Rose Red." He is full-on glaring at Roland. A muscle in his jaw ticks.

"Wherever Red goes, I go," Roland says gallantly, quoting the movie, more forcefully than his movie counterpart, however.

"Cut the crap, Prince..." Ethan struggles to remember his name and lands on "Prince *Whatever*." Ethan takes two more steps. Near enough to hiss, "I need to talk to you, Marin."

"I don't know any Marin." Roland stands in front of me. He's done this before, with a few dads who wanted me to know they always thought Rose Red was the sexiest princess. I can barely see Ethan over Roland's shoulder. "So, if you don't mind, we're on our way to the palace." Roland turns around and sticks his arm out.

I am frozen. Why can't I move? Ethan's staring daggers at Roland's back as he waits for me to take his arm. I should say something, but I am in character. There are guests everywhere, and Ethan Reve shouldn't be here, shouldn't bother me at work. People will talk. People will post. That's exactly what Ethan doesn't want.

"Please excuse me" is all I can muster. I take Roland's proffered arm again. We walk a few steps, then I glance behind me and mouth the word "LATER." Ethan's nod is almost imperceptible, his eyes dark, his stance aggressive. I whip my face forward, back in character. When I turn back a minute later, Ethan is gone.

At the hidden palace alcove, Roland brings me a diet Coke and granola bar and asks, "What was that all about?" His eyes are no longer warm.

"It's a long story. Ethan is—"

"Ethan Reve!" Roland smacks his hand to his forehead. "I thought I knew him from somewhere, but I wasn't sure. He looks different. Older." He bites into his protein bar before asking, "Why is Ethan Reve talking to *you*?" The dumbfounded disbelief on his face makes me defensive.

"Like I said, it's a long story. I'm helping him with something." A look of astonishment alights Roland's face. "It's not like that. It's not what you think."

"Sure. Of course. But Red, come on. Clearly the guy is into you. He looked like he wanted to rip my head off." Roland finishes his bar in two bites, throws the wrapper in the trash, and sits across from me.

"No, no. Seriously. It's not like that. I can't really talk about it, but it's for the park." I stand up and pretend to check my make-up in the mirror. I see Roland in the reflection. He takes a sip from his soda, a skeptical look on his face.

He joins me in front of the mirror, adjusting his collar and belt. "Well, be careful. I'm a guy, and I know how we think. He's definitely interested in more."

I want to tell him it isn't like that, but I keep quiet.

Roland's eyes find mine in the reflection, assessing me as if he's seeing me, *Marin*, for the first time.

Chapter Twenty-Four

Ethan

At the RP Lounge, I drink a mint julep in a back booth. They're going down easy. Too easy, but I don't care. It's been a day from hell. First my father, then that overgrown peacock putting on the Prince Charming show for Marin. I realize now that showing up like that was shitty, but it wasn't planned. I wasn't thinking.

I shoot Marin a text before I chicken out: *"Sorry about earlier. I'm at the RP Lounge. If you're free later, swing by. I gave your name to the host."*

After leaving the Little Lake marina, I walked around the entire park, subconsciously looking for her. I went to Mona Moon first, then the Lily Pad (the new Miss Maisy was not nearly as appealing), and after finding Princess Portia, Princess Bianca, and Princess Marie at the Revel Palace Hall of Enchantment, I finally made it to the French Village, all the while searching faces in the crowds for her.

I just need a friendly face, I told myself, which I try not to overanalyze now because I have enough neuroses to deal with for one evening. I can't eat. My stomach flip flopped as I tried to walk off my panic attack. If I'm honest with myself, the attacks started before Wade died and have only gotten worse since then.

So, I wandered, and before I knew it I was standing behind Marin, studying her beautiful profile as she smiled up at that prick. From where I stood, it seemed like that asshole might make a move, and Marin looked like she was waiting for a kiss, like a scene from the actual movie.

Something about Marin in that costume, waiting to be kissed, made me feel like that was my moment. Then I don't know what happened exactly. I just saw red. Yet another reaction I don't want to unpack. In fact, I decided that I didn't want to feel anything at all, so I ended up here. Again. On mint julep number, god-only-knows. Bobby had just left for the evening, and I thought about texting James, but he's gallivanting across the French countryside with the ghost of Morticia Addams. Elsie sent me a link to a *Secret Reveler* post with pictures of his trip last night.

Henri was god-knows-where. Probably on some tundra collecting the fecal matter of an endangered emu or something like that. Dom and Elsie, they're in school. They're young. Happy. They don't need this shit. I used to have friends. Well, people I was seen with. Not the same thing.

I'm about to open up my text thread with Wade and delve into my grief again when I feel eyes on me. A beautiful young woman in a slinky teal dress leans against my booth. Her hair is blonde, slicked into a high ponytail. Her skin is sun-kissed.

"Well, hello," I murmur, grateful for the distraction. Grateful for anything that keeps me from the maudlin act of reading my dead brother's text messages.

"You're Ethan Reve." She sits next to me, crossing her legs in my direction, inviting me to look at her tan, smooth leg.

"Last time I checked." I enjoy the view. I am a man after all. I throw back my drink, disappointed it's gone. Before I can call the waiter over, the blonde has her hand in the air.

"Another round." She points to my empty drink. The waiter nods. A few moments later, two mint juleps land in front of us.

"What are you doing here all by your lonesome?" She wraps her rosy lips around the straw and sucks. The show she's putting on is a bit much.

"I was thinking," I reply, intentionally vague.

"Do you want me to leave?" Her eyebrow arches, a challenge.

Yes, I think, but then I look at the clock. It's 10 p.m., and I have been alone with my thoughts all day and look where it got me. I check my phone. Marin hasn't texted back.

"No." I lean towards her. Decision made. Ethan Reve, sad sack, is now Ethan Reve, devil-may-care cad. "I bet you have a great name."

"Veronica," she whispers and wraps her hand around the tall glass. Her movements are feline.

"Nice. What's a Veronica like you doing in a place like this?"

Hopefully, Veronica can help me numb the sensation of perpetual angst. I can erase the meeting with my father, his parting epithet, "*You. Are. Not. Wade.*"

I can forget seeing Marin take her prince by the arm. I can ignore that I'm a mess.

Chapter Twenty-Five

Marin

It's late when I open the doors to RP Lounge, the sort of exclusive place that I could never afford. Apparently, there is an exorbitant annual fee for this private Reveler experience. The place is a stylish Revel version of a 1920s speakeasy. A shiny mahogany bar, a dance floor. Old black-and-white photos line the walls—Mick Reve cutting a ribbon with giant scissors, Mick twirling Marie Reve around at a party, Mick and Marie and little Gaspard and Alice at the opening of *The Scarlet Slippers*, their first live-action film in Hollywood. At the far end of the room, there's a stage, enough tables to seat at least a hundred guests, and intimate, cranberry-colored, high-backed booths.

It is in one of these booths that I spy a scantily clad blond woman, touching forehead to forehead with Ethan. He shakes his head playfully, their noses grazing. Her hand rests on his chest, toying with his shirt button. This is the Ethan I'm used to seeing. The party boy from *TMZ*. This juxtaposed with the image of Ethan I bonded with while watching *Island of Sirens* together. The Ethan who laughed at my dumb jokes. The Ethan who hugged me so tenderly. Dissonance makes my brain hurt. I remember Ethan from earlier today. I hear Roland's quip, "He is definitely into you." But here is *this* Ethan, practically making out with some clothing-averse maneater in public.

Feeling disoriented from the Ethan whiplash, I duck (okay, run) into the bathroom.

I hide in a stall. How can I leave without being seen? It shouldn't be too hard. They were about to play tonsil hockey out there. He wouldn't even know I was here. Decision made, I'm about to exit the stall when the bathroom door opens, and the clack of heels reverberates off the marble floors and walls.

"It's working! I can't believe you're going home with Ethan Reve," a woman with a raspy baby voice declares. I hear purses open and various makeup clasps clicking.

"No one will believe it unless you get some good pics." asserts another woman, who I assume is the blonde. I try to peek through the slit in the door frame. "Seriously. When I go back out there, I'll get close to him again. Make sure you zoom in."

"Got it. Ooooh, we should send them to *The Secret Reveler*," the accomplice suggests. I hear a smack of lips. Someone just reapplied lipstick.

"No, we're going to sell them, dummy." The faucet starts running.

For a moment, I think about letting them get their photo op; it serves Ethan right. But does it? He doesn't owe me anything. It's a bit weird that I'm this upset by this. I need to think about this rationally. We're colleagues. He can canoodle with whomever he chooses. But our proposal means a lot to me too. So yet again, I will save this project and Ethan from his big dumb self.

I open the stall door. They barely look at me while I wash my hands. Instead, they inspect their reflections in the mirror. The blonde sticks her hand down the front of her dress, pushing her boobs up to her chin.

I practically run to Ethan's booth. He's slumped over. Oh no. He's drunk again. I scooch in next to him, grab his arm, and wrap it around me. I try to get him to move, but I forget how heavy he is. I can't lift him. Lifting him and racing him out of here is not an option right now. His breath is minty. Flashback alert. I survey the table and spot an empty mint julep. I was right that night I pulled him from the moat! His kiss tasted like mint julep. I'll have to do option two.

Get yourself together, I tell myself. Focus and make this look real.

I grab Ethan's chin, his eyes flutter open. "Kiss me, you idiot," I say.

His eyes widen. He breaks into a goofy grin. "Marin?"

He's drunk, but at least he knows who I am.

"You came!" He beams at me, which breaks my heart, but I can't think about why right now.

"Less talky, more kissy." I lean in, but he still doesn't get the hint and gapes at me.

"Kiss the girl," I command him. Nothing. "Kiss me, Ethan." To hell with it, I think as I smash my lips against his. His lips don't move, but he doesn't pull away. This isn't the intoxicating kiss from the Mona Moon moat, but it must look real because our show has the desired effect.

"Excuse me," a twangy voice demands from behind the booth. The blonde from the bathroom has arrived. Huzzah!

I disengage slowly and turn. "May I help you?" Smiling at the blonde then back at Ethan, maneuvering his head, has the desired effect. It appears like he's nuzzling my neck. Ethan mutters incoherently about golden amber again, whatever that means.

"Ethan, not now, sweetie, you're incorrigible," I laugh and pet the back of his head.

"I was sitting there." Blondie motions to the seat next to Ethan.

"And now you're not. Thanks for keeping my seat warm, but poor Ethan here has had a few too many, and I'll be taking him home now."

My eyes lock onto hers. I don't look away, daring her to challenge me. After a few excruciating moments, the blonde's gaze averts. She glares at the empty drinks littering the table.

"Fine, whatever. He's too drunk anyway." She snarls a discreet "bitch" before she stalks off, no doubt disappointed at losing her fifteen minutes of skanky fame.

When I'm sure she's gone, I push Ethan off me. I look around to see if anyone has been watching. The coast appears clear, so I grab a glass of untouched water and throw it in his face.

"Whaa-whaat?" He is startled, more conscious now.

"Sober up! It's time to go." As I lead him out of the booth, Ethan leans into me, wobbly. We breeze past the hostess into the cool night air. This wakes him up enough so that I can guide him to the compound and use his key to get into his dark apartment. He keeps repeating, "Sorry, sorry, so sorry" and "Wrong son, so sorry, wrong son."

My anger completely dissipates by the time he face-plants on the couch. I get him a glass of much needed water and perch next to him, watching while he takes a few sips.

"More," I say, urging him to finish it.

I grab the glass and move to get up, but his hand grasps my wrist. "Don't go." His blue eyes pleading. "Please."

This reminds me of the last time he made this plea—his hands on my lower back, the minty taste of his mouth, his desire pressed against me.

I pull myself away. "I'm just going to the kitchen, needy," I say, before taking off his shoes and dropping them under the coffee table.

In the kitchen, I fill his glass to the brim again and find some Advil in a drawer. By the time I've brought it back, Ethan's fast asleep, mouth open and snoring loudly.

What a mess, I think as I shoot a text to Flora that I'll be crashing elsewhere tonight and will explain everything tomorrow.

An eggplant emoji pops up on my screen, followed by a question mark.

I write back, *"No, get your mind out of the gutter. Talk later. Promise."*

In Ethan's bedroom, I notice his sparse decor. There's a wide bed, a boxy dark dresser, and matching bedside tables with shiny silver pulls. I throw myself on the enormous king-sized bed, the expensive soft mattress feeling like a cloud compared to the twin cot I've been sleeping on the past few weeks. His gray duvet smells like him, a hint of cedar, and his pillows are firm. From here, I notice only one personal picture. It's on his nightstand. Ethan is standing next to Wade in his dress blues, their arms draped casually around the other. The look on their smiling faces reveals a closeness I long for in a sibling.

I've never seen Ethan smile like that, so warm and content, I think as I drift into a fitful sleep.

Chapter Twenty-Six

Ethan

An alarm blares somewhere in my apartment, an obnoxiously loud alarm called Five-Truck Fire. I throw myself off the couch to find it and turn it off, but it magically stops. It hits me. I am about to be sick. Making it to the bathroom, I retch up a vat of whiskey, simple syrup, and mint.

The tile wall across from the toilet feels cold and refreshing against my back. I will my stomach to stop heaving. Through the fog of what is sure to be one of the worst hangovers of my life, I attempt to retrace my steps. I saw Dad and Yasmin on the boat. I spent hours in the park. Then I saw Marin as Rose Red and that peacocking, two-bit actor. My stomach does a somersault, and I lean into the toilet and retch again. God, my nose burns. My throat burns. Everything burns. And aches. I lie flat, placing my cheek on the cool bathroom tiles, which seems to help the spins and my throbbing head.

This is bad. Why am I so hungover? It dawns on me that I didn't eat much yesterday. That might explain it. Why didn't I eat again? Oh, yeah. Anxiety. When it's pumping through my veins, the last thing I want to do is eat. So, when I couldn't talk to Marin, I went to the RP Lounge. The vague outline of a face appears before me, blonde hair, tan legs.

Shit. I take a deep breath. Did I take that woman home? Is she the reason my alarm turned off?

Will she have blabbed this to all her friends and the internet?

A small voice in my head says, "You do this to yourself, buddy."

Fuck.

I move to stand, but I wobble. Okay, I'll crawl; closer proximity to the ground means fewer chances of serious head injury. Although, I can't be sure I didn't fall and incur head trauma last night because, holy shit, I feel like I had twelve hits to the head with a two-by-four.

I crawl down the hall, looking like an asshat, but dignity went down the drain with last night's juleps.

I make it to my room, grateful for the runners in my hallway. I head toward the bed, wary of startling the mystery guest. At the foot of the bed, I listen for a few moments and hear light breathing. Shit. Okay. I leverage myself onto the bed as quietly as possible to get a peek at my guest. Instead of blonde hair, I see auburn locks sprawled across my gray pillowcase.

Oh, thank god. It's Marin. This is my last thought before I crawl my way towards the headboard, grab a crisp pillow, and fall onto the bed.

Chapter Twenty-Seven

Marin

I'm running on the levee, except I'm not running for fun. Something wild and shadowy is chasing me. When I glance back over my shoulder, it disappears, but I can still feel it there. I can't seem to catch my breath, and other runners are flying past me while ACDC's "Thunderstruck" plays on a loop.

What fresh hell is this? Then my brain finally drags me from the dream. The rock song is not in my head but playing somewhere close by. Where am I? I turn over and yelp. Ethan Reve is curled up next to me. His beautiful face smooshed against a white pillow. His crumpled shirt open. His hair an inky mess. His phone lighting up and "Thunder!" chanting on repeat. He doesn't move, not even a twitch.

I nudge him. Nothing. "Ethan, wake up," I whisper. No movement. His torso is tan and powerful, even at complete rest. I blush. I'm in Ethan's bed, ogling him, then I remember that I'm mad at him.

His behavior was atrocious yesterday. Between the confrontation with Roland, the reckless flirtation with the blonde, and the excessive drinking, I'm mad, but I'm also worried. This is the third time that he's done this, that I know of. This isn't party-boy behavior. Parties are supposed to be fun, and he doesn't seem to be having any. This is self-destructive, and I don't know why this rich, intelligent, handsome man wants to get black-out drunk. Why is he the "wrong son"? Once his dad called him the wrong son at his brother's funeral. I'd seen it in a dozen posts. Does Ethan actually believe that?

His phone stops ringing, finally. Then it buzzes a few times. Ethan rolls over, mumbling. His phone falls out of his pants pocket, and I grab it to put it on silent, but stop short when I glance at the screen.

From Ernie Guidry: *Where are you, kid? I called three times.*

Followed by: *Tilda called an emergency board meeting. She's up to something.*

Three blinking dots, then: *It starts in an hour. Palace Boardroom. You NEED to be there.*

Crap! Ethan is still out cold, his back expanding and contracting with a light snore. Sound asleep. I grab his shoulder and flip him onto his back.

I kneel next to him and start smacking his face. "Ethan, Ethan! Please wake up."

He groans but doesn't move.

"Ethan!" My volume rises, my pats become slaps. "Get up, Ethan!"

Suddenly his eyes flutter open. He looks at me, confusion clouding his blue eyes.

"Thank god," I mutter as I lean back.

"Marin?" He attempts to sit up. He squints, taking in the room and me in it. "Why are you in my bed?"

"I found you in the RP Lounge last night," I spit out, eager to get him up, showered, and to the conference room.

"Did we...?" His eyebrows are raised.

"Seriously, you don't remember anything?" I'm angry now. "How drunk were you?" I bolt up, pulling on the jeans I took off before landing in this dream bed, too angry to care that he's squinting at my bare thighs.

"I'm sorry, I..." His brows furrow. "I...I need to go." He leaps up, stumbling a bit, and rushes to the bathroom. The sounds of Ethan's retching and a toilet flush a moment later reach all the way down the hallway. I find him, the giant Ethan Reve, prone on his bathroom floor.

"Ethan, you have to get up." I push his splayed leg with the ball of my foot. He grunts in response. "Ethan, Ernie Guidry texted you. Tilda called an emergency board meeting. You have to go."

I step into the bathroom as he rolls onto his side and mumbles something.

"What? I can't understand what you're saying," I say, trying to calm myself down.

"I can't. Sick." He looks green. Sweaty.

"You have to get up, Ethan." I enter the enormous bathroom and balance on the edge of a soaking tub.

"Think about the proposal. Think about what we've been working on." But he isn't budging, so I say, "Think about Wade."

He forces himself to sit up. "Okay, okay. I'm up. I just need to shower." He uses the counter to lift himself. He pulls off his shirt. "Can you start the water?"

I sneak past without touching him, find the faucets, and keep the water cool.

Ethan is dazed. I hear him unzip his pants, and I hop to the door. As I'm closing it, I hear, "Oh, no," followed by more retching.

I wait in the hall. The toilet flushes again. I push it open a crack to see him holding onto the sink, his knuckles white. "I can't, Marin. I'm sorry. I can't move without the world spinning."

"What do we do then?" I ask, trying not to freak out, but 100 percent wanting to cry like a hangry toddler.

"I don't know." Ethan wipes his mouth and slowly crumples back to the floor. He points to the mouthwash on his sink. I hand it to him as he droops against the tub. "Can't...can't..." He's back to the toilet, dry-heaving now.

"Okay, okay. I'll figure something out." I leave the bathroom and pace into the dining room, noting the facts of this predicament. The meeting is in less than an hour. Before I can talk myself out of it, I grab some notes and my legal pad from the dining room table, and yell down the hall, "We'll talk later!"

I race out of the compound and all the way back to the dorm. Flora isn't home, thank god. I brush my teeth and hair and make myself as business presentable as I can be, then book it back across the park to the Revel Palace conference center. There, security eyes me skeptically when I tell him I'm Ethan Reve's assistant, but I hold his gaze until he directs me to the third floor. Eyeing my phone, I have two minutes to spare. In the elevator, I pull lip gloss out of my bag, apply it quickly and take a breath. When the doors open, I follow the ornate silver-plated signs to the conference room. Outside the board room, I throw my shoulders back and take a deep breath. I watched a TED Talk about power poses recently. My family would scoff at the "pseudoscience" of power posing, but I need all the help I can get. In a matter of seconds, I'm standing in front of ten professionals, including Tilda Olsen-Reve.

It's a record-scratch moment. All eleven board members turn to me, and before I can hyperventilate and run screaming back to the dorms, a portly Cajun man says, "Miss, can I help you with something?"

"Yes," I nod. "I work for Ethan Reve. I'm his assistant, Marin Vandersee."

The room somehow gets quieter. "His assistant?" The older man asks, his brow furrows.

"Yes, pleased to meet you." I hold out my hand, hoping it isn't sweaty from my run.

He takes my proffered hand and steps closer. "Where's Ethan?" His voice drops lower. Concern emanates across his wrinkled face.

"Unfortunately, he's got a stomach bug and is unable to join us," I say loud enough for the room to hear. Tilda snorts in disbelief. "But he sent me here as his proxy."

Tilda rises, her eyes assessing everything. Her curious non-expression seems to find me lacking. In an all-white jumpsuit, which shows off her tanned, toned arms and streaked blonde hair, she's a few inches taller than everyone in the room. Next to Tilda, I feel like a short, rumpled gnome.

A tall, handsome man in his forties sidles up next to Tilda, extends his hand and says, "Bill Symons." His eyes appraise me in a different way. Less icy and more appreciative. It gives me the heebie-jeebies.

An older Black woman in oversized red glasses stands beside me. "Nice to meet you, Marin. Shirleen Watson. This is Luca Conti, Barbara Staffield, Binky Dupuis, Claude Pitre..." A sea of faces blur together. "Why don't we get this started? I'm curious to know about this emergency." Shirleen indicates a seat at the table, and we all sit down.

The room is overwhelming. Clearly, an homage to the Coquille in Versailles—gold-inlay shell arches, intricate marquetry on the floors, a shiny, long mahogany table. If it weren't for the large television mounted on the wall and the brand-new laptops and smartphones littering the table, I would think I fell through time and landed in Louis XVI's court.

"Yes, let's." Tilda glides to the center seat, sits, and folds her hands on the table, as if to say, *this meeting can begin.* "I spoke with Gaspard yesterday."

"Is he okay?" Ernie Guidry leans forward, concerned.

He texted Ethan, I remember, which means he could be an ally. At least I hope he is. I make a mental note.

"Yes, yes. Recovery is slow, but smooth. He's curious about the progress of the island cruise project. While he is not currently able to vote, he wants the board to know I have his full support for this venture." She pauses, looking around the room. "He also wanted to let me know that he has concerns about his son's proposal and would like to table this for the foreseeable future."

A surprised "What?!" flies out of my mouth. I can't help it. It's out before I can stop it.

"Yes, Ms. Vandersee?" Tilda states coldly. "You seem confused."

"I am." I clear my throat and remind myself to show no fear. Predators feed on fear. "Ethan is expecting to pitch the proposal at next quarter's board meeting."

"Yes, but that was before..." Tilda's gaze slides to Bill's face who is grinning.

"Before what?" My feathers are ruffled.

"Before we, Gaspard and I, and a few members of the board, discussed our serious concerns with Ethan's image. Instead of waiting and wasting money and everyone's time, we felt it was important to meet now to move forward." She bares her teeth at me, and I assume this is meant to be a smile.

"Tilda, you're going to need to explain yourself here." Shirleen eyes her skeptically. Her tone matter-of-fact. Another possible ally?

"Of course." Tilda aims her smile at the board. "We're a family company. We value family, respect, integrity, and stability. And the image we project to the world should reflect that. Ethan, as you all know, hasn't met these expectations. The partying, the gossip, the revolving door of women." She lets her eyes rest on me for a beat.

Subtle.

Bill chimes in. "And that business with Bree Brooklyn didn't help. She's one of ours, part of the Revel family, and their breakup reflects poorly on us. The blogs really ate that saga for lunch. There's also word that there's a documentary about Bree's life in the works, and Ethan will definitely not be cast in a good light."

A few board members shift uncomfortably in their seats. A beautifully tan man dressed in Armani raises an eyebrow. The infamous Luca Conti probably finds the American obsession with celebrity sex lives puritanical.

Tilda nods enthusiastically. "Yes. And because of Gaspard's illness AND Ethan's less-than-stellar reputation, I think we should wait a year, maybe two. Let Ethan get settled. Give him a chance to rehabilitate his image, if he's up for it. If he's going to be the face of Revel moving forward, we need to make sure he's more..." She pretends to struggle for the words, "...more...brand-friendly, more stable."

I am stunned. This is clear sabotage. While I can see how Ethan's image isn't necessarily spotless, Tilda seems to be deliberately hurting her stepson, with his father's blessing, to push her agenda. I think about his excitement after watching *Island of Sirens*. His dedication to seeing his brother's dream become a reality. He's clearly struggling, and, yes, his reputation needs some work, but that doesn't mean he should be sidelined in such an underhanded way. There is more to Ethan than the party boy. And I have a sixth sense that this news could push him over the edge that he's been teetering so close to lately.

"I disagree," I interject.

"Excuse me?" Tilda leans back in her chair and crosses her arms. "And who are you again?"

"Marin Vandersee. Ethan's marketing assistant."

"His 'assistant' who happens to be young and attractive. By all means..." Tilda smiles and gives out an airy laugh. "Please, proceed."

"Thank you for the compliment, but Ethan hired me because I'm a die-hard Reveler who's helping him with marketing and development." I pause. "The *Island of Sirens* experience embodies Revel's values. It's exciting, educational, and entertaining. You all have the chance to create a cutting-edge exhibit and win back your critics."

"Well, thank you for your input, but you don't really get a say here." Tilda's phone pings, and she dismisses me, giving her attention to her screen.

Now that is just rude. "I don't think you can make a decision like this without including the person you're talking about in the room. This seems underhanded, which is certainly not aligned with Revel's values."

Shirleen nods, and Ernie adds, "I'm going to have to agree with the kid here."

Tilda doesn't appear to be listening. She's smiling down at her phone. "Tilda?" Bill says, trying to get her attention.

Her head snaps up, mirth lighting her eyes. "I'm so sorry, I just received the most interesting message. I must share it with everyone. In fact, I'll send it to the projector."

Bill picks up a remote and a screen scrolls down from the ceiling. A sinking feeling overwhelms me. Whatever is making this woman smile can't be good.

"Voila!" she gestures to the screen. Emblazoned, writ large, is the headline "Ethan Reve's New Flame?" and below it is a picture of me kissing Ethan in the RP Lounge. We are practically on top of one another. My profile is clear, and Ethan is looking at me like he wants to eat my lips.

My face turns beet red.

"You should have been clearer, Ms. Vandersee. Your title seems more like part-time assistant, part-time bedfellow?" Tilda looks like the cat who caught the canary. "What were you saying about values?"

The room closes in on me. A power pose will not get me out of this one. My heart races, sweat breaks out in the small of my back, my pits, the back of my knees, and my eyelids? Who gets sweaty eyelids? Shit. It was my idea to stage that kiss. I didn't think those girls would take pictures of me. Of us. Those opportunistic, conniving tarts! I have to think fast. I have to fix this.

"Um..." I hesitate, unable to find the words.

Ernie coughs. Shirleen turns towards me. Bill grins like the Cheshire cat.

"You want to explain this, Marin?" Tilda beams, losing the formality now. Confident in her win.

"Yes. I do." I take a steadying breath. "Ethan and I started working together. He hired me specifically for my knowledge of the Revel Pointe brand. I'm taking a semester off from Tulane where I'm in the second year of my MBA program."

A few board members look surprised. I ignore this and continue. "Obviously, our relationship has changed. We didn't plan to...we didn't plan on falling in love, but you all know that saying about the best laid schemes of mice and men?"

Bill watches my face, bemused.

Shirleen smiles at me and adds, "They often go awry. It's from a Robert Burns poem."

"Yes," I return her smile. Grins pass around the boardroom table like dominos. Tilda doesn't look convinced.

It spurs me to blurt out, "I'm his girlfriend."

Tilda's eyes narrow. "Ethan Reve doesn't have a *serious* girlfriend."

"Well, I guess people change because you're talking to her." I feel my chin lift a little in defiance.

"Why are we just now hearing about you?" She refers to the picture on the wall.

We do look cozy together, I think. Lovey-dovey, even. Ethan's looking at me like I'm a delicious piece of cake. I start to blush.

"Ethan and I have spent every night at his place this week."

Ernie lets out a chuckle, and I realize what I just insinuated. At this point, I'm sure my cheeks match my hair color.

"Wait, no. It's not like that," I correct.

Bill laughs, "Sure, sweetie."

And then my embarrassment turns to anger. "We haven't had time to go out because we've been working on Wade's proposal. Ethan has not stopped for the last month. He eats, breathes, and sleeps this project. Last night I forced him to take a break. You haven't heard about us because, imagine this...we wanted privacy." I hope they get my sarcasm.

"Too late for that now, isn't it?" Tilda points to the screen.

"We wanted the focus to be on this project, not on our personal lives," I explain. "We all know what happens when the public gets wind of his romantic life."

"Sometimes our personal lives get in the way of our professional lives," Bill Symons retorts. His glare looks wolfish.

"I get it, but didn't you just admonish him for not representing Revel's values because he wasn't in a stable relationship? Ethan is with me now, and we care for each other." Screw them and their double standards; ire fills my voice. "And I am not some pop queen or party girl. I'm not a floozy in a bar; I'm a nerdy ginger MBA candidate from Vermont!"

I pause and take a deep breath. The room is silent now. Ernie Guidry grins at me, nodding like he wants me to go on.

I stand. "If Ethan's tumultuous love life was really the dealbreaker, then consider that worry a thing of the past." I pull my bag onto my shoulder and continue. "I am not here to talk to you about Ethan's personal life. I am here representing Ethan Reve because he's unwell this morning, and because this project is the right move for Revel. He cares deeply about this and wouldn't want anything or *anyone* to sabotage his chance to share it with you. Including a stomach bug. Including this last-minute meeting, months before the board had planned." I inch towards the door.

In the glass, I can see that Tilda is standing now, her hands splayed on the table. "We aren't finished here. Just where do you think you're going?" Irate, her voice turns shrill.

I stare at her a moment and then look around the room. "To check on my sick boyfriend. Thank you for listening. I hope to see you all again soon. With a finished proposal. As promised." I turn and leave them to deal with the bombs I just dropped.

Chapter Twenty-Eight

Ethan

I've made it to the living room couch like a goddamn hero. I should be worried right now, but I can't make myself care about anything but not dry heaving until I die. I've never wanted to die, but at some point this morning, I accepted my fate, embraced it even. "Jesus, Buddha, Moses... whoever's out there, I'm ready to come home if that's your plan," I pray as I drift again into a restless, dreamless slumber. I wake up when I hear my front door slam.

Marin stands in my foyer, dressed like a sexy businesswoman, hands on her hips.

"How did you get back in?" I bumble, trying to sit up. Too hungover to be embarrassed wearing only my boxer briefs.

"I took your key." She stares down at me. Her slate eyes ablaze. She throws a plastic grocery bag at me. Pedialyte, crackers, and ginger ale tumble onto the sofa.

"Oh my god, thank you." I open the Pedialyte and feel judgment wafting off her. Let's hope this stays down. I take a careful gulp. "What's up?" I lean over, rub my face, and run my hand through my hair, which I'm sure is standing straight up.

"What's up?" She starts to pace. "What's up?!" I try not to check out her ass in those fitted pants. Who knew I was so into slacks?

"Is everything okay? Where'd you go? Why are you dressed like Jan from *The Office*?" I take another swig from the bottle. I can't stomach the crackers yet.

Marin stops pacing. She's so still I start to fidget.

"I went to the emergency board meeting."

I stand up so quickly that my vision blurs. "What?!" It's my turn to yell.

"Yes. And I saved your ass. *Again.*"

I wobble in place, spinning, dumbfounded.

"What does that mean exactly?" I feel like there's a delay in my feed. *Does not compute. Ethan Robot malfunction.*

"Tilda said you weren't fit to represent the company, that you don't represent Revel's values. That they should table your proposal for another year, until you can prove you're a stable, positive representative of the Revel brand." She's pacing again, hiding something. Her red hair, in a high ponytail, swings from side to side, lulling me into a light hypnosis.

"Oh."

"Oh?" She asks. "Oh? Is that all you have to say?" Her chin juts forward. "They use a bullshit excuse to torpedo your project, *Wade's* project, and all you can say is 'oh'?"

"Yes, *oh*... because they're right." I exhale loudly. "Marin, I'm a fuck-up. I'm nothing like Wade, and this is a family company, and my behavior has been anything but family friendly the last few years."

She just stares at me, waiting for me to go on.

"I can see it from their perspective. It used to just be an annoyance, my behavior—*Ethan's rebellious stage*—but now that I'm in charge, to everyone's surprise, including my own, it's different. It's a problem. I get it." I shrug before taking another sip, happy I'm able to keep the liquid down now.

Marin flops onto the sofa next to me, and I join her. "It seems like now that you want to produce something that might take resources away from Tilda's island cruise, your behavior matters. *You* matter," she retorts, angry on my behalf.

When was the last time someone's been angry for me, not at me? I guess the last time was with Wade. Jesus. I press my hands against my temples. When I look over at her, Marin's bright, round eyes are on me, hesitant.

She's about to say more but stops herself and sighs.

"What?" I ask.

"Well, I have to show you something. And tell you something, and it might make things weird." She averts her gaze to her bag and then pulls out her phone, her hands shaky. She opens a browser and on the screen is a picture of us. Kissing.

"What is this?" I whisper. I don't remember this. How drunk was I? I should remember kissing Marin.

"I...Last night, at the bar... I overheard some girl in the bathroom say that she wanted to take pictures of you two in a..."—she looks down, embarrassed—"...compromising position."

"The blonde?" I vaguely remember her.

Marin nods. "She wanted to sell pictures of you two, you know.... I knew you were drunk and so I intervened."

"By kissing me?!" I'm yelling again, upset that I keep putting myself in these positions, upset that I don't remember anything, upset that she's seen me like this multiple times. Fuck. I hate that she's seen me like this.

"Yes, I ran out to the booth while they were primping in the restroom. I wanted the blonde to get a clear message that she needed to leave you alone. I didn't really think; I just acted. They must have decided a pic of us was better than nothing." Marin nods to her screen.

"Girls?" I don't remember girls.

"It was a blonde and her friend." Marin starts picking at her right thumb nail nervously. Her eyes don't meet mine. "You seriously don't remember any of this?"

"No. I remember having some drinks, waiting for you, then talking to a blonde. Then...nothing."

"That's not good, Ethan," she says, concern in her eyes. I hate that pitying look, and I hate myself for warranting it. "This behavior is reckless, self-destructive..."

"I know!" My voice is louder than I intended. "I made another mistake. One of many. But so did you. This press is not good. This picture of us? This isn't good, Marin!"

I immediately regret lashing out, but before I can apologize she bolts up off the couch and crosses the room.

"Are you serious right now?!" Her jaw clenches and her chin lifts in such defiance I want to cower. "Without me, they would have killed Wade's project today, and you wouldn't have even known!"

Furious, Marin continues. "Tilda projected this picture onto a big screen in front of a room of very important people! People I want to work for in the future! Can you imagine how humiliating that was for me? To save your ass, to save this project, I had to tell the board we're dating. Seriously and exclusively. I told them that we were a team, and we accidentally fell in love. I told them you were serious about this project and that the only reason you weren't there is because you had a stomach bug."

Marin returns to stand in front of me and leans in so our faces are level. Her voice an intense whisper. "I lied, Ethan. For this project. For you, you...you...asshat."

She's right. I am an asshat.

"Why?" I whisper, barely able to keep my voice steady, overwhelmed again by her kindness.

"Why, what?" She crosses her arms, exhausted. Who wouldn't be?

"Why do you keep helping me?" I need to know why this woman has shown up for me, three times already. Why is she standing here now? How long before I push her away entirely, before she realizes there's no return on her investment?

Marin bites her lip; her eyes look glassy. "I believe in this project, and I thought you were a good guy, just that maybe you're going through something, and maybe you deserve a break. I guess I was wrong." She turns on her heel and heads for the door.

I follow, a bit wobbly. "So, what now? Are you leaving? After you lied to everyone and told them we were in a stable, committed relationship? Did they even buy it?" I sound harsher than I intend, but goddamnit, I'm pretty sure she's about to quit, to walk out on me, and I can't stomach that.

Marin faces me. I note the dark circles under her eyes. "Yes, I think so. I think Ernie Guidry and Shirleen Watson are allies. Check your phone. Ernie probably texted you the board's decision." She sounds so tired. Her bag slumps to the ground. She uses the wall as support. I chance leaving her alone and retrieve my phone from the bedroom. Ernie did text.

Ernie: *Tell your little lady to bring that fire when you officially pitch your project. Hope you feel better, buddy.*

"Well?" Marin hovers by my bedroom door. Her eyebrows raised, curious to know if her gamble succeeded.

"It worked." My voice cracks. "You did it." I show her the text. Happy to be near her, scared that I feel tethered to her like the moon in orbit.

She reads, quiet for a moment. Introspective. I take in her pale face, the freckles on her nose, her pretty, pink bow lips. I try to memorize her face before the inevitable. Before she walks out of here and never comes back.

But she meets my gaze. Her eyes scan my face for something deeper. I hold my breath, hoping Marin finds something in my eyes to keep her here.

She sighs. "We'll keep the ruse going until the proposal. And I'll keep working on the project. I believe in it and want to see it through." She takes a step towards me. Somehow, she seems taller.

"But, you are NOT going to sabotage this. No late-night parties, no public shenanigans, no mint juleps. I need you to promise me that. Otherwise, I walk away, and it is clear, more than ever, that you need me to pull this off." Her eyes are steely.

I nod and lean in. "You have to promise me something in return."

"Do you really think you're in a position to ask for anything?" Her mouth turns down and her brow rises quizzically.

"Yes, for the sake of the project. And for our deal, yes." Our eyes lock. "This committed, stable relationship you sold to the board has to look as real as possible."

Marin rolls her eyes, like she can't possibly be the problem in this equation. "You don't have to worry about *me*." She scoffs. "And what, pray tell, does a real relationship even look like to you?"

This stings a bit, but it's a valid question. "If we're 'in love,'" I air-quote aggressively, "then you should be over here every night. You'll have to stay the night sometimes. We'll go out in public. We'll touch, in public, a lot."

She lets out a breath I didn't know she was holding. Her lashes flutter up at me.

"And no more flirting with Prince Fuckface. If we're in love, you're with me."

Her mouth drops. "*ROLAND* and I were not flirting. We're professionals, and our characters flirt. Plus, I'm in full costume. Someone would really have to look to tell that it was me."

"Whatever. Just make sure you don't blur *those* worlds." Oh, the hypocrisy.

"Speak for yourself." Marin crosses her arms and huffs.

"What does that mean?" I take a half step, and our hands touch. My face is inches from hers. Her expression turns sardonic, and I wonder about how soft her lips feel.

"I just mean that you sound like a possessive boyfriend right now." Up close, she has dark smudges under her eyes. She probably didn't sleep well. If I were her real boyfriend, I'd tell her to quit working for such a shitty boss.

"I'm just making sure nothing gets in the way of Wade's project." My voice is low now. "I'm a public figure, like it or not, and this means there will be eyes on us. All of the time."

"Okay. I hear you. I agree to those terms. Make it look real. Stay the night. PDA. Got it. But like you said, no blurring worlds. *We* know what's real and what isn't," she draws an imaginary line between us. "This is a professional relationship. I'm a professional person. *Capiche*?" I can tell she is trying to sound tough, but this is undermined by her audible gulp. Marin holds out a hand. We are so close I have to look down at it between us. "We're making a deal, Ethan. We should shake on it."

I take her hand, give it one firm shake, but I don't let it go. "Deal."

With my pointer finger on her wrist, I feel her pulse pitter-patter. She freezes for a beat before extricating herself from my grip.

"I have to get ready for work. I'm playing Rose in two hours."

Back in the living room, Marin picks up her bag again. Her eyes linger a moment on my bare chest and abs, and quickly avert before they dip lower.

As Marin turns to leave again, her red ponytail flips to the side. "Take a shower, Ethan. You stink."

"Thank you, Marin, for everything," I call. She pauses mid-stride, so I know she heard me.

When she's gone, I sink back onto the couch. A shower, some bland food, and another nap, then I'll get to work. But before I do any of that, I grab my phone, google my name, and examine the picture of Marin and me kissing. I wish I remembered it, I think, before I push the thought away.

Don't blur worlds. Don't blur worlds. My newest mantra.

Chapter Twenty-Nine

Marin

Eight hours later, and I'm dead on my feet in full costume at Princess-palooza (as Carrie calls it). I'm taking pictures with guests as well as the whole squad: Princess Portia, Thumbelina, Princess Bianca, Kaliope, and Princess Marie. Revel uses a wing of the Revel Pointe Palace for these epic, exclusive, and expensive meet-and-greets. Each princess has her own section of stage for posing and quick banter with park guests, mostly little girls and boys, but sometimes couples and groups of girlfriends.

It's weird to be here as Rose Red just a few hours after that insane board meeting. Every blonde I see reminds me of Tilda for the first hour.

But the novelty of this many princesses in one room assuages any residual negativity from this morning. Guests absolutely freak out when they see us all together. Plus, I get to work with different cast members. I haven't spent much time with Marie, Bianca, and Kaliope. We always work in different sections of the park, and often at the same time.

Of course, I already know Lana and Carrie. Carrie is the runt of the princess pack, which makes sense as the petite Thumbelina. In her green fitted one-piece with her blonde pixie cut bedecked with flowers and vines, Thumbelina is the most androgynous character of this bunch. The David Bowie of Revel princesses.

We take our break in the green room behind the stage. The princesses sit, stretch, eat, drink, reapply make-up, and adjust our costumes. While resting at a small card table, Carrie leans in and asks, "Who's your favorite princess?" She digs into a peanut butter and jelly sandwich. "I can tell a lot about a person by their favorite character."

"Hm. I need a minute," I reply, taking the question seriously. "What are Thumbelina fans like?"

"Future softball players." Carrie winks at me.

I roll my eyes. "No, really."

Carrie huffs. "Thumbelina fans are the ones who don't quite fit in."

I nod. *Thumbelina* is an '80s movie. She's an impulsive live-wire who is reluctant to marry her prince, wanting adventure instead.

"I mean, my princess is the only one who grows wings." She shimmies so they dance behind her.

"Okay, what about Princess Marie?" I ask.

Marie is the put-upon peasant turned princess from *Diamonds and Toads*. She's taller than me by a head, and an old-school fan favorite. Apparently, she was based on a young Marie Reve, beautiful, bookish, and kind. She's a classic French beauty, naturally slender, with long brown hair and eyes. She's in her day-wear, a blue dress with a pale, yellow apron. Her classic ballgown look is only for parades and night events.

"That's easy," Carrie answers. "*Mariens* are bookworms and shy girls. I imagine there's a Venn diagram somewhere online that shows the propensity to love Marie overlaps with the propensity to love horses."

A laugh escapes from deep in my gut, and I start to feel lighter, like myself again after the stress-filled morning. My best friend and fellow Reveler in junior high, Gretchen, loved Marie and also had a horse named Buttercup. I cock my head at Lana, who preens in front of a mirror. "And our friend, Princess Portia?"

Princess Portia has platinum locks and electric blue eyes, which match her lapis sheath, cinched by a silver belt. She's the heroine from *Portia's Power*, a film based on the Norwegian fairytale of the same name. Lana, who plays Portia, calls her Revel's first good witch. She's powerful, able to control natural elements, but ultimately good hearted. The film came out in 1968, and she's definitely the first empowered, "hear-me-roar" princess protagonist.

Carrie says, "Control freaks and geeks love Portia. Girls who long for power, but you know, more like self-empowerment." Lana is painstakingly fixing her fake metallic lashes in the mirror. Carrie's eyebrows raise as if to say, see what I mean? "The class presidents of the world."

"What about Bianca fans?" I ask as I finish a bottle of water. Princess Bianca is the bossy, boisterous, fun-loving princess from *Princess and the Pea*.

Carrie just gives me one word, "Trouble."

She looks over as Ella, a dead ringer for Bianca, who adjusts her bosom and looks down forlornly like her boobs aren't cooperating. Of all the princesses, she is the most curvaceous, her frilly red, green, and white peasant dress cinched by a yellow corset. Ella applies a shimmery glow to her chest, highlighting her light brown skin and ample assets. Her voluminous black hair is piled up on her head, curled tendrils cradle her heart-shaped face and large amber eyes.

"Anyone got some baby powder?" Ella yells to no one in particular. "My girls are chafing today."

Carrie and I giggle. It's refreshing to laugh. I feel like I've lived ten lives today, sprinting across the park, fighting with Ethan, fighting with the board, fighting with Ethan again. My phone died, not that I could use it anyway, but I'd love to phone a friend right about now. I'm going to have to tell Flora everything, and I pray no one eventually recognizes me from the photo with Ethan. I'm in profile in the photo, but my hair is the major giveaway. People who know me could guess, but I'm so done up as Red right now that you'd really have to look past a wall of foundation, bronzer, and blush.

I wonder if Roland pays attention to celebrity gossip. My shoulders slump. It doesn't really matter. They're all about to stop seeing me as one of them. I'll be the girl working with, but most importantly, "dating" Ethan Reve. I need to enjoy this simple moment while it lasts.

I heave a sigh and rise back onto my tired feet. Our break is almost over. I turn to Carrie who rolls her neck around as if to get out a crick. To my left, Kaliope, a.k.a. Dionne, flips through a *Vanity Fair*, looking bored and as beautiful as an actual siren.

I don't need to ask about Kaliope fans. Kaliope is hands-down the biggest badass in the history of Revel princesses. Her purple hair and green eyes pop against her sorrel skin and black netting top that looks like scales and chainmail. She wears black sandals that tie up her calves with black leather. Her armor is covered in black barnacles. She is regal; she is otherworldly; she is fierce.

"What about Rose Red fans?" I ask Carrie, curious what she thinks about my character, who's not just my job, but my actual favorite Revel princess.

Carrie smiles and says, "Oh, they're the worst. They're the do-gooder, hopeless romantics. Insufferable, if you ask me."

"Hey, I resemble that remark," I joke as we head back to our places on stage.

If only she knew what this Rose Red fan was up to now. What sort of romantic agrees to a fake relationship to create a theme-park exhibit? That has to be the least romantic set-up in the entire world. Maybe I need to change my favorite to Kaliope.

Chapter Thirty

Ethan

This day will not end. The hazy sun fades through my windows before I finally pull myself together enough to check my email. I've spent the afternoon in and out of consciousness, watching talking heads yell about football on ESPN. My phone collected seven missed calls. Four from Ernie Guidry, two from Tilda post meeting, and one from my dear little sis, Elsie.

After keeping down a whole package of crackers, it's Elsie I reach out to first. She picks up after two rings.

"Hey, Bambino." I can barely hear her over the ambient background noise.

"Where are you, a rave?"

"No, I'm in a coffee shop on campus, writing a paper on stocks and bonds for my business journalism class." Elsie is getting her degree in journalism at Columbia, trying to commodify her natural nosiness. "What are YOU doing?" The knowing tone in her voice lets me know she's seen the photo.

"Avoiding the press. Watching Sportscenter. Trying to work, calling you." I hear the click-clack of typing on the other end.

She lets out a frustrated groan. "Ugh, you know what I mean. Who's the redhead from last night? I haven't seen a scandalous Ethan Reve photo in months."

Elsie, the Littlest Angel, is actually the devil.

"Not everything is what it appears to be, Elsie. You should know that by now." The typing stops.

"You okay, bro?" Her volume drops with worry.

"Yeah, just busy." I try to sound breezy and unconcerned.

"Tilda giving you hell?" Elsie's a smart kid. Well, a smart twenty-year-old. Too perceptive. It's hard to keep things from her.

"Always," I reply.

Elsie is silent for a moment. "Want to talk about it?'

"Not really." I stretch, wishing I'd texted Elsie instead of calling her. She always has a way of excavating information out of people.

"You sure?"

"Yeah, I just...I'm trying to do what Wade wanted, you know?" The ambient noise has disappeared. I can tell she's walked somewhere quieter.

I hear her yell, "Watch my things, will ya?" Then she asks, "What do you mean?" Her curiosity is piqued. I have to give her something, give her a bone to gnaw on.

"Before he died, he wanted to do an *Island of Sirens* experience."

"Really? Wow, that's awesome." She sounds genuinely enthusiastic, which is unusual. Her feelings about Revel have been lukewarm recently.

"You've seen it?" I ask. She's never been much of a Reveler, preferring movies like *All the President's Men* to *Princess and the Pea*.

"Yeah, it's the best thing we've ever done. Fuck what the ignoramus in Kentucky says about it."

She's referring to Senator Malaby. The idiot who started the boycott.

"Anyway, Wade really wanted to build this experience, but Tilda wants to launch another cruise line and buy an island."

"Sounds on-brand for her." Elsie and Tilda have never really seen eye-to-eye. In fact, Elsie downright refuses to acknowledge Tilda's presence when forced to spend time together. The icy feelings are mutual. Elsie is closer to our dad, but she doesn't talk about him with her half-brothers. She knows we have a different relationship with the man.

"I have until next quarter's board meeting to update Wade's proposal, get the financials together, and pitch it to the board."

"Whoa. That seems, well, frankly, unrealistic. Can I help?" She sounds concerned, definitely not my goal here.

"No, you need to focus on school." I get up and stretch my legs, slowly pacing my apartment.

"Seriously, Ethan. I can help. You haven't exactly been around Revel the last ten years. And your Revel knowledge is a bit..." She struggles for the right word.

"A bit nonexistent. I know," I concede. "But I got this, and I actually hired someone to help me, a graduate student from Tulane, a real Reveler."

I hear her sigh with relief. "Thank god. I'm glad you're using that big brain of yours to delegate."

"Aw, thanks, sis." I chuckle. "I think you'd actually like her, my..." Shit, I don't know what to call her. My girlfriend, my assistant, my friend? "The woman I hired. She's this walking Revel encyclopedia, without the crazy eyes."

Elsie is silent, so I fill the dead air. "She read Wade's proposal and has been fired up ever since. She's been a big help. Smart, opinionated, kinda nerdy." I smile thinking about Marin's eyes red-rimmed from crying, but also steely with the look of raw determination.

"Oh, I see." Elsie sounds smug like she does when she gets the Final Jeopardy clue and none of the contestants do.

"See what?"

"It's clear as day. This Reveler you hired is the redhead you're smooching in that photo."

Goddamn Elsie, the bloodhound. "I'm not having this conversation with you, Elsie."

"And you *liiiiike* her." She adds seventeen syllables to "like," solidifying for me that little sisters regress to ten years old when it comes to their older brothers.

"Seriously?"

"Aww, come on! Don't be mad that I figured it out. It wasn't hard. You've *never,* ever thought I'd like any of the girls you associated with before. Literally, never." She's right. Damnit, I should be more careful around Elsie. I'm hungover; my defenses are down.

She laughs, a guffaw filled with the pride of being right. "Go ahead, spill."

"Nope. No way, Els. I gave you all the dirt you're going to get."

"Fiiinnnee," she whines. A beat later she asks, "Ethan?"

"Yeah?" I need the interrogation to end. If she asks me another question about Marin, I'll have to hang up because I don't trust myself to talk about her and not give all the complicated details away.

Instead of pushing, Elsie surprises me. "I think what you're doing is great, and I one thousand percent believe you can do it."

I want to say something, but there's a lump in my throat.

"Wade would be proud," Elsie adds before hanging up.

It wasn't the pep talk I was expecting, but it was the pep talk I needed.

I open my text thread with Marin and type: *What time are you coming over tonight?*

A minute later, she returns: *I'm not. Not tonight. I have to talk to Flora, but I'm off tomorrow. I'll be there bright and early.*

I push back my twinge of disappointment before I reply: *See you tomorrow.*

And then, before I can stop myself, I add: *Girlfriend.*

Three little dots blink, then disappear, then blink again. A minute later she just sends me a meme of Rose Red looking exasperated. Apparently she's at a loss for words.

Chapter Thirty-One

Marin

It's strange, but today is the first day I feel eager to get out of my costume. I just want to be plain-old Marin Vandersee tonight. A very tired, stressed out Marin, but me nonetheless.

In the dorm, silence greets me. Normally, the couches in the dorm lobby are filled with cast members chatting, scrolling on their phones, watching the giant screen TV. Tonight, it's like a scene from a high-school movie. This is the second time in one day that I hear a figurative record scratch when I walk into the room. A couple of dancers in athletic clothes whisper as I walk past. "Oh my god, I think that's her." By the time I reach the elevators, my face is the color of a boiled lobster. They've seen the picture and know it's me, which means Flora has also seen the picture.

Crap. The anonymity of my costume beckons me once again.

In the room I share with my best friend, I am more nervous than I anticipated. I take a deep breath, watching Flora heat something in the microwave.

"Hi," I mutter.

Flora is wearing her Kiki the Croc pajamas. Her hair is in a messy bun, and her oversized glasses have replaced her contacts. She looks like the world's youngest grandmother. A stern grandmother who thinks I need a talking-to. And by golly, I probably do.

"Well, hello, Marin Anna Vandersee." Not good. She's using my full name.

"You've seen the picture." I drop my bag by the door and plop onto the stool, ready to take my lumps.

The microwave dings, and Flora grabs a large bowl. When she turns around, she's holding a vat of popcorn. She places this on the counter next to an open bottle of tequila. She pours two shots, and then hands one to me.

"I've got my tequila. I've got my popcorn. Let the hot goss commence." She shoves a few kernels into her mouth, then raises her glass in the air. As I mirror her, she yells, "Salud!", downs the tequila, and slams the shot glass back onto the counter. "Now spill."

It takes about an hour, but I tell Flora the whole story, about Ethan asking me to help him with his *Island of Sirens* project. I tell her about the deal, how if we pitch it, and it's successful, I can continue to work on the project as a full-time, salaried Revel employee. Her eyes go wide, but she doesn't say much, so I keep going.

I explain how amazing Wade's proposal is, how wonderful the exhibit will be, and how it aligns with Revel's core values. She nods a lot and absentmindedly shoves popcorn into her face.

"This all sounds great." Flora raises a perfectly arched, black eyebrow. "So, what's the problem?"

"Wade's proposal isn't the only one up for consideration." I go on, explaining how there's competition to use the capital for Tilda's island acquisition and cruise in lieu of Wade's *Sirens* experience. "But the *Island of Sirens* project is considered risky because of all that stuff with Senator Malaby."

Flora exhales, exasperated. "*Island of Sirens* isn't even that political! It's just about taking care of your home and helping others. These are actual lessons in the Bible, the book Senator Megabutt claims to have read. We are supposed to be 'good stewards' of the Earth."

"We know that, and I think the board actually knows that too, but they've been playing it safe ever since that controversy." I shove popcorn into my mouth, suddenly famished now that my nerves have settled. "It's also been hard between Wade's death and Gaspard's stroke. And I don't think anyone thought Ethan would actually show up and take his role seriously."

"And is he taking it seriously?" Flora challenges, skeptically.

"Yes, I think so. I mean, this is about more than just creating a great Revel experience and proving his business acumen. This is about his brother."

"Okay, but don't be surprised if he totally flakes. He's a rich kid who is used to getting whatever he wants, whenever he wants it, without actually working for it." She sounds flippant. Worldly-wise. And as mad as I am at Ethan, and despite the confused feelings swirling around my body, I don't think he's a flake.

I release the breath I've been holding and defend the cad Ethan Reve. "I think he's deeper than his public persona. And now he's being set up to fail."

When I explain about the deadline to revamp and update Wade's proposal to pitch to the board, Flora exclaims, "That's ludicrous!"

"I know. It's not enough time, but I think that was the point. Tilda wants Ethan to fail. She wants this project to fail so she can pursue hers."

Flora pulls her phone out of her hoodie pocket and eyes me warily before asking, "What is this all about?" On the screen, there we are again, Ethan and me, kissing in the RP Lounge.

I recognize the magenta background and the florid scrawl of the blog's masthead. This is a new *Secret Reveler* post. I knew it was only a matter of time before the definitive Reveler gossip blog would add their voice to the sea of tweets and posts.

I grab the phone and see the headline. My jaw drops. Flora snatches the phone out my hand and begins reading aloud.

"New Job, New Girl, New-and-Improved Ethan Reve?

"Well, well, well, what do we have here? After months of silence from our favorite bad-boy Reve, this picture dropped from the ether just last night. By the looks of it, Ethan Reve had an intimate "conversation" with this fiery redhead in the RP Lounge. After some serious sleuthing, I have discovered some fascinating information about the ginger canoodling with dear Ethan in the photo. The young woman in question isn't your typical Ethan Reve fare. She's no socialite, no model/influencer, no famous TV star-turned-singer (I'm looking at you, Bree Brooklyn). From my very credible sources, I have learned that the red-headed lady is a graduate student at Tulane University, and, get this, Ethan's new <u>girlfriend</u>*. Yes, ladies and gents. Ethan Reve, a notorious player, has a steady girlfriend. Apparently, they met working together on some big, secret Revel project and sparks flew. Between Ethan Reve's new job and his new girl, we can only wonder if this Revel has finally found a cause.*

"Argh." I put my face into a pillow, and then start pacing.

Flora's eyes follow me. "So...is this true? Are you two, you know, dating?"

I stop. "No," I admit. "But we're going to let everyone think we are, so you have to swear to the great gods of discretion to keep up the lie."

Flora moves the empty bowl of popcorn into the sink and sits across from me at the counter. "Why?"

Great question, I think as I struggle to articulate my stupid, silly plan. Ultimately, I tell her about the predatory girls at the RP Lounge. I tell her about Tilda and Bill's character assassination of Ethan, saying how he doesn't represent the company's values and how Tilda displayed the photo for all to see at the board meeting,

"She didn't!" Flora pours us two more shots.

"She did." We take this moment to throw back our tequila, which goes down smooth. Flora doesn't buy the cheap stuff.

"So, you told them, the board, that you were dating?" Flora's having a hard time keeping her mouth shut. It wants to stay open in permanent shock.

"Yep, and I told them our 'relationship' is proof that Ethan is a stable, committed person." The tequila warms my throat, but I still have trouble forcing the words out.

"So, just to recap..." Flora hands me a glass of water and preheats the oven. "You're working on an *Island of Sirens* project with Ethan Reve, and you have a few months to create a proposal for an entire Revel experience to pitch to the board." She pulls a frozen pizza out of the freezer. "Ethan wants to create the attraction for his brother Wade. You want to do it because it could land you your dream job, and no one at Revel headquarters wants you to do it because the project is considered too risky. And Ethan is too risky as well."

Flora slices open the shrink wrap on the cheese pizza. Then, gesturing with the scissors, she says, "And to make this venture seem less risky, you two will pretend to be a perfect, wholesome couple until you pitch the proposal."

"Yes, that's about it. Except, I think we have a few people on the board who actually care about Ethan and Revel's legacy, not just the bottom line." My stomach folds with nerves finally hearing it all out loud, and also from hunger.

"Okay, so I'm the only one who knows this isn't a real relationship." Her eyes are starry with intrigue.

"Yes, and it needs to stay that way." I purse my lips, shocked by how ridiculous my life has become in such a short span of time. I should be studying for Macroeconomics midterms, but instead I'm pretending to be someone I'm not by day and night.

Flora rolls her eyes, making it clear that I don't even need to ask her to keep mum. I should know her better than that, so I zip it and know I can trust her.

"Okay, I still need you to be Rose Red, but I'll try to limit some of your late-night shifts."

"Thank you, thank you, thank you." I grab Flora's hands and shake them up and down.

The oven timer goes off. She pops the pizza in, slamming the door closed. "One more thing," she says.

"Of course. Anything!" I rest my chin in my hands and drop my elbows on the counter. I need to sleep for a week, but the tequila is working its magic, shaving down the edges of my worries.

Flora leans forward too. Her voice is low and conspiratorial when she says, "I want in."

"What do you mean?" I stare at her.

"I've had my own drama recently. Problems moving up the corporate structure. I was going to lay it all on you this evening, but that was before you stuck your tongue down Ethan's gorgeous throat."

"I did not–"

"Sure thing, lady. But you know I'm not just a sassy best friend without her own plot line." She shakes her head and finger in the sassiest way possible.

I laugh. "Okay, go on, hero of her own life's story." I curtsy before her, and she beams at me for a moment before her smile morphs into a dramatic frown.

"I had my meeting with Marta." God, I can't believe I forgot about that. I'm about to apologize when Flora holds up her hand to stop me. "It did not go well."

"I'm so sorry, Flora. What happened?"

"She trashed my new costume designs. Said they were amateurish and "jejune." I had to look that word up, but I got the gist."

"It means boring," I offer meekly.

"Of course you know that word!" She pulls a salad mix out of the fridge along with a cucumber and carrots. She hands me a cutting board and knife. "Start chopping, nerd."

I stick my tongue out at her and slice while she continues.

"But that isn't even the worst part." Flora dumps salad into a mixing bowl. Her voice gets louder. "That woman, Marta, kept my designs, and when the VP came in for their monthly design meeting, that washed-up old hack showed him *MY* designs."

"Oh my god." I stop chopping and stare at her. "Were you in the room?"

"No, me and the VP's assistant are buddies. He told me how excited the VP was about the new designs. When I asked to see pictures, the dude showed me my drawings." Flora stops moving and bows her head for a minute, collecting herself, before saying, "I realize that anything I create here belongs to Revel, legally, and I get that, but I do not understand why I can't get any credit for the work I do."

I see red, ready to pounce on that statement-necklace-wearing harpy, Marta. "Can you complain to someone?"

"Who? To my boss? That would be Marta." She laughs cynically. I hate the sound. This is her dream, and this double-crossing witch is crushing it. This makes agreeing to her request a no-brainer.

"You want in, you're in." I push the cutting board towards her. She takes it and throws the veggies into the salad bowl.

"Are you sure?" Suddenly, she's quieter, less confident. I hate Marta for making her doubt herself and her talent.

"Absolutely. Neither Ethan nor I are designers. You would be helping us out. No Revel designers will work with us. They are too busy until...guess when?"

"After you are supposed to present to the board?"

"Bingo."

I point at her while tapping my nose with my other pointer finger. "We need you. I never thought to ask because you're already swamped and this was all supposed to be a secret, but the cat is out of the bag, and we absolutely NEED you."

And this is exactly what I'll tell Ethan when I see him tomorrow. Not only will Flora create our concept art and costumes, she'll be the lead costume designer if the project is greenlit.

Now so much is riding on this one proposal, I think, as the timer dings and Flora pulls the pizza out of the oven.

Ethan owes me. Big time. And I owe Flora. Big time. And it's true, she is really doing us the favor.

After dinner, I lie in bed trying to sleep, but I keep fixating on the fact that the whole world is watching me now, at least the whole Reveler world.

My future and my best friend's future are wrapped up in the success of this proposal. And I have to fake a relationship with someone who, let's face it, I'm attracted to, who is also a mess, and I'm not entirely sure I trust him.

If this doesn't succeed, what will happen to Ethan? To Revel? To Flora? To me?

No pressure, right? I think as I finally drift off into a fitful sleep, dreaming of the *Island of Sirens* scene when the storm washes away Nestor's island.

Chapter Thirty-Two

Ethan

It's early. Croissants, coffee, and fruit litter the kitchen counter. I am pacing, my heart rate way up. Maybe I overdid it on the coffee this morning, I think, when I hear three knocks on the door. I take a deep breath, put on my most devastating smile, and greet my new, fake girlfriend.

"Good morning, sweet baby-angel-muffin," I sing. Marin's hair is in a messy bun. She's cute in her fitted jeans and a faded Captain Nemo shirt. Vintage Revel. Bright red framed sunglasses cover her eyes. She grunts a reply.

"Uh-oh, you okay?" I ask. This is not the usually chipper Marin I'm used to, the real-life Revel princess.

"I had a date with tequila last night." She shuffles past me and groans as she throws her bag in the dining room. "We've since broken up."

"My turn to nurse you back to life, eh?"

"Ha ha." Marin lifts her sunglasses and rolls her eyes dramatically.

"Coffee?" I offer.

"Yeeeesss," she says as she flops onto a chair and puts her head on her hands.

I pour her a full to-go cup of black coffee and bring a croissant, which she turns her nose up at, so I immediately return it to the kitchen. She's cute like this, all disheveled and petulant.

She takes a few sips of coffee as I settle in across from her. She stretches and says, "Okay, let's get to work."

"I have an idea. Let's get a change of scenery."

She moans. "Noooo, moving bad."

"It's not far; you'll like it." I pick up my laptop, sling her tote over my shoulder, and grab her coffee cup, using it to lure her out the door.

In one of the turrets, there's a library and study replete with an impressive hearth, which I always thought ostentatious and useless in Louisiana. However, there's a long mahogany table that will be good for spreading out and working. Plus, there's a view of the park and river that even I can appreciate.

Marin's tired face lights up when I open the large wooden, double doors. She drops her tote and gasps.

"This is amazing," she whispers, hugging herself, walking to the long turret windows. The upper sashes are stained glass recreations of stills from movies. Fittingly, she stands at the Rose Red window. Pink, red, and purple morning light shimmers on her face, and I want to touch her. Desperately.

"It is so beautiful," she says, using her church voice.

"It is," I say softly, mesmerized by the color of her hair, the wonder in her eyes. Everything is better, newer, more beautiful to her.

She peels her eyes away from the view, and her eyes meet mine.

Before I can do something stupid, like brush my fingers across her cheek and into her hair, she clears her throat and asks, "Where are you on the financials?"

This snaps me back to reality, and the rest of the morning flies by, a whirlwind of logistics and numbers. Despite the hangover, she is sharp. She asks good questions and seems to anticipate my own. We're a good team. Around noon, I lean back in my chair, ready for a break.

Marin stretches again. Her short tee crawls up her torso, so I get a peek at her belly button. Does she wear crop tops to torture me?

"Do you think you can stomach lunch?" I ask.

She stands, her eyes following me. "Yes, honestly, I should probably eat something."

"I'll be right back."

I rush down to my apartment and throw together a tray of croissants, cheeses, olives, grapes, along with utensils and napkins. When I return, Marin's reading the proposal again, a pencil tapping, her lips pursed in concentration. I place the tray on the table in front of her.

She nabs a croissant, eyes it suspiciously, then takes a tentative bite. I find myself watching her pink lips again. When she takes another bite, she moans.

She licks a flake from the corner of her mouth. "This is the best croissant I've ever had." She takes another bite, closing her eyes in gastronomic ecstasy.

Who knew pastries could be so sexy? I shift my position, and suddenly my pants feel tight.

"So, I have an idea I want to run by you," she announces. Marin's food orgasm ends. Thank god. Her eyes level on me, clear and ocean blue today. I move away to recline in one of the two overstuffed tartan chairs in front of the fireplace, while she stands and paces.

"We need to develop some concept art," she says.

"Yeah, but do you really think we have time?" No designer will talk to us, let alone design.

"Yes. So much of Wade's vision for the attraction is based on an animated film. The aesthetics can make or break this project. We need to make them see what we see."

She's right, of course. "Do you have a designer in mind?"

"We don't have a lot of time, and I know just the person for the job. Flora."

"Your best friend," I say flatly.

"That has nothing to do with this." She grabs an apple slice. "She is talented. Scary talented. And she's like me; she knows this place in and out, and loves *Island of Sirens* too."

Marin spreads brie on an apple slice before she continues. Why is this adorable to me?

A moment later she adds, "She'll do it pro bono."

"No one does anything for free. You should know that by now." She puts the entire slice in her mouth, chewing and clearly working up the courage to lay out Flora's terms.

"She wouldn't be paid for her initial work, but if this proposal is successful, she'll be the lead designer on the experience."

"That's quite a jump from costume design assistant to lead designer." I'm just assuming this is true. I don't really know the design hierarchy. Yet.

Marin now strides like a tiny General Patton.

"I know it's a big jump, and I wouldn't even propose this if I wasn't 100 percent confident in her abilities. I've seen her work. She's transformed a black box theatre space into a magical, electric forest for *A Midsummer Night's Dream*. Flora has updated every costume for every character at this park, and some of her designs were just enthusiastically approved by the VP of Park Production and Design, so I think we're the ones getting the deal here." Marin's chin juts forward. The sass is back.

"Okay." I nod. The sun from the stained glass makes her hair glow, and I think of the first time I saw her. *Golden embers.*

"Furthermore, Flora is already a—" Marin continues her pitch, but I interrupt.

"Marin." I stand so we face one another. "I said okay."

"Oh." She pauses a moment, jumps up and down, then wraps her arms around me.

"Thankyouthankyouthankyou! You won't regret this!"

I pull my arms from her embrace, and she pulls back, as if startled to find herself hugging me. Her eyes are so big and her mouth makes a perfect 'O', and she's so fucking cute it hurts.

Before I can think too much about it, I grab her hand, pull her back to me and wrap my arms around her. Her arms remain at her side, so I pick them up and wrap them around my waist. It's like hugging a robot.

I rest my chin on the crown of her head. "We're supposed to be a couple, Marin. You need to at least appear comfortable showing the tiniest bit of affection. This is good practice."

I hear her exhale loudly, like she'd been holding her breath. Her soft body relaxes into me. Her hair smells like roses.

Of course, it does, I think. After a moment, she looks up at me, and I go absolutely still.

This seems so familiar. Perhaps my body remembers our kiss from the other night at the RP Lounge. But this is different, like a deeper memory.

She licks her lips, her eyes hooded. My mouth longs for hers. I lean down an inch and then my back pocket starts buzzing, AC/DC blaring.

"You better get that." She backs away, her voice raw. I swear inwardly.

The phone screen lights up, Ernie Guidry calling. I hit the green phone icon.

"Ernie, hello." Marin's eyes get bigger than dinner plates. I pivot towards the Rose Red window.

"Ethan, my boy. I have a request." Ernie has never once asked me for anything.

"Anything. What's up?" My voice must sound concerned because Ernie laughs.

"Relax. It's nothing bad, son. It's just my wife heard about you and the little spitfire. She wanted to see if y'all were free for dinner tonight." I haven't been to Ernie's in a long time. Last time, I was probably ten or eleven. His wife, Vangie, is a real Southern character. Wade was a frequent guest, but I have been gone so long, this feels awkward.

"I'm not sure if..."

"It'd really mean a lot to the wife, and it'd be a chance to talk and get to know Marin." Ernie's tone drops like he's speaking in code.

"She's right here, let me ask." I turn back to find Marin next to me, staring at my mouth intently. She's heard the whole conversation. "Marin?"

She nods. "Yes, I'm free."

"We're in. What time?"

Marin plays with a piece of hair nervously. Her brows knit with anxiety.

"Seven. Don't worry about bringing anything. It's casual. I hope y'all like jambalaya 'coz Vangie's making a vat of it."

"Sounds great."

"I'll have a driver come get you at the compound," Ernie says. "See y'all soon."

I pocket my phone again and find Marin perched awkwardly on the armrest of a tartan chair.

"So, we're going to Ernie's tonight," she says, biting her bottom lip.

"Yeah, unless it's a bad idea. I can call him back and tell him—"

"No, it's a good idea," she interrupts. "And it's my day off. What do you think that's really about?" She pulls a scrunchy from her wrist, puts her hair in a ponytail, and then immediately takes it down.

"I think he wants to check us out, make sure we're serious about this project." Marin is in the process of putting her hair up again, but I walk to her and grab the scrunchy out of her hand. "Make sure *we're* serious."

She won't make eye contact with me for some reason, so I lift her chin, forcing her to look at me. "Marin, no one will buy this act if you can't look at me or touch me."

"Oh, I can look at you. Obviously." Her eyes dart around my features. Awkward doesn't begin to describe how uncomfortable she seems at the moment.

"And touch me," I say. Her face turns a pretty shade of pink, and I can't stand it a second longer.

"Let me try something." I angle toward her so our foreheads are almost touching.

"Try what?" she whispers.

"This." I bend down and kiss her parted lips.

Chapter Thirty-Three

Marin

The tension of this moment overwhelms me at first, but then I can't help but be drawn in by his firm, warm lips. His gorgeous scent, like clean cedar. His stubble tickles my cheeks. His tongue finds mine and then the chaste, tentative salvo melts into a passionate kiss.

Ethan puts his hands on my lower back, and I can't help it. A moan slips out. He pulls back, so I open my eyes and stare into his. They're glittering, light blue, and smiling. He wears a devilish grin.

Okay, he's kissed me, and I've survived. I didn't burst into a million splendid suns.

Moment over, I think.

But I'm wrong. So, so wrong.

He drops his head again, kissing my neck. He's leaning me against the back of the chair, and to get a better angle, he picks me up and perches me against a deep window sill. My legs part for him as he leaves a trail of kisses from my ear to my clavicle. My hands explore his shoulders and back, muscles taut underneath his gray t-shirt.

He smells so good. Woodsy. Edible. His jet-black hair feels so thick and soft against my chin and neck.

With his hands on my low back again, he pulls me closer to the sill's edge, closer to him. I gasp as I dig my fingers into his back, yanking his tucked shirt out, wanting to touch his skin.

Pressure building, I pull him in with my legs, trapping him so he's even closer. He pulls back slightly, then against me again, harder. A tingling sensation shoots up my torso and throughout my body, and silver stars burst behind my closed eyes.

His lips find mine again, but I want more. I need more.

I moan his name, aching for him to scratch this overwhelming itch, "Ethan, please."

He stills. His lips pause on my neck. "Marin," he growls.

"Hmm-hmmm?" My eyes are still closed, but I feel him pull away.

"Look at me." His voice is low, heated. I open my eyes. The intensity in his eyes shakes me. In a gruff voice, he asks, "Do you want me to stop?"

I jerk back. Confused by why he's so far away now. But then it hits me like a cold shower. This isn't our *real* first kiss. This is practice for the cameras. This is for show.

And I, a complete fool, was just begging him to take me on this fancy windowsill. Could long lenses find us up here? Heat floods my cheeks again. He's probably so used to women throwing themselves at him, women far more experienced than me, that this is just a blip on his sexy scale.

I shift uncomfortably. Suddenly, the wood feels cold and hard under my seat.

I'm the one who admonished him about not blurring worlds. I'm the one who made a big deal about remaining professional. I'm the one who's panting like a dog in heat. I'm the freaking hypocrite.

I hop off the windowsill and create space between us. I look up at him again. His eyes search mine. I don't know what for, but I am grateful for this reprieve.

He's being a gentleman, and I need to think.

"Stop," I croak, then clear my throat. I place my hands on his chest and push him away, gently. A nervous chuckle escapes my mouth. I want to dissipate the tension. But he's just staring at me, not laughing.

"That was definitely enough practice," I blurt out, trying to be cool about my blazingly hot reaction to him. God, he must have sensed how inexperienced I am. That's why he stopped.

"See?" I pat him, *pat him like a good boy*, on his left hand. "I feel comfortable touching you, and other stuff..." I taper off, so awkward it physically hurts.

His eyes bear into mine for a second more, then he shudders slightly as he backs away. He turns around, tucks in his shirt, and takes a deep breath. I straighten myself out and try to flatten my hair.

When he turns back around, he's a different Ethan, composed again, sardonic, more like the Ethan from a week ago in my dressing room accusing me of selling pictures to the press.

We go to speak at the same time, but I insist he speaks first. I giggle again. Unable to control it. I always laugh at the worst times. I sound like an idiot, a besotted schoolgirl. Cue the self-loathing in 3...2...1.

"What I was going to say is *bravo*." He claps his hands together a few times. "You are quite the actress. I almost believed that was real." His voice is about 10 degrees colder than it was a few moments ago.

"I, uh..." I want to tell him that it was real, 100 percent absolutely authentic, so pure that I couldn't fake it, but he cuts me off.

"Very convincing." He runs his hand through his wavy, sable hair. "Everyone will buy it."

"Yes, good" is all I can get out. My mind left the building the minute his lips touched mine. I'm incoherent with lust and confusion.

How can I be such a walking, talking, heaving bosom while he's such a cool customer? Oh, right. He's Ethan freaking Reve.

"I think that's enough practice for today. I have errands to run and numbers to crunch." He walks back to the dining room table, looks down at his laptop. "Can you be back at my place by 6:25?"

"Uh, sure..." My face is heating up so much that I feel sweat bead at my temples. Can a head spontaneously combust? I grab my laptop and stuff it in my bag, zip it, and practically run for the door.

He's right behind me, but I barely get "See you later" out before I slam the door behind me.

Chapter Thirty-Four

Ethan

After Marin's abrupt exit, I count to sixty, then run to my apartment suite, tear off my clothes, and hop into a cold shower. I have been with my fair share of women, not as many as the media suggests, but a lot. Enough to know that what just happened between Marin and me was something special. I have never in my life been this aroused. Not with anyone. Including Bree. Including Bree and, occasionally, her special guest-star girlfriends. And Marin and I were just kissing.

Damn it, I felt completely out of control. I was about to take her in the turret. Tear her clothes off and lick every inch of her.

Until she said my name. Breathy and so goddamn sexy.

With her hands on me, stroking and scratching my back, pulling me in closer, I needed to make sure it was real. Not an act. When I asked if we should stop, I wanted her to ignore me, to tell me to keep going, to pull me back into her. To tell me she wanted this. Wanted me. But she didn't.

She was only kissing me to practice, to feel comfortable in our roles. Because we have a deal to make our relationship believable. Marin wants the proposal to succeed. What I've offered is her dream job, and I made myself her golden ticket.

As I step out of the shower and dry off, I glance in the mirror and see an idiot, ashamed and embarrassed by my lack of control.

Marin is a good person. She cried when she read Wade's proposal. She vociferously endorsed her friend's talent. She handled the board when I couldn't. Hell, she is the one who suggested the fake relationship to make me seem like a normal, stable guy. Of course she wanted me to stop.

I'll have to be okay with the fact that at least she seemed to enjoy kissing me, though she doesn't seem experienced. Her kiss was amazing, hot, but there's something innocent about her. No filter, no rehearsed moves.

Damn, I don't know how to deal with respectable women.

I will have to be more careful in the future, I tell myself. We'll only get close in public. No more "practicing" from here on out. She deserves more.

And as much as I wanted to hear her say, "Yes, Ethan, I want you to keep going," that has to be off limits. I clearly can't help but blur lines with her, and she deserves more than me messing with her. She deserves her prince-fucking-charming, not some lost, anxiety-ridden fuck-up playing at businessman.

The sooner we get this proposal done, the better. This is not going to be easy or simple.

I sit down at the dining room table and pull up a few spreadsheets. I make a few phone calls. Before I know it, I need to get ready for our double date at Ernie's.

When Marin returns, she's carrying her large San Fran Safari tote and holding a folder. Her red hair is mussed in beachy waves. Her porcelain skin looks soft and delectable in her mint green sundress. She smells like flowers and coconut. I want to devour her like an ice cream cone on a hot day.

Instead I say, "You're early."

She strides past me, turns on her wedge heel, and holds the folder out to me.

Curious, I grab it. "What is this?"

"I figure if we are actually 'dating,' we should know more about each other, so I compiled a list of biographical facts you should know if this—" she gestures to me and then herself— "were real."

She's a bit terse. Her arms cross; all business now, I suppose she's trying to affect a no-nonsense stance, but her crossed arms draw attention to her cleavage, which I can't help but enjoy for a moment before scanning her biographical one-pager.

Basics:

Marin Elizabeth Vandersee

Born July 13, 1991

Grew up outside Burlington, Vermont

Schooling:

University of Vermont, B.S. in Marketing

Tulane University, pursuing MBA

There's a section that has her complete family tree with professions, skills, and hobbies. I scan past this to her interests, allergies, and hobbies.

Interests:

All things Revel Pointe, running, true crime podcasts, reading (especially 19th century Brit Lit and contemporary romance), and one day owning a dog named Nemo.

Allergies:

Kiwi fruit

Favorites:

Foods: Crème brûlée, bread, and Waldorf salad

Movie: Three-way tie between *Island of Sirens*, *Rose Red*, and *The Godfather, Part II*

Color: Red, blue, green...actually, this is dumb. I like all the colors except chartreuse.

Music: I'm partial to the *Around and Far and Upside Down* and *Island of Sirens* soundtracks, as well as *Princess and the Pea*.

Non-Revel content: Neko Case, Nick Drake, and LCD Soundsystem.

I raise an eyebrow. "LCD Soundsystem and *The Godfather*?"

"I contain multitudes, Ethan." She shrugs her cute bare shoulders. "Any more questions?"

I have a million, but I start with, "So your entire family are scientists and/or doctors?"

"Yes." Her voice is brittle. She starts to sway a bit, her hands shoved into her pockets.

"And they all went to Yale and Harvard?"

"Yes." She looks anywhere but me.

"Impressive." Reading between the lines, I can sense that Marin isn't close to her family. That her resume isn't quite up to the family's snuff. I can't imagine they also have time to watch Revel movies with her. They're too busy being excellent. Maybe we're more alike than I imagined. But I don't press the subject.

"Why have you never owned a dog?" It seems like the most innocuous question.

"My mom doesn't like the shedding." She shrugs again, like it doesn't really matter to her that much.

"There are non-shedding dogs." I toss the folder on the counter and roll up the cuffs of my linen shirt.

"I know," she retorts. Then her posture changes, stiffens. And in a crisp transatlantic accent, she says, "Small dogs yip. Large dogs drool. All dogs require attention, so no dogs."

I laugh. "Is your mother Katherine Hepburn?"

"Basically." She's silent for a moment. It's awkward between us.

"About earlier..." I start to apologize, and she holds up her hand.

"No, don't. We just got a bit..." She searches for her words. "Carried away."

"Either way, I'm sorry I was abrupt. I won't do that again."

She steps closer to me. "Do *what* exactly?"

It takes everything in me not to bridge the gap between us. "Blur boundaries."

She is silent for a moment. Her head drops a bit, and she grumbles, "Thanks."

I stand there, trying to think of something to smooth this over. Thankfully, the heaviness in the room is interrupted by my phone. I pick it up on the second ring.

"Our driver is here."

"Great." Marin breathes deeply, as if putting on her game face.

Downstairs, a black town car awaits us. The driver opens the door. It's too intimate, too cozy in the backseat. Not what we need right now. We need a stretch limousine. I scooch as close to the other side without appearing as if I'm terrified of her.

She does the same, like if our knees touch, a rift in space-time will open, and she'll fall into an abyss.

"So, Ernie Guidry seems nice. What should I know about him?" She tucks an errant lock of hair behind her ears. I notice she's painted her nails a rosy pink.

"He's been at Revel for ages. PawPaw liked to help out fellow vets. PawPaw and Ernie would take me and Wade fishing sometimes. Then his wife, Vangie, would feed us and pinch our cheeks."

"He is Cajun?" She is hesitant, maybe afraid to get the terminology wrong.

"Yeah, how'd you guess?" I snicker. "He is the most Cajun man I've ever met. He grew up in the swamps, fishing on a pirogue. He bleeds LSU football and makes a great roux."

"A roux?"

I turn towards her, my face in mock shock. "You've been living in Louisiana for how long now, and no one's taught you how to make a roux?"

She smiles. Interest lights up her face. "Cajun men cook?"

"Yep. And hunt and fish and tell 'Boudreaux and Thibodeaux' jokes." I relax as the electricity between us is unplugged with easy small talk. "You've been warned."

Her head cocks to the side. I love that tic of hers, her inquisitive head tilt. "Boudreaux and what?"

"You'll see." I smile as we drive out of the curated beauty of the park into the back roads of the Parish, lined with sugarcane fields and thick, green cypress forest, deeper and deeper into the wilder, wetter sticks.

Chapter Thirty-Five

Marin

After an awkward half hour of talking around our sexy tryst in the turret, trading likes and dislikes—Ethan prefers mountains to beaches while I'm the opposite; we both prefer coffee over tea; we both love to ski; but I'm pro-karaoke while he's very anti-singing in public—we arrive at Ernie Guidry's.

I'm shocked by the rustic nature of Guidrys' place. I was expecting a mansion. Ethan called it a "camp," saying they've always preferred a modest life close to the water. The dark, rust-colored home sits on a bayou, elevated on huge stilts about eight feet above ground. Crickets chirp and wind chimes tinkle as we walk up a flight of stairs to the front door. A doormat reads "Bienvenue!" and there's a stone frog statue wearing an LSU Tigers jersey.

Ernie opens the door, a dish towel thrown over his shoulder. The inside smells like a mix of those flowery but fruity potpourri sachets my grandmother had in her drawers and a delicious, savory stew wafting from the kitchen. "They're here, Vangie!" Ernie calls out.

"Okay, just a minute!" a warm, feminine voice hollers back.

"Come in, come in." Ernie walks us to a very large sectional couch. "Have a seat. Make yourselves comfortable. You want a beer? Some wine?"

"Beer, and the lady will have..." Ethan looks at me. He doesn't know what I drink. Crap.

"White wine. Any kind. Thank you."

Ernie leaves, and it gives me time to notice the eclectic décor—a mash-up of high-end, mid-century modern and rustic, log cabin. Eames chairs paired with La-Z-Boys. A minimalist oval table next to a basket filled with crochet work. It doesn't make sense, but it's also perfect.

Ernie returns with an enormous glass of wine and an Abita Amber. He perches on the edge of a gray-blue recliner across from us. "Vangie'll join us in a minute. The food is almost ready. I hope you two are hungry."

We both nod enthusiastically. I haven't had anything since the croissant and apple around noon. I couldn't put anything in my belly after it was essentially occupied by a ball of nerves since whatever happened in the turret happened.

Ethan grabs my hand, and I try not to start, but I'm pretty sure I look jumpy. Damn. I am not doing a good job of selling this whole relationship thing.

"So, Marin. Tell me about yourself." Ernie smiles warmly. I give him the usual spiel—school, Vermont, yadda, yadda, yadda, but he interrupts me with a chuckle.

"I didn't ask for your credentials, chére. Those never tell us much about what kind of person you are."

I smile. My parents would disagree, and I say so. Ernie looks at me expectantly, so I continue down a different track. "Okay, then. Well, I'm an enormous dork and have been obsessed with all things Revel Pointe since I can remember."

Ernie leans forward, his eyes mischievous. "Is that so?" He pauses for a beat, then asks, "What's the name of Thumbelina's pet hedgehog?"

"Petal," I reply, lightning quick.

"The name of the magical broomstick Miss Prudent Pleasant rides?"

"Haberdasher."

"What is the name of Miss Maisy's lily pad palace?"

"Croakingham Palace," I answer confidently, then smiling smugly, I ask, "Is that all you got?"

Ernie puts on a mask of solemnity. "All right," he says, cracking his knuckles. "Now for some difficult questions."

Ethan shakes his head, smirking at me. "Those were the easy questions? I only knew one answer," he says.

I nod, eager now, having a blast. Ernie continues his quiz, blasting me with more obscure trivia. Of course, I get them all right.

Then he drops, "In one sentence, what's the main takeaway of *Island of Sirens*?"

Oh. This isn't all just fun and games. This is a test. I think for a minute. I can feel Ethan's eyes on me. Ernie's chocolate brown eyes bore into my own.

"The main message of *Island of Sirens* is that home is worth fighting for." Ernie doesn't say anything for what feels like an hour, but is probably just a few seconds.

He nods his head and says, "M'yeah. You got it."

"Dinner's served!" Vangie yells, and we leave the living room and enter a vintage eat-in kitchen. Lime green appliances and butter-yellow linoleum are a shock to the system, but not as much as the woman ladling jambalaya into bowls. She's a bigger lady, broad in a bright pink caftan with giant magnolia blossoms all over it. Her hair is a voluminous platinum blonde, and she's wearing purple cat-eye glasses accentuated by her black cat-eye makeup. Her lips are also pink, and there isn't a wrinkle on her, even though she's definitely in her 60s.

"Ethan, honey, grab that French bread and butter and bring it to the table," Vangie orders. Ernie grabs two bowls and brings them to the table, and I follow suit while Vangie takes off her caftan to reveal a pink sheath dress with rosette piping around the waist. She looks like she's been preserved in Tupperware for the last 50 years. I am instantly in love with her.

"All right, gang. I got my dinner dress on, I got my hubby and my guests. Thank the lord, now bon appetit!" We all sit in mid-century tulip chairs. If homey space-age were an aesthetic, Vangie's nailed it.

"Sooo. Lovebirds?" Vangie twangs after pulling off a piece of French bread and spreading a healthy pat of butter on it. "Ernie here told me all about how you two are working together on Wade's project—God bless his sweet soul—and how you started dating and dropped that bomb at Miss Tilda's little coup. I looked y'all up on the internet, I saw that picture, and y'all looked SO sweet, I told Ernie to invite you two over so we can get to know you better. I haven't seen Ethan here in ages and ages. Plus, I love a good love story."

There isn't a single question in her monologue. Ethan and I check in with one another. His eyebrows raise, as if to suggest I should be the one to reply.

"Well, thank you so much. This is delicious." I grin at her, and the compliment is genuine. This jambalaya is out of this world. The chicken is succulent, the sausage is spicy, and the rice is perfectly cooked.

"It's good, isn't it?" She returns my smile. "Well, it should be. I've been working on the recipe for decades. It was Ernie's mother's recipe, and her jambalaya was considered the best in Louisiana, which means best in the world. The mean old coot wouldn't share it with anyone, but I've been piecing it together ever since."

"Yeah, Mama didn't like to share," Ernie agrees and takes a pull of his beer. "A real madame têtue."

"Now, Ethan. Why haven't we seen you around? Wade used to come to dinner—God bless his sweet soul—but you haven't been around in ages. Where you been?"

Ethan looks uncomfortable. "I, well, I went away to school, then was in New York..." he stammers.

"That's no excuse. You're rich, and that's saying something because Ernie and me are richer than the Pharisees. You could fly one of those Revel jets down. I know your PawPaw misses you."

"I came when I was needed. After Wade..." Ethan breaks off. I rest my hand on his and take over.

"We're thrilled to be here now," I reply for the two of us and squeeze Ethan's hand. "Now I heard that Ernie tells 'Boudreaux and Thibodeaux' jokes. Am I saying that right?"

Ethan nods, a grin creeping on his face.

"I've never heard one before."

Vangie lets out a shocked "Oh! Well, you're in for a treat, Missy."

And Ernie doesn't miss a beat. In an even thicker Cajun accent, he begins, "Boudreaux and Thibodeaux were walkin' tru the woods de other day, when a flyin' saucer landed near dem. A door opened, and two little green aliens climbed out of the spacecraft..."

Ethan squeezes my hand back. I glance at him briefly, and he mouths "thank you." I feel my face go warm. When I look up, Vangie's considering us with a knowing smirk on her face and a gleam in her eyes.

"Thibodeaux turned to Boudreaux, 'Mais, look at dat. What you tink dat is?'" Ernie continues. "Boudreaux, aiming his shotgun at the little space critters, replied, "'Thibodeaux, I don' know, but you hurry back to de camp, put on de rice pot, and start makin' a roux!'"

"Shoot, that's terrible!" Vangie says, but she's laughing.

Her laugh is infectious. Ethan and I both giggle, but it makes me wonder what kind of meat is in the jambalaya.

"Ethan scolded me in the car for not knowing what a roux is," I say. "What is it exactly?"

Both Vangie and Ernie look at me, mouths agape. "Chére, you gotta lot to learn."

Chapter Thirty-Six

Ethan

Vangie and Ernie tell stories throughout the meal. It's good to have an evening to relax and laugh. Marin charms the hell out of the couple, and by the end of the meal, Vangie asks Marin to come over and she'll teach her to make étouffée, and Ernie tells me Marin must come on the boat with them.

Marin blossoms under their attention and care. After reading her fact sheet, I gather that warmth isn't a priority in her family. She doesn't wear her hurt though. She engages with the world, asks questions. Ernie and Vangie tell Marin about their three sons, their five grandchildren, their love of travel. "If there's a tiki bar and drinks with those little umbrellas, I'm there," Vangie says.

Vangie tells us to check out the new deck while she freshens up. On the deck, party lights glimmer, setting an inviting mood. The water is glassy and placid, and the furniture, large and comfy, waits around a firepit.

Ernie throws a blanket at me and tells us to get close to keep warm. Marin eyes me warily at first, but dons a fake smile and says, "How cozy!"

I wrap the throw around us, and we snuggle in tight. It's awkward at first because we don't know where to put our hands. I want to kiss her, to put my hands in her hair, to feel her hands on me.

"Just put your arm behind me," Marin says under her breath.

We both lean back at the same time and sigh loudly, which makes us laugh.

Vangie walks out carrying a cocktail.

"What's that?" Marin asks.

"This is a Cajun highball." Vangie can tell Marin needs more context, so she continues. "A highball is what my mamou used to call her nighttime drink. Basically, highball is a fancy way of saying Southern Comfort and Diet 7-up."

Ernie follows Vangie, and finally we're all seated snug around the fire.

"You know, my mamou was gifted with the sight." Vangie tips her glass back and drinks daintily. I wonder how much she's had to drink. "Tell 'em, Ernie. She met you and told you your whole life."

Ernie smiles. "Yeah, she sure did. I think she was just good at reading people."

"She saw everything," Vangie says. "She saw you were it for me. You were going to make lots of money, give me babies, and get shot in the ass."

"You got shot in Vietnam?" Marin asks, her eyes like saucers. Ernie had mentioned the service earlier in the evening. Made some joke about Vangie's red beans being hotter than Saigon.

"Yep, but it turned out to be a blessing because I got to come back to Vangie, who was being courted by another man, taking advantage of my absence," Ernie harrumphs.

"I hadn't heard from you in months, Ernie!" Vangie declares. "And I was young and beautiful. You can't leave a beautiful lady all alone for months on end." She leans over and smacks my knee. "You hear me, boy?"

"So, you get shot in the ass, then what?" I'm suddenly dying to hear this whole story.

"Well, Vangie was right. I stopped writing her. It got too hard. All my letters were awful, filled with sadness and violence. It hurt to write them. But it hurt to write the happy ones too because those were lies. So, I just stopped writing altogether."

"But you came home and found her?" Marin places her elbows on her knees, engrossed. I rub circles slowly into her back, and it feels good, natural. She doesn't flinch beneath my touch, so I continue.

"I did," Ernie confirms and glares at me, saying, "Turns out you can't keep quiet and keep your lady." Then he continues. "And wouldn't you know it, when I came back, the woman was engaged to Polycarp Benizet." Ernie's mouth puckers like he's eaten a worm.

"That is NOT his name!" Marin laughs. "This can't be real!" Her eyes twinkle at me, looking for confirmation. I just smile and nod.

"The man was definitely real. And in real trouble. Because I decided to take my Vangie back," Ernie boasts.

"Such a man, isn't he?" Vangie shakes her head, a sly smile on her lined pink lips.

"The problem was I had no job and no prospects. I didn't go into fishing like my brothers. I went to LSU for a business degree, but then I joined the Marine Corps, went to OCS, then headed to Vietnam in 1966. But old Polycarp Benizet... That man owned a slew of car dealerships in this neck of the woods. And all I owned was a stinking medal, and that couldn't buy me much."

"How'd you two meet?" I ask, also engrossed.

Vangie chimes in. "We met at LSU. On a double date, except we liked each other better than our actual dates."

Ernie picks up the narrative. "So, we ditched them and went and necked in my rusty old Chevy Impala."

Vangie's eyes twinkle. "I decided this one's it and took him to meet my entire family the next week. My mamou read him and told him his life. And everything she said came to pass."

Ernie grins. "It sure did, and that's what gave me the confidence to approach you even though you were engaged."

"You sure did use the whole 'mamou foretold our union" angle,'" Vangie laughs and takes another swig of her highball.

"I did use it, and the fact that Mick Reve gave me a job and an advance so I could show up at your mama's house in a new stylish coupe and a new Brooks Brothers suit to woo my sweet Evangeline didn't hurt neither."

Ernie and Vangie hold each other's gaze for a moment. Marin sniffles.

"Are you crying?" I look at Marin, incredulous.

"No!" She denies it, but her eyes are watery.

"You are! You are crying."

Marin's face is red. "It's just a beautiful love story. I always cry when I'm moved."

"Like with Wade's proposal," I add gently.

She nods. Our eyes lock for a moment. When we look away, I notice Vangie and Ernie both grinning at us.

"Well, I get it, honey. It *is* a beautiful story, if I don't say so myself," Vangie says, laughing at herself. "But the story was also a ginormous tangent because what I had meant to tell you was that I have the sight too, just like my mamou, and I wanted to do your readings tonight."

For some reason, I want to stand and run back home. Just leave all of them there and tear through the swamps, mosquitos and gators and all. I don't want anyone "reading my life."

I'm about to decline when Marin perks up, claps her hands, and says, "Me first! Me first!"

Chapter Thirty-Seven

Marin

Vangie pats the empty seat next to her on a wicker loveseat, and I leave Ethan's warm side to rush over to her. Pretty string lights glimmer above us, and Vangie lights three large citronella candles. "The boys can talk while we get down to business," she tells me in a low tone.

I nod and think about the pack of tarot cards Flora bought in college. We'd play around with them sometimes after a few Moscow Mules. I got a particular thrill out of it because my entire family would roll their collective eyes so hard when I'd tell them about a reading.

"It isn't based in empirical fact," they'd say. *"It's just mumbo-jumbo for weak-minded mid-wits."* Just because something hasn't been peer-reviewed and/or replicated and validated by multiple, disinterested parties doesn't mean it isn't fun and insightful.

Vangie pulls a black velvet bag from a lacquered box on the end table. Her deck of cards has delicate designs of stars on the backs. She hands them to me, with a direct order: "Shuffle till you're done."

I shuffle the cards, admiring the way silver flecks of stars enhance the constellation illustrations, and I feel particularly mystical out under the vast, dark night sky.

Vangie says, "My mamou didn't need cards to read people, but I find them helpful. Gives me something to bounce off, you know?"

Before I tune them out completely, I hear Ethan and Ernie talk about fishing for tuna in the Gulf.

He's in good hands, I think. Ethan tried to bring up the proposal earlier in the evening, but Ernie shut it down, saying, "This is a social visit, Ethan. No business." Ethan seemed more relaxed afterwards.

Secretly, I kind of don't want him to hear my reading. If the cards are true and Vangie is any good, he may play a prominent role. Suddenly I'm nervous. We're lying! And she's about to read me. *What did I agree to?*

It's too late, I guess. I stop shuffling, and Vangie tells me to cut the cards three times. I put them into three neat piles on the glass top bamboo table.

Vangie puts one pile on top of the other, takes a deep breath, and starts flipping cards into a pattern. The cards are beautiful, colorful and playful without being childish. They look like they're painted by a local folk artist. As she lays out twelve cards, Vangie squints, pondering what she sees and then begins interpreting.

"All right, this is interesting to say the least. This first card sort of sums up the heart of the matter right now. Who you are. And boom, look at that, the Queen of Cups."

The Queen of Cups is a mermaid with long turquoise hair and tail. She carries a giant golden cup in both hands.

"The Queen of Cups is a highly passionate woman. She is vulnerable, caring, often the emotional rock of the family. Some people see this as a weakness, but it is absolutely her strength."

I nod, and Vangie continues. "She has so much to offer, creative and hardworking, and see how generous she is, letting us drink from her cup, but she has to be careful. This particular queen can be too giving; she can give her cup to the wrong person. "

Vangie's amber brown eyes lock with mine. "The Queen of Cups loves people with her whole heart, but she must learn that some people can't reciprocate. They're limited and not worth her time."

Vangie points to the next card, which overlaps the Queen of Cups. "This is the Moon card. A very powerful card. This position is what is challenging you right now. The Moon represents only having partial knowledge and the fear and uncertainty that come along with being in the dark. You struggle with self-doubt."

Vangie taps my hands, which are clutching my knees. "Don't let self-doubt eat at you, precious."

Vangie places a manicured finger on the Tower card.

I gulp. "That is a scary-looking card."

"Yeah, it's not good, but it's in the past. What I'm sensing is a home built on faulty ground. A home that doesn't feel like a home. Sound right?"

My eyes well up, I can't speak, so I just reply with, "Mmm-hmm."

"Well, sweet thang, you have left that behind, but it follows you. Maybe that's where a lot of the self-doubt comes from. Let's look at your hopes and goals."

She picks up the card above the Queen of Cups. "Oooh, this is a magical card." On it, two disembodied hands look like they are about to clink golden cups together. The Two of Cups.

"You hope for a partnership built on a union of trust and respect. Don't we all?" She smiles. "This can be a romantic union as well as any other kind of partnership. Either way, this kind of partnership, it's a biggie, having a profound effect on both partners."

Ernie laughs, breaking Vangie's attention for a moment. Her eyes linger on him, her gaze soft and warm.

She looks back at the cards. "Anywho..." Below the center card is the Ten of Pentacles. "This card is in the unknown influences position. Essentially, these are forces affecting your fate. Completely out of your control." Vangie bites her lip. "Hmm."

"What?" I ask.

"Well, I'm not seeing this as clearly, but this card is about family legacy and societal pressure. It's not one force, but many. It's hard for me to get a clear read on it." Her brow furrows.

"What's this one mean?" I point to the card to the right of the Queen of Cups. I don't like the look of it. It's a giant red heart and three swords skewer it like chicken satay.

"Ah, this is the future." Her brow creases even deeper. "So, listen. I know it looks bad, but it's about learning more than anything."

I lift my eyebrow skeptically. Vangie sees it. "I know that sounds like some Pollyanna flimflam, but hear me out." She scoots forward on her seat. "Heartbreak is in your future. I'm not going to pull any punches with you."

I nod, wishing she would pull them just a little.

She continues, "But this heartbreak isn't what this card is about. Do you see the rainbow emanating from the heart?"

"Yes," I whisper.

"That rainbow is important. Your heart will bleed, but what determines your fate is what you do when you're knocked down. It's how you respond to the punches. That rainbow is what you learn about yourself, about your resilience. Your future shows some challenges, but the next card lets me know you are up for it." She beams at me as she picks up the Ace of Pentacles.

"This, Marin, is in the position of your overall outcome."

In it, a giant hand offers a large silver pentacle. "This is a good card, precious, a card of new beginnings, an abundance of wealth and love and adventure. See the angels in the corner, blowing their horns? These little cutie pies are celebrating your spiritual homecoming. You, baby girl, are going to find that home you've been missing."

I can't tear my eyes away from the card. Almost like if I can keep eyes on it, the future it offers will materialize before me.

"Now, some guidance and a warning." Vangie waits until I look at her before she continues. "I want you to pay attention now." She picks up the Seven of Swords. A man is on his stomach and seven swords are shoved into his back. "You'd have to be a complete dunce to not figure out what this means."

"Betrayal," I whisper.

"Yes, ma'am. Someone with a secret agenda will hurt you if you aren't careful about who you put your faith in. You'll get unwanted attention."

"What does that mean, exactly?"

"I'm not quite sure; it's just that it's a consequence of the betrayal."

"Who is that?" I ask, indicating the Knight of Swords, wanting to change the subject.

"He's handsome, a man of action, see how he charges into battle, sword drawn. He is ambitious, intelligent, and creative. He can be erratic, but he's a knight so he knows how to lay the charm on thick. Because he is in the warning position, I would be wary of this fella."

I'm quiet for a moment, and then I place my hand on the last card, the Knight of Cups.

Vangie squeals a bit. "This is another man in your life. I call him my sweeper-off-yer-feeter. Romantic, chivalrous, and loyal. He's the mate to the Queen of Cups. He's a real Prince Charming. Surely, you've got yourself a prince in your life." She wiggles her eyebrows at me, and I giggle.

It is then that I notice Ethan and Ernie have moved. They're down at the edge of the dock, looking out over the water and at Ernie's boat. Ernie must've said something funny because I see Ethan's face light up, and he throws his head back for the full-body laugh that does something gooey to my insides. When I turn back to Vangie, she's smiling at me.

"Last thing before we rejoin the boys.... The hardship coming at you, there's no escaping it. That's life, right? It's like those Buddhists say, life is pain. The only way is through, not around, over, or under it, it's *through*. You gotta walk *through* it to get your piece of the happiness pie."

Her eyes crinkle as she smiles at me. She grabs my hands, gives them a squeeze and says, "Let's go see what those boys are doing."

Chapter Thirty-Eight

Ethan

On the ride home, Marin is quiet, so I give her space and gaze out the window, remembering PawPaw telling us about the time he saw a feufollet, a lightning ball, in the swamps. He pointed out the cypress knees, poking up like gnome dwellings from the water, and made up elaborate stories about why trees grow knees. I smile, watching the half-moon silhouette the landscape. I forgot how much I liked Ernie and Vangie and their house on the bayou, their warmth and humor.

Eventually, I break the silence and ask Marin about the tarot reading. She gives a noncommittal answer, claiming it was "very interesting."

"Do you really believe that stuff?" I ask.

"I don't rule it out immediately," she snaps.

"Hey, no judgment!" I hold my hands up as if to protect myself from her.

"Sorry, it's just that my family thinks all of that stuff is hogwash." She shrugs, her defenses lowering.

"Hogwash? You've been talking to Ernie and Vangie too much." I smile at her. She reciprocates.

"Didn't you want a reading?" She crosses a leg over a knee, turning toward me. I try not to gaze at the few inches of thigh visible beneath her hem.

"Nah. Vangie seemed pretty wiped after yours. Maybe next time." But I honestly wasn't sure I wanted the Cajun seer looking into my inner workings and future. I've had enough people speculating about me and my life for my taste.

We spend the rest of the ride talking about how great Ernie and Vangie are. She asks when we could see them again, like we are a real couple. Like this wasn't just a façade to make me seem less morally dubious to the board and investors.

I need to burst this bubble for myself, for her, for Wade's project, so I douse the good feelings with business talk. "Listen, if we're going to have Flora do concept art, she needs to be at our next meeting. What's your day like tomorrow?"

Marin stares at me for a moment, recalibrating to the topic change, then says, "Busy. I'm Rose Red. Roland and I are doing meet-and-greets all day."

I inadvertently scoff.

"What's your problem with Roland?" she asks, her pretty pink lips hinting at a smirk. It makes me want to "practice kiss" her again, so intensely that she could only view Prince Dink as a dopey little brother.

"Nothing. Also, Roland? Doesn't he have a real name?"

"Of course, he does, but we only see each other at work," she replies.

Good, I think. The guy is a royal asshat. "He takes his role very seriously, don't you think? I mean, it's not like this is actual theatre. You aren't Marlon Brando, dude."

"I like that he's professional. In fact, we should make sure everyone has that same dedication to the craft that Roland does when we hire for *Island of Sirens*." She crosses her arms, and sticks her chin forward, which, I've recently discovered, is sexual catnip for me.

I scooch closer to her and say, "I just think he's a bit of a creep, okay."

She stares at me for a beat. "That's your prerogative, I suppose."

"Thank you for being so magnanimous." I smile, enjoying riling her up.

"He's been lovely to me." She huffs. "But we'll just have to agree to disagree on Prince Roland."

"Agreed," I say. "So, what time can you and Flora meet at my place?"

"After my shift, around seven."

"Good," I reply.

"Great," she retorts.

"Looking forward to it," I counter.

"Likewise," she snaps.

"Good," I volley.

"You said that already." She's grinning like a goofball.

"Oh, shut up" are the last words I say before she hops out of the car and says, "See you tomorrow at seven."

~

It's almost midnight, and Flora, Marin, and I have destroyed my dining room. The table is covered in Chinese take-out cartons, sketches, laptops, colored pencils, beer cans, and a bottle of Sauvignon Blanc. I try not to stare at Marin, at her kissable lips, but I fail over and over.

Flora clears her throat and stands abruptly.

"Where's the loo, Reve?" She smirks at me while twisting her torso side to side. The multi-colored bangles on her arms create a tinkling tintinnabulation when she moves, like an old-timey gypsy woman.

"Down the hall on the right," I yell, but she's halfway there already.

Nothing stands in my way now of admiring Marin's copious red hair atop her head in a messy bun, her pale skin bedecked by freckles, her brow slightly furrowed in concentration, and her rosy lips puckered slightly as she examines Flora's drawings. I almost wish I had never kissed her, never felt her warmth, never gotten close enough to inhale her sweet scent, never tasted her lips, her neck. Knowing exactly how her body feels in my arms makes this so much harder. Makes me harder.

I decide that I need another beer and dash into the kitchen to grab another local lager. I jump when I discover Flora behind me.

She nods at my beer selection. "Good taste, Reve. I hate IPAs."

I throw her one. I like Flora. She's a gifted artist and the ultimate hipster Reveler.

But I also like how much she cares for Marin. There's a protectiveness there, between the two, a fierceness that reads more like family than friends. It reminds me of Wade. I pull a swig of beer and set it down abruptly, startling Marin at the dining room table.

"You okay?" she asks.

I nod. "Sorry."

"It's late; we should probably go. We have work in the morning." Marin closes her laptop and finishes off the last sip of wine in her glass.

"Aww, I was just getting warmed up." Flora does a little dance, vaguely reminiscent of the running man.

Marin snorts. "Well, I'm turning into a pumpkin."

"Fiiiine," Flora whines. "Reve here looks like he's revving to go?" She nudges me slightly in the side.

"I'd like to apologize on behalf of my friend Flora here." Marin slings her bag over her shoulder. "You feed her beer, and the dad jokes appear."

"Whatever, poet. Stop trying to hide my light under a bushel." Flora stuffs her material in an oversized duffel, made from quilted Revel sheets from the '80s and '90s. She grabs her purse and another tote as she says, "We'll see you tomorrow evening, Reve."

When they are gone, my suite feels emptier than usual. I am struck by how quiet the place seems without them.

Without her.

Chapter Thirty-Nine

Marin

Today is another perfectly warm and sunny day in Louisiana, a meet-and-greet day in the French village. I always feel more like myself when the sky is a bright, clear blue to match my default positive disposition. The crowds are, well, crowded today. Spring has sprung and the Revelers are here in droves. Roland and I have hit our stride, entertaining scads of oohing and ahhing kids, charming the adults, and bantering in character. I was initially worried about working with Roland since the news broke about my "relationship" with Ethan Reve, but I shouldn't have been. Roland is as professional and kind as ever. In fact, he seems more attentive than before. And he never asks me about Ethan or the photo.

After our shift ends, Roland walks with me through the cast member tunnels to our HQ. Usually, he lets go of my arm when we enter the tunnel. Today he does not. I look up at him, and he winks. It's charming, and I can't help but giggle. Fangirling about my co-worker, who I don't even really know outside of our characters, feels oddly comforting, like wearing broken-in shoes after a long day of heels. Flora was right to warn me about keeping the fantasy world and reality separate. In fact, this seems to be the theme of my life lately.

When we get to our dressing rooms, Roland hesitates at my door.

"What's up?" I ask. He's never lingered before.

"Would you like to walk back to the dorms together?" His shirt is open at the collar, and he lifts one arm up above his head to lean on the door jamb, a sexy Revel prince calendar come-to-life.

"Um...sure. It takes me a minute to, you know...Flora is usually here..." I gesture down at my complicated costume.

"Of course. Do you need some help with the back thingy?" He moves his hands to mimic tying a bow. Such a dude.

"Actually, that would make this go faster." I turn around, and he finds the tightly tied laces beneath a large red bow.

"Here?" he asks and reins me in a bit.

I nod. He pulls the laces, loosening them, and I sigh in relief. "Jeez, the princesses really do have it rough," he says, then taps my shoulder to let me know he's done. I turn around, and he's right there, my face nearly touching his chest. I look up instinctively. His face is so close.

But before I can react, I hear Flora. "Excuse me, big guy."

He flinches, then takes a big step out of the room to make way for our fearless costume leader.

"I can take it from here." She gives him a narrowed look. He recovers so quickly I think I may have imagined any awkwardness.

"Then I guess I'll walk you home another night, Red." He gives me a devastating smile.

"Bye, Roland." I wave lamely and feel Flora staring at me. "What?" I ask as I pull my layers off.

"Why is he suddenly wanting to walk you home?" Flora asks, rearranging her makeup caddy on the vanity.

"I don't know. Just being nice, I guess." I don't know, honestly. "We have been talking more on our breaks, and you know, we spend a lot of work time together."

"It wouldn't have anything to do with the fact that everyone knows you and Ethan Reve are a thing?" Flora looks at me then, her black eyebrow raised again in her patented skeptical expression.

"Wouldn't that have the opposite effect? Like, if I'm off the market, he's barking up the wrong tree, right?"

"To some guys, yeah. To others, that might tap into some caveman, competitive shit." She shrugs her shoulders. "All I know is that if you're with Ethan..." She gives me an exaggerated wink. "Then you might want to avoid long sunset walks with Prince Charming."

"Number one: He just offered to walk me back to the dorm." I use my fingers to enumerate. "Two: He hasn't even mentioned Ethan over the last two days, so who knows what he knows? And three: Ethan has made it very clear that this 'relationship' will end in a few weeks. While I'm not going to do anything to jeopardize this project, I am also not going to shun a co-worker and possible friend."

"Who happens to be your cartoon dream man?" Flora smirks so hard I think her cheek muscles might harden in place. I say nothing as I pull on my jeans and throw on a vintage *Secret Questbook* tank top.

"Sometimes, Mare, I worry about you."

"Why?"

"You don't see yourself clearly. You..." She grabs me and squares my shoulders, forcing me to look in the mirror. "Look at you. What do you see?" Her voice is stern. This seems important to her, so I follow along.

"Um, I see me." I shrug, tired and anxious to get to Ethan's. Flora rolls her eyes, and says, "Seriously! Look."

"I don't get what we're doing." I fidget, not wanting to dilly-dally, not wanting to reflect on my reflection.

She shakes her head. "Your family....Sometimes I wish I could slap them all the way to Timbuktu for the number they did on you." She takes a deep breath and continues. "Look again, my clueless friend. You are a knockout. Like, a bonafide, real-life Revel Pointe princess, who is also hella smart and super kind and generous and fun and so much more."

Our eyes meet in the mirror. Heat rises on my cheeks. I hate this so much. I hear my sister Arista telling me that I must be adopted. I see my mother's judgmental eyes, disappointed in my B in Calculus. I hear Alana discouraging me from talking about the latest Revel movie because I sound childish.

"I know this makes you uncomfortable." Flora reads my mind. "But you need to hear this. You're a catch, and you need to see yourself as one because you are freaking blind to how people, men especially, react to you."

"Okay, okay." I turn around to look at her. "I'll admit that I'm pretty clueless about guys. And thank you for thinking I'm a catch."

Flora's liquid brown eyes emanate concern. "You still don't see it, do you?" she whispers.

"What?"

"How *he* looks at you." Flora crosses her arms.

"I don't know what you're talking about." I mirror her posture.

"Okay, I'll back off. I just care about you. I don't want you to get hurt." She pulls me in for a bear hug.

"Got it, mooooom," I reply sarcastically.

"Now, do your chores or no TV for a month!" she admonishes in a 1950s Donna Reed voice.

On our way back to the dorm, we get banana smoothies from the San Fran Safari Hut and sing along to "Monkeying Around" for the millionth time as a cool front sweeps down the foot paths. Tourists in shorts and tank tops scurry into souvenir shops to purchase overpriced sweatshirts. After inhaling our smoothies, we drop our gear at our place and head to Ethan's, talking about the *Island of Sirens* designs the entire way.

I'm getting used to the Reve compound and Ethan's chic apartment, but this makes sense with the sheer amount of time I've been spending here. We all get to work immediately, eating the Pad Thai and spring rolls while talking shop. I don't know when Flora had the time, but she's produced more costume and ride designs to review. They are so imaginative, whimsical, and deeply moving that

I have to hide my emotions to keep it professional. She has created a look book with characters' aesthetics, Pantone color palettes, fabric swatches, and drawings. A separate book includes ideas for the set, including the Sirens' cove, the Jade Palace, and Naxos, as well as the island that disappears. We want to use old-school animatronics, live characters, and holographic images.

At midnight, Ethan says, "Marin, are you a pumpkin yet?"

It surprises me how much he pays attention. He had a glass of Sauvignon Blanc waiting for me this evening. He remembered Flora preferred lager. He was focused and, after seeing Flora's work, he was genuinely excited and complimentary. Flora beamed. Finally, I thought. Someone else recognizes her talent.

When we leave, I fight the urge to hug him in the same way he hugged me after watching *Island of Sirens* together.

Flora doesn't struggle at all. She wraps her arms around Ethan and says, "Thanks so much for this opportunity, Reve."

"You deserve it," he replies softly. His eyes meet mine. My heart sends lightning bolts into my stomach.

Chapter Forty

Ethan

Marin and I have barely touched since our dinner at Ernie's, let alone kissed. To keep up the dating façade, I met her at Le Bleue Tortue for a coffee one afternoon, which produced a quick new array of candid photos that popped up online. Leave it to Revelers to find semi-discreet ways to take our photo without us really noticing, to find our best angles and make us look wholesomely in love.

With all the cramming both day and night, we hit our respective mental and exhaustion walls. I told her it would be good PR to go out again, maybe to the RP Lounge where Revel executives might see us together. Really, I just wanted to spend time with her outside the confines of work again.

The lounge is fairly quiet. In our booth, with her daiquiri and my beer, I move closer to her, our bodies finally touching, and whisper in her ear, "Eventually, there's bound to be someone who'll take our picture. I'm going to hold your hand. Is that okay?"

I feel her shiver, but she nods. I lace my fingers through hers, feeling like a starving man being given a crust of bread. Her skin is velvet. Her long, slender fingers touch me, and it's my turn to shiver. I find myself staring at our interlocking hands for a beat too long.

"Holy palmers' kiss," I quote under my breath.

"Weird, I was just thinking that!" Her face lights up. Her nose scrunches up. "Can I ask you a question?"

"You just did."

"Argh. You know what I mean." Her eyes roll dramatically.

"Shoot." I relax, placing my hands behind my head, a picture of openness.

"What's with the Shakespeare?" she asks hesitantly, not wanting to offend. "I mean, not many guys I know quote him like you."

"It was PawPaw. When we were little, he took us to Shakespeare in the Park. He's memorized the sonnets and most soliloquies. The man has a quote for every possible situation. The language was impossible at first, but I found that having the words, more beautifully constructed than my own, for a moment, a feeling, a situation helps me experience it fully. If that makes sense..."

"Like two people holding hands." Her smile is coy.

"Exactly." I take her hand again. She stares at our hands a moment, a wistful look on her face.

She sighs. "I remember thinking Shakespeare knows how to write a meet-cute."

"A meet-cute? What's that?" I ask. She looks at me like I just asked what planet I'm on.

"It's a romantic comedy term. It's, like, how the couple first meets. It's usually memorable, often funny or embarrassing. The most famous one I can think of is from a Billy Wilder movie–I don't remember the name–but a woman goes to the store to buy a pajama top, and the guy is there to buy the bottoms. Let the romance commence!"

"Lame," I retort, just to flirt. "*Romeo and Juliet* is not a comedy, and I don't think their first meeting is funny or embarrassing."

"Well, duh, and they both end up dead." She rolls her eyes. "It's just *too* perfect, isn't it?" She takes a sip of her daiquiri; I would give one million dollars to be the straw on which her perfect lips land.

She's on a roll now. "It's this huge party. Romeo is able to sneak in because it just so happens to be a masquerade. And they just so happen to be the children of their parents' enemies, and of course, they meet and speak in sonnet form and fall instantly in love."

"I guess it would be a meet-cute if they end up living happily-ever-after," I counter, enjoying arguing with her.

"So, let's just agree to disagree." Her eyes are twinkling, and I can't help myself. I act.

"Then move not, while my prayer's effect I take," I pull her hand up to my mouth and kiss it. Marin blushes. We are frozen in this moment until a light from a camera phone in the dimness of the lounge interrupts us. I'm both thrilled and annoyed.

Later, this picture fills the top post on *The Secret Reveler* with the caption "Prince Ethan Woos His Lady."

~

A week of working and not touching later, I am agitated. In the gym, I punish my quads with squats and my biceps with curls. Moving to exhaust my body with cardio, I increase the speed on the treadmill and run until my lungs burn, but my progress is interrupted by a text from Elsie: Give me a call.

I hit the Stop button on the treadmill and press Elsie's name.

"Well, hello there, lovebird." Her voice is saccharine. I already regret calling her.

"What's up?" I reply, curt as can be.

"Ah, nothing. Writing a piece on the global supply chain and another human-interest piece on a local soccer hero. It's all very boring. I want to hear about you and your new girlfriend." She elongates the word *girlfriend*, really making a meal out of it.

"You know you're a juvenile dork," I chuckle. I can't help it.

"I'm the baby. It's allowed. I'm dying to know more. Please give me one little fact, one minute detail, an iota of information, anything to let me know this isn't some sham relationship."

"Why would it be a sham?" My voice drops an octave.

"I was kidding, Ethan." She pauses. "Wait, is it a sham?"

"No, of course not." Shit, shit, shit. Damn it, Elsie.

"You sound pretty defensive." Her tone is matter-of-fact. Again, too fucking smart for her own good.

"Why would I be in a sham relationship?" I reply, then deflect. "Jeez, you think I can't get a date?"

"I think you can always get a date, big bro. Now, whether you can handle subsequent dates, in a row, like a real-life boyfriend, well, that's a bit more difficult to believe. Especially since The-One-Whose-Name-Shall-Not-Be-Spoken."

This is one of her pet names for Bree. Elsie has always hated Bree, said Bree is the exact personality type who longs for fame even though it's the worst thing for her, and anyone else who happens to be along for the ride. Elsie has used the term "fame whore" several times since we broke up. In retrospect, she was right.

"Thanks for the vote of confidence, kid. Marin and I are doing well." I feel like I need to give her something. A name, a detail, to throw her off the lie. "We're going out tonight. I'm taking her to La Provence."

"Marin what?"

"What do you mean?"

"I mean her last name, silly."

"Ah." What's the harm in that, I think. "Vandersee."

"She's Dutch?"

We've never talked about it before, but I suppose she is, so I just say, "Yeah."

"Okay. So... La Provence, huh?" She affects a posh British accent. "Fancy."

"You sound like James." James, despite denying it, speaks in a clipped, hybrid Anglo-American accent. A real Cary Grant of a man.

"Cheers, DAH-ling. Anyway, it sounds like you really like this girl. La Provence is super romantic."

"It's a great place." PawPaw hired a Michelin star chef, Andre Renard, to run the place in the early '80s. It's right outside the park, and it's a big deal. Gaspard proposed to Yasmin at La Provence, and I just made up a fake date that is apparently happening there tonight.

Shit, I'll have to let Marin know ASAP. And, I'll have to reserve a table.

"Anything else? Jeez, you'd think you'd be dying to talk about your new lady." Elsie is doing what she does best—investigating, a.k.a. digging into my personal life for her own entertainment. Unfortunately for her, I can see it a mile away.

"Talk about my new girlfriend with the nosiest Little Angel? I think not. At least Dom has the decency to never call." I hear her huff on the other end. "But to get you off my back for now, I will tell you one juicy detail."

"Go on..." Elsie urges.

I wait a moment, really letting the tension build.

"She... is..."

"Yes..."

"From...Vermont."

"Dude! I knew that already."

"How did you know that? But not her last name?"

"I wanted to know if *you* knew her last name. Plus, I may have talked to some people."

"*Elsie*," I say, laying the warning tone on thick. "Do NOT, I repeat, Do NOT, meddle."

"I'm not meddling. How is being curious about my big brother's life meddling?"

"It is meddling when you talk to people other than your big brother about your big brother."

"Oh, like you're the most forthcoming—"

"Elsie, who did you talk to?"

"Oh, I gotta go. Late for class." Before I can say another word, she hangs up. Who did she call to pump for information?

I head up the elevator, hop in the shower, and rack my brain for who told Elsie what. Lathering my shampoo, it hits me. Ernie. Of course. He had a relationship with Wade, why not Elsie too? Ernie and Vangie adore the Little Angels like their own grandkids.

Standing in a towel, with my screen fogging, I text Marin: *"Hey, change of plans. Instead of coming to my place tonight, I'll pick you up. Wear something nice."*

"What's going on?"

"More PR."

"Roger that." A few moments later she texts, "How nice?"

"Fancy-dinner nice."

"Got it."

Short and sweet. I want to keep texting her, but she's probably on her way to work. Now I need to get a table at La Provence. I could probably just walk in tonight and push some unsuspecting couple out of their table, but I hated when famous people did shit like that in New York. "Do you know who my dad is?" syndrome was rampant in my old crowd.

I phone the restaurant, and they tell me they always keep a four-top open for any member of the Reve family. It's Revel's attention to detail like this that overwhelms me at times. Impeccable taste and specificity are what make this whole place successful. Everything is accounted for.

Speaking of success, I review the final costs for our project. I'm nervous. Now more than ever. Tilda and Dad have been too quiet, which can't be good.

It's funny, but I've been so focused on Wade's project, on succeeding, on Marin, that I haven't felt that familiar tug of panic. Despite all of the high-stakes pressure, my mind feels clearer. And despite all of the confusing, mixed-message feelings swirling around Marin, I feel grounded. I try not to dwell on it too much. Afraid to jinx this good streak.

It's easy for me to stay grounded, I think, because I only have one job while Marin and Flora are running themselves ragged. Just last night, Marin asked if she could take a power nap, at 9 pm. She looked a bit rundown when she walked in that evening. The fact that she works all day in that heavy-ass dress and wig and then comes here for another full shift of developing this project blows my mind.

I told her, "It'll be quieter in my room, come on." And I led her into my bedroom. I don't know why, but I felt the need to tuck her in. Instead, I turned around and whispered, "Sweet dreams." I wanted to kiss her good night.

Not real, I reminded myself. I had to reinforce my conviction constantly. It was like a record skipping in my head, playing the same refrain over and over again.

~

Tonight I'm waiting outside the cast dorms, leaning against the black town car for my fake girlfriend to appear for our fake date, wearing a tailored Burberry suit courtesy of James's recommendation. He had us all go to Saville Row for suits last year in London. I'd only worn it once. It made me think of Wade. That outing was the last time all four brothers were together: Wade, James, Henri, and me. Wade was scheduled to leave—where, he couldn't tell us— so we took a pre-deployment trip to the UK. In the mirror, in our tailored suits, Wade laughed, saying we looked like the Reservoir Dogs.

My memory is interrupted by the click-clack of heels on pavement. And now, I see only her. Marin shines in an asymmetrical, beaded black dress. Her hair swoops up in some sort of twist that I'm sure there's a name for. Her makeup is darker than usual, but still tasteful, and her skin seems to glow. Her legs are breathtaking in her black heels.

"Hi." She stands in front of me, a few inches taller than usual, and I suppose I should say something back.

All I manage to croak out is, "Hi."

She smells amazing, like orange blossoms and sweet olive trees, a scent that makes her seem edible. What is happening to me? I'm Ethan fucking Reve—experienced beyond most men—and I'm standing here with my mouth open, hopefully not salivating at the sight of my fake Revel princess girlfriend.

"You look great," I blurt as I open the car door for her.

"Thanks, you too," she says as she maneuvers into the low sedan seat in her tight dress. I don't mind that she's struggling because I get an eyeful of her peaches and cream thighs through the high slit in her dress.

Keep it PG, Reve, I reprimand myself and shut the door before I do or say something stupid.

Chapter Forty-One

Marin

We park outside a beautiful restaurant. La Provence is a sprawling, single-story building nestled in an old copse of 300-year-old live oaks. It's a simple, elegant French country-style ranch with a gas lantern-lit cobblestone path that guides us to the front door. The exterior isn't as ornate as I expect; instead, it reminds me a little of the French Village at the park. It's rustic, with stucco walls and ceiling, wood beams, and chic, antique sconces that filter soft light around the perimeter. The enormous windows are framed with wide wooden shutters. I love it. Ethan grabs my hand and leans towards me.

"Hey, remember. We're a couple. We're in love. So, we're going to touch more tonight, okay?" His breath whispers against my ear. I shudder all over.

"Are you cold?" He smiles at me, knowingly.

"No, I'm good. Okay. Let's do this." I nod a few times, and he thankfully moves out and holds the door. I pull my dress down, which has ridden up in the car.

Flora lent me this little black number. I don't know where she got it, but I was so grateful to have something that fit. La Provence is formal, and I left all my fancy clothes at home. And by fancy clothes, I mean my winter formal dress from junior year and the boring, matronly numbers my mother curated for me.

Ethan must see I feel uncomfortable as we enter. He pulls me close at my waist and puts his mouth near my ear. "Stop fidgeting. You look beautiful."

I still myself and take in the beautiful surroundings. The natural lighting—a stone fireplace in the center, white candles and white linen tablecloths on every table give everyone an inviting glow. The furniture is old. The oversized, antique chandeliers remind me of the Prince's palace in *Diamonds & Toads*. There's a definite fairy-tale, Old-World quality to the place. I feel immediately transported.

A tall man in a dark suit greets us. "Ah, Mr. Reve, so glad you could join us this evening. Please follow me."

We're led through the main dining area. Guests turn their heads to watch us pass. I don't blame them. Ethan cuts a striking figure in his tailored suit. If this whole theme park dynasty gig doesn't work for him, he can always model for Armani.

I attempt to keep up with the host and Ethan, but these heels aren't meant for walking, and I inevitably lag behind. Ethan, god bless him, turns and grabs my hand. "Come on, slowpoke."

I smile, and before I realize what is happening, his lips are on mine for the briefest of moments. Like, he just couldn't help himself and had to kiss me right then. My heart flutters.

"Oh my god. It's Ethan Reve," I hear from somewhere close by, and this breaks the spell. I remember that we are in the middle of a busy restaurant, and everyone just watched Ethan kiss me, which I suppose is the point.

He gives me a quizzical look. "You coming, Marin?"

It's a show. *It's all a show*, I remind myself as I pick up the pace, and let him guide us to a table in front of an enormous window overlooking a garden patio rimmed with bare trees that are coiled with twinkle lights. We're in a small alcove, a little removed from the other diners, but it's not completely private. Privacy is not the point.

Play your part, I tell myself.

We sit down and Ethan orders us a bottle of white. "I think you'll like it. It's a Pinot Gris from Alsace."

"Thank you." I sound stiff.

"You're welcome." I glance at him finally. He is grinning like the Big Bad Wolf.

"What?" I whisper.

"You."

"Me what?"

"You're adorable." He takes a sip of water. "You're all uptight." He mimics my posture. Apparently I'm sitting like a soldier at attention.

"I am not," I argue, but he's right, I am totally uptight. I need to loosen up. We have an audience and we need to put on a good show. But I've never liked being on display, not as just the regular old Marin Vandersee. I wish I was in full costume. Well, a different costume.

Where is that wine?

"Okay, you're not uptight." His voice drips with fake sincerity.

"Darn tootin.'" I smile. Let's see if he remembers this little inside joke.

"Bah!" A bark escapes him. "What are you, eighty?"

"Why?" I ask coyly, happy he remembers. "Are you into octogenarians?"

"If they all looked like you"— his voice drops seductively—"then, hell yes."

"Oh, you're good." I pick up my napkin and place it in my lap.

"What do you mean?" He's relaxed now, curiosity arching his eyebrows.

"You're a good flirt, Ethan. I'm complimenting you."

"Well, thanks, I guess. You're not so bad yourself."

I snort, which makes him smile wider.

"Are you serious? I'm terrible at flirting." I gesture to the entirety of my being. "Clearly."

"Could've fooled me." He reaches for my hand and beckons me with his other. "Come closer," he whispers.

A giggle escapes as I tilt toward him, our foreheads almost touching.

"I have an idea. Let's kill two birds with one stone. You can practice your flirting skills on me. I'll provide some constructive feedback, perhaps model some effective flirtation techniques, and everyone within a mile radius will buy that we're madly in love." Both of his hands are holding mine. Warm and strong.

I think of them on my back.

Do not blur worlds, I remind myself, but I shove those thoughts aside for now. And before I can stop myself, I whisper back, "Deal."

I hear ice rattle in a bucket. Our wine has arrived, and we break apart. Ethan tastes the wine, and nods, and the waiter pours. Finally, we clink glasses.

"To future flirting and business endeavors," Ethan toasts.

I laugh and take a delicate sip of the Pinot Gris.

"It's lovely," I say and take another, much bigger gulp.

"Glad you like it," Ethan replies. "I hope you don't mind, but I ordered ahead of time from the prix fixe menu. Whatever André makes is brilliant."

"No, of course not. I'm excited to see what he has prepared." And I'm secretly glad I don't have to try and order something in French. Despite wanting to speak the language of Marie Reve, my utilitarian parents said Spanish would be more useful in America.

"So...let's see what you've got." Ethan sits back and places his folded hands on his abs.

"See what exactly?"

"Flirting. Give me your best material."

"Material?"

"Yes. What's your winning technique?"

I blush and mess with the folded linen napkin in my lap. Biting my lip, I say, "I don't have a technique."

He eyes my lips. "Bullshit. That was good."

"What was good?"

"The whole blushing, lip-biting act." He claps his hands a few times. "Brava."

"That wasn't an act."

"Aw, come on. Marin. That was super sexy." He sounds disbelieving.

Now I'm super blushing. "Well, this is news to me because that definitely wasn't the flirting demonstration."

He stares at me for a moment, his blue eyes dark and probing. "Wow. Okay. I can't wait to see the flirting demo." He gestures for me to get on with the show. "Go on then."

I throw my shoulders back, then put my elbows on the table, and drop my chin into my hands. I look up at him through my lashes. He looks intrigued.

In a breathy voice, I whisper, "Did it hurt?"

Confused, he stammers, "Did it hurt?"

"Yes, did it hurt?" I ask more insistently, pouting a little, pushing my arms together, showing off cleavage, doing my best Jessica Rabbit impersonation.

He shifts in his seat. "Did what hurt?"

I grab his hand and start to massage the flesh between his thumb and pointer finger. I purr my response, really laying it on thick. "When you fell from heaven."

He bursts out laughing. The whole restaurant screeches to silence and looks our way. Ethan is howling, wiping his cheeks. "I don't know why I'm laughing so hard..." He's doing that whole body laugh that I like. I can't help but laugh too. "That was so...so..."

I help him out. "Cheesy?"

"Yes. Holy shit. I need a minute." His laughing fit slows, he dabs at his welled-up eyes, and takes a big gulp of water. Watching him laugh sends heat waves throughout my body.

Before I can stop myself, I say, "I like making you laugh."

He gets quiet, his gaze intense. I start to feel silly again. Blurred-world silly. Then he threads his fingers in mine, palm to palm. "That was the best damn flirting I've ever experienced. The master has become the student." He bows to me, and it's my turn to laugh.

"Oh, here comes the food." Two plates and a steaming pot of mussels are placed on the table. It smells like butter, thyme, and garlic. I inhale deeply, in gourmet heaven.

"Let's eat, princess." And we dig into the best meal of my entire life. The food, the wine, and the company—all so delicious, so much so that I forget about the prying eyes and cameras pointed in our direction.

Chapter Forty-Two

Ethan

When the town car pulls up to Marin's dorm, I do something stupid. I don't want this night to end. Our date, our fake date, is the best date I've ever been on.

I put a hand on her sweet knee and blurt, "I'm having fun. You want to get a nightcap at the RP Lounge?"

She sizes me up, eyes narrowed. "If you promise not to drink twenty-seven mint juleps, yes."

"I promise." I cross my heart. She smiles.

"Can we walk there? I love the park at night."

I nod, hop out, and tip the driver.

Once the driver leaves, she takes off her heels, her bare feet on the concrete. "Do you mind if I go up to my room so I can grab different shoes?"

"Not at all. Let's go," I reply, but she looks hesitant.

"What?" I ask.

"Nothing. I guess we are dating, and it would be weird if you never came over." She sounds like she's trying to convince herself it's okay, like if we caused a scene it wouldn't be a problem.

"I don't have to come up if you'd rather I didn't..." I offer, secretly wishing to throw her over my shoulders and declare to the world that this is my woman. Caveman-style.

"No, no, no," she interrupts. "I'm just being uptight again." A soft smile spreads on her face. "Come on." She reaches for my hand. It seems natural.

As she unlocks the front door, she says, "Flora should be home, but she sleeps with earplugs and a mask, so don't worry about making noise." She tiptoes around the small apartment regardless. A conscientious roommate.

"My shoes are in the bedroom, hold on a sec." Marin opens the bedroom door slowly. I hear "Huh?"

"What?" I follow her to the bedroom.

"Flora isn't here. Weird." Marin looks around the room for a moment, trying to locate her shoes. "She's probably out with the princesses."

"The princesses?"

"Lana and Carrie. They play Princess Portia and Thumbelina. They're sort of a squad."

I have no idea what to say. This Revel shit is all so niche and strange. But I'm fake dating Rose Red. Who am I to judge what's weird?

"Got them!" She announces as she plops down on her bed and puts on some worn red Chuck Taylors. After she ties them, she lifts up a leg and says, "Punk rock, right?"

It's the red sneakers that are my undoing. Her sleek leg, her black dress hugging her curves, her unaffected pose on her bed. I grunt my affirmation.

She stands up quickly, rubs her hands down her dress, and says, "So...you ready?"

"Are you?" I step closer to her. My jumbled mind becomes laser focused. On her lips, on her hips, on her smell. On her taste. On feeling her beneath me. This visceral need is so intense—she's so intoxicating—I feel high with wanting her.

She gazes into my lustful eyes. "Ethan, what are you doing?"

Then she goes and bites her lip again. The straw that breaks my back. I cup my hands on her face, drawing her to me.

My mouth claims her, opens hers, plays with her tongue. She isn't tentative. There's a lit fire between us in every place we touch. And this time I don't think it's an act. I want her, and I can tell she wants me, too. Consequences be damned.

My hands move down her back, and I crush her against my hips. She can feel how much I want her, and she gives a little appreciative moan. I bend and reach to feel her plump, perfect ass in my hands. Before I know it, she jumps and wraps her legs around me. Her thighs squeeze, and her breasts press into my chest. Holy hell.

We crash into a tall dresser. Bottles clink together and crash to the floor. "The bed," I growl. She nods, and I lay her down.

It's a tiny twin cot, and it can barely support our weight, but I couldn't care less. My entire body aches for her, has ached for her for so long that I may incinerate.

You've got to slow down, I tell myself. I've dreamed of showing her one of the perks of being in a relationship with me. Fake or otherwise. All that I know I can make her feel. Raising myself over her, I kiss her throat and move my hand to her inner thigh, caressing slowly, softly, taking my time. A little moan hums in her throat and I push my hand up, and up, until she shivers when I feel her thong wet with anticipation.

"May I?" I pat two fingers on the silky satin of her panties.

"Yes, please, yes," she whimpers.

"Thank god." I move the thong to the side and slip a finger slowly into her. Her breathing hitches. "God, Marin."

She moans louder this time in response.

"Let me make you feel good." I search her eyes, desperate for permission, and when she nods slightly, I make my dream a reality.

Her hands grip my head, and her fingers play with my hair as my mouth finds its way down home. I pull my finger out of her, soaking wet. I push her dress up around her waist, pull her thong all the way off, and make love to her with my mouth—kissing, sucking, and claiming her. Making her mine. I drive my finger back into her warmth, then join it with a second, and feel her thighs clench, her nails on my upper back.

"I'm so close, Ethan." Her breathing is louder now.

"Mmm-hmm," I reply, my voice muffled in her sweetness. Then her back arches.

She gasps, "Ethan, Ethan, yes, yes!" Her climax is intense. She's so loud that she covers her face with a pillow. I hear a muted, "Ethan, yeeess!"

I leave a trail of kisses on her inner thigh down to her knee. She twitches a little, a bit ticklish it seems, her face still smothered by the pillow.

"Are you still alive?" I smile, knowing my work has had such an effect on her, when she mumbles "Maybe" through the pillow.

"Princess? Are you alive under there?" I move up and over, so I can lie next to her, stroking her arm.

"Mmm-hmm." She's still hiding her face.

"Care to show me?" I try to peak under the pillow.

"In a second." I run my fingers across the light, glistening sweat on her chest, admiring her heaving curves, her taut, pink nipples, the way her ribcage hitches under my touch. Her dress is scrunched up around her stomach. I want to pull it off, but I'm way too excited to explore more.

Finally, Marin emerges from her hiding place. Her eyes are filled with satisfaction, but also a little trepidation.

I don't like the trepidatious bit.

"What's up? You okay?" I ask.

"It's nothing," she whispers, biting her lip again. "I mean, yes. I'm okay." God, she has to know that every time she digs her front teeth into those flower-petal lips I go a little crazy inside, but it's clear something is up with her.

"Liar," I tease. Her eyes warm up. I can see her warring with herself, on the verge of revealing something precious.

"It's just..." She hesitates. Is she about to say this was a mistake? How can her screaming my name be a mistake?

I fill in. "...Just that I'm amazing and rocked your proverbial world and..."

She laughs. "Well...." She brings her hand to my chest and looks into my eyes. "That was a first for me."

"A first what?" I begin kissing her neck.

"The first time...well, that I, you know...with a guy." She squirms a little. I pause, lift my head, and peer into her eyes, which can't quite settle on mine.

"Are you a virgin, Marin?" I ask, quiet, recognizing she's being open with me, not wanting to scare her off.

"No, not technically," she says softly.

"What does *technically* mean?" I match her volume.

"I've had sex before, but I never... came with a guy before." She throws her face in the crook of her arm.

"Only with girls?" I smile at her, trying to break the tension, open to whatever she wants to tell me.

"No, no." She elbows me a little. "Just, you know, by myself." The diffused streetlight shining through the small bedroom window is just bright enough that I can see her embarrassment. And how beautiful she is. I shiver as I imagine Marin touching herself.

"I'd like to see that."

"What?" Her voice gets high and breathy.

"I'd like to see you make yourself come." I press against her. She can feel how hard I am for her.

"Really? That doesn't freak you out." She turns, propping up on an elbow, resting her head in her hand so we completely face one another. She's gazing at me level through long lashes the color of the crisp October maple leaves that line the paths of Central Park in October.

Jesus, Marin makes me poetic. She has no idea how sexy she is, which is, in itself, sexiness personified.

"Absolutely not," I say.

"No, I mean, about not having a partner give me...you know."

I think about her question for a moment. Am I bothered that I am the first man to give Marin Vandersee an orgasm?

Fuck, no.

"No, I like it." I kiss her. "I really like it." I kiss her again. "In fact, I fucking love it."

And I do. I like that I'm her first in this way, and a little voice in my head wants to tell her I'll be the last man, too, that no one else will ever make her come again. Just me.

But that's crazy talk. Too much, too soon. Too intense. I need to take a moment to breathe.

"Well, good, then." She rolls into me, snuggling her head into my neck. She slowly glides her fingernails lightly over my chest, my sternum, my stomach, and before I can even think about freaking out about my reaction to her confession, Marin unbuttons my pants.

"Let's see if I can return the favor," she purrs.

All I can do is groan. I intended to fuck her brains out, but she pulls at the waist of my boxer briefs. "A little help, please."

She maneuvers up and over me, so she's off the bed. I stand up, pull my briefs down, and sit back on the bed, all while watching her movements in front of me. As Marin gets down on her knees, it's all I can do to hold back in anticipation, watching her wavy, disheveled hair cascade over her shoulders. With her black dress still technically on, although rumpled and barely covering those puckered nipples, Marin takes in how much I want her.

"Wow, Ethan, you're... impressive." I can tell she's blushing, but she smiles like she's plenty ready for the challenge.

"Please, Marin. Touch me."

And she does. Her hand is tentative at first, but she picks up a steady rhythm. Her grip becomes firm. Then she licks the length of me, and I almost explode right then. But I want this moment to last. I watch her pretty pink lips open as she takes me into her mouth, all the while stroking me, up and down, up and down.

She moans, and flashes of light flood my vision as an explosion of pleasure reverberates through me.

Chapter Forty-Three

Marin

I crawl up Ethan, kissing his belly again, teasing him after his release, like he did to me. When he flinches, I lie beside him. We catch our breath together, squished on my single bed. Then I hear the familiar sound of the front door opening. Flora is home.

Shit, shit. Double shit. This is not good roommate etiquette.

I look over at him and whisper, "Flora."

Ethan pops out of bed like a ninja and pulls on his pants. I pull my dress back up and then down, smoothing it quickly. My red Chucks are still on, and I don't even want to think about what my hair looks like. This looks bad, and it smells like sex in here. I put my fingers over my lips to silence Ethan. I spray some of Flora's lavender room spray and hold my hand up to indicate I'll be gone one minute.

I find Flora in the kitchen, drinking a giant glass of water.

"Heeyyyy, lady! You're up. Thank god. I am a little bitty topsy...tipsy," Flora giggles, her voice overly loud. "You have a good night? That dress!" She does a chef's kiss. "So fab." She is more than tipsy.

"Yes, yes. A good night." I'm trying to figure out what to say to Flora. Ethan Reve and I went on a fake date, then we gave each other very real orgasms, and it just occurred to me as I stand here with my sex hair and fancy dress how many levels of discombobulation I'm dealing with now.

Fortunately, Flora doesn't seem to notice my hair or my terse response.

"I've got to get this makeup off my teeth and brush my face." She hiccups. "And then try to fall asleep." She leaves for the bathroom and closes the door.

I run to the bedroom, grab a very handsome, very disheveled Ethan, pull him through the kitchen, and back out into the dorm hallway.

In a whisper, I push him towards the elevators, "I'll see you tomorrow."

Ethan's eyebrows shoot up. "Is the evening over?"

"'Fraid so. Flora is about to pass out, and I have a long day tomorrow, but I'll see you after work, right?" I realize I'm speaking New England fast talk, pulling him by his coat lapels.

"Okay, are you sure you don't want to come with me?" he asks, a hopeful glint in his eyes.

I slow down so he knows I'm serious. "No, I can't. Sorry. You really should go." I look up and down the hall to see if anyone is around. I can hear water running in someone's bathroom. "I'll see you tomorrow."

For a moment, I see something in his expression, disappointment, hurt, maybe. He nods and gives me a sideways smile.

"Tomorrow then." His voice is clipped.

I hate to see his expression shift back into business mode. We're almost to the elevators, and even though this is Rubiks Cube-level confusing, I can't help but kiss him deeply on the lips. Part of me worries if he shuts down I'll never feel this connected, warm feeling again.

"Thank you for an amazing evening, Ethan," I say.

Scared of his reaction, I run back down the hall to my dorm room.

~

When I finally fall asleep, I dream that I'm a medieval queen and two knights are jousting for my favor. I can't see their faces as they are obscured by armor. One knight wears red, the other, blue. The blue knight stabs the red knight, and instead of blood, money pours from his chest. I wake up sweating. I have no idea what it means, but I feel off when I wake up.

By the time I make it to the French Village as Rose Red, I've shaken off the dream and feel like I'm floating on air. Turns out that having a mind-altering, world-blurring orgasm has lasting effects. The world is shiny and beautiful. The sky is bluer, the air smells sweeter than cotton candy. Every crying kid is adorable; every rude selfie-taker is just trying to document the wonder of Revel Pointe; every overbearing parent is just protective.

I catch Roland side-eyeing me a few times, but his expression is unreadable. As long as I don't think too much about what last night meant for me, for Ethan, for the project... I can exist in this blissful plane.

Of course, this is me, Marin Vandersee, so overthinking overwhelms me a few hours later, especially once the orgasm-induced endorphins wear off and the slew of guests taper to a trickle. On autopilot, I wander the village and go into full post-mortem mode, analyzing the evening from every possible angle.

Hands down, last night was the best date I've ever been on. I didn't feel awkward. Well, I did at first, but Ethan somehow helped me forget we were on display. He helped me forget that this wasn't a real relationship. So much so that we crossed the line last night. And I don't know what that means. I don't know how he feels. I mean, he *seems* to like me.

I decide to take my break away from Roland. I head to the cast cottage and down a bottle of water. All this introspection makes a girl thirsty.

Here's what I know for certain. Ethan is attracted to me. But also, this relationship is for show, and the stakes couldn't be higher. We have to be careful.

I think about Vangie's reading. Is Ethan the good knight or the bad one?

An image of a heart stabbed with three swords appears in my mind. I am so out of my element. I'm liable to get hurt here. In fact, if an idealistic, inexperienced Reveler told me she was in a fake, maybe real relationship with Ethan Reve, I'd tell her to run screaming, to protect her heart, to go slow.

The more time I spend with him, the more I open my heart, and I'm 99 percent sure this will end with three swords slicing through it.

Also, what is going to happen after the pitch? Will this all end? What if it fails? What happens then? What if it succeeds, and he doesn't actually want to pursue a real relationship? I'll be working with him closely for years. I need to prepare myself for that eventuality. Despite the rainbow Vangie mentioned coming out of my heartbreak, I am not interested in those swords piercing my heart.

"Ahem." Roland stands before me in all of his princely regalia.

Taken by surprise, I yelp.

"Whoa, sorry." He holds his hands up in mock surrender. "I didn't mean to scare you." He goes to the mini-fridge and pulls out a Diet Coke.

"No worries. I guess I was just lost in thought." I've been alone, sitting at the round table, staring off into space for at least ten minutes. I must look batty.

"I get it. You have a lot to think about these days, it seems." He gives me a strained version of his Prince Roland smile.

"What do you mean?" I ask.

"Well, I guess I was right about Ethan Reve liking you after all." He takes a swig from his soda and stares at me with a pointed expression.

I don't know what to say.

"Listen, you don't have to play coy with me." He sits across from me, his hazel eyes posing an unasked question. "I've seen the pictures."

"The *pictures*?" So, he's seen them all.

"Yes, pictures." He emphasizes the *s* at the end, sounding like a snake.

"You have?" My voice squeaks.

"Aww, come on, Red. They're all over the internet right now." His beautiful mouth twists into a sneer.

"I haven't actually paid much attention." I look down at my hands, fixating on my nails, which have grown too long.

Roland hasn't been anything but nice to me the past few months. He's helped me, he has been gallant, chivalrous even, and I think, maybe, he did mean to ask me out the other day.

Not that long ago, I would have jumped at the chance to go out with him. I wished for love at Mona Moon, and Roland's face was the one that came to mind. A perfect, fairytale love with a perfect, fairytale prince. Talk about an amazing meet-cute.

And then Ethan's sloppy self fell into the moat.

Roland snorts, as if reading my thoughts, and walks to his personal items thrown in the corner. "You haven't paid attention? I find that hard to believe, but here, this is just from last night. See for yourself."

He pulls his phone out of his messenger bag and hits a few buttons. We're not supposed to use our phones in here, but I'm curious. On the screen, there's a picture of me and Ethan in La Provence; it's when he kissed me in the dining room before we sat down. I scroll, and there are so many more. Me flirting at the table, him laughing with a hand on his chest, our hands touching. There are all different angles, too. I didn't even notice the phones. I was hyperfocused on Ethan.

I hate that our evening wasn't ours. But I knew that was the deal. In fact, that was the whole point. Ethan told me the evening was a PR stunt, so why do I feel like throwing up?

The caption reads, "Ethan Reve in Love?"

I shove the phone at Roland. "Here. Take it." I can feel his scrutiny, everyone's scrutiny.

"You really didn't look at these before, huh?" Surprise laces his voice.

"No." I glare at him for a moment. He stares back and then shakes his head.

"Sorry, I figured you'd like the attention. It could be..." He struggles to find his words. "*Beneficial* for you, for your career." Now he's looking at me like a rare species in a zoo. "I would have 100 percent checked my phone every five seconds if I was in your shoes."

"Not me. I actually feel sick looking at them. I don't like all of this attention." In costume, I'm able to hide behind a character. But these are pictures of *me*. And while it was a publicity-stunt version of me in a dress fancier than I've ever worn, it turns out that the idea of something and the reality of it are very different. Same goes for the whole idea of a fake relationship and what it's really like to actually be in one.

Would this be easier if it were real? Is it real? I take a deep breath and put my head in my hands. The stakes are so high and everything feels so complicated. I try to stave off tears. A blotchy Rose Red is neither canon nor attractive.

Roland moves his chair so he is next to me. He rubs my back in giant circles. "Hey, Red. I'm sorry. I'm just..." He pauses for a moment and looks down. "I was being a jerk. Take a deep breath."

I count my breaths and feel the tension release. I feel better, not great, but better enough to say, "No worries."

He stands, chugs the rest of his drink, throws the can in the recycling bin, and then looks at me, earnestly. "I have to say something. And you might not like it, but I'll say it one time and never again."

He takes a deep breath, trying to collect his thoughts. "Be careful. Guys like Ethan Reve don't know what it's like to have to work for things, like you and I do. They get everything handed to them on a platter, so they take everything for granted. You and I have to work harder, we have to exploit every advantage and opportunity." Roland starts pacing our cramped cottage quarters. "Ethan Reve and his type take what they want, when they want it, and then..." He sits back down suddenly and grabs my hands. "Then they move on, Red. You and me? We have to fight harder and smarter to get ahead."

The cold, steely gleam in his eyes makes me shiver. He lowers his head for a moment then continues. Warmer now.

"I care about you, Red. I don't want to see you get hurt. Okay?" His thumbs run over my fingers.

"Okay," I whisper and manage a lame smile. He's just being protective of me, ever the Prince Charming, the knight-in-shining-armor. I think back to Vangie's reading, but I shake my head, dispelling the image.

His voice softens considerably. "I just don't want you to be some rich boy's plaything. And people are already starting to connect the dots. You can only hide in costume for so long. Gossip around here spreads like wildfire."

He's right. My days as Rose Red are numbered. Before I can say anything, he rises abruptly. "Play this smart, Red."

"This isn't a game," I say, but there isn't a lot of conviction in my voice. Technically, I am in a fake relationship to land my dream job.

I am playing a game of sorts. Even though I think my feelings for Ethan are real, I feel dirty.

"Sure, just be careful." And with that, he leaves the cottage, his red cape swishing behind him.

I'm so out of my depth right now, and the proposal deadline is looming. I promise myself that moving forward I will just focus on work, and I'll wait to see Ethan's next move.

Chapter Forty-Four

Ethan

I'm enjoying a 30-year Macallan Scotch in the turret by the fireplace the next afternoon and gathering my thoughts before I scan *The Secret Reveler*, looking for a new post. When it pops up, I don't know what to think.

Ethan Reve in Love?

Well, hello, Revelers. Could it be that the rakish Reve brother has finally met his match? Marin Vandersee (pictured right in a stunning black dress) looks longingly at a devilishly handsome Ethan Reve who has apparently heard the funniest joke ever told. Look at those eyes, Revelers. Miss Vandersee wants to eat that man up!

I stare at the picture, and it's true. Marin looks like she's truly into me, and after what happened last night, I'm pretty sure this fake relationship has morphed into a version of a real one. And the fucked-up part about it... I am ecstatic. I've been grinning like a kid who just rode his bike for the first time. My mind wanders from the emails piled up before me back to Marin. How beautiful she looked last night, how hot she was in bed, her bee-stung lips, her quivering legs, her hands pulling my hair when she came.

I scroll through the post to find more pictures of her, of us, and I'm not disappointed. There are so many. It's a bit much, actually. I'm used to pictures of me on the Internet, but this is ridiculous.

I wonder how Marin is doing with all of this. She's not like the girls I dated in New York. They understood the paparazzi, the hustle and the game of it all. Most of them courted it. Marin is different.

And while she agreed to this whole scheme, it still can't be easy for her. She seems like a naturally private person.

But we need the publicity to solidify our steady relationship to Tilda and the board. This is exactly what sells it, makes us look valid, lasting. It makes me look stable. Though, while this whole fake relationship was her idea, the reality of what we're doing is a big ask for a person who's not used to the scrutiny of a blinding, worldwide spotlight.

Marin's life is about to change drastically, with her name out there now in bold next to mine. Phone calls, emails, requests for on-the-record interviews. The good thing about being in Southern Louisiana is that the media apparatus here is fairly limited, and we can protect her in the park. But not completely. Everyone with a cellphone is a potential reporter.

I realize we need to talk seriously, and not just because we are pitching soon.

To that end, I review our work from the last week. Flora is ready with some stellar mockups. We've heard back from a few designers despite the probable help embargo courtesy of Tilda. Some of them remember Wade, and I think, from some subtle hints in conversation, are not particularly thrilled with the direction Revel has been going the last few years. Cricket, the designer who told me she's working on some sort of secret project, actually called me when she got back to town. When I told her about the proposals, she asked, "Does the world need another shitty cruise line?"

Maybe not always subtle.

I try to focus, I really do, but I'm like a fucking teenager. My mind—and body—keeps wandering back to thoughts of Marin. And it isn't just snapshots in my imagination of intimate poses from last night. It's the way she flirted with me last night, how she stretches like a cat before she stands up, how she made Ernie and

Vangie laugh. How she makes *me* laugh. How smart and capable she is. Who knew competence was a turn-on for me?

Suddenly, the reality of our setup hits me like an asteroid from space crashing to Earth. If we get the board to approve this pitch, Marin can stay here. At Revel Pointe. With me. But if we don't, what's her plan? Would she consider me as part of it? Would staying as my girlfriend freak her out? Do I really want that? I feel so uncool, so out of sorts, way beyond my comfort zone now.

My phone dings.

James: *Hey, Bambino. Saw some interesting photos of you.*

Of course. No doubt Elsie has sent them to the siblings. Probably to everyone she knows.

James: *Elsie says you're in love with a Revel adult.*

This is followed by another one before I can respond.

James: *Also says you're working on Wade's project and pitching it to the board with said bombshell.*

I respond with a simple: *Yes.*

James: *Yes to the pitch? Yes to the love?*

It's way too soon to say love, right? Lust and extreme-like perhaps. Admiration? Immense respect? Enormous desire? Fuck. I don't know what to write, so I just re-send: *Yes.*

James: *Your loquacity knows no bounds, big brother.*

Me: *Busy. Talk later. Go back to your goth chic, I reply.*

James: *Already moved on. I'm having an Italian renaissance;)*

A moment later he sends a photo of a building under construction next to an ornate church.

Ha. I write, *Buon fortuna.*

James's always had tunnel vision on his interests. One thing at a time, full-speed ahead.

James: *Good luck yourself.*

Luck. I'll take all that I can get. I don't want to push it, my luck, or Marin for that matter. I feel like we're on the precipice of something. Something big. And I don't want to fuck it up. I'll let Marin's behavior dictate my own.

She will need to make the next move.

Chapter Forty-Five

Marin

It's been three days since "the boom event." We haven't had much alone time to talk about it. Ethan's flirty and attentive, but no more than he was before "the boom event." I'm calling it "the boom event" because Flora saw the photos the next day, and when I walked woozily into the dressing room after my shift, she pointed at me and immediately said, "This isn't fake anymore, is it?"

"Ahh..." I'm not a good liar, especially with Flora. "What gave it away?"

"Your skin is currently the color of your hair." Flora shrugged knowingly.

"Argh!" I kicked off my shoes.

"So...?"

"So?"

"I have to ask." Flora paused, then blurted out, "Have you two done the dirty yet?"

"What?! N-n-no."

"Something happened. Give me details. You two look like you want to jump each other's bones in those photos." She rolled herself over the back of the couch and plopped down.

"We made out, and a bit more. I won't go into detail because it's weird, and we all have to work together for the next week. But..."

"Seriously, Marin. You finish that sentence, or I'll burn your original *Miss Prudence* cast recording."

I dropped down next to her, sinking into the old brown sofa, and covered my face with my hands. "He did something no one else has been able to do," I whispered.

Flora knew exactly what this meant. Back in college, I confessed to Flora that no one has been able to make me climax when my boyfriend Jonathan broke up with me in our junior year. I cried and yelled, "I think I'm deficient!" And Flora soothed me, telling me that it's likely that my partners were deficient, and I would find a guy someday I had chemistry with, and "BOOM! Ya come!"

Flora leaned forward, excited for me. "He made you boom?"

"Oh, yeah. Big boom." I felt a little hot just thinking about it.

"Hell, yes! We need to throw a party or something. To honor this momentous event." She clapped her hands together. I could only imagine the cake she'd make me. I envisioned a Red Velvet cake shaped and frosted like a cartoon bomb.

"No, no, no. I have enough attention on me to last a lifetime." I shudder when I think about all the photos of me. Fortunately, my social media is all set to private, but I've already had a few interview requests through my Tulane email.

"Only you would be bummed about the attention." Flora grabbed her mug and took a gulp of her leftover coffee. "But I get it. It's fame for dating someone, not for doing anything awesome."

"Yeah, and it's personal." I gathered my many skirts and heaved myself up. "And it wasn't *supposed* to be real."

"Would it be easier to handle if it were fake?" Flora helped me unlace my corset.

I considered this for a minute. "I think so. Kind of like how I like being Rose Red. I'm not me, I'm a character. It's an escape from the neurotic, insecure me. If it was fake, I don't think I'd feel as weird about all the press. The messed-up part is I completely forgot that last night was a PR stunt, not a real date. A real date with thirty cameras seems like an invasion of privacy."

"What are you going to do about it?" Flora asked, her brow furrowed.

"I don't know. I guess I'll focus on the work at hand, and Ethan and I can figure out our stuff after the board pitch." I stepped out of my dress and paced the room.

"You know he looks like he's over-the-moon in love with you in those pictures, right?" Flora's eyes twinkled again.

"I think he likes me. I do, but it's Ethan Reve, and I'm me. I have no idea what I'm doing."

Flora picked up my costume. "Mare…"

I went on. "I'll let him take the lead here. We have too much to lose, and I don't think we should make any decisions about anything yet."

"If we succeed with the pitch, will you date him for real?" Flora asked tentatively.

"I can't think that far ahead or I will freak out." At the mirror, I started pulling pins from my wig.

"Right-o, cap'n." Flora headed to the door, stopped, and turned around. "Hey, Mare."

"Yeah?"

"I can't wait to be the awkward third wheel at tonight's meeting." She deadpanned and closed the door.

~

Life continues to follow our routine. Flora and I both work during the day and head to Ethan's every night. "The boom event" only made things awkward that first night, then the weirdness got lost in the pressing details of the proposal. But this tension between Ethan and me is getting ridiculous. We need to talk. And apparently he isn't going to initiate the conversation.

I can't go into that board meeting with my head (and panties) in a twist. So I made a plan and worked it out with Flora. Tonight, Flora would say she had a thing and leave early. That would give me enough time to bite the proverbial bullet and talk to him. I've caught him staring at me the past few days. And I'm positive he's caught me staring at him an embarrassing amount of times, but it never goes anywhere because we're never alone, and we're always swamped.

Tonight we'll be alone and we will talk. I'm fed up with this stalemate and my meek, wait-and-see tendencies.

Chapter Forty-Six

Ethan

The last three days have been torture. I am trying to be patient. To let her take the lead, something I don't usually do with women. Marin is different; she's savvy in so many ways, innocent in others.

But goddamn, does she have to wear those crop tops to our strategy sessions? Does she have to stretch every five seconds? Okay, maybe not five seconds, but too much for me to stay focused. And does she always have to smell like sex and home simultaneously, that musky coconut-rose scent that makes me want to rip her jeans off and take her on the table?

Flora, and the deadline, have kept me on task and on my original plan, which is to let Marin's behavior guide my own.

But it's too much. I am a nuclear ball of frustration and desire. Tonight I have to make a move, I think when Flora coughs dramatically, more of a stage bark than a throat clear.

"Earth to Ethan... Are you in there?" Flora collects the seventy bags she carries.

"Sorry, what's up?" I am staring blankly at my screen, envisioning a black lace bra under Marin's pink crop top.

"I gotta run a little early tonight. I got a...thing to do."

It's music to my ears, and before I can ask what this vague thing is, Flora is out the door, and Marin and I are finally alone.

Across the table, Marin brushes a lock of freshly curled hair from her eyes. A vision in pink. She looks edible. An adult, sexy Strawberry Shortcake.

"So..." Marin looks uncomfortable. Maybe she doesn't want to be alone with me after all. But then she smiles. It's a shy smile, but there's something seductive in it.

Losing my ability to remain cool, I blurt out, "I want to kiss you."

Her mouth drops open. She recovers quickly. "About that..." She straightens her posture. "I thought we could talk about the other night. Sort of check in." She's blushing, playing with her hair again.

I stare at her for a moment and hear strings. I vaguely remember I put some classical music on earlier. She stares back at me, and then we are scraping our chairs back, colliding in the middle of the room. Her mouth, her body. I can't get enough of her. The tension of the last few days, the last few months, it's been too much. I need to feel all of her.

"Ethan..." she whispers as I kiss down her neck, her hands grabbing fistfuls of my hair.

"Marin..." I respond, knowing we should talk, but the ability to think straight diminishes with every fervent kiss, every desperate touch.

"Ethan..." she says with force, pulling me out of my stupor. I press my forehead against hers.

"Marin..." I repeat, my breath heaving.

"I...we should talk..."

I kiss her cheeks and move to her ear. I swallow hard, my mouth going dry. "Let's talk."

She trembles. I'm thrilled to know I affect her as much as she does me.

"It's hard." She sighs.

I push against her. "It is."

"Ha!" She nudges me away playfully. "No, not that. I mean, yes, it is."

"You're cute when you're flustered." I move back into her neck, noting her moan as I kiss the place between her hairline and ear.

"Ethan. Give me a second."

I pull away. So reluctantly that it physically hurts. "Proceed."

"Things are blurry. Our worlds have blurred." Her lips purse.

"So, what I'm hearing is that it's all a blur?"

"You know what I mean, and I wanted to check back in with you. There's a lot at stake, and this..." She indicates the space between us. "This is complicated. It's not supposed to be real, but the other night..."

I lean in and whisper. "You want to know what my intentions are?"

"I guess, yes." She exhales so much so that her body shrinks from me.

"I intend to fuck you, Marin. I intend to make you come multiple times tonight. I intend to hear you scream my name."

She's red now, but she's biting her bottom lip. Before she can speak, I continue.

"Turns out I like the blurred worlds. I like you. A lot. And I'm tired of fighting it. I want you."

She tips her head up, looks me in the eyes. "I want you, too, but I don't want to get hurt, and..."

It's clear this admission is difficult for her. I am blown away by her willingness to admit that I could, in fact, hurt her. She's utterly, perfectly guileless, and I want to pull her in my arms and never let her go.

"Marin, the last thing I want to do is hurt you. Ever." I kiss her lips, chastely. A silent promise.

"I want to believe you, but..." She studies her shoes. I finish her thought for her.

"But I'm 'Ethan Reve.'" I can't help but let bitterness seep into my voice. "Listen, I get it. I wish I had made different decisions when I was younger. Hell, six months ago. As much as I want to, I can't go back in time. But please know that most of what you've seen in the media is an illusion. You more than anyone knows that the shit online isn't real. The publicity. The posts, the tweets, the photos. It's all fake. All of it is fake."

Marin takes a step back, hurt briefly washing over her face. But it's quickly replaced by detachment.

"Yes, it isn't real."

Fuck. I'm going to have to lay it on the line with her. "Except with you." I pull her towards me and lift her chin up so there can be nowhere else to look but in my eyes. "The other night. The date, afterwards...That wasn't fake for me. I want this to be what it is."

"And what is it?" she asks, her voice barely above a whisper. Her eyes big and expectant.

"Real," I press my forehead to hers. "It's real."

And then my lips meet hers.

She kisses me back. Tentatively. I pull away. I need to make sure she's with me. I need to hear her say she wants the same. I'm already in so deep, but I can maybe salvage some of my heart and dignity if the feeling isn't mutual. I pull back and look at her square in the face.

"Do you want this to be real?" I ask.

Her blue-gray eyes meet mine. A soft smile creeps on her face. "It already is."

And then she's all over me.

Chapter Forty-Seven

Marin

I come up for air after unleashing days of my pent-up sexual frustration through a deep, long, passionate kiss. Ethan's eyes narrow, and there's a wolfish quality to his features now. Sharp and intense. Before I can move in for more, Ethan picks me up by the waist and swings me into his arms.

"Where are we going?" I ask, laughing, my heart pounding.

"To my bed," he says as he kicks open his bedroom door and then gently lays me down. "A proper bed to bed you in." He nuzzles my neck. "Properly."

"Not too proper, I hope," I suggest, surprised by my own forwardness. He makes me feel like the sexiest woman alive, which makes me braver.

"Absolutely not." He takes off his T-shirt. I ogle his olive skin, his broad shoulders, the dark spray of hair on his chest, crawling toward the sculpted abs—a Greek god of a man.

I'm greedy to see more, but he, unfortunately, leaves his jeans on. He grabs my ankles and drags me down so I'm under him.

"This isn't fair." He tugs on my t-shirt, so I lift my arms as he pulls it off, throwing it away in one swift movement. I came prepared, just in case, wearing a lacy pink bra, which I see he appreciates. Wait until he finds my matching panties.

He gazes at my body beneath him and licks his lips. "Now the bottoms. I'll do mine, you do yours." I love how he tells me exactly what to do.

Trying not to appear like I'm in too much of a hurry, I smile and slowly unzip my jeans. He, on the other hand, stands before me in gray boxer briefs before I can blink.

Ethan lies next to me, caressing my hip, my side, my arm, until he cups my face.

"Just one more thing," he whispers.

"Yes." My voice sounds like a whine. I am done waiting.

"Are you sure about this?" His blue eyes meet mine, and I take a second to think about it, though I've already made up my mind.

"Absolutely," I say as I lightly scratch my nails down his back.

Ethan releases the breath he had been holding. "Thank god." He grins and then kisses me again, his tongue playing with mine, his hand reaching around to unclasp my bra.

"As much as I like looking at you in this bra, I need to feel you against me." He moves down, kissing my neck, and then my nipples, each getting equal attention. His knee parts my legs, and he moves down to kiss my inner thighs.

"So beautiful, Marin. You are so beautiful," he murmurs between kisses. "Inside and out."

He hooks his fingers and pulls my pretty panties down.

"Now, you," I whimper, desperate in a way I've never been before. There's an aching emptiness inside of me; I need him to fill me up.

He is standing again, next to the bed. He rolls his briefs down and I hop up on my knees, eager to see him, and before he can protest, I lick the length of him.

"Fuck, Marin." I put my mouth around him, and he moans. I have never really been into this before, but with Ethan, I just want more. He pulls my hair, forcing me back, "Not now. Now I need to be inside you."

I can only nod. He lifts me up, wraps my legs around his waist and lowers me back onto the bed. His hand moves down my stomach and rests between my legs.

"Are you ready for me?" His fingers find the answer.

"Yes," I cry as I move into his hand, raising my hips.

"Just a second." Ethan's arm reaches his side table, grabs a condom from a small drawer, and I watch as he rolls it on.

He seems to sense my hesitation, and cajoles, "I'll go slow... at first." On top of me now, he slowly sinks into me. There is some discomfort at first, but my body wants him and eases as he moves in waves, slow and sensual.

"Is that okay?" he asks, his neck muscles strained. I can see he's holding back.

"Yes, but I need you inside me." His eyes get darker. "All of you, Ethan." Then he gives me exactly what I want.

We spend the rest of the night in his room. Boom after boom after boom, and it is nothing short of spectacular.

Chapter Forty-Eight

Ethan

At dawn, I wake up. Marin sleeps like the dead, barely moving in the night, on her back, arms at her sides. She looks like a princess, waiting to be kissed. I decide to wake her up with one. Her eyes flutter open, and she yawns. It's early.

"Good morning," she says as she stretches. Damn it, I want her again.

"Good morning. How do you feel?" She rolls so we're facing each other.

"Tired, but satisfied." She grins conspiratorially. "How do *you* feel?"

"Ready for round four, but I figured I should give you a break."

"Maybe for a few hours." She kisses me and whispers, "Can I take a shower?"

"Only if I can help you."

She nods enthusiastically.

In the shower, I take my time, shampooing her hair and soaping her body. I rinse her off, then lick her clean until she screams my name. Her body flushed with heat, her eyelids heavy, she massages me until I come. Then she washes my body with so much care it aches.

When I go to shampoo my hair, she says, "Let me." I can't remember feeling so cared for. We dry each other off, giggling like kids, and I feel like I could take on the world with her at my side.

"Marin," I whisper and kiss her forehead.

"Yes?" she asks as she pushes back a hair from my forehead.

"I'm glad you stayed." I kiss her clavicle.

"Me too."

When she embraces me, I think, *This... This hug in my bathroom is the most intimate moment of my life.*

An alarm blares from my room, breaking the spell.

"I wish I could spend the day in bed with you, but we've got to get to work," I say, racing to my phone. "The lark, no nightingale..."

When I turn back around, Marin is pulling up her jeans, singing, "*Back to life, back to reality...*"

I could do this every morning of my life, I think. Then do a quick scroll on my phone.

Ernie texted this morning, checking on our progress. "*Almost there*," I text back.

~

Later that night in the turret, I set up a projector. Flora puts finishing touches on the concept art, a dreamy sea of greens, blues, and iridescent scales. Marin has proofread the proposal a million times. The numbers add up; the t's are crossed, and the i's are dotted. We did a run-through with our slides yesterday. Both Flora and Marin's eyes were glassy with tears when I finished. I am proud of the work we've done. Scared out of my mind, but proud.

Today, Marin and Flora work, and then tonight we steelman the proposal. Marin told us to come up with at least ten objections and opposing questions to anticipate at the meeting.

Tilda has not been in contact with me. The meeting time has not changed. My father hasn't summoned me.

As I walk Marin out, an eerie feeling overwhelms me.

It's quiet—too quiet—and I don't like it.

Chapter Forty-Nine

Marin

It's another meet-and-greet day with Roland and Rose Red. Prince Roland has been the consummate professional since our last discussion. When we take our breaks, he doesn't pry, but he does ask me lots of questions about myself. My favorite books, movies, songs. He asks about Vermont and my family.

Today is no different, but after hours on my feet and so little sleep, I'm not my bubbly self. Roland doesn't seem to mind, and I'm happy that we can move forward as friends.

I also can't stop thinking about Ethan. I see his face above me, his blue eyes piercing and intense with desire. I feel his hands on me, caressing my breasts, my stomach, his five-o'clock shadow scratching my skin pink. I hear his baritone voice: "It's real, Marin. It's real." I do my best to remain professional for the rest of my shift, but I can't wait to get out of this costume and back to Ethan's.

If someone had told me six months ago that I'd tell off my family, take a break from school, get paid to cosplay as Rose Red, work on a dream project, and moon over my sexy sleepover with Ethan Reve, I would have laughed until I passed out. But here I am. Beyond tired on my feet in the best way.

"Look, Mommy! It's Rose Red and Prince Roland!" A little girl drags her mother to the cottage where we've set up today. The sun is setting, and the sky is that perfect coral color for photographs. The girl is about ten and decked out head-to-toe in Rose Red regalia.

"Well, hello there, young lady," I say in my best Rose voice, which has become second nature to me. "What's your name?"

"I'm Ros-EE, but I'm not named after you. I'm named after my grandma, but sometimes, I tell people I'm named for you." Her brown eyes beam up at me, and I feel Roland stride over.

"Well, your secret is safe with us, Rosie." Roland winks at her. "Would you like a picture with us?"

Rosie simply stares for a few moments, takes in a huge breath, and then bellows, "MOM! CAN YOU TAKE A PICTURE OF US!?"

Roland and I bend down, maneuvering Rosie into the middle. The exhausted mother gives a thumbs up, snaps a few photos, and says, "Okay, Ro, it's time to go. The park is closing soon."

"Wait!" Rosie motions for Roland to lean down; he hunches over so she can whisper in his ear. I watch as a smile breaks over his face. He nods and says, "Rosie has a request."

Rosie runs back to her mom and says, "He's going to do it!"

Before I can figure out what "it" means, Roland grabs my hand, spins me towards him, dips me, and lays one on me. The infamous Roland twirl-dip-and-kiss.

"I got it, I got it!" Rosie screams, jumping up and down. "It's sooooo romantic!" Her mother finally pulls a reluctant but satisfied Rosie out of the village. Roland still has me in a dip when I hear her yell, "Bye, thanks!"

Roland slowly lifts me up, grinning the entire time.

I am speechless. Roland has never done this before. He has kissed my hands, pecked my cheek. While this was straight out of the last scene in the movie, it is definitely not protocol.

Once we're both standing, I try to find my voice.

"That was—" I stammer.

"Thanks for indulging little Rosie." He fixes his cape and beams at me. "Ready to call it a night?"

He holds out his arm, and I just nod, my body just going through the motions. A few months ago, I would have literally swooned if he pulled the Roland dip. Now, I am simply surprised and a bit uncomfortable.

During the walk back to my dressing room, I find my voice. "I don't think we're supposed to really kiss."

"Red, it was just acting. The kid was cute, and she said it was her 'totally and completely favorite part.' I had to do it." He looks down at me. "I didn't think it would rattle you so much." I detect a bit of a smirk on his handsome face.

"I'm not rattled per se, I just–" I struggle to articulate my thoughts. Roland slows down his pace and drops my arm. He looks me in the eye.

"It was a special treat for a cute kid. I couldn't say no. I won't do it again, okay? I didn't mean to cross a line." We've made it to the dressing room. He opens the door for me and gestures for me to enter. Once inside, I turn around, and he's right in front of me, his hand still at my waist.

"Do you forgive me?" His hazel eyes are expectant. His expression contrite.

"Sure. Just don't go Method actor on me, okay?" I exhale then let out a chuckle, wanting to dispel some tension.

He laughs a little, too. "As you wish."

He bows. I curtsey. It's become a sort of ritual between us. He leaves, and I fall onto a bench.

I went for years without being kissed by anybody, and now I'm being kissed by two hot men in one day.

Who am I?

Currently, I am someone who's making a big deal out of nothing. Roland was just acting. He's been nothing but professional this entire time, and that little girl was particularly cute. Maybe he just knows I'm with Ethan now, so it wouldn't mean anything to either of us.

My face heats up when I think about Ethan. I should tell him about the kiss, even if it was all an act. However, Ethan is not Roland's biggest fan, and he doesn't seem to get the castmate culture. He'll think the worst of the situation, and that could have possible repercussions for Roland. No, I'll keep this little misstep to myself.

Plus, I'm probably making a bigger deal out of this than I need to. Ethan doesn't need to know anything because nothing actually happened. It was fake.

What Ethan and I have is real, and the sooner I get out of this costume, the sooner I can get to him. The sooner we can make the *Island of Sirens* experience a reality.

Then we can get back to business in his big, comfy bed.

Chapter Fifty

Ethan

Flora, Marin, and I work later than usual. Flora spends the evening smiling knowingly at us. Subtlety is not her forte. Then again, neither is ours. When I say I'm going to fill Marin's wine glass for her and she follows me into the kitchen, we return ten minutes later, pink beard burns on her face from my stubble. When I brush a lock of hair out of Marin's eyes and tuck it behind her ear, Flora stops smiling and starts gagging.

"Okay, you guys are too gross. I can't even." Flora mimics puking profusely, then huffs to her feet and grabs her thirty billion bags. "I'm tapping out for the night. See you tomorrow, lovebirds!"

Alone at last, I think. Marin has seemed a bit frazzled all night. I know she needs a day off, but the proposal is right around the corner. I want her to stay the night, but I also want her to get a solid night's sleep and not run herself ragged.

"Why don't we go to bed early tonight? Try to get some sleep," I offer, trying not to sound too crestfallen.

Marin pouts. "Is that what you want?"

"No, I want to worship your body all night long, but you worked two jobs today, and I don't want to be selfish."

"Ethan Reve, you are not living up to your devil-may-care image right now." Some of her long hair falls out of a messy bun, and her Mona Moon T-shirt is just cropped enough that I can see her pale stomach. The shirt reminds me of our meet-cute in the fountain.

"Come here," I order, and she sways her lovely hips over to my chair. I pat my leg, and she sits on my lap. Her coconut rose scent envelopes me.

"Can I ask you a question?"

"You just did." She snuggles into me, and I am instantly ready to whisk her off to bed, but I'm curious about something.

"The night you pulled me out of the fountain..." I say as I kiss her neck. Just a taste before I look into her eyes.

"Yes?" She looks wary. "What about it?"

"I get the feeling that you haven't been completely honest with me about it."

"What do you mean?" She squirms, and I try not to let her ass on my thigh distract me.

"You blush whenever I bring it up." Pink already spreads across her cheeks. "Did anything else happen?"

"Um..." She readjusts again. Goddamn, the ass on this woman. She has no idea how sexy she is.

"Yes?"

Marin crosses her arms and blurts out, "We made out, okay?"

"Oh." I'm sad I don't remember Marin all wet in a corset. *Dear god.* "Is that all?"

Her mouth drops open. "What do you mean, 'Is that all?'" she cries, exasperated. "It was really hot!"

"Was it, now?"

She pushes me and tries to get up, but I wrap my arms around her waist.

"You don't even remember and that's embarrassing!" She won't look at me.

Genuinely confused by this reaction, I ask, "If I don't remember it, then why are you so embarrassed?"

"Because *you* don't remember, and it was more than just kissing. It was more...like sex!"

"But we didn't have sex, right?" Surely I would remember that, I hope.

"Of course not!" She tries to get up again, but I snuggle into her neck.

"Tell me all about it."

"No." She's sulking, limp in my arms.

"Please, it's not fair that you have this hot memory of me. Also, you basically took advantage of me. I should be the one who's upset."

She turns to face me. "What! You were all over me, asking me to 'please stay' with you, calling me your angel, or some other sappy nonsense about golden ambers."

"I don't know...sounds fishy." I smile, but it's my turn to feel embarrassed. God, I was such a mess that night.

"You're making fun of me? I can't believe I made out with such a jerk!"

"Such an irresistible jerk, you mean."

She pushes my shoulder, and I grab her arm, pulling her into me. "It's not every day a Revel princess saves a drunk idiot and makes out with him in the middle of the park."

"You didn't even know it was me. I could have been anyone," she whispers back, a sadness in her voice.

I put my hand under her chin, forcing her to look at me. "I knew it was you, Marin."

"Sure you did. You were drunk as a skunk."

I wince. "Seriously, I may not have been fully aware of what I was doing, but I knew it was you."

Her eyes peer into mine, skeptical. "How?"

"I called you an angel. I mentioned glowing embers, not amber." Her eyes flare with recognition. "That's how I know it was you."

"Lots of people call lots of people 'angel,' Ethan."

"No, not me. I remember seeing you before. Had to be in January. Do you remember? It wasn't my finest hour."

Marin straddles me on the chair. I'll remember this position for later, but now she needs to know I was thinking of her even in my drunken stupor.

"You mean, the night you were retching in the bushes?" she asks. "I thought you didn't remember me."

"I did. I remember thinking you were going to take a picture of me, sell it to the highest bidder. But instead you just seemed concerned. The sun was setting, and I couldn't really see your face, but your hair was like a halo. It made me think of the way a fire looks when it's close to being out, golden embers..." I let her hair down. "A halo of glowing embers. Like an angel."

"Oh." She seems thoughtful. "Why, Ethan?"

"Why what?" I ask as I run my fingers through her hair. So grateful to have her in my lap. To have her in my life.

"Why were you doing that to yourself?" Her brow knits together.

"Ah, the million-dollar question." I don't want to talk about this, about all of the ways I'm deficient. I don't want to ruin whatever is growing between us.

"You don't have to talk to me about it, but..." She pulls away, and that's the last thing I want. "It's not a big–"

I cut her off. I sigh with my whole body, letting long-held tension release, and decide to not let her go. "Yes, I do have to talk about it. You saved my life. If I owe anyone an explanation, it's you." I shift, uncomfortably. This is going to take a while. "Come with me?"

Her brow raises skeptically. I smile.

"I'm serious. If you keep squirming around on me, I will have to ravish you right here, and I'll forget about everything else." I stand, picking her up with me. "Let's go to bed, and I'll tell you a story."

Chapter Fifty-One

Marin

After he throws me on the bed, I demand we take care of business before we get comfortable under the covers. We brush our teeth next to one another in his marble bathroom. I can't stop looking at him, his square jaw, rough with black stubble, his white teeth, his perfect lips. He's wearing gray pajama pants. I'm wearing one of his gray tees, our own Billy Wilder meet-cute outfit. I eye his bare chest.

He catches me checking him out in the mirror and wiggles his eyebrows suggestively, which causes me to burst out laughing. Unfortunately, I still have toothpaste in my mouth. It goes everywhere, including the mirror. Ethan starts laughing but has enough control to spit in the sink first.

"You're such a dork," he says as he kisses me, our minty fresh breath mingling. "I'll clean this up later." He picks me up again, and I wrap my legs around his waist while he keeps kissing me.

Cozy in his crisp, cool sheets, Ethan lies on his side, facing me, cradling his cheek in his hand.

"Okay, bedtime story." He exhales as he rolls on his back and stares up at the ceiling. Clearly, this won't be an easy conversation. I am curious though. Curious and concerned.

"I've been lost. I could say since Wade's death, but that wouldn't be honest, and I want to be honest with you." He rolls onto his side, so we are facing one another again, our heads so close together it's hard to focus my eyes on him.

"Wade was my best friend. He was the best everything, actually. He could do anything he put his mind to, and he had this way of making people feel like the best versions of themselves. My dad pushed us hard, and it never fazed Wade." He looks down and plays with a thread on my sleeve, his mind seemingly back to some memory of his brother.

"But it fazed you?" I surmise gently.

"Yeah, you could say that. Nothing is ever good enough for my father. His standards are so high for us kids that he can't see us as individuals. Wade and I got the brunt of it, but Wade could talk sense into our dad. Wade had Dad's respect because he didn't care what he thought, but I wanted the man to like me. I wanted his approval, so I'd never get it."

I find his hand in the sheets and grasp it. Ethan brings it to his lips and kisses.

"When I got older, I got resentful. Furious. I saw the way he treated James and Henri, too. The same distant way he was with us. We were an occasional obligation. In some ways James and Henri had it worse. They weren't a priority for their mom, Tilda, either. And then Yasmin and Elsie and Dom came along, and Dad changed. He became an entirely different person with them. An actual father. He went to basketball games and dance recitals, bragged about them. He had pet names for them. He seemed like he actually loved Dom and Elsie."

"Ouch." My heart aches for young Ethan, as well as this Ethan next to me. I understand, on a visceral level, what it feels like to be less-than in a family. My stomach muscles tense up, but I try to relax and be here for him.

"Yeah, the kids were adorable. I love the Little Angels, but—"

"The Little Angels?" I ask.

"Each pair of siblings have different nicknames. Wade and I are the Bambinos because my mom's name was Bambi. James and Henri are the Pride & Joy, ironically, and Dom and Elsie are the Little Angels."

I smile. I am aware of the family tree already, but I've never heard about these private nicknames.

"Cute." I poke him in the ribs. "So you do call other people angel?"

"I guess so, but the Little Angels moniker was initially a dig, not affectionate. It also helped us keep track of Dad's wives and progeny."

Ethan brings my hand to his heart.

"Anyway, I left for school. I've always loved math and wanted to pursue an advanced degree, but Dad thought it was useless, so I studied finance instead. I interned at Goldman Sachs right out of college and landed a position there. I hated it, but I was good at it. I made my own money and invested well, so I quit after a few years. Good timing, too, right before the recession. I called to tell Dad that I quit and was going to stay in New York, and he and Revel could go fuck themselves. That was when the attacks started happening."

"Attacks?"

"Panic attacks. The first one I had, I swear, I thought I was dying, like having a massive heart attack. I would have gone to the emergency room if it weren't for my last name. I was partying pretty hard earlier that night, and I knew I'd be another gossip headline the next day if I was tested and treated. I just figured I was having an adverse reaction to something I'd taken."

Ethan takes a deep breath, probably remembering, regretting, before he goes on. "The partying kicked into high gear after that. I started dating Bree Brooklyn and surrounding myself with idiots who were even bigger fuck-ups than me. The attacks eased off, but when I had one, I self-medicated with bourbon, vodka, anything I could get my hands on, really."

"Did you ever think about getting help?" I ask timidly, afraid I might be insulting him.

"Sometimes. It just felt like admitting I needed help was admitting I couldn't hack it on my own." He rolls onto his back again, bringing me with him to lie in the crook of his arm. "Plus, at that stage in my life, I didn't have responsibilities. Obviously, that was part of the problem. I'm privileged in so many ways, what the fuck do I have to complain about?"

"Having an overbearing yet distant father, your personal life scrutinized by millions, a lack of direction," I say. "Sounds like the good life."

"Well, when you put it like that..." Ethan pauses for a long time. His chest heaves and retracts with a few long, deep breaths. I can feel his healthy heartbeat, and I'm glad he seems to have stopped abusing his body.

"I was pissing away my privilege and pissing off Dad," he goes on. "No one had expectations of me anymore, and I thought that would make me happy. I was starting to get restless though. Wanted to make a change, was looking into grad schools, then Wade..." Ethan's voice cracks.

I rub his chest for a moment, listening to his heart rhythm race. "You don't have to go on if it's too hard."

"No. I do." Ethan clears his throat. "I need to stop avoiding all of this. I've spent years of my life dicking around. So, I'm going to finish this story." I feel his jaw clench on top of my head. "I need you to understand this about me."

"All right." I stretch my neck, reaching to leave a kiss on his collar bone. "Go on."

"Wade signed up for the Marines without telling a soul. He changed a lot—pulling away from everyone, dropping weight, keeping strange hours. When I finally asked him what was up, he told me he'd enlisted. Said, 'I want to do my part.' He lost a high-school buddy in Iraq and decided to join. He always had a fascination with service. Loved our PawPaw's World War II stories. Dad was furious. He had a rough time in Vietnam. But I think it was more about the business. Wade was being groomed to take over Revel one day, and his altruism was fucking up the timeline."

"He was probably scared for Wade, too," I whisper.

"Sure, but it's hard to tell which he was more upset about—Gaspard Reve's ultimate business plan or his first-born son going to war." Ethan's arm muscles tense around me. I rub his chest again, letting him know he doesn't have to keep reliving this right now.

"As you know, the last thing Wade worked on before he was shipped off was the *Island of Sirens* proposal. He even told me about it, which was sort of unusual because he knew I didn't care about Revel business back then. You know, I barely paid attention. I was also still mad at him for leaving. I was so wrapped up in myself that I didn't spend enough time with him. Didn't tell him..." Ethan breaks off, overwhelmed.

"Sshh, shhh, it's okay," I squeeze him, wrapping my arms around his middle, feeling his ribcage vibrating now against my cheek.

"It's not okay. When you saw me that first time, puking in the bushes, I was thinking about Wade's funeral. I had shown up to the service blitzed out of my mind. Dad was furious. Told me that the wrong son was in the ground."

"Oh, god. Ethan, I'm so sorry." I want to take his pain away.

"The thing is, he's not wrong. Wade was better than me in every conceivable way." His voice is so matter-of-fact that it makes me furious with the man who would say such a thing to his son. "Dad had a stroke a few weeks later. The stress of it all. I'm sure I contributed to it, and..."

I can't think of anything to soothe him. To make him feel better. I rub his chest lightly.

"So, every time I thought about Dad's words, I had another panic attack and tried to drink it away. You saw the results of that. Several times. I was walking around this place, and all of these memories of Wade and me and PawPaw kept surfacing. PawPaw used to take us to Mona Moon Lighthouse when we were little and told us to make wishes. I guess I ended up there because I wished to make Wade proud. I wished to be better for him." He stops, and I think he might be crying because he reaches up with his free hand to press his eyes. "And if it wasn't for you, Marin, I might be in the ground, too."

We are both silent for a moment, letting the gravity of his statement sink in. Our breaths sync in the quiet.

"I'm glad you aren't," I whisper.

"What?"

"Dead."

He's silent for a beat and then bursts out laughing. It's infectious. We're both holding our stomachs, completely overtaken by the absurdity of that statement, the truth of it, and laughing away the pent-up tension of the whole story, of his trauma, of what could have been.

"I'm glad I'm not dead, too." He wipes tears from his eyes.

"Good," I say.

"Yes, excellent," he replies.

"Quite," I assert.

"Indeed," he concurs.

And I don't know how it happens, but I'm on top of him and we're kissing manically, like this is the last time. His fingers grip my ass, and I grind into him while he pushes his hips into me.

"Ethan, I need you."

He throws me onto my back and pulls my shirt off. In seconds, we're panting and naked.

"Marin, you have me." He almost growls. Then he enters me slowly, and the frenzy of overwhelming feeling blurs any thought. We do not take our time, climaxing together. I feel somehow both disembodied, and more in my body than ever before.

I'm so content and so tired from the day and the revelations that I struggle to keep my eyes open. The last thing I hear before drifting off is "Goodnight, angel."

Chapter Fifty-Two

Ethan

I'm standing alone at the future location of the *Island of Sirens* experience, waiting for Ernie Guidry to join me. Though now there's only a levee of tall grass where starlings dip for bugs, I can picture what Marin and I have been developing for weeks now. This is where Wade imagined the location. It's perfectly situated, on the water, on the outskirts of the park, far enough away from where the cruise lines disembark, that it feels isolated. There's a walking path that meanders with the Mississippi and a few benches that face the water. I take a seat and watch the river in all its glory. A single freighter grows on the horizon down-river. Usually the river's a churning brown beast, but today it has a calmer, gray-blue cast.

Like Marin's eyes, I think. Then I smile to myself, knowing I've got it bad for this girl. And how much I have changed in just the short time I've known her. How much I want this project to succeed, not just for Wade anymore, but for her. I want to help her hard work and dream become a reality.

She's spent every night with me for the last week, as a real couple. The more I learn about her, the more I like. Conscientious and considerate—two traits that have never been top of my must-haves in a romantic partner, but I appreciate the hell out of them in her. Marin turns off the lights when she leaves the room, she picks up after herself, and whenever she goes into the kitchen, she asks if I need anything. Kindness personified.

A ball of kinetic energy, her eyes spring open in the morning. It's like Marin's part fish; she needs to move constantly to breathe. The only time she sits still is when we're working or watching a Revel movie. She thinks it's a *travesty*, her word, that I haven't seen most Revel movies. We've only watched two, however, because I can't sit next to her for more than twenty minutes without touching her.

Touching leads to more touching, which results in taking four hours to watch a 90-minute movie.

Like me, she runs to think, so we ran together a few mornings. Although one morning she asked me to slather SPF lotion on her back and shoulders, as it's been sunny and warm recently. I got distracted by how amazing her ass looked in her running shorts, and we ended up working out horizontally on my couch.

An "ahem" tears me from my daydream. Ernie is standing by the bench. I've asked him to meet me here to talk logistics. Also, I'd love to pick his brain about Tilda and Gaspard. Their radio silence is freaking me out.

"Ernie, thanks for making it." I stand up, and we shake hands.

"Of course, kid. I haven't been over here in a while. It's pretty and quiet." He turns and surveys the land, the grasses rippling in the wind and the giant river. "This is what you had in mind for the new experience?"

"Yes, luckily for us, Wade had this location picked out already, but I wanted to run it by you. See if there would be any logistical issues Wade overlooked."

Ernie nods his head and says, "Tell me what you're thinking."

We spend the better part of an hour talking shop, mostly about water, flooding, electrical, and cable networking. I take notes in a small Moleskine notebook.

"It won't be a walk in the park; it'll take some serious elbow grease and some innovation, but we're in the business of building worlds." Ernie's face is determined. "That's exactly what we've been doing at Revel for over fifty years."

I smile into the morning sun, struck by the pride I feel in his words. Proud to be a part of this family, this place, this world for the first time since I was just a kid.

Ernie sits down on the bench. "Gotta rest my gams a minute."

I sit next to him. We're both quiet for a moment. Taking it all in.

"Your PawPaw is proud a'you."

I don't know what to say. I haven't seen the man in months. He never leaves his damn cottage.

"Does he know what's going on?" I ask, trying to keep my resentment at bay.

"Of course. He keeps an eye on everything," Ernie says matter-of-factly.

"You talk to him?" I ask. Curious. Ashamed that I haven't.

"Yep, not as often as I'd like, but I went up to the cottage to bother the old grump a few days ago."

"Oh." I cross my arms. Not sure how to feel that this man has more access to my grandfather than I do.

"You know, you can do the same. Don't have to wait for an invitation," Ernie says. "Just go on over."

"He hasn't been around much the past few years." Well, not in the last decade or so. Not that I can blame him.

Ernie snickers a bit. "He's not much of a talker, always in that head of his. Since Marie...well, you know." He rubs his hands up and down his pant legs like he's dealing with a little pain. Well, the man is definitely past a dignified retirement age.

"Yeah," I sigh. Their romance was legendary. He was the dreamer, and she kept him grounded, tethered to reality, to us. Without her, Revel Pointe would have just been pie in the sky.

"I showed him a few pictures of you and Marin on a jog. It was on some website." Ernie says *website* like it's a dirty word. "Those paparazzi are really giving you the once-over."

I haven't checked on our "PR campaign" lately. I stopped caring about appearing like a couple for the public when we actually became one. Not sure that's smart, but it seems to be working without my machinations.

Ernie continued, "I told Mick all about how she came to that meeting, too. How she took Tilda on. Fought for you and Wade's project."

Wow. Now I'm really curious. "What did PawPaw say about that?"

"He said, 'Though she be but little, she is fierce.' Apparently, that's a quote from something. I don't know. I'm more of a math guy."

"Me too, but if it's PawPaw, that's Shakespeare." I take out the notebook and write the quote down. I think it's *Midsummer*. Dad said PawPaw's quoting Shakespeare all the time was an affectation because PawPaw never went to college. I call bullshit. PawPaw's affection for the Bard is sincere.

"I told Mick you were working hard, trying to do right by Wade. Told him about Tilda and Gaspard's vision. Apparently, he already knew all about it."

"How?" I still find it hard to believe he cares enough to keep tabs on the park and us.

"Like I said, he's got eyes all over this park. It's his legacy. He may have stepped down, but he hasn't stepped out." Ernie stands and stretches his bulky frame.

I join him, heading back the way we both came down the levee. "Any news on Tilda and Gaspard? Haven't heard from them in a while."

Ernie shakes his head. "They're being mighty quiet. Yasmin has Gaspard on a tight leash still, although he's taking some calls and meetings despite her griping. And Tilda's been in and out of town quite a bit. She just got back from New York. Some sort of big meeting... she was real hush-hush about it."

Three brown pelicans crest a stand of trees across the river and dip low before soaring overhead. They capture our attention until they're out of sight.

My mind hasn't left my Tilda inquisition. "A big meeting? Interesting." What is that woman doing? I imagine her as a witch in her lair, surrounded by Louboutin heels and piles of money, concocting poisonous potions and preparing to strike.

"'Let him who desires peace prepare for war,'" Ernie quotes solemnly.

I raise my brows. "Who said that?"

"Some Roman general." He shrugs. "Vegetius, I think."

"I thought you said you didn't read much." I slap him on the back, and we continue as the park comes back into view—the tops of the lighthouse, coasters, and Thumbelina's Ferris wheel, gracing the swampy skyline.

"I read history. No poetry or novels and such," he says, his tone indicating his disdain for fiction. "Anyway, I gotta run. Vangie says hello and wants you two to come over for étouffée soon!"

"Will do." We shake hands. "Thanks, Ernie." I feel grateful to have such a good man on our side. I watch him hop in his white Ford F150 and turn onto the gravel service road back to the main byway.

I take it all in one more time before heading home to Marin.

I stop in my tracks. *Home to Marin.*

This is moving so fast. So many feelings, so soon. I can't think about it too much, but a dark thought bursts open. *What is she doing with me?* I'm a mess, and she's perfect.

I wish I could call Wade and talk about it. I can't though. The only thing I can do is go with this momentum and make this proposal so good that no one in their right mind could reject it.

For Wade. For Marin.

Chapter Fifty-Three

Marin

"How do both Hansel and Gretel's costumes lose most of their buttons at least once a week?" I ask, sitting in Flora's office, sewing gold buttons back onto vaguely German, 18th century lederhosen-esque jumpsuits.

Flora's smile is wicked. "You know they're a thing, right?"

"Hansel and Gretel?!" I can't help but shriek. The two cast members are in their early twenties, 5'5 and 4'11 respectively. "They play brother and sister!"

"Not off the clock." Flora laughs as she laces Lana's intricate corset. "Off the clock, they screw like horny Grimm's Brother bunnies."

I survey the piles of costumes that require attention. Between our work on *Sirens* at night, the day-to-day maintenance, and Marta's mock-ups for "her" new designs, Flora has been spinning all the plates. Technically, this is my day off, but my bestie needs help, so I'm here.

Flora knows how to make everything a party, so we are sipping ridiculously large Mississippi Mud iced coffees and oscillating between the *Island of Sirens* and *Princess and the Pea* soundtracks on repeat.

We've been at it all morning. My fingers are starting to cramp. "How do you do this without having gnarly claw hands by the end of the day?"

"Practice, silly." Flora grabs another costume. It's Roland's red cape.

"What's wrong with Roland's cape?" I ask as I stand to stretch my back.

"The collar needs starching." She goes to the small ironing board hooked up in the corner next to a steamer and a Singer sewing machine.

I haven't told Flora about Roland kissing me. Roland and I have worked together since then, and it's been completely professional, so the twirl-dip-and-kiss seemed like an outlier. In fact, he's continued to really make an effort to get to know me during our breaks. I've learned about him as well. Except his real name, strangely. Maybe I wanted to keep it fake, keep it safe.

His childhood seemed idyllic. His dad is a mechanic and his mom a first-grade teacher. He lettered in three sports in high school, went to business school, but fell in love with acting after dating someone in the theater department. His parents are supportive, and he is close to his brother, Jonathan, who is much older than him and has recently come out of the closet. "It's like I have three parents," he quipped. He complained that money has always been tight, but his loving, supportive family sounded like a dream to me.

I have caught Roland checking me out a few times, but overall he's been great, and I don't want to make a big deal out of nothing, especially if the twirl-dip-and-kiss could hurt him.

Flora interrupts my reverie. "Earth to Marin."

"Sorry, completely spaced out." I grab a sip of my iced coffee and turn to face her. "What were you saying?"

"I was asking about you and Ethan."

"Oh," I smile. "It's...he's...well, he's meeting with Ernie at the location Wade scouted. I've run by there before, and it's perfect—"

"No, Mare. I mean how *are* you guys, you know, romance-wise?" Flora wiggles her eyebrows and humps the air.

"Oh my god, you are such a perv." I pass Flora's drink over to her and then take a break, curling up on the couch.

"A curious perv." She leans away from the cape, takes a sip, and places her fist under her chin. "Do tell," she says in a posh English accent.

"It's amazing." I struggle to find words to encompass all that I feel.

"Well, duh. The chemistry between you two is pal-pa-ble."

"I can't not touch him." The familiar heat rushes to my face when I think about him, his body, his everything.

"Well, he seems smitten." Flora's smiling as she hangs Roland's cape. "How do you feel?"

"I'm also smitten, which is scary."

"Scary?" Flora says as she grabs a wig and a brush. The wig is pure white, so it must be for Princess Portia.

"Terrifying. I'm so out of my depth, Flor. He's beautiful, smart, sophisticated, and has way more experience than I do."

"Honey, that doesn't matter." Flora's eyes flash sympathetically. She leans against her dressing table, brushing out the wig, then placing it on a head to redo the complicated plaiting.

"I mean, I know he likes me a lot. He explained why I had to pull him out of a fountain a few months ago." I take a breath. "But he's still 'Ethan Reve.' When I forget that he's American royalty, then I'm fine."

"I sense a 'but' in there somewhere."

"But... it's hard to forget." To have something to look at and focus on, I get back to work. I find black thread and work on sewing a tail onto a zebra costume. "I don't know what will happen if the proposal isn't approved. And I don't know what will happen with us if it is. Is this a blip in Ethan's life? Am I just a supporting character in his story?"

"You're definitely not just a supporting character. You're the swashbuckling heroine." She throws a thimble at me, which I catch. We're both surprised at my sporty reflex. "Plus, he seems so different from his persona. I definitely didn't love the guy at first, but I think I'm guilty of judging him through the lens of celebrity gossip. Plus, I may be a wee bit of a class warrior..."

"Yeah, you've been known to rail against the system a few times," I tease.

One of the few criticisms Flora has about Revel is its corporate pay structure. They do value creatives, but it seems like Gaspard and Tilda have no qualms about the shareholders earning fatter and fatter profits, while the lifeblood of the park, the public-facing workers, have stagnant salaries, year after year.

Flora laughs. "But I love how dedicated he is to the *Sirens* project and how he treats you, so I'm definitely Team Ethan now."

"As opposed to?" I ask.

"Team Roland," she says as if that was obvious.

I flick my hand at her. "Oh, well, you don't have to worry about that. Me and Roland, we're just friends." I look down at my lap. So much sewing to do.

"Mmm-hmm." She isn't buying it.

"What?" I feign innocence.

She smirks. "He'd like you to be more than friends."

"No, he knows all about Ethan, and he's been very respectful."

Except for that one kiss, I think, but let it go.

"Marin, remember what I said, for some guys, competition is like gasoline on fire."

"Argh." I slump and finish pinning the tail to the zebra.

"Don't argh me." Flora throws a button at me this time. "Flora knows all."

"Okay, okay," I laugh and throw the button back at her but miss by a foot. So much for my sporty moment.

My phone beeps, and I still. Flora notices.

"What? Is it Prince Ethan?" She says in a sickly-sweet, Rose Red voice.

"No," I reply, stunned with fear. "It's my sister, Arista."

The message reads: *What the ever-loving hell?*

Below the text is the picture of Ethan kissing my hand in the RP Lounge. Before I can reply, Arista sends three more messages.

My research assistant shared this with me.

Another picture of us in La Provence.

Do you know how embarrassing this is for us?

Below this is a headline: "Mixing Work with Pleasure? Who Is Marin Vandersee?"

I thought you at least had some real goals, but Ethan Reve's new fucktoy? This is a new low. Try to get ahead in life without putting out, Marin.

My stomach drops through the floor. I feel like I've been punched.

Flora grabs the phone and reads.

"What a bitch!" She seethes while she paces the cramped room.

I don't feel angry. I don't feel anything. My mind sort of hovers above my body, detaching completely. This is what I do when it comes to my family. This is how I manage. Some people fight, some people flee. I disassociate.

"It's fine," I say, picking up the black thread and looking around for something to sew.

I can feel Flora stare at me before speaking in her uber-heated voice. "No. It is *not* fine."

I shrug. "It's just Arista being Arista. I'm used to it. Also, I probably should have told them. I just didn't think to. I was so wrapped up in the project and Ethan. She's just shocked. I mean, it is shocking. And my family, they are pretty private people. To them, the only good publicity is an article in a peer-reviewed journal or a fellowship announcement, not a tell-all blog post."

Flora remains silent, but I can feel her watching me as I sort through a nearby pile of Lycra.

I reach for my phone. "I'll text her back and apologize."

Flora steps back. "No, you fucking won't."

"Flora!" I yelp, surprised.

"That's abuse, Marin! You don't apologize to your abuser!" She says between her teeth.

I shake my head. "That is not abuse. We're sisters, we fight."

"No, that is not normal sisterly fighting. It is unacceptable behavior. And what is really freaking me out is how you don't seem to see it that way."

I stand up and turn away, busying myself with a wig. Flora is not letting me ignore this, and I want to ignore this. She's pulling me back into myself. Pulling me down like a string on a balloon that just wants to float away.

I turn back. "Give me my phone." I reach out my hand expectantly.

"No. I can't in good conscience let you apologize to *her* for calling you a slut." Flora crosses her arms, holding the phone.

"She didn't call me a slut." I sound whiny, which makes me madder.

"She did, Mare." Her voice is gentle. "A normal sister would be curious about her sister's life. She would know that you would never, in a million years, be some guy's fucktoy. A good sister would not shit on you and every decision you make. Also, how are they just now learning about this? Are they so far up their own asses that they haven't called you in months?"

"Flora–" My voice ticks up, impatient.

She puts a hand up. "No. I love you, and I need you to see that your family may not have *physically* abused you, and though they may have provided for you, fed and clothed you, you have been *neglected* and made to feel less-than your whole life."

I sigh. "What do you want me to do about it?"

"I want you to fight back!" Flora shouts. Two tears stream down her cheeks. Frustration tears. She's feeling for me, but I'm numb.

"May I please have my phone back?" I hold out my hand again.

She waits a beat, then resigned, hands it over.

"Thanks," I mutter. Then I open up my text messages and type: *Sorry that I didn't talk to you about this sooner. It's been crazy the past few months.*

When I look up, Flora is still watching me. Her expression dejected.

"Does Ethan know?" she whispers.

"Know what?" My phone beeps again.

Another message: *Just think about how this looks for the rest of us who actually want to be taken seriously.*

"Know about your family. About how they treat you?"

"No." My tone is matter-of-fact. "We haven't talked about it."

"So you know all his trauma, his deep, dark secrets, and he knows diddly-squat about you." Her arms cross.

I say nothing. Just avert my gaze.

"You've got to reciprocate." Her eyes are welling up again, and I can't stand how she's looking at me. "Tell him about your family."

"That's the last thing I want to do." I enunciate every word.

"But you said he's shared with you—"

"Yes!" I interrupt. "And I get to be the capable Marin with him, the smart Marin, the desirable Marin, his goddamn angel!"

I throw the sewing on the ironing board. My phone beeps again, but I shove it in my pocket.

"But you aren't an angel. You're an amazing, generous, kind person, but you're not actually a Revel princess; you're not some perfect angel saving his life and his project. You're a real person who has some baggage, too."

"Gee, thanks." Sarcasm drips from my mouth.

"I don't mean that you aren't–"

"No, I get it. I'm damaged. I'm broken. A neglected, dyslexic ginger who doesn't know what's best for her. Is that right?" I am being unfair, but it's like I'm possessed. I can't stop this flood of words and feelings.

"You're putting words in my mouth–" She steps towards me.

I step back. "Why are you even friends with me? If I'm so delusional?" My voice is flat again, like I'm floating above myself, watching myself attack Flora.

She recoils as if I've hit her. "You're not delusional. But you need to be real with Ethan, and your family, and most importantly, yourself." Her voice lowers. "You're my best friend, and I hate to see you hurt."

"Well, *you're* hurting me." My tone is accusatory. "I just want to be happy, to be a part of this." I gesture around the room, but I mean Revel in general. I mean Ethan. "Part of this whole world. I want to feel like I'm worth something."

Flora grabs my hands. "You *are* worth something. *You*. Not some idealized version of you."

"I have to go," I interject, moving towards the door.

"Okay, but–" Flora wipes a tear from her cheek. "Marin–"

"We only have the weekend to do finishing touches on *Sirens*." I stop and turn back. "Your designs are perfect. We'll do a full run-through tomorrow night."

"I–" Flora moves towards me again.

"I'm sorry. I just have to go." I close the door behind me.

My phone beeps again. It's Ethan this time.

The meeting with Ernie went well. I'll see you in a few hours. A few seconds later: *Can't wait.*

I "like" his last message and put the phone in my pocket.

Now I need some time to think.

Chapter Fifty-Four

Ethan

Dinner is waiting in the turret—a Margherita pizza, Caesar salad, and bottle of Chianti. I light white votive candles in the center of the mahogany table and shake my head at this man I've become. Never once have I set the table for my date, let alone shared this much of my life. When Marin walks through the door, there's a noticeable tightness in her features. Red rims her eyes. Her lips seem pursed in a reserved way.

"What's wrong?" I ask.

"Nothing." She drops her bag, sort of hiding her face from me. "Just tired."

"Bullshit. What's going on?" I move to her, attempting to squelch the need to fix everything.

"Seriously, I'm fine." She smiles, but I notice how it doesn't reach her eyes.

"Do I need to kill someone?" I wrap my arms around her, my hand holding the back of her head.

She snorts. "No. Just a long day."

I kiss her forehead, then lead her to the dining room table. "Liar."

"We'll talk after dinner."

As we eat the mouth-watering, wood-stove pizza, Marin asks about my day, for specific details about Ernie's thoughts on the site, about last-minute changes we need to make to the proposal. I feel her deflecting, trying to engross herself in the work and keep the subject off anything personal. After her last bites, she stacks the plates, readying to bring them down to the kitchen.

"Stop." I grab her plate and utensils and place them back on the table. She stares off into space. Something happened today. I take the nearest seat and try to pull her into my lap, but her body language is stiff. I grab her hand, standing close to her again.

"I can feel something's off. What happened earlier?" I wait for her to volley. "I'm right, right?"

She sighs and takes a sip of wine, another diversion.

I continue. "Come on. It's just me." I place my hand on my chest, trying physically to recall how I poured my heart out to her. "What's wrong?"

"Flora and I had a fight." Her voice is detached. "We'll get over it. Everything will go smoothly on Monday. It's just a bit of drama. Nerves, probably." She throws a hand in the air and rolls her eyes as if it's nothing serious.

"Are you nervous?" I ask. She always seems so sure of herself, so sure of the project, so sure it's the right path.

"About the proposal?" She shakes her head. "I mean, a little, but I think it's brilliant. I think we'll kill it on Monday, and then it's up to the board to see the light."

"Then what's going on?" I ask again.

"I'd rather not talk about it." Her mouth forms a determined, thin line.

"Well, I want you to." I'm getting frustrated. I crack my knuckles.

"Well, I don't." She huffs, crossing her arms.

"Okay, you've forced my hand. I've told you all about me and my neurosis and family drama," I say archly. "Turnabout's fair play."

She is quiet, glaring at me. Then her eyes well up.

"That's what Flora said," she says, then bursts into tears. I sit before her, pulling her down into my arms.

She cries for a few moments, then mumbles, "I'm so sorry, I didn't mean to get so weepy. Let me go, please." She pushes me back then retreats to the Rose Red window, overlooking the park.

Wanting so desperately to follow her, to fix whatever is causing pain, I force myself to give her space and move to the fireplace. Why did Flora talk to Marin about sharing something with me? What have I missed? I've been so wrapped up in work and my own shit. Did I miss something? A ding goes off in my pocket, but I ignore it, wanting to be present for her.

A few moments later, she turns around, her eyes red-rimmed and glassy.

"Come here," I say, taking a spot on the loveseat and patting the cushion next to me. She crosses the room, but plops in the chair across from me.

"I need to tell you something." Her tone is solemn, resigned.

Oh, shit. She's breaking up with me. My mind starts to tailspin. I keep myself sorted, lean in slightly, and focus on her instead of the creeping panic.

"What's going on?" A hitch in my voice betrays my concern. I hand her a box of tissues from the side table.

"I-I-I'm not perfect, Ethan." She exhales then blows her nose. "That's what Flora wants me to tell you."

Huh? Marin is perfect. To me, anyway. But it's strange that she thinks I need to hear this.

"Did you kill a man in Reno?" I joke.

"Ha! No." She chuckles. "Nothing like that."

"Did you traffic illegal drugs and weapons for the mob?"

"No!" She's laugh-crying now.

"Did you blow up a bus of orphans and puppies?"

She throws a pillow at me. "Of course not. I just had a shitty childhood."

Her eyes grow wide like she's surprised by her own admission.

"Oh." I pause, not sure what to do with this information.

"Yeah, and I got a text from one of my sisters today. I haven't talked to my family in months, and they just found out about us dating."

Even with my dysfunctional family, I do talk to my brothers and sister often. Some more than others. At the very least, we text. Whether I want to share or not, I have them. I know they have my back, and that's everything in this weird family that is itself a business.

"Why haven't you talked to your family in months?" I whisper, concerned that if I speak loudly, she'll shut down again.

"Well...it's complicated, but I'm the black sheep of the family."

"And you thought I wouldn't understand that?" I try not to sound surprised.

"No, no, no. It's..." She struggles to find words.

"Complicated." I nod. "I get that."

"Yes. My sister Arista accused me of sleeping with you to get ahead. She told me I was an embarrassment to the family." Her head drops, and she fiddles with her tissue.

"Well, it's clear your sister is a raging bitch," I seethe.

"That's what Flora said. She said I should tell her off."

"And did you?" I'm irate on her behalf. I want to call the harpy myself.

"No." Her voice grows meek. "I apologized."

"What the hell." I stand. "Why would you do that?"

She recoils. "Because I'm messed up. Flora said I was neglected and emotionally abused my whole life."

"Were you?" Keeping my voice down is becoming harder. I grab the fireplace mantel, steadying myself. It feels awkward, so I sit back down, on my hands.

"I don't know. I don't like those words, but I have never been good enough for my family. They are all these uber achievers. Top of the class, celebrated intellects. And I have a learning disability, which they told me never to admit. No one even acknowledged it until an English teacher in high school noticed I had problems reading and worked with me." She shakes her head in frustration. "They hate that I went to a state school. They hate that I'm in business. They hate how much I love Revel, they hate how I look, they hate me," she says flatly.

"How could anyone hate you?" I ask, flabbergasted by her admission.

"I just never fit into their world, and they certainly let me know it." For the first time, she sounds bitter, which is an improvement over resignation. "The last time we spoke was over winter break. They made fun of Flora, made fun of her for working here, sarcastically told me I should just quit my silly grad program and work here. And I don't know why, probably because they were picking on Flora, but I finally lost it. I told them I was going to do exactly what they said. I didn't plan on actually following through with it, but when I saw the Revel sign on the way to school, I just drove here." She sniffles. "I haven't actually spoken to anyone in my family since then. Until today."

"Why didn't you say anything before?"

"Because I finally felt like I was part of something. I felt like I finally fit. I could be part of this project we're building together. A part of Revel."

"You do," I say emphatically. "You are. More so than me. You brought me into this world in a way I didn't think was possible."

She smiles weakly and continues. "I didn't want to ruin it. Ruin our partnership. Our relationship. I didn't want to be seen as broken or deficient, like how they see me." She wipes a tear from her cheek. "I wanted to escape, to become someone else. At first, it was Rose Red. But then, it was about becoming this perfect, capable person."

"Jesus, Marin." I close the gap between us and kneel before her, bleeding for her, understanding what she's saying exactly, but not knowing how to help, and it's breaking my heart.

"That's why I was at the lighthouse that night, wishing to be loved and to find a place where I belong. It's silly, really. I thought I could just forget that I was this damaged, delusional, dyslexic dork..."

I push a beautiful lock of cinnamon hair from her face. "With a penchant for alliteration?"

She snorts. "Yeah."

"Look at me." The pain in her eyes makes me ache for her. "I don't need you to be a perfect person. You know I'm certainly not. And you've found it in your heart to help me, to care about me. If anything, the strength you've shown, the resilience and joy for life despite everything you've been through, is nothing short of miraculous." I touch her face, wipe away a tear. "I admire you."

Marin hiccoughs and nods, looking down at her hands again.

"Look at me." I lift her chin. "You aren't broken. You're beautiful, intelligent, creative, and kind, and I find it tragic that anyone would find you deficient. You are eminently lovable."

Her eyebrows quirk up in surprise. Her lips tremble. "Thank you."

Late sunset light streaming through the stained-glass windows makes her look like a Vermeer painting, and I have to tell her how I really feel.

"And this may be too soon, and terrible timing, but I don't care. I was going to wait to say this after the board meeting, but I can't wait." I bring one hand to my heart and the other to hers.

"I am so fucking in love with you it scares me."

Tears fall down her rosy cheeks. Her lips part as she draws in a quick breath. She says nothing. One second, two seconds, three, and I'm convinced. I've spoken too soon, said too much. I start to pull away, but then she speaks, halting me.

"I love you too," she says breathlessly. My heart feels like it may detonate.

Later, with the full moon shining through those wide windows, we make love on the soft rug. Her skin glows. There's never been anything more beautiful than Marin in the moonlight. I kiss her and do everything in my power to show her how much I love her, on and on.

~

Once Marin falls asleep back in my apartment, I grab my phone and check my text messages. Tilda's radio silence has ended. She has cordially invited me to a meeting in New Orleans.

I have found a solution to our little problem where both of our proposals can succeed. Meet me at the Sazerac Bar at 7pm tomorrow night. It will be worth your while. Your father will not be there. Just you, me, and a possible investor. Please hear us out. For our family's sake. For Wade.

I want to punch a hole through the wall. That woman doesn't give two shits about my brother. She saw him as competition, and I'm sure she still does.

Then something Ernie said earlier slips forward in my mind. *"Let him who desires peace prepare for war."* I will hear her out. If anything, I'll appear magnanimous, even if I reject whatever scheme she proposes. I think about another famous quote from my pal Sun Tzu, *"Keep your enemies closer."*

I reply, *I'll be there.*

I decide not to tell Marin about the meeting. It'll just worry her, especially after the backhand of a text her sister sent and the emotional upheaval it caused. Plus, this meeting is liable to be a waste of time. I'll tell Marin I'm meeting with a former Revel designer in New Orleans for last-minute advice. Tilda used to be a designer,

so this is technically true, I think, as I lie down beside my sleeping
Marin.

Chapter Fifty-Five

Marin

The next morning, I find Flora on the dressing room floor, sewing as usual. Her black hair is swept up in a messy bun, with about six colored pencils sticking out of it. She sports dark circles under her eyes. I feel terrible. She's been working nonstop, and I bailed yesterday.

Not today.

"Hey," I utter. Sheepish.

"Hey," she says but doesn't look up from her stitching.

"Um, I brought two bags of beignets and coffee," I offer, holding up my treats.

Flora looks at the goodies and says flatly, "Put them on the table. I probably won't eat them. Beignets don't travel well. They get goopy."

I sit down on the couch's arm. "I...okay...I just want to apologize for freaking out yesterday."

Finally, Flora locks eyes with me. "Go on."

"You were 100 percent right, and I wasn't prepared to hear it, so I lashed out." My voice cracks a little, but I soldier on. "I am so, so, so sorry."

"I get it." Flora pushes a pin into her wrist cushion and stands, her knees snapping. "Apology accepted."

That was fast. I planned to grovel. "Are you sure? I mean, I completely ran out of here and left you with a mound of work to do and–"

Flora interrupts. "Yeah, that wasn't cool, but it is my job, and you're here now, and you don't have to be." She picks up an iced cafe au lait and takes a sip. "Can you start re-lacing the Princess Bianca corset?" She hands me a corset and a spool of string.

My spirits lift tentatively as I thread a needle. After a few minutes of sewing in silence, Flora asks me what happened with Ethan and the text, and I explain everything to her, glad to have my friend back.

I pull in a fortifying breath before talking about my family again. "And you were right about my family."

"I don't want to be, if that's any consolation." Flora reaches over and grabs my hand.

"I know. I just didn't want to face it. I spent years just sort of existing in la-la-land to avoid thinking about it. I didn't know that the world I was living in was so void of love until I met you, Flora. But I just thought you were special."

"Past tense? Harrumph."

"Are. Special." I squeeze her hand. "Then I came here and felt like I really belonged. I wasn't this weird aberration. I mattered. My ideas mattered. My voice was heard." I try not to completely lose it again, but I can feel heat behind my eyes. "I really, truly feel what I've been missing for the first time, and it hurts."

I'm crying again. This must be a record. Flora finds tissues in her fanny pack and hands them to me.

I blow my nose. "Anyway, thank you for sticking up for me all these years."

"Oh, of course! And I'm so sorry there was a cause to." Flora embraces me. I pull myself together after a few moments.

She leans back and whispers, "What are you going to do?"

I sigh. "Well, I'm going to get through the next couple of days, and then I'm eventually going to have a little heart-to-heart with the Vandersees. At least, I'll try."

Flora nods vigorously. "I think that's a brilliant idea, but..." She picks at her lip.

"What?"

"Do you think they'll be able to hear you?" Flora's concern is clear.

"Probably not, but I'll find a way. I'll use this newfangled voice I've found."

"Heck yes, you will."

I sit up straighter. "And if I can pitch a proposal to the board at Revel Pointe after just three months of working on it while being Rose Red by day and boss-bitch marketing guru by night, then I can talk to my family about the new rules for being in my life moving forward."

Flora throws both of her hands in the air. "Don't leave me hanging, this calls for a high ten!"

Our hands smack together. We beam at each other.

"I am so proud of you."

"I am so proud of you, too."

"Now these goopy beignets aren't going to eat themselves." She grabs the bags and hands me one. "Let's eat copious amounts of sugar, wash our hands, then work on these costumes while you tell me everything Ethan said last night before we move onto the proposal."

I take a bite of my beignet, and without really thinking about it, I declare, "Ethan told me he loved me last night."

Flora coughs, ejecting a cloud of powdered sugar. "What?!"

"Yes, he said he meant to wait until after the proposal, but he couldn't not tell me after I shared about my family. He said he admired me, and that I was 'eminently lovable.'"

"What is he, like, eighty?" Flora laughs.

"That's what I'm always saying!"

Flora waits a beat, then whispers, "What did you say?"

"I said I love him too because, well, because I do." I feel the blush overwhelm my face.

"Oh my god!" Flora waves her hands, her beignet releasing a blur of powder all over her navy blue *Coven Academy* T-shirt, making it look like snow in a night sky.

"I know," I laugh. "I am scared and happy and nervous and excited all at the same time."

"Yep, that's love." Flora brushes the sugar snow off and wipes her hand on a napkin. "What are you scared about?"

"The usual. How fast everything happened. How complicated it all is. Mostly, I'm freaking out about getting hurt." I see three swords in a heart then seven swords in my back.

"Yeah," she says, nodding. "But nothing risked, nothing gained, right?"

"Yep, and I trust him." I know I am smiling like a goofball now, and I wonder how much powdered sugar is on my face. "Ethan Reve makes me feel at home."

"Awww, vomit," she says and pantomimes puking.

"Yeah, I know, we're gross." I laugh.

"In the most adorable way." Flora's eyes sparkle. "I'm so happy for you. And if he hurts you, I'll destroy him."

"You're the best." I pluck out a wet wipe and clean my sugary hands and grab the corset to return to work.

"I know."

This feels like what I always hoped sisters would feel like. *Revel sisters*, I think. Flora really sees me and even loves me unconditionally. We spend the rest of the day working, laughing, and dreaming about life after the board approves our proposal.

Chapter Fifty-Six

Ethan

The Sazerac Bar is an Art Deco masterpiece in the Roosevelt Hotel downtown. It's covered in hand-painted murals from the '30s and dark, rich hardwoods. This place used to be where crooked New Orleans politicians would wheel and deal while drinking Sazeracs and smoking Cuban cigars, so it makes sense that Tilda would choose this place. It looks classy, but there's a seedy underbelly.

I make my entrance right on time. Tilda has found a bit of privacy in the back of the bar. She's elegant in a white blouse and white linen pants. As I draw nearer, I see the back of a man's head, the blondish hair slicked back. Tilda clocks my presence, and both stand to greet me.

"Ethan! Hello." She kisses each cheek—an affectation that seems continental but is about establishing control from the outset—"This is Harrison."

We shake hands. He's average height with a good build. He gives me the up and down, smiles, and reclaims his seat.

"Pleased to meet you, Ethan. I've heard a lot about you and this project."

"Really." I can only imagine what Tilda has told him.

A waiter in a white smock comes over and takes my order. Tilda and Harrison have French 75s. Champagne? A little peremptory celebration, I suppose. This Harrison cat looks familiar. Actually, he looks like a lot of guys I graduated with and worked with on Wall Street, dressed in a Tom Ford suit, replete with a blingy Bugatti watch. Maybe from family money, used to getting what he wants.

"So, yes, I met with Tilda last week in New York," Harrison starts. "She told me a little bit about your current predicament, and I think I can help."

The waiter brings my Sazerac. I take a sip, taking my time. "No one helps without getting something in return." I level my stare at him. He smiles.

"Well, of course, I see this as an incredibly lucrative investment." He chuckles slightly. "And I would want to see a healthy return on said investment."

Tilda chuckles along. "And Ethan, this could mean we both get what we want. There doesn't have to be this..."—she reaches for the right word— "this discord between you and me and your father."

I lean back. She never seeks compromise, never shies away from a fight. It's what has got her where she is today. She's up to something, but I'll play along to find out.

"Okay, so you will invest in the cruise line then?" I lead, intentionally misreading Harrison's offer.

Harrison glances quickly at Tilda and then replies, "Well, no. I wanted to invest in the *Island of Sirens* experience."

"Oh, really?"

"Yes, Tilda has told me a bit about what you plan to do, and I want in."

"You want a cut," I retort cynically.

"Yes, that tends to be how these things work." Harrison smiles. Smarmy.

I had a German calculus professor in college. Loved the guy. Sometimes he'd tell us fun, untranslatable German words. One of my favorites was *Backpfeifengesicht*—a face that's begging to be punched. Harrison's face longs for a right cross.

Tilda crosses her legs and continues. "We can work out all of the details in the office on Monday."

"Hold on, what percentage?"

"Obviously, we don't have all of the numbers in front of us, Ethan."

"Bullshit. Why even have this meeting if you don't know the potential profit? What's your cut, Harrison?"

He looks to Tilda, who nods almost imperceptibly. "Fifty-one percent," he mumbles.

"That's insane. That'd be giving you ownership of the IP, something Revel is highly protective of."

"Well, it's a risky project, what with all the controversy surrounding the film's political agenda and Senator Malaby's boycott campaign—"

I cut him off. "Why don't you invest in the cruise then?"

Tilda answers for him. "Because the cruise will be approved by the board on Monday." She looks at me with pity in her cool blue eyes, like it's a foregone conclusion.

"So, you'd invest and expect fifty-one percent control." This is a waste of my time.

"Really, I think that's fair, given the risk." He downs his drink, then snaps his finger to get the waiter's attention and points to his glass. The waiter, barely hiding his contempt, nods.

"Let me ask you a question," I say, pivoting.

"Shoot."

"Why *this* project? Why the *Island of Sirens* experience?"

"Let's just say I see the potential, and I'm a fan." He splays his hands out on the tablecloth as if he has nothing to hide.

We'll see. I take a play from Ernie's playbook. "What's the name of the island Nestor's from?"

"Um, let's see..." Harrison sits up straight like this will jog his memory.

I answer for him. "It's Ikaria."

"Right, it was on the tip of my tong—"

"What's the name of Laurel's sister?"

"Well, it's been a while, let me—"

"Ethan, do you really think a pop quiz is necessary?" Tilda interjects.

"Would you want to hand over fifty-one percent to someone who demonstrates ignorance of the source material?" I snap back.

Harrison's face is a blotchy red now. His cool has left the building.

"It's Daphne," I answer again.

"Daphne, that's right." He wipes his hands down his pants. "I—"

"One last question," I say, holding up one finger. "What is the theme of the movie in just one sentence?"

"Hmm." He puts two fingers to his chin. If he had a beard, he'd stroke it. "Give me a second to think."

"By all means." I grin and take another swig of my drink.

He stalls and then takes a swing. "It's about finding true love and living happily ever after?"

And it's a miss, a *palpable* miss. "Sorry, Harry. You're wrong."

I stand and throw a hundred on the table. "I don't know what you're up to, Tilda, but don't ever waste my time like this again."

"I don't know what you're talking about." Tilda stands up, too. Her voice is icy and defensive. "I just wanted to help."

Harrison remains sitting, fuming. I don't care. Fuck this guy. This was clearly a Hail Mary play on Tilda's behalf. A lame attempt to throw me off my game and waste my time. God, she must be slipping if she thought this plan would work. As I turn to leave, I stop dead in my tracks.

Walking towards us in a ridiculously short, tight purple dress is my ex, Bree Brooklyn.

Chapter Fifty-Seven

Marin

We're the flavor of exhausted that has morphed into embarrassing giddy nonsense. Our arms ache after mending costumes, detangling and re-braiding wigs, and cleaning shoes, but Flora and I walk back to the dorms making up new lyrics to the theme song of Revel Pointe's silly '80s puppet movie, *Prehistoric!* (emphasis on the exclamation point). We stop periodically to bend over, tears-in-our-eyes, giggling. The amount of work and hours of lost sleep are on the verge of lifting off our shoulders, and we can feel it. Finally, the sacrifices will be worth it.

After we pop a frozen pizza in the oven, down a few glasses of cabernet a little too quickly, and Flora yells, "Fashion show!"

I try on six different outfits for the proposal on Monday. She plays that ridiculous "I'm Too Sexy" song followed by RuPaul's "Supermodel" on her phone. I can't keep a straight face when Flora sings, "*You betta work!*" and tries to vogue hopelessly.

We end up deciding on a simple black blazer, a blush camisole, some wide-leg trousers and some sensible heels. With this outfit and a power pose, not to mention that I know the pitch better than I know all of the words to the *Rose Red* movie, I know I'm going to murder that meeting. It just feels right.

Back in our PJs, I run through the proposal with Flora in the style of Ethan Reve.

"*Island of Sirens* is an important artistic film that needs to be celebrated." I lower my voice in the style of Ethan Reve, emulating his cool baritone and cocky swagger.

"Strut more!" Flora instructs.

I hop off the stool, puff out my chest, and swing my arms. "Bwahahaha!" Flora holds her belly and bends over. "You look like a silverback gorilla!"

I pound my chest. "Me, Ethan. Me, alpha male." I start to knuckle walk. "Me, super sexy and smart."

"Stop, stop, I can't breathe!" Flora's giggles transform into a silent seizure. It takes a solid two minutes for her to control her breathing and composure again. We are slap-happy on wine and sleep deprivation.

"Okay, can I actually keep practicing now?" I feign impatience, folding my arms and tapping my foot.

"I don't know, can you?" Flora jokes. "But, of course, of course. Let's do this." Her own serious tone of voice makes her burst into hysterics again. Flora is famous for her laugh attacks. In college, friends would compete for who could get her going. Once, her boyfriend ordered one of those huge blowup T-Rex costumes and planned the exact moment to join Flora in the library, just to stun her into a laugh attack. They are that epic.

It takes another few minutes to get this new chuckle fest under control, but eventually we do. I get my laptop out, and we tweak the presentation, timing the slides perfectly.

At 9:05 p.m., we are watching *Island of Sirens* again, and I get a text from Ethan:

Hey, this is taking longer than I thought. Get some sleep tonight. I'll see you tomorrow.

Weird, I think. I was supposed to head over to his place soon.

I text back: *Hope everything is okay.*

My fingers hover above my phone screen. Is it too soon to write "I love you"? I mean, we said it to each other. In person. But I don't want to seem too eager. *Screw it*, I think. New Marin is brave.

I write, *Love you. Stay safe. XO.*

I don't hear from him the rest of the night.

Chapter Fifty-Eight

Ethan

Bree has followed me into what used to be a payphone alcove but is now just a private seating area to confront exes. I stare at two black leather chairs and a marble table, collecting my thoughts before I direct my rage at Bree. I do not sit. Nor do I turn to face her. I need to get calm first.

"Ethan," her husky voice pleads, "please turn around, baby."

"Don't call me that." I finally turn around and really look at her. She's thinner than she was. Bordering on scary thin. I wonder how much coke she does with Gordon Gecko out there.

"Ethan, I—"

"Can it, Amy." I use her real name. She hates it. When she emancipated herself from her parents, she legally changed her name to her stage name, Bree Brooklyn. "Why are you and your boyfriend here?"

As soon as Bree walked in, I remembered who Harrison was. Elsie had sent me a link about them dating. That seems like so long ago and so insignificant.

"He's here to talk to you about some investment thingy." She steps towards me. I step back, the back of my knees hitting the seat of the chair.

"Bullshit." I cross my arms and try again. "Why are YOU here?"

"Ethan, I wanted to see you, to talk to you." She's stammering a bit. Normally, she's so sleek and cool. This is new. A crack in the armor.

"Mmm-hmm, about what?" I keep my voice distant, not wanting to get a breath closer to this snake charmer.

"I wanted to say that I am sorry I didn't come down for Wade's funeral." She starts picking at her nails, looking sheepish. "That was shitty of me."

"It was," I concur, losing patience with whatever this act is. "Now cut the shit. Why are you here?"

Her eyes flash at me briefly. A hint of annoyance creeps in, but it's gone a second later, replaced by something that looks like real human emotion—remorse maybe? She's definitely acting, something she's not that great at.

"I'm serious," she whines. "I feel terrible about how things ended. I was selfish. I've been selfish forever, and it wasn't until this past year, without you around, without you looking out for me, that I realized I royally fucked up." Her eyes plead for contact.

"It's fine. Forget about it. I have." My jaw clenches. *Something wicked this way comes*, I think.

"I completely understand that you hate me. When Harrison said he was meeting with Tilda about something and then flying down here, I basically forced him to take me with him. I had to see you. To just say I'm sorry, and, and—" Actual human tears form in her eyes. Putting it on, that's what she's good at.

She wipes her cheeks and continues. "And I love you and I messed everything up and I know you're with someone else, and that killed me when I found out, but I had to try, to try—"

She moves directly in front of me, putting her face in her hands, her shoulders bobbing up and down. In all my time with Bree, she has never apologized, acknowledged fault, or cried. I'm at a loss for what to do, wondering if this isn't all an act.

"Oh, Ethan, I'm so sorry!" she cries and then slams her head into my chest. Unable to compute what's happening, I awkwardly pat her a few times on her back to console her.

She cries for what feels like two hours but is probably only two minutes. She starts to rub her head into my chest, like a cat seeking affection. No way, I think, and push her so she's an arm's length away from me, my hands resting on her shoulders.

"Bree, thank you for apologizing. I really appreciate it. But I think you should go back out there to your boyfriend and go home."

She looks up at me through long, wet eyelashes. "You don't miss me at all?" Her mouth is pouty. A year ago this come-hither look would have been sexy to me. Now I just find it sad.

"No. And I'm sorry, too. I wasn't fit to date anyone or be in a real relationship."

"Until now, I guess." She sounds bitter. Her arms cross her body.

"Yeah. Until now, I guess." I shrug, wanting to resolve this so I can get home to Marin.

She sniffles again. "I'm just so messed up without you, Ethan."

Before another word can come out of my mouth, she is on me like a jungle cat. She hops up and swings her legs around me. She clings with her thighs. And her mouth is on mine. I still for a second, offering nothing back, except for catching her by her ass when she wriggles, so she doesn't fall to the marble floor. Damn my reflexes. I should've just dropped her.

Instead, I disentangle her legs and push her away. "No, Bree," I say firmly.

It's then that I see Harrison leaning against the door jamb, smiling and holding his phone up.

"That'll do, Bree," Harrison says as he pockets his phone in his suit jacket and taps it against his chest. "Time to run." And that's exactly what Bree does, in four-inch heels no less.

She turns around briefly, a devious smile lights her face. "Ta, darling!" she yells before I realize what just happened. Dumbstruck, I stand there like I'm nailed to the floor.

A few moments later, my freeze thaws, and I run out into the lobby, but they're gone. I go back to the Sazerac Bar and scan the room. Tilda has fled the scene of the crime as well.

Well played, Tilda. This'll teach me to ever underestimate her again. But I know she's fucked me. I sit at the bar alone, my heart pounding ten thousand beats per minute.

The bartender saunters over to me and asks, "Another Sazerac, sir?"

"Yes," I respond. Dejected. Confident that suggestive pictures of me and Bree will be on the internet in no time. I can feel a panic attack simmering. One of the worst things about anxiety is the anxiety about having an anxiety attack. I do some deep breathing, put my feet on the ground, and steady myself.

I need time to think. I need a plan. Clearly, the goal of this charade was to divide and conquer. Tilda will show the world that I'm not to be trusted and make Marin hate me, thus poisoning our *Sirens* proposal before we even walk in the room.

After finishing my drink, I shoot Marin a text, telling her I'll see her tomorrow. After her shift as Rose Red, we were going to meet afterwards for dinner and last-minute planning.

A few seconds later, I see her reply. *Hope everything is okay.*

I notice my phone is about to die. Shit. I need to turn it off. I need to think. To figure out how to save this project, and most importantly, how to convince Marin to trust me after this idiotic Bree Brooklyn story breaks.

I scan the mural behind the bar. It's a party scene. In the middle of the mural, there's an old man in a brown three-piece suit, smoking a cigar. His eyes pierce through to the viewer, clearly in the crowd, but also apart somehow.

Then it hits me. I know what I need to do, who I need to talk to. Let's just hope he's willing to help.

Chapter Fifty-Nine

Marin

Roland has been strange all morning. I repeatedly catch him giving me puppy-dog eyes. And I never thought I'd say this, but there's a fine line between charming and officious. He's too attentive, asking if I'm too warm, too cold. Should we stand in the shade? Should we move into the sun? Do I need to take a break?

Finally, I've had enough. "Roland!" I whisper-yell after he asks me if I need a water break about ten minutes after our last one.

He quirks his eyebrows up. "Yes, my Rose."

"I'm fine, please stop with the coddling." I smile up at him, staying in character and talking through my teeth.

His smile wavers for a moment, but then he nods. About fifteen minutes later, I catch him looking at me quizzically. His look is inscrutable, like I'm a patient on concussion watch. Something between concern and anticipation.

I try to ignore it, as well as the fact that when I started this shift eight hours ago, I had not heard back from Ethan. Normally, I love being phone-free. Today it is torture.

When our shift finally ends, Roland extends his arm, I take it, and we retreat towards the tunnels.

"So...how are *you*?" Roland slows down his stride.

"Fine, how are *you*? Why have you been acting so weird all day?" We are almost to the cast members' egress door to the tunnel, so I'm still whispering and smiling.

He stops, which jars me a bit. He looks down at me, astonishment on his face and in his voice. "You don't know, do you?"

He's starting to freak me out. "Know what?"

He grabs my arm again; our pace is now brisk. "Come on, let's get in the tunnels. This isn't for guest ears."

He opens the door for me, and I immediately stop and ask, "What's going on?"

Roland pauses a moment, then digs his hand into his back pocket. He pulls out his phone.

"Roland! You're not supposed to have that in character." He's not listening to me, tapping furiously.

"I know, I know, but you need to look at this." Then his phone screen is mere inches from my face. I back up a step, my eyes focus, and I cannot believe what I'm seeing. I grab the phone and scroll.

The headline reads, "*Ethan's Reunion with Bree.*" Then the pictures.

Ethan looking down at Bree.

Scroll. Ethan hugging Bree.

Scroll. It looks like Ethan kissing Bree.

Scroll. Ethan holding Bree up by her butt.

I want to vomit, to scream, to wail, but what I do is just stand there, my eyes glued to the pictures, to Ethan's hands. Her dress is so short I can see the curves of her bare ass. Ethan's hands cupping it. I practically throw the phone at Roland.

"So, this is why you've been so weird all day?" I mutter more to myself than him. I need to think. I need to move, but I can't seem to do either.

Roland shoves his phone in his pocket and stands in front of me. "I thought it was weird that you came to work today. I didn't think you would. You seemed a little tense, but not what I was expecting. Not how you would be if you checked *The Secret Reveler.*"

I snort. "Yeah, turns out I should check it more."

I want to scream. I turn from him to head to our dressing rooms. Roland grabs my arm. "Marin, slow down." He looks to his left and right. "I'm worried about you. Stop for a second."

I stop. We are only halfway to the dressing rooms. I can't catch my breath. I want to get out of this corset now.

"Red—" He takes my hand. "Is there anything I can do?"

"I can't breathe," I whisper, panic rising. "I—" I lean against the tunnel wall. He starts rubbing circles on my back.

"Okay, deep breaths." He inhales loudly. I try to mimic his breathing, but I can't seem to catch the first breath.

"My corset..." I wince as I try to breathe deeply.

Roland starts unlacing it, and the relief is almost immediate. It is then I start to cry.

Roland turns me around and embraces me. "Don't cry, Red. He's not worth it."

"I don't understand what happened—" I stammer.

"Sssh, I know. I know. Ethan Reve is a monster for hurting you. I hate to say I told you so, but..." This makes me cry even more. I feel like such an idiot. Always seeing the best in people when I should just take them at face value.

I hear rustling and footsteps. I don't want anyone to see me like this. Roland must hear it too because he says, "Come on, let's get you out of this dress."

We practically run the rest of the way. I throw open the door, hoping to find Flora, but find it empty. I need her. I need to find Ethan. There must be some explanation for this. I pull pins out of my hair and take my wig off in record time, then let down my hair. I shimmy out of the dress so I'm just standing there in a chemise and petticoats.

"Ahem." Roland walks through the door, closing it, but leaving it open a crack. He stands in front of me again, and I don't care that I look crazy.

"Where's my street clothes?" I turn away from him and look on the director's chair by the mirror. "I have to go, I have to—"

"Red," Roland says quietly but authoritatively. I pause and face him.

"You need to calm down." He reaches for me and pulls me in for another hug. It is warm, and he has been so kind, but I have to get out of this place.

I struggle to move away from him, but he holds me tighter. "Shhh, it's okay, Red."

"It's not. Nothing is okay, and I just want to go home right now." When I think of home, I think of Ethan's place, his smell, his bed, *him*, and that makes me go limp in Roland's arms.

"Maybe this is all a misunderstanding..." I offer limply.

"Did you talk to him last night?" he asks quietly.

"No, he said the meeting went long." I think about the unanswered text. Oh god. Did he read that while he was with Bree?

"He's Ethan Reve, Red. He takes what he wants and dumps people when they are no longer useful." Roland's voice is bitter. "Weren't you guys working on something?"

"Yes, a project," I say into his chest. And we're almost done. Why would he screw this up before the proposal? It's just a few days away. Also, the whole point is to convince the board he's different now. This makes no sense, unless he thought he could get away with it.

"Well, maybe he doesn't need your help anymore? This is his way of breaking up with you." He hugs me tighter. "Didn't he break up with Bree Brooklyn by hooking up with someone and getting tagged on social media?"

Oh god, Roland's right! Ethan's so aware of cameras. Maybe this was meant to leak? Confused, I begin to weep again.

"Just let it out. I've got you," Roland coos as he rubs my back. I'm sure I am ruining his costume with wet mascara and gunky foundation.

Roland keeps talking in a calm, steady voice. "He doesn't deserve you. You are perfect. You are too innocent and good for him. A real-life Revel princess."

This makes me cry even more. Ethan and I just talked about this. And he made me feel loved for being me, not some perfect version of me. But the day after I open up and share, this is what he does?

And that's when it happens. That's when I start to float above myself. I watch myself being comforted by Roland. The tears stop, and I go numb. Hello dissociation, my old friend.

I barely feel his hand at the curve of my spine. Or his other hand as it moves up my arm. Then he's looking into my eyes, and his hand lifts up my chin. "You are so beautiful, Red. He's an idiot."

I am a cipher. A blank.

Roland kisses my forehead, my tear-stained cheeks. When he kisses my lips, I stand there. Not moving, just a doll being manipulated. My mouth responds mechanically.

Oh look, he's kissing my neck now, I think.

When his hand grazes my décolletage, I wake up.

"What are you doing?" I whisper.

"Hmm?" He's distracted, kissing down my chest, groping me.

"Roland, stop," I say loudly. He doesn't stop.

"Roland, no!" I say more forcefully as I push him away.

For a second, he looks like a toddler whose toy has been taken away, but he recovers quickly. He straightens up and glances at the door, which I notice is slightly more open than before. Oh god. I hope no one saw that.

"I'm so sorry, Red, I got carried away." He steps towards me again.

"Okay–" I put my hand up, not wanting him an inch closer. I don't know what to say. I feel like I'm in the Twilight Zone.

"The thing is, I've liked you for a long time, and you were so sad, and I wanted to make you feel better. And I lost my head for a moment." He smiles his winning smile, and I still feel nothing, except an overwhelming desire to hide from the world under a blanket.

"Thank you for your help, but I need to be alone now."

His eyes go wide, surprised. "Are you sure? I'm happy to stay and–"

"Yes, please. I mean no, I want you to go. Thanks for your help, but I need to be alone."

"Okay, well, you have my number. If you need *anything*, give me a call." He grabs my hand for a moment, kisses it, and is gone.

I close the door and lock it. I sit at the make-up mirror in silence and wipe away the tears along with layers of cream blush and foundation. I don't know how long it takes, but eventually I find and change into my street clothes and wander into the humid night.

Chapter Sixty

Ethan

I hesitate in front of PawPaw's cottage in the marshy woods a half-mile down the road from the park. A beautiful recreation of MawMaw's French provincial cottage, surrounded by her immaculate rose bushes, the place is a scene out of my childhood. The stairs to the front door have been recently swept. I smell lavender and hear spring birdsong instead of traffic. It's like entering another world through a magic portal.

I knock on the large wooden door, hearing nothing for a moment, then three latches clinking. PawPaw stands before me in light blue slacks, and a white button down and a yellow cardigan. The newspaper is in his right hand and he wears his frameless glasses, which show off his twinkling, teal-blue eyes. He is still as tall and thin as he ever was, with broad shoulders and a bit of a limp from a war injury. For a ninety-four year-old, he moves with surprising ease. When I was a boy, he told me the secret was squats. "You can squat, you can move."

"Ethan," he says warmly. "Come in, come in."

I enter the foyer and follow him to his snug living room. It is clear I interrupted his morning routine—breakfast, the news, then work. I don't know what his work is now that he's retired. By the look of him, he's keeping busy, not a lethargic bone in his body.

"Coffee?" he asks. I nod, and he retreats into the kitchen and brings me a cup.

"So, what can I do you for, Ethan?" PawPaw sits down and places his newspaper on the side table.

"I, well, I–" I had it all worked out in my head—what I'd say, how I'd convince him to come to the board meeting as a show of faith both to the board and to Marin.

But now, in front of the old man, I struggle to put two words together. I feel like I'm about to ask for too much after being absent—and frankly a problem—for so long.

"I don't know where to start," I admit.

"Well, let me see if I can help you..." He sits up a bit straighter, and using his story-time voice, begins his tale. "Once upon a time, there was a prince named Ethan. Ethan was lost for a very long time and suffered much heartbreak as a child, losing his mother and having a father who didn't know how to raise two young boys. As he grew up, young Ethan didn't think much of himself and wandered about looking for meaning and love. But in the wrong places." PawPaw pauses for a moment, letting me know how he felt about my gallivanting.

He continues. "The greatest tragedy of his life was losing his best friend and brother." PawPaw's eyes get glassy. He clears his throat. "The king suffered this loss dreadfully and became ill, so the crown and responsibility went to the second son, Ethan. At first, Ethan did not want the crown. It was so heavy but discovering his brother's plans for an ambitious, imaginative project, he found his purpose. He would honor his brother's memory and make something beautiful for the world. How's the story so far?" PawPaw asks, genuine curiosity on his wrinkled, rugged face.

"Spot on," I reply, a frog in my throat.

"Good, good. Now, Ethan struggled going up against his wicked stepmother and his grieving, distant father. He was alone, and he needed a helpmate. Along came a plucky, kind, resourceful princess. Who, in an interesting turn of events, saved this prince-in-distress." He smiles. "Multiple times, if I heard correctly."

I nod, wondering how many ears he keeps to the ground.

"You two work together, you fall in love, and everything is going swimmingly, and even though you're the underdogs, you just might win the day."

He leans forward. "Now I must be missing something; otherwise, I don't think you'd be sitting in that chair right now if the course of true love ever ran smooth."

"*Midsummer Night's Dream*, right?" I whisper. Overwhelmed by his story, by my own shame for never visiting him, for thinking he didn't care.

"Very good, you were always the best at picking up my Shakespeare." He pats my knee. "Now, what's wrong?"

"Tilda asked to meet me last night. It was a set-up. She had Bree Brooklyn—"

"The *Twinners* girl you used to see?"

My mouth is agape. Why did I think he didn't pay attention? "Yes."

"Never liked her much." His voice gruff. "Or that inane show."

I smile. "Yeah, well, Bree shows up and apologizes and starts to cry, and then she jumps me."

"I'm sorry, is that a euphemism for something?" PawPaw's bushy brows knit, but his eyes are knowing. He's toying with me, I can tell. Making me work for it.

"I wish. No, she literally jumped on me, wrapped her legs around my waist and laid one on me."

"Ah, and I imagine there was someone in the corner taking pictures."

"Yes..."

"And they're all over the interwebs, aren't they?"

"Yep." I laugh at his tech nomenclature.

"And Tilda's whole game plan is to sully your reputation and break up the crackerjack team that is you and Marin."

"And while the project is important to me—"

"Marin is more important." He nods. "I understand." His blue eyes shade a little cloudier for a moment. He's thinking of MawMaw, and I think I truly understand him for the first time.

PawPaw slowly stands. "So, how do you want this story to end?"

Chapter Sixty-One

Marin

Instead of going straight to the dorm, I brave the crowds and walk around the park in a daze. Strangers are preferable to knowing looks and under-the-breath comments from gossiping co-workers. Finally, I land in front of the lighthouse, the very spot of our beginning—mine and Ethan's—but also, just mine. This was where I came to make a wish before I'd even laid eyes on him. I take out my phone and see three texts from Ethan.

At 9:33 a.m., he wrote, *I know you're at work right now. I'm sorry I was MIA last night. It's a long story.*

Then the *Secret Reveler* story must have been published sometime between his first text and second.

At 1:03 p.m.: *Please call me as soon as you're off work. I promise I can explain. Please trust me.*

Two minutes later: *And for what it's worth, I love you, too.*

I can't reply. Not yet.

Then came a series of texts from Flora:

Come straight home when you get off work.

Where are you?

Seriously, I'm starting to worry.

I should text her back, but I need to think.

None of this makes sense. Why would Ethan do this? Like picking a scab, I scroll through the pictures again, unable to keep from looking at them.

Something about this doesn't add up. I want to believe him, but why would he lie about his meeting? Why wouldn't he call me or return my texts until this morning?

Maybe he hasn't actually changed at all. Why would he tell me he loves me on Friday and play tongue hockey with his ex on Saturday? What if what Roland said was true? Am I really this naïve girl being used by the savvy rich guy?

I bolt up. *No.*

I'm not this gullible, perfect princess who just doesn't know any better. And screw Roland for thinking that. And screw anyone who thinks I'm stupid enough to fall for this hackneyed setup.

I race home to the dorm. I open the door to my place and literally run into Flora.

"Ohmigod, I was just going to go looking for you!" She's out of breath, her bag slung across her body.

"I'm here," I declare, needing it to feel true.

Flora pulls me in for the tightest hug and says, "You've seen the pictures."

"Yes," I whisper.

"Have you heard from Ethan?" Her brown eyes fill with dread.

"Sort of," I reply. "But I am not sure everything is as it seems."

She eyes me warily. "What do you mean?"

"Roland showed me the pics in the tunnels after work. And I had a complete meltdown. I couldn't breathe, he had to unlace my corset–"

"Say what now?" Flora interrupts.

"I asked him to." She exhales a sigh of relief.

I continue. "Roland brought me back to the dressing rooms and said all of this stuff about how I'm perfect, and how Ethan was using me, and how this is the sort of thing guys like him do."

"Way to make you feel better," she says snarkily. "Then what?"

"Then he started kissing me."

"What?!" Flora's voice goes up an octave. "Noooooo!"

"Yeah, he said he's liked me for a long time and just got 'carried away.'" I look down for a moment. Embarrassed beyond belief.

She snorts. "What does that even mean?" She gives me the death stare. "Did you kiss him back?"

"No, not really. I didn't do much of anything but stand there. Eventually I told him to stop, and I walked around the park for a while to think."

"And..."

"And I don't understand it. Any of it. Why make our fake relationship real? Why tell me he loves me on Friday to do this on Saturday?" I take a breath, keeping my tears at bay. "And why would he do this now, just two days before the proposal?"

"Maybe he didn't think he'd get caught?" Flora offers reluctantly.

"Maybe, but you know how weird he is about the paparazzi. He's super aware of cameras."

"Hmmm." Flora purses her lips, takes her hair down and puts it back up into her signature bun.

Her eyes light up. "Plus, the initial reason for 'fake dating,' was to prove he was a good guy, representative of Revel's family values, their image."

"Right," I assert. "And the timing is a bit convenient, don't you think?"

Flora nods slowly. "Ohmigod! It was a set-up." She covers her mouth with both hands, her eyes bigger than sunflowers.

"Yeah, the more I think about it, the more convinced I am that it was. Remember those scheming floozies in the RP Lounge that wanted to take pics with Ethan? What if it was something like that?"

Flora paces the room. "And *who* would benefit from something like that?"

We look at each other, and say, "Tilda" at the same time.

"What do we do?" Flora asks, her mischievous I'm-up-to-no-good glint in her eyes.

"We find Ethan." I leave to retrieve a brush from my bedroom.

"And then what?" Flora asks, following me.

"I don't know, but we're not going to hang around waiting—quiet, meek, and mild—while that witch tries to fuck with our lives." I pull on a hoodie and change into my Chucks.

"Wow, Marin," Flora says, leaning against the door.

"What?"

"That's the first time I've ever heard you say *fuck*."

"Well, I've never needed to before."

"Atta girl."

As we walk out the door, she says, "Let's go save the day."

Chapter Sixty-Two

Ethan

After our morning brainstorming session, PawPaw made us turkey sandwiches for lunch. In the afternoon, we took a drive down to the proposed *Island of Sirens* site, and I filled him in on the particulars. He asked insightful questions and seemed impressed by the answers. I told him Marin is the brains behind the experience. He said he couldn't wait to meet her. Around seven, after my grandfather and I ate dinner together, I called, but she didn't pick up. I tried texting Marin, asking her to meet me by the lighthouse in an hour. I'm positive she's seen pictures of Bree and me by now, and this situation is beyond damage control for the proposal. This is our personal lives at stake.

I got to hand it to Bree. The pictures look scandalous. Her acting skills have improved.

I just hope my plan works. I bring our dinner dishes to the farm sink, wash them, and lay them in the wooden drying rack. No dishwasher. PawPaw believes hands are the best dishwashers.

I turn, and PawPaw stands there, smiling.

We embrace. He's thinner than he used to be. A tickle forms in my throat.

"Thank you, PawPaw. For everything."

"I'm sorry I haven't been around as much, I just can't—"

"No need to explain yourself, PawPaw."

"Ach, well..." He pats my back and walks me out. "Go get your girl!"

I rush home to make myself as presentable as possible for Marin. It's ten minutes to eight when I arrive at the lighthouse, and I'm glad I'm here first.

My plan is simple. PawPaw told me to just lay it all on the line. "An honest tale speeds best being plainly told."

When he saw I didn't know the reference, he said, "*Richard III.* Ignore the source." He smiled. "Tell it like it is. No baloney. Good luck, kid."

I'll ask if I can explain what happened plainly, then I will grovel like my life depends on it, because it does. It's clichéd and unexpected—but the thought of not hearing Marin's voice, not seeing her stretch like a cat before she stands up, not feeling her beside me, feels like a punch in the gut.

The clock chimes eight. No Marin. I gaze into the moat, thinking of her trying to pull me out of the water. I try to imagine kissing her back then. Even blind drunk and stupid, my body knew I belonged to her.

"Ethan!" I turn and see Marin and Flora running towards me.

She's adorable in a Rose Red hoodie and her red Chuck Taylors.

I run to her. We stand apart, facing one another square. Flora discreetly moves toward a bench and sits down the path to give us privacy.

"I am so sorry about everything. Let me explain–" I begin, taking a step toward her.

"You were set up by Tilda," she says matter-of-factly.

My mouth drops open. "Uh, well, yes, so–"

"So Bree shows up, ambushes you, and someone is conveniently there to take pictures, which just so happens to go up the day before our meeting."

"Well, yes, and–" I stammer.

"And you're worried about me." She takes a step closer.

"Yes, if you'd let me talk," I groan and throw my hands in the air. "You're ruining this whole thing!"

"I'm ruining what exactly?" She crosses her arms, her head cocked to the side.

"I was going to explain all that, that my phone was dead, which is why I was MIA last night, and then grovel profusely for lying to you about the meeting."

"Well, I've figured out the first part, but I'd love to hear the groveling bit." She takes a step even closer and looks up, batting her lashes flirtatiously.

"I was going to tell you I lied because I didn't want to burden you after what you shared on Friday, especially since I knew the meeting with Tilda would be bullshit."

"You should have told me." She huffs, blowing a lock of russet hair out of her face.

"I know. I'm sorry. Lesson learned." I pull her into an embrace. "You know that I never wanted to hurt you, and I understand if this life, this spotlight, is too much. If you want to, need to–"

She pulls back and glares at me. "Listen, Ethan. If I can handle the last six months, I can handle anything. Don't you worry about me, buster!"

"Buster?" I laugh. "What are you eighty?"

She laughs, too. "Darn tootin'."

I bring her in again, feel her head rest on my heart.

"I love you, Marin." I kiss the top of her head, the coconut and rose smell of her washing over me. The smell of home. "Thank you for trusting me."

"I love you, too."

Gazing into her large slate eyes, I kiss her gently on the lips.

Flora calls from the bench, "You call that a kiss, Reve?"

Challenge accepted. I show them my secret weapon. Something I've been doing since I was a teenager to woo girls. My friends called it "The Move," but it is formally known as the twirl-dip-and-kiss.

I take Marin's hand, swing her out, twirl her back in, and when I have her in the dip, I bring my mouth to hers. Flora squeals and claps. "Woohoo! That was epic!"

When I stop kissing her and gaze into Marin's eyes, they are soft and inviting. "So, you're the real Prince Charming, huh?"

"Darn tootin'," I reply and pull her upright. "I was just saving that move for the right occasion."

"Why did you want to meet here?" she asks.

"I was going for saccharine sentimentality. I hoped it'd remind you of us."

"Of when you got drunk, fell into a moat, and shamelessly made out with me and didn't even have the courtesy to remember it?" Her mouth twitches to the side.

"Well, when you put it like that, maybe this was a bad idea." I start to back away, but she catches me and pulls me back.

"Seriously, why here?" she insists.

"I think I wished for you, and it worked once. I thought if it wasn't going well, I could try again."

"Oh." Her eyes are glassy, her voice a whisper. "Let's make another wish."

"Flora, get over here!" I wave her over, and Flora skips gleefully to the fence.

Next to Marin, she asks, "What's up?"

I pull out three quarters. I hand one to Flora and one to Marin. I hold mine up and say, "Make a wish!"

I kiss mine, say my wish in my head, and throw the coin in the moat. Marin and Flora do the same. It's cheesy as hell, but I don't care. I've never believed in luck, but these two have made me believe in a bit of magic. We are quiet as we watch the coins glimmer to the bottom, then we grin at each other like goofy kids.

"Alrighty, now what?" Flora bounces on the balls of her feet.

"Now we plan. Let's order take-out and collude," I say, as I rub my hands together like an old-timey villain.

"Bruhahahah!" Marin cackles.

"The princess has become the witch," Flora giggles.

"Let's go, witches," I say. "We don't want to be late to the hurly-burly."

Chapter Sixty-Three

Marin

The morning of our *Island of Sirens* proposal presentation there is a freak cold snap. This happens in a Southern spring. We'll have three straight weeks of warm weather and then, *snap*! Everyone rushes to cover their plants. This "cold" is child's play for a Yankee like me, but everyone else in the park is dressed like they're going Alpine skiing.

Flora, Ethan, and I stayed up most of the night. The proposal itself is solid. Ethan's a math whiz, and the proposed budget is balanced with a healthy contingency. Flora's designs are fresh and respectful of the source material. The narrative journey of the experience mirrors that of the heroine, and the marketing plan, if I do say so myself, is original and targeted.

On that front, we feel confident.

On the ad hominem-attack front, not so much. We role-played every nasty trick we could imagine Tilda pulling. Ultimately, the pictures are a PR nightmare, and we can't pretend otherwise. However, we hope that the board can divorce this image from the concept. After all, these Bree photos are a blip in the public image we've kept up as a solid, happy couple for months.

Plus, we have a few tricks up our sleeves ourselves. Revel fans like me and Flora have been studying villains our entire lives. We were made for this challenge.

Flora crashed on Ethan's couch. At the butt crack of dawn, Ethan went for a run while Flora and I rushed back to our place. Because of her tenuous relationship with Marta, Flora opted out of being present for the proposal today, but she'll be on standby the entire morning. She also has a very special mission to accomplish.

I take a quick shower and think about Ethan's arms around me last night—his face nuzzled into my neck and his sleepy "I love you, Marin. Thank you for believing in me."

"Of course," I whispered back. "I love you, too."

I grin away while Flora does my make-up. She gives me what she calls her "tasteful boss bitch" face. I wear my hair down and wavy; my lips are a muted red.

I feel like a different person from the Marin who came here months ago. Confident, strong. A woman with a voice.

"I'm ready," I declare.

"You look amazing." Flora holds up two palms in the air. "High ten for luck!"

We look at each other's elbows—the key to an excellent high ten—and smack.

"Go get 'em, Mare." Flora hugs me at the door.

Ethan waits for me outside. It's like *Sixteen Candles*, but instead of a red sports car, my man leans against a theme-park golf cart with Miss Maisy Moreau, the frog, painted on the side. If it's a callback to that morning when I stood there before him in green paint, I get the reference and it makes me chuckle.

"Wow," he says as I walk towards him. He looks devastating in a tailored navy suit, with a blue v-neck sweater and a red tie.

"Wow yourself," I reply, pecking his lips.

"Hey, before we head over, I wanted to say that no matter what happens, you and me? This?" He indicates the space between us. "This is what I wished for yesterday."

"Do NOT make me cry right now! Flora would kill me if I walked into that room with raccoon eyes." I kiss him again, thanking god for 24-hour lipstick, and say, "Me too."

We hop in the cart and travel in silence, reaching the Revel Palace conference room a full thirty minutes before the others arrive. We set up the space.

Clicker works, check.

Presentation slides work, check.

Sound works, check.

Twelve bound proposals in front of each seat with a few extras in the middle of the conference table. Check, check.

We are ready, standing at the front of the room by the screen. A stunning illustration Flora drew of the Sirens' island, Naxos, is our screensaver.

Five minutes before the meeting starts, board members trickle in. Most just nod to us. When Shirleen arrives, she shakes our hands and whispers, "Good luck."

Ethan looks like a bored *GQ* model while my nerves run a marathon in my body. My heart warms when I see Ernie walk in. He beams at us, shakes our hands, and says, "Vangie sends her love." He winks at me. "Remember, home is worth fighting for, chére."

The gorgeous Luca Conti saunters in, his eyes on his phone before meeting mine. He gives me a devasting smile. Like he's won already. Tilda walks in a minute later, shocked to see me at first, but quick to hide it. She's wearing a black peplum suit coat with a purple pencil skirt. Bill Symons is right behind her, smirking. And that's not all.

Gaspard freaking Reve walks in. I try not to visibly gasp. Cameras do not capture the looming physical presence of this man. Enormous and handsome, of course, with black hair, silver temples, and olive skin. I gulp audibly, and Ethan squeezes my hand.

"Dad, I didn't know you'd be here," Ethan says politely.

"Tilda asked me to come." He nods at Tilda who gives him a sweet smile, then he turns his attention to me. "And this must be Marin?"

Instead of waiting for Ethan, I stick out my hand. "Marin Vandersee, pleased to meet you."

His eyebrows furrow a bit, then he smiles, his white, straight teeth gleaming, the wrinkles around his eyes crinkling. "Enchanted," he replies as he shakes my hand.

Oh, my. I step back. Ethan's hand finds my lower back.

"Dad, why don't you sit over there? Ernie, can you hand him an extra copy?"

Gaspard finds a seat near Tilda, and Ernie throws the proposal on the table in front of him.

Shirleen clears her throat. "Well, I think that's everyone. Let's begin."

Chapter Sixty-Four

Ethan

Marin dims the lights, and we finally begin. Marin and I finally pitch the proposal we believe in with all we've got. We walk them through the actual experience from a guest's perspective, which follows Princess Kaliope's journey from Naxos to Ikaria to King Staffan's Jade Palace and back to Naxos. Flora's renderings of each location, each monster, each costume makes the vision come to life. Next, I talk numbers, then Marin lays out the marketing plan. Most board members follow along, taking notes in the binders we provided. Many of them nod along, and even Luca Conti looks intrigued. I acknowledge possible challenges and pushback, and our plans to address them.

Forty-five minutes later, I finish with Wade's reasons for wanting to do this. *"What is the point of money and power if we don't use it to protect the defenseless, as well as entertain and educate the public?"*

"That is his call to action," I say.

Marin hits the clicker, and a picture of Wade in his dress blues floats on screen. I pause and look at Wade's face. I think about his kindness, his honor. I hope he can hear this.

"We need to decide if we want to heed his call," I continue. "If we do, Revel will not only make money, we'll be the place we say we are. This is about our home and the home of future generations. And as you know, home is worth fighting for."

I look at the board members squarely. "Thank you."

"Any questions?" Marin asks and brings the lights back up. She has tears in her eyes, and she's not the only one who's moved.

But I don't have time to dwell on emotion because there is a slew of questions. Many about logistics, some about money, and a few about marketing, which Marin handles with aplomb.

It's all going swimmingly until Dad coughs. The room goes silent. "If this board does approve the proposal, who will be working on this day-to-day?"

The tension in the room is back. "We would obviously need to gather a team, but we have an astounding amount of people here who would love to work on a project like this," I say, placing a hand on the proposal binder in front of me. "I would oversee finances, Marin would have a role in experience development and marketing, and the artist behind the beautiful concept art has already agreed to work on the project immediately."

"So, you'd actually be here, you'd be responsible for the work?" Dad raises a cynical brow.

"Yes, that's the plan," I say.

"No heading back to New York once things get boring here?" He isn't really asking questions, just hurling thinly veiled insults.

I don't bite. "No, of course not."

Ernie breaks in. "Gaspard, what are you getting at here?"

Dad turns a cold eye on Ernie. "Well, I think this proposal has merit, but it's Wade's proposal, and Wade isn't here to see it through, to make sure it succeeds. We'd be putting millions of dollars into this, and that's investing a lot of money and energy in someone who's not been here the last decade."

Marin steps closer to me. I try to calm my racing heart.

"I see your point, Dad." I pause, then look him in the eyes. "I did leave, but I also earned a degree in finance and worked at a top-tier investment firm. I've made my own money. I don't need to be here. I *want* to be here."

Marin's hand finds mine, and I continue. "When I read Wade's three-page proposal, I was inspired in a way I never have been before.

Marin and I turned Wade's proposal into the 100-page plan you see before you. I am committed to this. I am not going anywhere." I look at Marin, who smiles encouragingly at me.

"Interesting," Tilda says loudly.

My head whips to her. "What do you mean?"

"We've all seen the latest gossip, Ethan." She looks around the room. No one says a word. Some people look down at the binder, averting their gaze.

"No? Not everyone?" Tilda opens her laptop. "May I?"

I grit my teeth. "By all means." I know what she's about to do. We planned for this. I squeeze Marin's hands, preparing to see Bree and me on *The Secret Reveler*. But that is not what is on the screen.

It is *The Secret Reveler* all right, but instead of Bree and me, it's Marin.

The first picture is that fucking Prince Fuckface unlacing her corset.

In another, he's holding her in her underclothes. In another, his hands are on her and he's kissing her.

"Oh, look at this," Tilda practically squeals with glee. "I meant to find Ethan in a compromising situation with his ex, but what's this?"

She bends down to read. "Don't Worry about Ethan's GF; She's Met Her Real Prince Charming."

I look down at Marin. Her face is bright red. I want to kill Tilda and maim Prince Asshat. Then punch my smug father in the face.

Marin lets go of my hand. "Those pictures are not what they seem. They're fake." Her voice is wobbly.

"Well, they sure do look real," Bill Symons says, leering at the screen. I add him to my maim list.

Dad harrumphs. "Listen, we know the course of young love never did run smooth, but this is ridiculous. We're supposed to invest in this project and the two leads are already in the news for reckless, irresponsible, and let's call a spade a spade, immoral behavior."

Oh, the hypocrisy of this man. The room explodes into a cacophony. Everyone is talking at once. I notice Tilda sits back, her arms crossed, a triumphant smile tugging at her lips.

Marin whispers to me, "Now?"

I nod. I pick up my phone. A moment later, I place it in front of us, and we lock hands again.

Last night, Marin told me about Roland. I wasn't prepared to see pictures of it, but if we've learned anything from the mess, it's that honesty is the best policy. And she thought something seemed off about the whole Roland exchange. She told me about his behavior over the last month, the increasing questions, his warnings, his twirl-dip-and-kiss (assuring me my moves were better). We covered it all. Anticipating that Tilda would cover her bases, we prepared.

Flora did a little digging, saying she's never trusted Todd Jared Michael, a.k.a. Prince Roland. She expressed how Todd is always "on," always horny, and always hustling. Flora had an idea of how to expose him for the opportunist he was. She was shaky on the details last night, but said she thought she knew of a particular weakness.

I only hope it will work. As if on cue, a message from Flora pops up on my phone. It's go-time. I give Marin a signaling look. "Okay, you're on," I whisper.

Chapter Sixty-Five

Marin

All of the board members are talking at once, except Tilda, who's sitting back and enjoying the chaos, and Luca who sits quietly, sphinxlike. I take a drink of water to buy myself a few seconds and calm my nerves.

"Excuse me, excuse me," I say, but no one hears. I try again. Louder. "EXCUSE ME!"

The room goes silent.

"Thank you." I take a breath and continue. "Since it's our reputations that are being besmirched, Ethan and I should be able to speak to these accusations." I lock eyes with every member in the room. Ending on Gaspard. I plan to win this staring contest. After what seems like an eternity, he gives an almost imperceptible nod.

That's my cue to continue. "We live in a different world these days. A world where everyone has a camera, and everyone's a reporter. Because of Ethan's profile and past, he's a target, and I've been caught in the crossfire multiple times. We're learning how to manage this exposure and *when* this project is approved, our public image will be high on our list of priorities. We need to control the narrative."

I walk around the table. "On Friday night, Ethan got a message from Tilda asking to meet her on Saturday. Can you pull up the message, Ethan?"

"On it," Ethan says as he changes the screen to his text thread.

Tilda: *I have found a solution to our little problem where both of our proposals can succeed. Meet me at the Sazerac Bar at 7 pm tomorrow night. It will be worth your while. Your father will not be there. Just you, me, and a possible investor. Please hear us out. For our family's sake. For Wade.*

I give them a moment to read. Gaspard whips his head and stares at Tilda.

"I don't see how this is relevant." Tilda rolls her eyes. "I was trying to help you, Ethan."

I cut her off. "Ethan went to this meeting with this investor who said he wants fifty-one percent control of the project and profits. Obviously, Ethan said no. That was a ridiculous offer, but it was a Trojan horse. Do you know who this investor was?" I pause. "Harrison Matthews... Ring any bells?"

There's some hubbub among the board members. Binky Dupuis, an older woman with a deep tan and a perfectly coiffed silver bob, reluctantly offers, "I believe that is Bree Brooklyn's new flame."

"Bingo!" I yell and put my finger to my nose. "And who should stroll in but Ethan's ex, who follows him out of the bar, cries, apologizes to Ethan and then jumps him, literally, all while Mr. Matthews takes pictures."

It's so quiet we can hear the log flume whistle from across the park. Gaspard's brows knit in a perma-furrow. Shirleen takes notes. Ernie's smile is bigger than his boat.

"When Ethan went back to the bar, Tilda was gone, but the damage was done."

Tilda huffs. "I had nothing to do with what Bree and Harrison did. Ethan made those choices, not me." She throws her hands into the air. "*I* was trying to *help* him. He always sabotages himself." She's talking too fast now. "I–"

Ernie interrupts her with an incredulous snort and then nods at me. "Keep going, chére."

"Now, as for me." I walk back over to Ethan. "I worked all day yesterday. In addition to working as Ethan's assistant, I work in the park as Rose Red. As you know, there's a strict no cellphone policy for cast members in character." In my best Rose Red impression, I say, "Princesses should never scroll on their phones. It ruins the magic."

A few board members smile. Some chuckle.

"What does this have to do with anything?" Tilda interjects, her manicured nails tapping on the table.

"I'm getting to it," I say. "So, I didn't have my phone on me all day. On the way back to my dressing room, the actor who plays Roland, who I've recently learned is really named Todd, showed me *The Secret Reveler* post."

I let this sink in. "I am in love with Ethan Reve. You can imagine how seeing those photos impacted me at first." I look at Ethan, who smiles and nods sympathetically.

"I had a bit of a freak-out, I couldn't breathe. I asked Roland, I mean Todd, to unlace my corset so I wouldn't pass out. I got back to my dressing room and wanted to get out of the costume ASAP. I cried, and Todd was trying to 'comfort me.'" I lean hard into those air quotes. "But really, he took advantage of my distressed state to take photos to sell to the highest bidder."

Shirleen shakes her head. Ernie looks pissed. Even Gaspard has the good sense to appear surprised.

"Could you show the pictures again?" I ask Ethan. He winces.

"Sorry!" I add. I hate making him look at them again, but it's necessary.

He pulls up *The Secret Reveler*. "If you look, you'll all notice I am not reciprocating. I am not touching him or kissing him. I am just standing there."

After giving everyone a few uncomfortable moments to inspect the photos, I continue.

"Think about it. All of this comes out a day before, and the day of, this proposal presentation. Pretty convenient if you ask me. And the last time I spoke to this group, Tilda asked you all to consider whether Ethan could represent the values of this company. If his reputation is tarnished, who benefits?" I let that nugget sink in. "As a lifelong Reveler, I can assure you Ethan does represent Revel's values. But I am not so sure the current leadership does. And I am absolutely certain that another cruise line and island acquisition would not."

"I will not sit here and..." Tilda stammers and stands up.

"Sit down, Til," Gaspard growls.

Luca's eyebrows rise. Bill's mouth opens, but no sound comes out.

I look at Ethan. He nods vigorously and gives me a thumbs up. "Oh, and one more thing," I add.

Ethan picks up his phone. "I'd love you to listen to this," he says as he hits the play button.

"So, you stole Ethan Reve's girl? Wow," a young woman says. Her voice is low and flirty. *"I'm intrigued."*

"A gentleman never kisses and tells." It's Roland's voice, his charm on full blast.

"What are we even listening to?" Tilda snarls.

Ethan hits pause. "You'll see." Ethan grins and hits play again.

"Good thing you are no gentleman," she purrs. The voice sounds familiar.

"True." There's some rustling sounds.

"Why, Prince Roland, I thought your heart belonged to the fair Rose Red?"

"That wasn't real. It was a career move," he says matter-of-factly. *Ouch.* He did tell me that people like us have to exploit every angle. God, I was so blind.

"What?" She sounds surprised but encouraging. *"Do tell."*

"Think about it: I'll forever be known as the guy she thought was hotter than Ethan Reve. I'll be on TMZ. This could launch my acting career."

Some more rustling. *"Plus, I'm more of a Thumbelina guy anyway."* He's talking to Carrie! There's some audible lip smacking.

Gross. I'm going to have to buy Carrie all of the margaritas from now until the end of time.

Breathlessly, Carrie asks, "*You come up with this idea all on your own?*"

"*No,*" Roland says. The rustling and lip smacking stops. "*Wait...why?*" He sounds suspicious.

"*No reason,*" she says quickly, too quickly. "*Ta, darling!*"

"*Hold on, where are you—*" Ethan hits pause on Roland's words. Again, the room is quiet.

"So," I say, "There you have it."

"I don't like what you are insinuating." Tilda's tone is deadly yet over-the-top saccharine.

"I don't like being manipulated," I retort, my eyes landing on Tilda. "And I especially don't like being assaulted by a fellow Revel co-worker."

Tilda sits back in her chair. Finally, she is silent.

Satisfied, I continue, "Ethan Reve isn't perfect. I'm not perfect, no one is. If you wait for people to be perfect to invest in a project, good luck with that. What I can promise you is that we are committed to Wade's vision, our vision. We are committed to each other." I grab Ethan's hand and look the board members in the eye around the table. "And we are committed to Revel Pointe and its values."

"Here, here," I hear a gruff voice cheer. I turn to see the source.

Mick Reve stands in the doorway.

Chapter Sixty-Six

Ethan

A shockwave ripples through the room. Only Ernie seems calm.

The look on Marin's face is frozen awe. I think she might faint when she sees PawPaw walk in the boardroom. I squeeze her hand to give her a signal that this is real. I forget that to a die-hard Reveler like Marin, Mick Reve is essentially the President of the United States, Mother Goose, Mister Rogers, and her beloved kooky grandfather all rolled into one.

"Pop, what are you doing here?" Gaspard sputters. Only PawPaw makes him sputter like this.

"Well, I thought if you were going to be here, son, it must be a family affair." PawPaw makes his rounds, shaking hands with the board members. "Barb, good to see you. Claude, how's the grandkids? Shirleen." He nods at her and winks.

Ernie pulls up a chair for him. "Here ya go, Mick. Take a load off."

"Thanks, Ern." PawPaw takes a prominent seat. No one says a word. "Well, how's it going?" He levels a supportive look at me.

I answer, "We finished our *Sirens* pitch, answered some questions, and restored our reputations."

"Ah, that's good. 'Good name in man and woman is the immediate jewel of their souls.'"

"*Othello*!" Marin says loudly. Too loudly. *Ah, my adorable dork.*

"That's right. I like her already, Ethan." PawPaw smiles brightly at Marin. "So... sounds like I missed some fireworks?" He gestures to Shirleen. "You took notes, I imagine."

"Mmm-hmm." She taps her legal pad before her.

"I don't know why you do. Shirleen here remembers every word ever spoken. It's uncanny."

"I take notes for accuracy," Shirleen replies, a Cheshire cat grin beaming at PawPaw. "For everyone else."

PawPaw nods, friendly but all-business. "What's next?"

"The board has received both proposals now," Ernie says. "So, we vote."

"Ooh, I'm just in time then." He rubs his hands together.

"Pop, what are you really doing here?" Gaspard scoots his chair up. It looks like a rod has been shoved up his ass.

"I just wanted to show my support for Ethan's proposal," he says innocently.

"Have you even read it?" Tilda snaps, then realizes her misstep. Throwing shade at these upstart youngsters is one thing; being rude to the living legend, that's unforgivable. She backtracks. "I mean, you've retired. I didn't think you were staying up to speed on the day-to-day."

"Hush, now. I may be retired, and a bit of a hermit, but I built this park. I love it like a child. Gave it to Gaspard, so that makes it my grandbaby, I suppose. And you know how grandparents dote on grandbabies." He winks at me. The man could charm paint off the wall. And he isn't even trying. That's just him.

"You don't have a vote, Pop." Gaspard looks uncomfortable. I wonder if he's as uncomfortable around PawPaw as I am around him.

"Neither do you." PawPaw stares him down. The number of Dirty Harry stare-downs today have reached astronomical proportions. "I'm not here to vote, I am here to shamelessly sway some voters."

He picks up the proposal, holds it up, and says to Gaspard. "This right here would make your mother proud." He pauses for effect. Gaspard looks at his feet. "I have kept to myself the last few years because I didn't want to be King Lear. Mad with grief, running around, yelling at the sky, making pronouncements about how young people these days don't know what's for, et cetera, et cetera...."

Ernie chuckles at the picture PawPaw has painted.

"I needed to cede authority. So, I stepped back." He looks at Gaspard and Tilda. "I couldn't stand to see the direction y'all were taking at times, but I felt it wasn't my place to intervene. But I had hope because I knew that Wade understood what Revel Pointe means to people, and I knew he could usher the place into an even brighter future. And when we lost him–" His voice cracks, and Dad's head drops. "And then when Gaspard got sick, Ethan stepped up. He's always been smart, creative, kind. It's no secret he was a little lost there for a while, but now he's home. And he's fighting for it. And I won't be quiet anymore. I can't."

"Home is worth fighting for," Ernie says, using the slogan we've uttered several times in the presentation. He smiles over at us.

PawPaw stands up. "*Island of Sirens* was the last film I ever worked on." A collective gasp reverberates around the room. I blink a few times, caught off guard. PawPaw continues, "It was top secret, of course, until now. Wade kept me in the loop, helped me stay stealthy."

"I knew it!" Marin screams. She points at him, and she can't help but jump up and down.

PawPaw laughs. "Yeah, I guessed some Revelers would figure it out sooner or later."

He walks toward the door. "And before you vote, I want you to know that I fully endorse Ethan and Marin and Wade's proposal. Do with that what you will. Thanks for listening."

Then just as he arrived, PawPaw turns and leaves the room.

Tilda stands. "What a shameless stunt. That was completely out-of-line. This is not the proper procedure. I demand we break until–"

"Tilda!" Dad barks. "Sit down."

Shocked, she sits. Bill Symons looks mesmerized by his pen, avoiding Tilda's gaze. Luca looks like he wants to throw her out the window.

Shirleen adjusts her giant red glasses and says, "It's eleven o'clock, and I would like to see my own grandbabies sometime this century, so I say we vote. All in favor of voting now?"

"I second that," Ernie calls out.

"Okay, let's proceed." Shirleen sends me a huge smile. "All in favor of supporting the *Island of Sirens* project?"

Marin holds my hand so tightly I think she might break my pinky finger, but I don't care. I look at her and mouth, "I love you."

She mouths back, "Ditto."

And I hear Shirleen say, "Ten ayes. Two nays. Congratulations, you two."

"Congratulations, everyone." Ernie stands. "This is a win for Revel."

I don't care if it's unprofessional, I sweep Marin up and do the twirl-dip-and-kiss.

Ernie yells, "Woo-ey! You're gonna have to teach me that one, boy!"

"I love you," I whisper in Marin's ear. "Thank you. For everything."

Chapter Sixty-Seven

Marin

I'm alone with my thoughts, itching to get out of the Miss Maisy costume. The cold snap fizzled. Spring is now just summer. It's a humid 85 degrees. I fantasize about removing my bald cap later, imagining visible steam lines rising from my head. It's my last day on the job as a character, and for the first time since I drove off the highway back in January onto the Revel Pointe lot, I'm ready to be me full-time.

Plus, I couldn't go back to Rose Red. Being Revel internet famous made it impossible. But I couldn't leave Flora in a lurch, so the current Miss Maisy was swapped to Rose Red, and I have spent two weeks as the iconic frog in front of the Swamp Ride. It's not all bad. I'm happy to be incognito and relieved to get some time to process everything that's happened.

After the board meeting, we were exhausted, but Flora refused to let the momentous occasion pass by without some sort of celebration. She dragged us to a hipster karaoke bar in New Orleans where we ate pierogis and drank cheap beer. After a mean rendition of "Hit Me With Your Best Shot," Flora and I got a wee bit tipsy and may have forced Ethan to sing along to "Kaliope's Promise." Turns out a baritone earnestly singing a Revel song is hipster catnip. He brought the house down. Too tipsy to drive home, we got hotel rooms in the Quarter. Flora brought a skinny-jeans-wearing hipster back to her room for some "reveling." Alone at last, hot and sweaty from the day, Ethan and I showered and had what can only be described as victory sex before falling asleep, satiated.

The next day, a little hung over, we got to work. It's been go-go-go ever since. Listening to the sounds of the park all around me, I think about this evening's agenda, the list of accruing meetings, decisions to be made, deals to be struck, but my reverie is interrupted by a guest.

"Miss Maisy!" a little girl screams. I look up from my lily pad, and we hop-walk toward each other. Like me, she is wearing all green. Miss Maisy is on her backpack, shirt, and sneakers. Her mom already has her phone out.

"Miss Maisy is her favorite," she says and takes pictures.

In my best Maisy twang, I ask, "And what's yer name?"

"ZOE!" She is about five years old and hasn't learned volume modulation. She's my favorite.

"Do you want to take a picture, Miss Zoe?" I bend down and she throws herself at me, little arms holding my neck.

"YES!" My ears will ring for the rest of the day, but it was worth it.

We pose for a few pictures, and then I ask, "Why am I your favorite, Miss Zoe?"

"Because you're the SMARTEST and because you're in charge of EVERYBODY!"

"Good answer!" I high five her, and she runs back to her mother, who thanks me for making her daughter's day.

No one ever said Rose Red was the smartest or in charge. She was a favorite because she was beautiful, kind, and sometimes silly. This makes me pause. Another life status update overwhelms me before I can stop it:

- *Family...* I need to put a pin in this one. I'm one hundred percent not ready to deal with them yet. I want to bask in this post-win love-fest a bit longer before dealing with those people.

● *Friends...* Amazing! No notes.

● *Love-life...* Speaking of love-fest, Ethan and I can't keep our hands off each other. It's a lot. So much so that Flora has instigated a "No Touching" rule in her presence. I'm in love, and it's gross, and I don't care. The multiple booms help.

● *Reputation...* After the Roland-Bree debacle, the first thing we wanted to do is confront Roland, a.k.a. Todd, but he disappeared. Someone must have tipped him off. I wonder who that could be? (It rhymes with Schmilda). Ethan and I needed to restore our reputations quickly. In a stroke of amazing luck, The Secret Reveler did a lot of work for us, like a digital fairy godmother.

In a post titled, *"Ethan Reve Set Up! Shocking REVElations!"* The *Reveler* got an exclusive interview with Harrison Matthews, Bree Brooklyn's now ex-boyfriend.

Apparently, Harrison's father, and boss, was unhappy with the optics. Harrison broke up with Bree, and in a phone interview with yours truly, he incriminated her, saying this stunt was the last straw: 'I played along, but it was clear she was still into the guy. Life is too short for this bullshit. Last thing I need is to get pulled into a defamation lawsuit.'

And then somehow, Roland's conversation with Carrie was leaked.

"Here at The Secret Reveler, we admit when we are wrong. It doesn't happen often, but when it does, we apologize... In the following audio clip, Prince Roland, (pictured below), admits to being bribed into kissing Rose Red, a.k.a. Ethan Reve's girlfriend, Marin Vandersee...

After that post, Ethan and I were fully in the clear. The posts that followed were of us jogging together, going to a Saints game with Ernie and Vangie, eating a celebratory dinner at La Provence. Only sweet, and TRUE, gossipy news. Our good names are restored. Huzzah!

- *School...* Hm. There's a tug at my solar plexus when I think about school. I'm supposed to go back in the fall, but as I dig into this *Sirens* project, gaps in my marketing knowledge surface. I want to learn more. I need to. Also, being referred to as "Ethan Reve's New Girlfriend" is nice and all, but I don't like that I'm famous for being someone's girlfriend. One, I don't want to be famous at all. Two, if I am known for something, I want it to be for accomplishing something, and three, doing an amazing job at that something. This means I need to get back to school pronto.

After our work meeting tonight, I will tell Ethan and Flora that I'm signing up for summer classes. It will make my schedule crazy, and I'll have to spend some nights in New Orleans each week, but I need to do this. Not just for the project, but for me. I want to be more Miss Maisy and less Rose Red. Scratch that. I want to be both.

Chapter Sixty-Eight

Ethan

PawPaw asked me over a few weeks after the board voted for Wade's project. Marin told me I had to start saying "my project" or "our project," but to me, it will always be for Wade. Although, I am surprised by how much I love the day-to-day operations, the logistics of such an enormous undertaking. I guess it makes sense. I love math because it's problem-solving, and the more complex the better. This is complex problem-solving, not in abstraction, but in the real world, with real stakes. Instead of caving under the mounting pressure, I find myself calm, like I'm a superhero who moves so fast that the world around him appears to stand still. Turns out I'm a Reve after all. But I still have my moments where I feel the world is closing in, panic rising. Right now, things are good.

PawPaw didn't say why I needed to come over, or why I needed to come alone, but we've talked more in the past month than we have in the last decade. Mick Reve is eccentric, but goddamn he's a genius. I've learned more from him in the last three weeks than in the few years I was at Goldman Sachs. I pull onto the road that leads to PawPaw's cottage.

Strange, I think, that Marin wasn't invited. The two of them hit it off immediately. When Ernie saw PawPaw and Marin talking about the Easter egg in *Island of Sirens* that connected to *Portia's Power*, which lent credence to the Revel multiverse theory, Ernie laughed and said, "Peanut butter, meet jelly." They just click.

When I park, I notice a giant Land Rover. "Shit," I huff as I walk up the driveway. Dad's here. Before I can think about turning around, PawPaw opens the front door.

"There you are. Get in here. I already poured you a glass of lemonade." He waves me over and pats my back three times, leading me to the kitchen table where Gaspard sits, looking like he's waiting to get a root canal.

"Good morning," I greet Gaspard formally.

PawPaw gestures to the open chair. The tension in the room is palpable. The last time we were together, *alone*, the three of us... God, I can't remember the last time. Maybe it never happened because Wade would have been there.

"Well, you got us here, Pop. What now?" Gaspard looks at his watch.

"And I thank you for taking time to meet with me. Both of you." PawPaw pauses, takes a breath, and starts. "We need to clear the air."

"Why?" my dad says as I blurt out, "What?" simultaneously.

"Now, I don't expect everything to be hunky-dory from one conversation, but I was thinking about *Island of Sirens*, about home being worth fighting for, and blast it, I need to get back in the ring. And I need you two to be able to sit in a room together for this home of ours to survive. We owe it to the family. We owe it to Wade."

I look to my dad. There's a hint of shame in his eyes. It dissipates quickly.

PawPaw continues, "Now, I'll start. I've been a right ass. Swallowed up by my own grief for too long, letting myself retreat to the corners of my mind, which I don't have to tell you is vast, but easy to get lost in. I've been a ghost, and I am so, so sorry." He tears up. I think my dad may die from mortification. I pat PawPaw's hand.

"Shoot, I'm more weepy than Ophelia." He takes another breath and says, "Okay, now Gaspard, your turn."

"My turn to what?"

"To apologize."

"Excuse me?" he scoffs. "To whom?"

"To your son, Ethan."

"I'm not sorry." Dad turns and looks at me. "I think the cruise line made more sense financially."

"Not about the business." PawPaw shakes his head.

"This isn't necessary..." I tell him.

"I didn't know about the other stuff," Dad blurts out gruffly.

I get quiet, waiting for more details.

"What other stuff?" PawPaw whispers, afraid to rock the boat.

"The whole setup—Tilda's goddamn meddling, the photos. That was too far. I won't apologize for it, though, because I didn't know about it and would've shut it down if I wasn't forced to stay at home like a goddamn invalid." He pounds the table on the word *invalid*. The ice in our drinks sloshes and clinks.

"Well, that's good to know," I say. "So, you didn't actively try to sabotage my relationship and the proposal." I sigh. Dad's been working with Tilda for over twenty years, so it's good to know there are lines he'd draw when it comes to the lengths she will go to get what she wants.

"I was surprised you even showed up," Dad mutters.

"Whoa, now," PawPaw warns. "We—"

"No, let him talk, PawPaw," I tell him. "He's right. I haven't exactly been a model of decorum and responsibility the last decade. I own that."

Gaspard scrutinizes my face, lets out a breath, and then quietly says, "I didn't think you had it in you."

I nod. "Well, I didn't, but now I do. And I had a lot of help."

"We'll see," Dad says, rubbing his tired face. "I still think it's too risky, but we lost, fair and square. I won't do anything to impede you, and I'll rein Tilda in."

"Well, thanks, I guess." The moment is awkward, but the tension in the room has eased.

"That little redhead of yours is something else." Gaspard wears a smirk and what I think might be begrudging respect.

"Yeah, she believed in his project and for some reason, me, from the beginning."

"And that's all it took, huh? For you to turn your life around?"

"Sometimes people need to know they're worth fighting for, too," PawPaw adds solemnly. It's a little on the nose, but he's never been subtle. "You should get that better than anyone, son."

Gaspard nods slowly then stands, heavily favoring one leg. "I gotta run. Yasmin has me scheduled for some sort of PT."

"Good woman." PawPaw has a bit of trouble standing as well but refuses to let me help him.

I follow Gaspard outside. He turns around suddenly, and his hand shoots out. Shocked, I take it and give it a hearty shake. "Good luck, Ethan," he says.

When I turn around to see PawPaw, he's wiping another tear from his eye.

"Come here." PawPaw gestures to me. "I got a new project in the works and want to pick your brain a minute." As I follow him back inside, I feel a weight I didn't know was there lift.

PawPaw shows me mockups of a beautiful building—a library to house the Revel Pointe archives, our family's legacy. With a twinkle in his eye, he tells me James, my little brother, is the lead architect.

PawPaw, Ernie, Vangie, Flora, Marin, and now James are all here in Louisiana. Suddenly, I feel overwhelmed. For the first time in a long time, Revel Pointe feels like home.

Chapter Sixty-Nine

Marin
Three months later

I'm jogging on the levee, trying to work out my stress. It's way too hot, but I've been working my tail off in the turret for the last few days and need to move, to get into my body and sweat it out. I just finished an essay for my Advanced Strategy summer course entitled "The Power of Personalization: How to Connect Younger Markets to Older Content."

I'm turning 26 in a few days. To celebrate, Ethan's taking me to dinner, followed by a "surprise." We've both been working like crazy since we broke ground a few weeks ago, and we need a night out. I've been driving to New Orleans a couple times a week and studying every free minute, trying to get my head back into finishing my degree. Ethan's been overseeing the project, so we pass each other like ships in the night. Good thing we live together. Otherwise we'd never see each other—or touch each other, which we definitely make time to do.

In addition to going to school and working on the *Island of Sirens* Experience, I've been seeing a therapist. In fact, both Ethan and I started going this summer.

Ethan had a bad anxiety attack on the Fourth of July. I had never been to the Revel Pointe fireworks display, and I wanted to enjoy it with him, so Flora, Carrie, and I dragged him to the show. He left halfway through, saying he wasn't feeling well. The crowd started to close in on him and he could feel his chest tighten. He and Wade used to watch the fireworks and a hot-dog eating contest every year together. He just needed to get out of there. In bed that night, he told me this panic attack gave him a three-hour migraine on top of the usual vomiting. He said it was finally time to get some help. Turns out, finding purpose and love helps, but is not actually a cure for grief and anxiety.

With Flora's encouragement, I found a therapist at Tulane, mostly to deal with my own family baggage. Despite receiving multiple messages from my family about my relationship with Ethan and my promotion at Revel Pointe—a lot of mixed messages at best—I didn't respond to any. I even blocked Arista's number, whose messages were the most aggressive and cruel. I want to talk to them face-to-face, to have that heart-to-heart, but I want a few more tools in my toolbelt before I can confront them. I'm making progress though. We both are.

I pass the two-mile mark and turn back, only able to jog four miles in this humidity. The repetitive sound of my feet on this dirt path works its magic. I feel calmer, focused. Running past the *Island of Sirens'* temporary production office on my way back to the compound, I stop dead on my literal track. Shocked.

My mom, dad, Arista, and Alana, all blonde, tall, and sleek in their summer linens, are standing outside the office, mere yards away. Ethan exits through the office doors and shouts over to me, "I was just trying to call you!"

I'm frozen, sweaty, staring at them, mouth open.

"Close your mouth, Marin. You look like a fish," my mother says. I close my mouth. Ethan makes his introduction to my family as I still can't move or say anything.

"This must be your mother. I'm Ethan Reve." He puts out his hand, which she shakes begrudgingly.

"Yes, we know who you are," she says tersely.

"Mr. Vandersee." Ethan shakes my father's hand, then my sisters'. "Pleased to meet you." Alana is polite. Arista looks conflicted, like she wants to bone him, but also like he's yesterday's trash.

"So…this is a surprise! How was your trip down here?" Ethan asks as if this ambush is a planned visit.

The first thing they do is complain about the stifling heat.

"It feels like walking in soup," my mother gripes, fanning herself with her black-and-white beach hat.

"It's the Deep South, in the middle of summer," I retort, standing by Ethan for moral support.

"So, you're just here to see Marin?" Ethan Reve, ever the diplomat.

Arista snorts and steps forward. "We wanted to see that she hadn't been abducted into some sort of cult."

Alana groans, crossing over to give me a polite hug, and says, "Ignore her. I came because it's your birthday this week and I wanted to make sure you were okay."

"Oh, yes, happy birthday, pumpkin," my father offers absentmindedly.

"We haven't been able to talk to you in months." My mother crosses her arms. "Except for pictures and posts on the internet, we would have no idea whether you were alive or dead."

"I didn't think you cared." The words fly out of my mouth before I can stop them.

"Excuse me, young lady!" My mother clutches her invisible pearls. "We flew all the way down here to see you. Arista, Alana, and I had to reschedule several important meetings. And—"

"Enough!" I bellow. Some tourists, curious about this new exhibit, turn and look at us. "If we are going to have an actual conversation, let's do it in a less public place. But if you are just going to stand here and criticize me, then I suggest you leave."

I glance at Ethan who tries to hide his smirk, not very successfully because Arista glares at him.

"We aren't criticizing you. But yes, a change of scenery would be lovely. Do you live on the premises?" my father asks.

Ten minutes later, after we've crossed through the park, my family gawks up at the huge Reve compound castle.

As we enter the cool air-conditioning of the main foyer, my dad quips, "Do you really live here?"

"Dad, of course they live in a castle. She's a princess," Arista says with the tone of an angsty teen.

"How about we all go up to our suite, and I'll make some Arnold Palmers to cool you off." Ethan holds my hand as we walk towards the elevators, "If that's fine with you," he whispers to me. I nod. I need a shower and to collect myself.

He makes idle chit-chat as we head upstairs. Alana keeps looking at me, like she wants to talk but doesn't know how to start. Arista stands with arms crossed. Mom and Dad ask Ethan questions about his family, his job title, where he went to school. They breathe a sigh of relief when he says MIT. When we walk through our apartment door, my mother asks if Ethan has any plans to get an advanced degree.

"Well, I'm a bit busy at the moment, Mrs. Vandersee, but yes, I've always wanted to pursue Applied Math one day."

He tells them to have a seat and he'll be right back. At least in the kitchen, he's safe from the pedigree inquisition.

"So..." I mumble, wanting to beam myself out of this place.

"Well, he *is* charming," Mom says, like it's an insult. "He has some academic chops, it seems."

Alana adds, "I love this place; it's Middle Ages meets modern industrial."

"Swamp royalty," Arista stage whispers to no one in particular.

Ethan returns to ask, "Sweet tea or unsweet?" He definitely heard Arista's snide remark.

"I need to take a shower," I announce. I also desperately need a mental reset and drag Ethan back into the kitchen. "Are you okay with those snotty beasts out there for ten minutes?"

"Anything for you."

In the foggy bathroom mirror, after I've washed away the grit and sweat and panic, I examine my features and look into my eyes. I'm different now, I tell myself. I've battled Tilda, Roland, random sabotaging meddlers, the press. And, I've won—I have my dream job. I'm working on my degree. I live close to the best best friend in the universe. And I found the love of my life. I didn't do it alone, though. I climbed this mountain with the help of my newfound family, my Revel family. I'm so not ready for my actual, biological family to be here. There's a literal lifetime of hurt there, twenty-six years to be exact. But, I've made so much progress, externally as well as internally. I square my shoulders and tell myself, "I'm ready."

Back in the living room, feeling refreshed and almost confident. "Okay, family," I announce to an awkwardly silent room. "You're here. You see that I am alive. Now what?" I give Ethan a glance, and he raises his eyebrows at me. I can just imagine the stilted conversation he's just had with these snobs.

My mother turns her icy glare on me. "*Now what*? I think you owe us an apology for making this trip necessary. Clearly, this was a cry for help. A classic case, really—the outburst at Christmas, the reckless decision to quit school, to work in a theme park?" Her voice wobbles on the words "theme park."

"And don't forget the inappropriate pictures," Arista adds. "With two different men."

"And we come all the way here for 'now what'?" Mom heaves a sigh so dramatic I want to give her an award. "Typical."

Ethan jolts up, his hackles raised. "Now, wait a second–"

I grab his hand and sit with him on the sofa. "I've got this," I say quietly, taking a breath. "It took *months* before any of you reached out to me, and I'm pretty sure that had my picture not been all over the internet, you would not have reached out at all."

My mother tries to speak, but I hold up my hand. "I am not done talking." I look around the room. "No one talks until I'm finished."

I pause, waiting for dissent. When there is none, I continue. "You have always made me feel less than. Like I don't belong. Like I wasn't a part of this family or your overachieving world. And it wasn't until I came here, lived with Flora, worked at this wonderful place, and fell in love with this wonderful man..." I tap Ethan's knee. "That I understood how messed up your treatment of me was. I thought love meant being quiet and pleasing and perfect, even though I knew I could never live up to your insane expectations."

"Marin, you shouldn't compare yourself to your sisters—" my father says.

I cut him off before he can say another hurtful thing. He doesn't even hear how hurtful he can be. "No. I am talking now."

I point at my mother. "You." And then my father. "And you. You should not compare *any* of us. This isn't a competition for who can accrue the most accolades and credentials. You should love us without us having to jump through all these hoops!"

"Mom and Dad were just preparing us for the real world, where some people, apparently, can't hack it," Arista says.

"Arista, be quiet," Alana huffs, annoyed. "Marin has the floor."

I look at Alana and see her eyes are glassy. She gives me a nod.

"I am done, but thank you." I nod back at Alana. "Clearly, this conversation isn't going anywhere. I will not apologize for no longer accepting how you treat me."

I stand then, striking one of my power poses, the Superwoman pose, hands on hips. Shoulders back. Chin forward.

"And what do you think, young man?" my mother asks Ethan. "You've been sitting there quiet this whole time as she's berated us." She stands, her pose mirroring my own.

The better to look down on me, I think.

"Honestly, I'm confused." Ethan raises his eyebrows at me and continues to address the Vandersees. "I just don't understand."

"What don't you understand?" Arista spits out impatiently.

"I don't understand how this beautiful, kind, intelligent woman is related to any of you." Ethan stands next to me. "Now get out of our home," he growls.

I would pay money to have a photograph of my family's appalled faces at that moment.

"I can't believe you would..." my mother stammers. No one tells this woman what to do.

"You heard me. Out." He strides toward the door, opens it, and gives a slight bow. "Have a safe trip back to whatever frozen hellscape you came from."

When they file out into the hall, I run to Ethan, throwing myself at him. "That was amazing! Thankyouthankyouthankyou!" I picture them all out there, stunned and lost in the Reve castle, and I don't care.

He hugs me, kisses me. "You were amazing. When you said, 'I am talking now,' I almost yelled, 'Fuck, yeah!' I am so proud of you!"

"Thanks, I'm exhausted and exhilarated at the same time," I mumble into his chest. "Is there a German word for that?"

He chuckles and says, "I don't know. Probably."

He brings my chin up so I'm peering into his concerned blue eyes.

"You told me about them; Flora told me about them, but there's nothing you could have said to prepare me for that." He exhales loudly and squints like he has trouble seeing me. "How?" he asks.

"How what?"

"How are you so well-adjusted?"

"I don't think I am," I say and promptly burst into tears. Ethan holds me and guides me to the bedroom, kissing me, melting away some of the hurt.

~

A few weeks after the ambush, Alana texts me while I'm walking Nemo—my birthday surprise, our new, fluffy, spotted, pound mutt—in the shady oaks around PawPaw's cottage.

Just so you know, I am so sorry about what happened at Revel Pointe. About everything. You really inspired me.

Apparently, Alana felt terrible for how she's treated me in the past, how Arista and our parents still treat me. When she left Revel Pointe, Alana had a complete nervous breakdown, the pressure to succeed and her complete hatred for her field of study, finally overwhelmed her.

When you stood up to them and said that you were done, something snapped. I had to change.

She quit her post-doc program and has been working as a vet tech because, get this, she's always loved animals despite never being allowed to have any.

I sit on a stone bench next to the Mardi Gras roses, a blend of yellow and pink double blooms that Marie planted years ago. I bombard Alana's phone with pictures of Nemo. I send one of Nemo eating Ethan's shoe, Nemo sleeping on Ethan's chest, Nemo on Ernie and Vangie's boat (his floof magnificent in the wind), and Nemo with his favorite dog sitter, PawPaw. Alana "hearts" all of them.

I want to spend time with her, make her a part of my new world, so I invite her to our Reve family Christmas in a few months. Ethan told me the entire Reve clan comes to town for a Christmas ball, including all of his siblings.

She replies, *A ball! Who are you? What portal did you fall through? I'm so there.*

I walk leisurely around the romantic, immaculately kept garden. Nemo has to stop and literally smell every rose. PawPaw agreed to hang out with Nemo while Ethan takes me out to dinner at La

Provence tonight. I can't wait to tell Ethan about Alana coming for Christmas. It'll be a sibling meet-and-greet, although I did meet one brother already.

James is here, working on a new project that his mother, Tilda roped him into. He's tall, like Ethan, more striking than classically handsome, and somehow scruffier than Ethan, which is at odds with his posh accent. He's brilliant, has a dry sense of humor, and is devoted to Ethan, even if he's a pretty buttoned-up guy. I like him. We've all been so busy with our projects we barely see James. I'll bring this up at dinner tonight.

I head inside the cottage, and Nemo, the goofball, races to find PawPaw. It still feels strange to call him PawPaw, but he insisted. To me, he still looms large—the icon, Mick Reve, the creator of all I live and breathe these days. *I'm not just a fan anymore*, I think as I greet him with a hug. *I'm part of this amazing place that PawPaw shared with the world.*

We chat for a few minutes, but I need to head home and get pretty for this evening. Tomorrow we are meeting with our virtual reality contractor, but tonight is about us. Ethan and me. I want this dinner to be really romantic. I bought a little red negligee as a surprise. Ethan has become a connoisseur of lingerie the past few months. We had to buy another dedicated dresser.

We'll worry about sleeping tomorrow night.

Tonight we celebrate our successes and growth.

Tonight we love each other.

Tonight we revel.

Epilogue

The Secret Reveler
A Blog Devoted to All Matters Reve

Silver Balls, Silver Balls...It's Christmas Time at Revel
The holidays are just around the corner, so you know what that
means—more family drama. Gaspard Reve seems to be on the
mend but still taking a backseat in the boardroom on doctor's (and
Yasmin's) orders. Things remain icy between Tilda and the rest of
the fam since the *Island of Sirens* experience was approved by the
board, but she's moved on to another project, the Grand Revel
Library. She's pleased as punch that her son, James Reve, is home
from across the pond. The dreamy James has been putting his
architecture skills to work on the library. Rumor has it that James
and Mommy Dearest are already clashing.
Here's a picture of Tilda and James at the jobsite. I included the one
of James in a hard hat for your viewing pleasure. Note his posture.
He's as rigid as a statue. More gargoyle than man. It doesn't take a
body-language expert to see James would rather be anywhere than at
this meeting. His granite gaze could freeze the Deep South.
Mick Reve, Recluse No More
Another bit of exciting gossip is Mick Reve will make a formal
appearance at the annual Christmas Ball. In fact, we've been
inundated with "Mick sightings" lately. See photographic evidence
below. Here's Mick with Ethan and Marin at the Island of Sirens
groundbreaking.
Here he is riding in a park golf cart with James.

Here's Mick fishing with Ethan and the COO, Ernie Guidry. Notice the puppy. Yes, the puppy Ethan apparently got Marin for her birthday. But that's not all he got her...

Ethan Reve Seals the Deal

Yes, I have buried the lede, my dear Revelers, saving the best for last. Here is a picture of Ethan, on bended knee, proposing to Marin Vandersee at La Provence, the site of their infamous fancy date. You can see from the kiss that followed that she said yes.

A Revel wedding? A prodigal son returned?

Did we mention there's a puppy?

Stay posted, my fellow Revelers. More intrigue is afoot.

The End?

The Revel Pointe Romance Continues

Stay tuned for the next book in the Revel Pointe Romance series, *Summer in the Stacks.*

James Reve, the talented, aloof architect, has been called home from England to build the Grand Revel Library for his PawPaw, the founder of Revel Pointe.
Summer, a Midwestern girl wanting more than her small-town life, accepts a highly coveted job as an archivist with a special assignment to uncover lost memorabilia.
Both James and Summer must navigate the usual high-stakes politics of Revel Pointe, the ever-watchful *Secret Reveler*, and their intense attraction to one another.
James is Summer's boss—a real beast at work and socially cold as a marble statue.
But appearances can be deceiving.

Did you love *Marin in the Moonlight*? Then you should read *Summer in the Snowfall*[1] by A.E. Merriweather!

Longtime wallflower Summer York is suffering some major impostor syndrome. Not only is she leaving Ohio to start a flashy new job as an archivist at Grand Revel Library—a new feature in the famous Revel Pointe theme park—but she's also suddenly in an unlikely love triangle. Her high school crush, Grainger McCloskey, and her new superior, James Reve are vying for her attention at every turn.

Summer must reconcile her guilt for leaving her provincial life and bereaved father while navigating Revel Pointe politics and the dynamics of her budding workplace romance. James Reve—the brilliant and moody architect behind the Grand Revel Library—makes Summer feel beautiful and capable. The more time

---

1. https://books2read.com/u/b5PN8l

2. https://books2read.com/u/b5PN8l

she spends with James, the more possibilities she can see for herself. But, his life is complicated. With the library project in the balance and a looming Christmas deadline, will James become a beast under pressure? As Summer uncovers Reve family secrets James does not know, their future seems doomed. How can Summer possibly keep everyone happy, including herself?

Read more at www.aemerriweather.com.

About the Author

A.E. Merriweather is a pseudonym that represents three writers. Combined, they have published short stories, essays, poetry, and have written for TV. The next book in the series, SUMMER IN THE STACKS, is a modern retelling of Beauty and the Beast, and the third book, CYNDA IN THE SWAMP, a retelling of Cinderella.

Read more at www.aemerriweather.com.